# PRIDE

ALSO BY NATALIE KELLER REINERT

*Ambition*
*Courage*
*Luck*
*Forward*
*Prospect*
*Home*
*Flight*

# PRIDE

A Novel

*The Eventing Series*
BOOK TWO

NATALIE KELLER REINERT

FLATIRON
BOOKS
NEW YORK

PRIDE. Copyright © 2016, 2024 by Natalie Keller Reinert. All rights reserved. Printed in the United States of America. For information, address Flatiron Books, 120 Broadway, New York, NY 10271.

www.flatironbooks.com

Designed by Gabriel Guma

The Library of Congress Cataloging-in-Publication Data

Names: Reinert, Natalie Keller, author.
Title: Pride : a novel / Natalie Keller Reinert.
Identifiers: LCCN 2024039450 | ISBN 9781250384966 (trade paperback) | ISBN 9781250384973 (ebook)
Subjects: LCGFT: Romance fiction. | Novels.
Classification: LCC PS3618.E564548 P75 2025 | DDC 813/.6—dc23/eng/20240830
LC record available at https://lccn.loc.gov/2024039450

Our books may be purchased in bulk for promotional, educational, or business use. Please contact your local bookseller or the Macmillan Corporate and Premium Sales Department at 1-800-221-7945, extension 5442, or by email at MacmillanSpecialMarkets@macmillan.com.

Originally self-published in 2016 by Natalie Keller Reinert

First Flatiron Books Edition: 2025

10  9  8  7  6  5  4  3  2  1

# PRIDE

# 1

I REINED BACK the big gray Thoroughbred as we reached the top of the hill, and together, we gazed out over the landscape.

The starting box waited at the base of the slope below us, its single open wall an invitation to come and stand inside, dancing, nerves jolting, fingers trembling, waiting for the countdown and the whistle and the jovial *"Have a great ride!"* from the starter. It was the gateway to our favorite world: the cross-country course.

Beyond the starting box's spindly wooden confines, a collection of cross-country jumps were scattered over hillsides and fields, the scenery of logs and brush a siren song to people (and horses) like us. Eventers—we were the lucky ones, happiest of horse people, calling a gallop through woods and fields a competition. My horse and I were about to go charging across that patchwork of forest and pasture on this north Georgia farm, taking the fences as they came to us, flying over them with our fearless hearts. Cross-country day was my greatest joy. All I needed for inner peace was out there on those green hills, in a zigzag of hogsbacks and coffins, trakehners and tables.

Still, I hung back for a moment, studying the slopes before us. Our hills in Ocala were more moderate than these steep foothills, stout cousins of the nearby mountains. Their azure humps wavered in the early summer haze like approaching thunderclouds. I wasn't used to seeing such heights—every time I looked up, I thought a rainstorm was about to descend upon us.

Mickey shifted beneath me, ready to go, and I closed my fingers on the reins to steady him, still trying to picture the course map. The steep hills played tricks on my eyes, and it was difficult to put the little black squares on a flat sheet of paper into position along the hillsides. That awful construction-sign fence, the one with the yellow-and-black barricades on either side—wasn't that supposed to be at the top of a hill? From up here, the jump looked like it sat in the middle of a broad empty field, flat as a pancake. I'd walked the course twice, but things still looked different from horseback and far away. Hopefully, the course walks would kick in once I was out there, my muscles taking over for my lapses in memory.

"I need a portable map," I told Mickey, who flicked an ear toward me with modest attention. "Maybe a nice laminated job I could clip into your mane."

That wasn't such a bad idea, actually. I could make them at the kitchen table on rainy days, sell them on the side. Make a little extra cash. Why not? Jules Thornton, star eventer and Etsy entrepreneur. Anything would make more money than training horses. My professional life was one large black hole of debt. Maybe I should learn knitting while I was at it; there seemed to be a tremendous market for knitted things, according to the internet.

"I could knit adorable gray ponies for all of our fans," I told Mickey.

The adorable gray pony shook off flies with a tremendous full-body shudder, all sixteen-plus hands of him shaking like a dog climbing out of a bathtub, flapping his head so hard the spare leather on his throatlatch went flying out of its keeper. I leaned forward, grunting as my belt caught me in the stomach, and tucked the loose end back into place. *That's* why the amazing portable eventing map would flop; it was cursed with a fatal flaw, like so many of my bright ideas. "You'd have sent my map flying and I'd be out of luck. If that happened to all the maps I sold, riders would go off-course and sue me."

"What map?"

Up rode Pete, sitting comfortably on his blood bay mare Mayfair, with his feet dangling out of the stirrups, reins loose and shoulders slouched. His hat was tipped back and a few strands of red-chestnut hair fell over his forehead.

"You didn't go back to the barns?"

"Thought I'd stay and see your round before I take her in. She's barely blowing."

Five years old and fighting fit, I thought wistfully, looking at the little mare with admiration. She had a light sheen of sweat on her neck and a dancing glitter in her eyes, as if she'd found the gallop refreshing and good for her complexion. Pete looked fresh and cool as well, which should have been physically impossible, considering the weather. Eighty-five degrees in the shade, not a cloud in the sky, moderate humidity; my smartphone told me all that, but I could feel it already, with the surety of a born Southerner. If only I looked the part! I knew full well I was red in the face and drenched in sweat, as if I'd just run a marathon.

"I had an idea for a mounted course map," I explained, ignoring Pete's dewy movie-star good looks. "A million-dollar idea, if I could figure out how to keep it on the horse's neck."

Pete grinned and lifted one eyebrow at me in that familiar quirk of his. "You don't need a map, Jules. You got this. Keep the red flag on the right and the horse between your legs and you'll be home in no time."

"Wouldn't that be nice." Home in the bathtub, with about a pound of Epsom salts and a chocolate bar and a bottle of something cold and bubbly. Home with the air-conditioning blowing down my neck. Home was still hours away. I stroked Mickey's light gray neck, feeling his heat and sticky sweat through my gloves. May was halfway over. It was barely even summer up north, but in Florida we'd been baking for months, and Georgia was happy to get in on the action. I was dying for a break in the weather, but we'd be waiting at least another six months before we saw one. I awoke sweating from dreams about cool nights and hoodies.

The loudspeaker nearby crackled to life. "Number thirty-eight, Louise Demaret on Rushing River, now on course. Number thirty-nine, Juliet Thornton on Danger Mouse, you're on deck."

Pete reached over and placed a gloved hand on my thigh. I resisted the urge to lean into him. His little mare was desperately in love with Mickey, and I was trying to discourage their inappropriate romance. "You got this," he repeated, eyes crinkling, a gift from the sun for a life spent outdoors. "One more little Training course, and you can go Prelim this fall."

I nodded, lips tight. *Thanks for the reminder.* We were sitting in fifth place after the dressage and show jumping. All I needed now was a clean cross-country round and a little bad luck for one of the riders ahead of me. With two more finishes in the top three this summer, I'd qualify for the annual championships. Then I just had to get a top finish in the Training level championship, and I'd have no trouble convincing Mickey's conservative owners that it was time to pick a three-day event and start training toward it.

My stomach lurched and I swallowed down something bitter. After all these years, horse show nerves were still part of life. You'd think it would get easier, but instead, the stakes just kept getting higher.

Pete leaned in for a kiss. "Good luck," he whispered, cupping my cheek. I pressed against his gloved hand for a moment, warm from his mare's neck, and smelled the good scents of our life: leather, liniment, horse.

"Thanks, Pete," I whispered, managing a real smile, and gathered up my reins. "Time to go for a little gallop," I told Mickey, and he tilted his black-tipped ears toward me, listening and ready, instantly at attention.

He was so good like that. I gave Pete a wave and sent Mickey forward with a nudge from my seat.

I let Mickey pick up a little jog down the hillside as we headed for the nearby starting box, scattering Pony Clubbers and gawkers who had come to see the horses set off on their runs. The starting box can be a pretty entertaining place to hang out at an event, especially in the lower levels. It takes time and experience to figure out what your horse wants from you before a cross-country round—some horses need to be kept wide awake and pacing in circles, some horses need to stand very still and gaze out at the field before them. Give them the wrong idea, and they start jumping around with their legs in the air well before it's time to run. Especially, God love 'em, the Thoroughbreds.

Mickey was an ex-racehorse too, but after a pretty tumultuous year together, I knew just how to keep his head firmly on his neck and his hooves on the ground. We jogged in a few neat little circles, scarcely more than fifteen meters wide, and as the starter glanced up and said, "You're up!" I brought him down to a walk, circled the starting box, and waited for the final countdown.

"Five—four—three—" The starter was giving me a warning look, her stopwatch held up so I could see she meant business.

I walked Mickey into the three-sided starting box, as big as a stall but with just one spindly railing around it. Once, I'd taken him in too soon, and he'd jumped out of it. I'd gotten a stern talking-to from the event organizers, and some interesting press on the blogs. Now I took him at the last second, which still annoyed the starters. There was no pleasing some people.

"Two—one—have a nice ride!" The usual recitation.

I gave Mickey a little nudge and he went springing into a trot, and then an easy canter, and we were on course.

"Here we go, buddy boy!" I gave him a rub on the neck and let him stretch out a little bit, feeling the footing. All the trepidation of five minutes ago was long gone. I waved at the jump judge as Mickey studied the first jump, a nice easy picnic table, hardly Novice height, and popped over it with inches to spare. The jump judge, who looked like a little kid with her ponytail and pink breeches, giggled at us.

"See you later!" I called back, but we were already continuing on too quickly for her to hear me, Mickey's hooves finding the well-worn track of the horses who had come before us, moving through the big open pasture at a hand gallop. Ahead there were a few more easy introductory fences—a coop in a fence line, a wood-lined ditch ominously labeled "the Snake Pit" on the map. They actually threw some rubber snakes in the ditch, which I found hilarious. If your horse had a problem with ditches, toy snakes were the least of your problems.

Unless, I considered, the snakes were put there to scare whomever ended up *in* the ditch. Landing in a pile of snakes would quickly teach you to put your heels down and keep your upper body back before a fence.

Mickey didn't notice the snakes and he didn't threaten to tip me into them either; he was too busy looking at the dark smudge of forest ahead. As we leaped over the ditch with scarcely more than a lengthening of stride, I was already beginning to adjust my weight backward, picking up his head and asking him to bring his hindquarters beneath his body. Mickey was not a naturally balanced horse when he was out galloping. He was more interested in covering ground as quickly as possible, and didn't seem to mind that running downhill on his forehand could end up sending us both head over heels. He was also heavy as an anvil this morning, dragging his head down against the bit.

I grunted, giving him a simultaneous tug on the reins and boot in the ribs. "Get your big old head off the ground, dummy."

We swept down the slope toward the woods, the heat rising up from the fields around us in sizzling waves. At least the woods would be cooler than this, I thought, blinking at the sweat starting to trickle down my forehead. The backs of my leather-palmed gloves were cotton, specifically designed to wipe sweat away from my eyes, but I needed two hands to balance Mickey, who was evidently determined to stay top-heavy. My eyes would just have to burn.

We jumped a hanging log into the woods and cantered cautiously along a mulched path through the oaks, Mickey's pricked ears watching out for potential bogeymen in the shadows. Beneath the shade trees, the air temperature seemed to drop twenty degrees.

The breeze became a cooling caress instead of a furnace blast. Why wasn't the entire world shady?

"Let's just give it all up and stay here forever," I told Mickey, but like a good sport horse, he was only focused on the finish line. He didn't even know he was hot. He wouldn't notice until we had pulled up and he was satisfied he'd won whatever race he was running in his mind. Then he'd drag me to the nearest hosepipe and quiver impatiently, pawing at the mud puddles, until I doused him all over.

A creek presented itself in our path and he splashed through it rather than jumping. "Good decision," I told him. "Save your energy." Ahead, the trail slanted uphill again and I could see the hot sun waiting for us.

Mickey was happier galloping uphill than downhill, and he picked up speed as we tackled the steep slope and burst back into the open field. The weird road hazard jump was waiting for us atop its hill, yellow-and-black stripes blazing in the white summer sunlight. The center planks were painted in a chevron of the same colors. The resulting palette was garish and off-putting, but did horses even see all the colors in our spectrum? I knew they liked blue buckets. Maybe the whole challenge was psychological.

"Road closed!" I shouted, feeling giddy as Mickey took the bit and lengthened his stride. He liked a good uphill fence as much as any other horse with a powerhouse of a hind end, and my hollering had him hyped up. I let him go plunging up to the fence at his own pace, content to revel in his power, sure he'd make the right decision about when to jump.

Mickey took off a full stride too early, catching me off guard. I lurched backward in the saddle and felt the cantle touch my breeches, then I regained control of my body and folded over his neck to stop my hands from catching his mouth on the other side.

My legs slid up behind me, but I managed to keep my knees pinned to the saddle to maintain a semblance of security.

I heard the jump judge gasp. Oh yeah, it was *that* kind of jump.

We landed like a ton of bricks on the far side and I slumped over his shoulder as we started downhill again, letting him straighten himself out while I regained stirrups and reins and seat. Luckily, there was plenty of time before the water complex to get myself situated again.

"Messy," I told Mickey, sorting out my slippery reins. "But who cares what we look like, as long as we're clear."

Pretty doesn't count in cross-country.

The main problem with having the cross-country after the show jumping, in my opinion, is that there's no mounted ribbon presentation, no slipping the rosette into your horse's browband, no victory gallop around the arena. It's highly anticlimactic to cool out your horse, pick up a gallon of Gatorade from the cooler, and march over to the jumping arena or wherever management has placed the leaderboard so you can stalk the final scores as they come in, one by one. Especially when you're already disappointed by your dressage score from the day before. I'd spent the past twenty-four hours knowing that unless someone ahead of me screwed up royally, I wasn't going to get what I'd come here for. I had about five more minutes for someone to make that golden mistake, and at this point it wasn't looking good.

Pete was managing to look nonchalant about the incoming scores, maybe because he was first after the dressage and had a clear jumping round. He'd picked up a couple of time faults in the cross-country, which had put the next finisher within a hairsbreadth of beating him . . . until that unlucky challenger picked up a refusal. There'd be a blue ribbon on our truck's rearview mirror tonight, it just wouldn't be mine.

"Looks like you're still on track to take fifth," Pete observed unhelpfully, surveying the whiteboard. The day's results so far were scrawled across them in an uneven attempt at a grid.

"Mm-hmm," I agreed around a gulp of Gatorade. I hadn't come all the way out here on a boiling-hot day in hopes of a pink ribbon, but I didn't bother saying that. He knew already. He knew I didn't like pink.

"Too bad it isn't first, I know, but, hey—you got around without any problems. That's a good sign. No sloppy mistakes, no messy fences, right? Good job, hon. You two have come a long way."

From anyone else, I would have bristled at these words. Pete got a pass. He'd been around since the rocky beginning. He knew that Mickey and I had overcome a few misunderstandings to get to this point—and by misunderstandings, I meant training issues that had exploded with roughly the power of your average island-destroying volcano. If it weren't for Pete's intervention, Mickey and I might not have been competing at Training level today, or ever.

Owing people a debt of gratitude was not really my favorite thing, but, luckily, Pete was pretty high on my list of People That Don't Suck. In fact, he was at the very top.

Which made it kind of hard to lie to him.

I peered over the lip of my Gatorade bottle at Pete. He squinted back at me. "Something you want to tell me?"

"We were kind of messy in the end," I admitted.

"The skinny hedge? Yeah, I could see it. That could've been tighter."

Sure, the skinny hedge. Let's leave it at that. Why mention blowing the takeoff at the road-hazard fence, or the monumental scramble we'd had over the two-stride log fences on the second sweep through the forest? We'd gotten over them, hadn't we?

I shrugged. "I just couldn't hold him together anymore. He was so heavy on the forehand by that point, just dragging himself around the course."

"He's not fit, you're saying. What do you think he's missing, in terms of conditioning?" Pete loved discussing the science of conditioning and nutrition. I didn't feel up to a research forum at the moment, though. The steward was over by the board, writing up some numbers. My stomach clenched and released as another pair of riders were added to the list of clean cross-country rounds.

"We've done the same fitness works as you and Mayfair," I said, averting my eyes from the whiteboard. "But she's ready to go out and run a race, and Mickey was blowing before the course was over. I guess we have to change something. Still, it was a clean round. No time penalties."

Pete smiled absently, no doubt thinking of how angelic his little Mayfair had been. She might have been a hair slow, but Pete wasn't really bothered with time penalties so long as he got an absolutely beautiful round. He truly *rode* his novices every stride of every course, showing them where to put their feet and when to jump the fences, using their dressage schooling to create picture-perfect bascules. He said that over-riding a horse a little in the lower levels gave them skill and confidence they'd be able to use to his advantage in the upper levels.

Personally, I thought he could use fewer cues from dressage and a few more from racing. Poetry in motion was lovely in theory, but optimum time was no joke. At the upper levels, only a few quarter-time penalties might divide the top three finishers—and at a big event, that could be the difference between paying off the show bills, or skipping Starbucks on the long drive home.

Pete seemed to live with a placid understanding that there would always be time to fix these things down the road. I, on the other hand, needed everything to be top-notch, all the time. I needed to win, I needed to know I was drawing ahead, I needed to know I was getting better all the time. I needed to know there was light at the end of this tunnel. I needed to know I could get a venti black coffee with a shot of espresso to see me home.

Living on the edge of bankruptcy was exhausting. I wasn't sure how much longer I could take it.

That was why a fifth-place finish hurt so much. It wasn't a leap closer to any of my goals. I couldn't see any point of having come here at all.

I scooted out of the way as the steward came over with a dry erase marker and added the last score to the whiteboard. I peered over her shoulder while she totted up the figures and started scrawling in the final placings. There you had it: Peter Morrison and Miss Mayfair were first in the Novice Horse division. A few rows down, Juliet Thornton and Danger Mouse were fifth in Training Horse.

"I'm just going to get my pink ribbon and go home," I said, starting for the registration tent.

"Hey!" Pete caught my arm as I tried to slip past him. "This is good news!"

I gave him a skeptical look.

"You had a good round, right? So you didn't get a top-three finish. I know you wanted to take him to the AECs later, but if you're not going to qualify by now, why worry about it? Don't spend your summer worrying about getting two more qualifiers. Just concentrate on getting ready for your first Prelim event."

"I want to move up, but . . . it's a *championship*." What a magical word that was. The American Eventing Championships had felt like an attainable goal a few months ago when I'd first moved

Mickey into Training level. We'd only got one qualifying finish though, when we'd won first place last month at Sunshine State. I was aware part of the win had been the venue—we'd shown so much at Sunshine State, the showgrounds just south of Ocala had started to feel like our second home.

"A *Training* championship," Pete pointed out. "What does that prove, when you're trying to get a horse ready to go Advanced someday? This time next year, you could have done your first three-day event. *That's* the goal. *That's* what you should be focusing on."

Those were the true magic words: three-day event. I started flicking through calendars in my mind. A one-star three-day event in the spring—compete all next summer—run a two-star in the late fall—then just like that, two years have gone by and we are going Advanced and competing with the big boys, for the big medals. If you spend enough rainy afternoons reading the United States Eventing Association Omnibus, you know exactly what weekend belongs to which event. I could see the next eighteen months unfurling before with me with thrilling clarity, and the thought of spending another moment worrying about the Training level championships suddenly became laughable.

"You're right." I threw my arms around Pete's neck. "It's time to think bigger!"

Pete stumbled back under my embrace. "Oh my God." He started laughing. "Those are the most frightening words Jules Thornton could ever say."

# 2

PETE'S WORDS HAD their tiny sting, but I guess you could say that I had a bit of a reputation. In fact, the only way I was allowed to share a truck cab with Pete on the way to and from events was if I promised to keep my mouth shut about plans, points, or priorities for the upcoming six months. I had a bad habit of living in the future, he said, and not spending enough time in the present. But it was such an interesting future, I argued, how could I be blamed?

This evening, as the sun sank in a lavish yellow spectacle over Georgia's rolling hills, I had mentally fast-forwarded past the hot summer ahead. My mind was on the upcoming fall and winter seasons. Through summer, I'd take Mickey to a few moonlight jumper shows to keep his show-jumping game sharp. We'd skip events in August, run at Training level in September for a tune-up, zing through the Modified courses in October and November to make that step up to Preliminary a little easier, and then we'd make our Prelim debut by Christmas. Fast? Yes. But Mickey was talented and eager. With some good placings over the winter, we could qualify and enter a one-star three-day event by spring. I gazed out at the endless pines and saw only cross-country courses and cheering crowds.

"Yes," I said aloud, so content I forgot the ban on audible ambition.

Pete grimaced at me from the other side of the cab. The blue, yellow, and pink ribbons of our rosettes were fluttering between us in the ripples of cold air from the laboring air-conditioning. The yellow one was mine as well as the pink; Dynamo had taken third in Intermediate, proving once again that he was my stable's solid workhorse, although I had no doubt Pete thought he would've beat us if he'd brought along Regina.

"Stop planning," he scolded. "Relax for a minute."

I laughed. "Not in my DNA."

"How many Olympic medals have you won by this time in ten years?"

"Oh, dozens."

"Ms. Thornton, you've won the three-day eventing gold medal four Olympics in a row! Any plans for retirement?"

"Never," I announced. "Never, ever."

Pete grinned. "I believe it, too."

"What's wrong with that? I love eventing. It's everything to me. Why would I ever give it up?"

He reached across the wide truck seat and gave my thigh a squeeze. "No reason," he said. "Every now and then I like to pretend

I'll get you to take a vacation with me, that's all. I figure you'll have to reach the pinnacle of your sport and get bored before you'll consent to a week off."

I snorted. "A vacation. You're a very funny man." As if either of us would ever have the time for that. With three competition horses in the trailer behind us, and two barns' worth of horses in training waiting for us back at the farm, there was hardly a chance of anything more than an afternoon off in our near future.

Not that I minded one bit, of course. This life was everything I'd ever wanted, and I was so close to having it all. A few more horses in my barn, a few more dollars in my pocket—well, it was the same complaint year after year, but I had to be closer now than I had been a year ago, right? A year closer, anyway.

"Heard anything new about sponsorships?" I asked idly, flipping through my email on my phone. I had been hoping a championship run would send a few brands my way. I would be happy to sit in just about anyone's saddle and give it total credit for my wins, but so far, no one was responding to any of my pitches. Meanwhile, the flaps on my cross-country saddle were wearing to wafer-thin beneath my knees and calves, and my dressage saddle's billets and tree had been born in different generations.

"Just . . . no. Nothing."

I turned and looked at his profile. "Are you sure?"

"Of course I'm sure." He chuckled.

I thought the laugh sounded forced. "You can tell me," I said, making an attempt to sound like a reasonable and empathetic person. I wasn't either of those things, which is probably why Pete laughed again, for real this time, and told me there was absolutely nothing going on.

"You'd be the first to know, obviously," he reminded me.

"Because I'm not taking anything that doesn't include you. We're a package deal."

I reached across the truck cab and squeezed his leg. I knew he meant it. Pete wouldn't leave me behind. He'd said so a hundred times, to the point where I was finally starting to believe him.

It was near midnight before our exit finally appeared in the truck's headlights. We went bouncing down the rutted country highway, west into the heart of Marion County, winding through the endless black-board fences and moss-hung live oaks. Yearlings woke from startled slumber and peered at us from their pastures. A white-tailed possum gamboled across the blacktop, its eyes reflecting our headlights like bright golden coins, and when Pete braked to avoid running it over, there was a barrage of complaining kicks from the horses in the backseat.

As Pete turned the truck up our own road, I felt a new surge of excitement at the thought of getting home, even though in these late hours there would be no one to greet us—or help us put the horses away. Lacey and Becky, usually our show grooms, had stayed behind this time, and they'd be long asleep. That was just fine; I was too tired to give a recounting of the event, who had been there, what they had been wearing, what their horses had been wearing, who had won what. I was just looking forward to the long walk back to the house from the annex barn, where my string of horses lived, with the bright Ocala stars over my head and the dark Ocala hills sloping away beside me, gazing up at the infinite beyond and knowing exactly where I belonged in the big sweeping universe.

Mickey and Dynamo were settled into their stalls, the tack and trunks had been shoved into place in the tack room, and there was no reason to put off heading home for a shower and bed. Still, I lingered, peering into stalls one by one, and the horses looked up from their hay and wondered why I wasn't leaving them to their nighttime rituals.

I didn't know, either.

Certainly not because the weather was nice. The hot, still day in Georgia had faded into a hot, breezy night in Ocala. Although the palm fronds along the barn drive were rattling with every gust, the sea breeze did nothing to cool the night. I could tell already, we were going to have an unreasonably hot summer. Extreme weather was the new normal: last year an unusually rough rainy season had featured a devastating hurricane, then an unusually dry winter had given us blazing wildfires all through spring. Why should this coming summer be any different?

My barn wasn't exactly a cool refuge, either. Briar Hill Farm had two main barns: the big gorgeous training barn, built in the shed-row style with open aisles around all four sides and high, open ceilings; and the annex barn, built in an old-fashioned broodmare-barn style, with thick cinder-block walls, low rafters, and a center aisle running between the dark stalls.

Pete had the training barn, and he would have been happy to share with me, but I didn't think I had the temperament to share a barn with anyone, let alone a boyfriend. So in the interest of domestic tranquility and sanity, I kept my little string of trainees in the annex barn, a good fifteen minutes' walk from the house and the training barn. At least as a former broodmare barn, it boasted big stalls and a wide center aisle, designed to give protective mares and their foals plenty of room to bounce around. That was the good part. It had been built back in the '60s by horsemen from up north, which was the bad part.

So naturally, instead of being sensibly built with the barn windows facing east and west, to catch the sea breezes from the

Gulf and the Atlantic, my barn's windows looked northeast and southwest. Nothing good ever came from either of those two directions—at least, not in Florida. The upshot was that the barn was cold all winter and hot all summer.

At each stall, a box fan was roaring away, speed set on high, blowing back the horses' forelocks when they pushed their noses up against the grill for some extra air. The fans' white noise was part of the summer soundtrack—everyone learned to shout a little louder, and turn the radio up a couple notches, when the fans were on. When the horses went outside and the fans were switched off, the silence was deafening.

In tonight's crushing heat, everyone was either making love to their fan or eating their hay over the aisle, hoping for a bit of breeze and making a huge mess for Lacey and me to sweep up in the morning. Dynamo was one of the former; he took no notice of me when I stopped outside his stall and peeked in at him. He'd been with me for two straight days, he was probably thinking, and the sooner I went back to wherever humans stabled themselves, the better.

Mickey was one of the latter, cheerfully strewing hay across the aisle with a glutton's abandon, though when I leaned against his stall door, he kindly decided I was more interesting than the hay. Ordinarily, I wasn't a huge fan of having a horse rub his hundred-pound head all over my torso, but getting this kind of attention from Mickey was flattering. He'd had a long, hot weekend, and he would have been well within his rights to ignore me for a day or two, which was what Dynamo was surely planning.

I let Mickey get his head rub on while I busied myself playing with his stubby forelock. He'd sheared it off in a barn accident last year, the very night he'd arrived at my farm. When it had grown back to a proper length, it would be absolutely gorgeous, like a unicorn's. Although the rest of his coat and mane were pale gray, shot through here and there with darker strands, the forelock had grown back pure white. I thanked the eventing gods every day that the hair had grown back, and so spectacularly beautiful.

"You look so dashing," I told him affectionately. "Such a heartthrob. The most handsome man I know."

"It's about time you realized that."

I jumped about fifty feet in the air, more or less, sending Mickey ducking back into his stall in alarm.

"Pete, dammit, don't *do* that!"

He was leaning against the doorframe at the end of the barn aisle, arms folded across his chest. The orange light hanging over the barn door, studded with flying moths, turned his lanky frame into a black shadow against the artificial glow. I couldn't see his expression, but I knew that lazy grin was spread across his tanned face, that laughing sparkle was dancing in his eyes, and that faintly patronizing eyebrow of his was arched in its usual display of amusement. Pete had decided early on that he found all my sulky moods and arrogant airs rather entertaining, like a hoity-toity filly who is too busy being a brat to pay attention and trips over her own two feet. He was essentially trying to train me out of being such a brat by laughing at my bad behavior. I wasn't sure if it was working, or if I just saved my sulks and moods for the isolation of the barn, like tonight. I guess he won either way.

"Sneaking around my barn again, huh?" I challenged. "Trying to find my secrets?"

"I know all your secrets, baby," Pete said. "You come out here at night and hug and kiss your way to blue ribbons. I just wish you'd do that with me."

"Hah." I turned back to Mickey, but the horse had rediscovered the joys of alfalfa. He was done with me. "I'm going to have to do a lot more hugging and kissing if I'm going to start beating you again."

Pete started down the aisle toward me. "I know you have it in you. Typical horse-crazy teenager. I'm surprised you don't sleep in the barn."

"Hey, I'm twenty-four whole years old," I reminded him. "I'm all grown up."

"And still horse-crazy? Shouldn't you have grown out of that by now?"

"I'll never grow out of it. Just like you won't."

"I'll admit that." Pete stopped in front of me. "But if you could be boy-crazy for just one minute, I sure could use a late night in front of the TV with a pretty girl." He opened up his arms, and after a moment's pretend hesitation, I stepped into them.

Wrapped up in Pete's arms, feeling his easy strength around me, I could just let go. Let go of all of it—the daily demands of caring for the horses, the bowing and scraping to my handful of owners, the constant fear someone would overtake me, leaving me with nothing again. I'd been so close to losing it all, and not very long ago. Last year I'd lost my farm to a hurricane, and I'd lost most of my business in the wake of the storm.

Still, hadn't I come out on top? I had to remind myself of that a lot. Yes, losing my farm had been like losing a piece of myself. But I had clients, I had horses, and I had Pete, the only person in the world I trusted enough to take charge every now and then.

I admit, there were occasional sleepless nights when I woke up beside him and wondered what would happen if we fought (*really* fought, not the silly fights I provoked simply by being me), and I had to move out. I was constantly aware I was living on *his* property and in *his* house. "But," Pete explained gently, one night when he woke up and saw me counting out down payments and mortgages on my fingers, "relying on someone else—that's how love *works*."

Now I rested my chin on his shoulder and closed my eyes, blocking out the view of the shadowy barn. There was nothing but the sound of his heartbeat and the sound of horses chewing their hay, snorting into their water buckets, pacing through their shavings. For a brief, shining moment, I felt peaceful.

Someone kicked a wall and someone else whinnied, and the moment was gone. I stepped out of his embrace and glared up the barn aisle. "Knock it off!"

There was an intense quiet as the horses gauged my level of outrage.

"We should be turning them out at night," I mused. "It's easier having them inside for breakfast, but it's too hot to leave them in. And they train better when they're out all night. They run around playing and they're worn out the next day. Less arguing. What do you think?"

"What, turn them out right now? Can't we go to the house, and take showers, and not work for, I don't know, four or five hours?"

"I'm just saying, tomorrow night, my guys are all going back out after dinner. Yours should, too, or they'll hear mine and fuss in their stalls all night."

"Anything, if you'll just come inside now." Pete mopped his brow dramatically. "You're so worried about them being hot, when are you going to start worrying about me?"

"When you're as delicate as a horse," I said, casting a glance around the aisle to make sure that all the stall doors were latched and all the light switches were flicked down. I couldn't resist one last night-check, and, holding up a finger to let Pete know I'd just be a second, I headed down the barn aisle, looking for trouble.

He sighed.

I paused by Dynamo's stall once more. The chestnut Thoroughbred I'd had since I was a teenager stood with his hindquarters to me, face deep in the hay pile he'd dragged to the back corner of the stall. "Dyno," I called gently. "Dyno-saur . . ."

He flicked one ear toward me and snorted into his hay. I bit my lip, disappointed. There was a time when he would have come over for a kiss.

To my right, there was soft nicker. I turned and saw Mickey leaning over his stall grill again, watching me with pricked ears. Even in the gloom, his gray coat was luminous, that snowy forelock nearly glowing. He saw me watching him and nickered again. My heart lifted.

Pete chuckled. "That horse sure does love you. You two have come together nicely."

My heart was in my throat, and I could only nod. It was a changing of the guard, and it was bittersweet. I didn't want to leave it this way. I would stay, I thought, until Dynamo gave in and said goodnight to me.

Pete sighed again and caught my hand in his. "Come on. I have a beer waiting for you in the kitchen." I took one more look at Dynamo, still ignoring me, and gave a parting kiss to Mickey's soft gray nose. Then I let Pete lead me away.

We walked quietly for a few strides, boots crunching on the gravel drive. The stars glittered overhead.

"My favorite time of night," Pete said. "I don't see it much, though."

"It's beautiful," I agreed. "But it's so hot."

"Fall's only a few months away. You gonna make it? We can always run away to Canada."

"I don't have enough blankets for them. That would cost a fortune. Anyway, as long as they're okay, I'm okay." I looked back over my shoulder at the annex barn, squatting low on the hill-side under its shade of live oaks. The barn had its faults—missing shingles, flaking paint, airless stalls—but the twilight hid them, and the barn was sturdy and strong and had survived many a hurricane. That had recently become paramount in my mind, and I knew I wasn't the only one in Ocala who was living with a new-found respect for nature. "We can live with a little heat."

"Now it's time to take things a little easier, anyway," Pete said, slipping his arm around my shoulders. "A little time off, and I have a secret plan to make you leave the farm and go to the beach with me."

I laughed. "Fat chance of that!"

Time off, with the prospect of prepping Mickey for a three-day event? Time off, with Dynamo still jumping strong? Time off, with only a handful of horses in a big barn just begging to be filled? Time off, with bills to pay and mouths to feed?

I had work to do.

Vacations were for other people.

# 3

MORNING CAME TOO soon, the sun peeping through the windows, then blasting in. I got up with much groaning and sighing; Pete grinned at me as he went out the door, but I could see he was tired too, so I let it pass.

I had a horse-show-weekend hangover. Too much coffee, Gatorade, and cheap granola bars, not enough real food and water. Staying in bed all day was the obvious, impossible answer.

"You'd like that, wouldn't you, Marcus?" I looked over my shoulder for my beagle.

Marcus snuffled around the base of a tree, his whip-tail wagging, and ignored me.

The walk down to the annex barn had been peaceful enough: an easy amble down an oak-lined drive, the trees whispering and rustling above, the black-board fences running with pleasant symmetry along either side of the road. I had views a king would envy: Briar Hill was practically a mountain by central Florida standards, and the drive-way ran right through the center, giving me a bird's-eye view of the neighborhood.

I gazed out over the rural patchwork of Marion County while the mockingbirds gossiped in the branches overhead, taking in the ovals of training tracks where young racehorses were learning their trade, the stern rectangles of dressage arenas, and the generous sweeps of open pasture, full of animals and humans very occupied at the business of life before the hot sun took control, and felt deeply lucky to be me.

I still missed my old farm, although now it was just a flat spot of ground grown over with weeds, but there was no denying I'd landed on my feet at Briar Hill. Sure, the past year had been rough, both competitively and financially. I'd lost a good chunk of busi-ness right after last summer's hurricane destroyed my farm, and I'd lost even more horses in training in the months since. I knew potential clients didn't like that I was a renter instead of an owner. They'd see my temporary status as the possibility that I'd pick up in the night and move like so many horse trainers loved to do when the going got tough. They didn't know how good I had it, though, or they could put their fears to rest. I looked across the green fields. *Good morning, darling farm! Good morning, lovely hills!* Pete wasn't the only one who was just a bit delusional.

"Good morning, kids!" I called down the aisle, but the horses were eating their grain and didn't have time for me. Also they couldn't hear me, since Lacey was blasting the radio station spe-cializing in '80s pop, evidently because she knew all the words to every song, even though they were older than she was.

I considered going back to bed, if only to escape her singing.

The horses would probably come with me. We could all run away together, and save our eardrums.

Lacey, her back to me as she raked the aisle, decided to really go for it, announcing to the world at large her devotion to expensive jewelry and designer clothes.

The words were pretty funny when you considered Lacey was wearing ripped khaki shorts, a pink tank top so stretched out and worn it was hardly a shirt anymore, and a pair of canvas sneakers from Walmart that had taken on the color and texture of the dirt beneath her feet.

"MATERI-AL-HUL!" Lacey wailed, in very loose synchronization with the radio.

I turned off the radio. "Hey, Spirit of the Eighties, you're going to colic my horses."

Lacey didn't even blush. She just looked at me over her sunburned shoulder and stuck out her tongue. "Oh good, the *boss* is here." She turned back to her raking. "Did you hear that, horses, *the boss is here*! Everyone be super good or you'll get in trouble!"

I switched the radio back on and went into the tack room to escape her. Lacey returned to her singing.

"Hello there, coffee," I greeted the dusty Mr. Coffee, which was rumbling away industriously from atop its perch on the ancient mini fridge. The machine reached the end of its cycle and cheeped a welcome to me. "Now that's the kind of sound I want to hear in my barn first thing in the morning."

While I sipped my coffee, I took thorough stock of the feed room. It wasn't much to see, just a twelve-by-twelve concrete cube doing double duty at holding everything my tiny string of sales and sport horses needed. Bridles hanging on the wall, plastic shelves holding everything from electrolytes to galloping boots, and a corner crammed with trash cans to store horse feed. I had a big wall calendar hanging on the door, marked with upcoming shows, galloping days, farrier visits, dewormer due dates, and all the other fun little things that break up the monotony of training barn life. Day in and day out, we performed the same tasks so often that if you really gave it any thought, you'd go slightly insane—had I really just meticulously cleaned that stall in order to put a horse back inside and watch him destroy it again? Was this really all going to happen again tomorrow, in the same order, in the same way? Only the big personalities in those stalls out there saved us from total boredom.

Dynamo was still king of the barn. The red chestnut Thoroughbred was fighting fit, with the build and swagger of a prize-fighter. I'd kept him eventing at Intermediate level for the past season. I was holding back on going Advanced, waiting for the right moment. When Dynamo took on the bigger, wider jumps at the top level of eventing, we needed to be ready to wow everyone. Especially any US Equestrian Team selectors who might be pulling for the next international championship.

If Dynamo was king, Mickey was prince and heir apparent. The good-looking ex-racehorse had matured over the past year, and was now a stunningly handsome performance horse with all the right proportions: long legs with plenty of bone; a deep, wide chest; powerful hindquarters; and an elegantly muscled swan's neck, which gleamed nearly white in the glaring Florida sunlight, all crowned with a salt-and-pepper mane. With those flashy good looks, his kind dark eye was a blessing. At seven years old, he was developing into a thoughtful horse who considered the things I told him and mostly agreed to do them.

I didn't own Mickey, but that was okay. Every now and then, when I felt like torturing myself, I imagined what life would be like if his owners pulled him from my barn and sent him to a bigger, more accomplished, arguably far more deserving trainer than myself, and I would walk around the rest of the day with a creeping sense of unease, jumping every time my phone rang or a truck's tires rattled over the gravel drive.

Of course, there was no real reason to imagine they'd take him away—not when they'd left him with me this long. I'd kept Mickey sound and happy through a year of Novice and Training level eventing, going as slowly as they had asked me to. I was doing everything right.

In my version of the future, Mickey and I were together forever, from Novice to the Olympics to retirement, a storybook saga as rich and beautiful as the one I had with Dynamo, only better because I was farther along as a rider now, so we could fast-forward some of the early scenes and get right to the good parts. He was the shiny white pony of my childhood dreams, the sleek gray sport horse I'd sketched into school textbooks in my teenage years, before I'd replaced that dappled hero with an emotionally damaged red chestnut who was at least *real*.

"Jules!" Lacey's insistent voice cut into my musings at just the right moment. "Jules, come and help me turn out!"

"Can't you do it? I have to go over my training calendar." I picked up the little agenda where I wrote detailed descriptions of daily rides, temperature-pulse-respiration numbers from fitness days, and hopeful training epochs I expected to reach in the future. Today being the Monday after an event weekend, I'd already written "day off" or "hack" across most of the horses' entries.

I blinked at the words in surprise. I'd completely forgotten what day it was. I really did need more sleep. "Never mind, I just did it," I called.

"Duh," Lacey said, leaning in from the aisle. She had Margot's lead rope in her hand, because these days Lacey was obsessed with the pretty chestnut mare and always turned her out first, hayed her first, gave her grain first . . . kind of the same thing I did with Dynamo and Mickey, my wonder boys. "It's Monday, goofball. It's our day of rest."

"Good, then I'm going home and you handle this mess."

"If you go home, I'm going home."

"If you go home, who will clean all these stalls?"

"Becky," Lacey suggested coyly. "We'll just tell her we're sick."

I laughed. The idea had merit. Becky physically could not let a barn go uncleaned. She'd do all of Pete's stalls and then march right down here and do all of mine. We'd never get away with it, though. "Pete would find out," I said regretfully.

Lacey sighed. "It's a shame *you* caught Pete and not me. He'd be putty in my hands. He'd think he was in charge and it would be me the whole time. With you, he's just plain in charge."

"He's not in charge. Well, he's not in charge of *this* barn."

Lacey smirked and towed Margot along. "Let's just get these animals out of the barn so we can mop up their filth, and then you can tell me how Pete's not the boss of you and I'll try not to laugh. Sound good?"

"Whatever," I said, queen of comebacks as always. "Get out of my barn, and take that bitchy mare with you."

Barney, a rough-coated Thoroughbred-draft cross with rolling white eyeballs, shoved his head over his stall grill as Margot went by, whinnying with desperate love. Margot aimed a hind leg in his general direction.

I waited until the mare was a safe distance away, then snatched up Barney's halter and lead, sliding the strap behind his ears while he was still watching his lady sashay out to the mare pasture. "She doesn't love you," I told him, "and she never will."

Barney wasn't very smart, though, and he cried after her all the way out to the gelding pasture, and then proceeded to run the fence line for the next fifteen minutes, shrieking out his endless passion, while we turned out Maybelline (also known as the Chestnut Mare of Doom, because she was much worse than Margot), and the geldings Mickey, Dynamo, Jim Dear, and Hart, none of whom paid the slightest attention to lovesick Barney. We were all used to him.

"Now, to muck," Lacey announced. "I guess you're helping, since you turned out your horses instead of riding them."

"We can hack them out together after we do the barn, and take a nap this afternoon." I felt in dire need of an easy day after melting in the Georgia heat all weekend. "Sound good?"

"Sounds awesome!" Lacey started flinging manure rakes and brooms into a wheelbarrow with fresh enthusiasm. Then she flipped the radio back on. That was the problem with Lacey, I decided, as she began to belt out the lyrics to a song I didn't even recognize. She didn't appreciate silence nearly as much as I did.

For me, cleaning up a silent barn is a form of meditation. You scoop and you fling, you rake and you dig, you smooth and you spread, all of your movements fluid and mechanical—after all, raking up manure and wet bedding and wasted hay isn't exactly rocket science. Your brain is free to wander. I usually did my best thinking when I was mucking out. I planned out training calendars, worked through complicated math to figure out if I could afford grain, gas, hay, a new set of open-front boots for Dynamo. I could probably have written a book while I was shoveling shit, quietly dictating the words into a little clipped-on microphone.

As Lacey howled along with Bon Jovi, I felt cheated out of a good wallowing worry. Nothing really brought home how little money I was making quite like going to an event, which was basically a large festival you threw money and time at, worked your ass off to win, then came home from empty-handed (except for your pretty ribbons), just hoping someone with money had seen you and been impressed. So far, no one had.

Meanwhile, the horses I owned seemed destined to stay with me forever.

Dynamo was a given, but Maybelline and Margot? It had something to do with their personalities and talents: one had too much personality, one had too little talent.

Maybelline was an empress of evil, a chestnut off-track Thoroughbred who went off the deep end every few months. Last month she'd been performing a solid First Level dressage test; this month she would have been more suitable for a bucking competition. Her pasturemate, Margot, was polite enough as a sort of advanced school horse for the occasional students who floated in and out of my daily planner. Lacey adored her, but there was nothing above-average about Margot.

Unfortunately, selling mediocre Thoroughbred mares in this market was next to impossible. Everyone in Ocala knew that if you wanted a mare, you just drove up to a breeding farm and asked for one until someone handed you a lead rope with a horse attached. There were always open mares after breeding season, mares who hadn't gotten pregnant or wouldn't stay pregnant, and didn't have any other use for their owners. To stand out as a Thoroughbred mare in Ocala, you needed to be a goddess among horses, talented beyond belief *and* regularly winning at rated shows.

Much like broke event trainers, average horses were a dime a dozen in this town. I had a couple of nice sales horses sent to me by a few friendly owners who weren't in a hurry and didn't want to pay higher fees for a more established trainer. Hart, Jim Dear, and Barney were all learning to event so they could be sold as amateur-owner mounts. I was pretty good at making solid horses who jumped what they were pointed at and stopped when they were told. It was a useful skill, because push-button horses are expensive. The check for my last packer, Virtuoso, was paying this spring's bills. I wasn't sure who was going to pay the summer ones.

I emptied a pair of water buckets out of the stall window and peeked out at the grazing horses, dotting the hillside below the barn. The sight calmed me, reminding me all this worry was worth it.

At least there were opportunities on the horizon. Pete had been in talks with a potential sponsor, someone who would step in and throw some money at us in exchange for being their brand ambassador, using their tack, hashtagging them on Instagram, talking them up at competitors' parties, that sort of thing. It was more about Pete than me, since he had Regina placing nicely at the Advanced level and was getting some buzz on the eventing websites for being young, hot, and talented. This was a double-edged sword, something no one had told me about attaining (relative) fame: people talked about you, and not just about what an awesome equestrian you were. Yes, getting plenty of mentions in the blogs was great for convincing sponsors to send us free stuff, but I wasn't sure how I felt about the captions questioning my choice in riding breeches or the lively comments sections debating whether I really had what it took to keep up with Pete on the upper-level circuit.

Scratch that, I knew exactly how I felt about those comments. I *hated* them. While Pete was getting all the adoring attention online, the attention I got was mainly for being the crazy eventing diva who managed to ensnare #SweetPete, and entire comment threads on Facebook were devoted to how lucky I was to have him/how I didn't know how good I had things. The *Eventing Chicks* blog had an entire category for us in their archives. And yes, everyone read *Eventing Chicks*. The main trio of writers, Cassidy, Chloe, and

Christina, were basically celebrities at events these days. No one loved gossip like horse girls, and these three could sniff out a controversy from fifteen strides away. Last month at Sunshine State, Chloe overheard me arguing with Lacey about a broken pitchfork and immediately wrote a lengthy social media post about abusive young trainers who took advantage of willing working students (with a photo of me walking several feet in front of Lacey, taken while I had an unfortunate pout on my face).

It should be noted that Lacey admitted to breaking the pitchfork on purpose because the tack truck had a fancy new one she wanted me to buy, but did Chloe cover that in her editorial? Of course not.

I was pretty sure that as long as the Eventing Chicks insisted on reporting on my every move as the latest proof I was unhinged and unworthy of Pete, there wouldn't be a lucrative sponsor knocking on my door. Still, Pete insisted any sponsorship deal he negotiated would be for the trainers (plural) at Briar Hill Farm, not just Peter Morrison (singular).

I slammed my manure rake on the metal wheelbarrow, knocking a few stubborn road apples out of the tines. "If I ran Dynamo at Advanced, they'd pay more attention to me," I told the wheelbarrow. "I wouldn't be the crazy girlfriend anymore."

Lacey's freckled face peered around the stall door and I nearly jumped out of my skin.

"Jesus Christ, Lacey, where did you come from?"

"What were you muttering?"

"I wasn't muttering. I was trying to get this fork clean on the side of the wheelbarrow. Did you finish the other stalls already? Can you pull out some shavings for me?"

"You were muttering."

"What if I was?"

Lacey's grin was diabolical. "You've been looking at *Eventing Chicks* again."

"No, I haven't. I don't have time for blogs. I have real, actual work to do."

She leaned against the wall and crossed her arms. "I saw what they wrote about you this morning."

I hadn't even looked this morning. "What? What did they write?"

"A haiku devoted to Pete's ass in white breeches."

"What about *me*?"

"You're not worried about the haiku to Pete's ass?"

"That's Pete's problem."

Lacey raised her eyebrows. "Some people might think it was a girlfriend's problem?"

"Fine, I'll just look myself." I wriggled my phone out of my back pocket.

"It's just a little comment," Lacey hedged. "Not even a full article."

I typed in the blog's address—of course it popped right up— and skimmed the morning entry:

Jules Thornton was in over her head this weekend, which is pretty bad considering she was actually in contention for the AECs. The championships will be a little less interesting without her personal brand of crazy, but a little safer considering the way she took some of the cross-country fences this weekend. All we can say is, Jules might want to invest in either some tougher bits, or some tougher riding lessons. Otherwise her horses are going to run away with her, and we don't think her boyfriend will be far behind. How much longer will Pete Morrison stick around with a girl who rides like *that*?

I chewed at my lip and read it again.

Then again.

"Goddammit," I muttered at last, and brushed away something hot and ticklish that was definitely not tears. "What do I do with this? Is it libel? Can I sue them?"

"Sue them—for God's sake, Jules, it's just a blog. They're basically written for high school girls sitting in the tack room after riding lessons looking at their iPhones and giggling. You do not need to do anything about them. Or . . ." She looked thoughtful.

"Or what?"

"You could be nicer, and give them less to grab hold of. You're never at the parties. You're never at the rail chatting. You're never meeting up with anyone on the course walks. You're hardly ever with Pete. And it makes them all think you hate them, and they probably think you really hate Pete, too."

"Why should they care about me and Pete?"

"Because they all want to *be* with him, dummy. He's their celebrity crush. Do you pay attention to anything besides horses?"

Lacey marched off to finish bedding stalls, leaving me alone to seethe. It was all about Pete, wasn't it? Pete and Regina, mare extraordinaire. Sweet Pete in his white breeches, winning everything in sight and looking cool as a cucumber while doing it.

"When's *my* name going to be in lights?" I asked the empty stall, tossing manure into the wheelbarrow with a vengeance. "Why should I be the celebrity's girlfriend?"

"That's the million-dollar question," Lacey called down the aisle. "That's what they all want to know—why you?"

I guessed there was a cold comfort in that.

# 4

WE WERE SLOGGING up to the house for a late lunch. Dark clouds billowed up in the west and the magnolia tree near the dressage arena turned from dark green to white as the wind flipped its leaves. "Here it comes, just in time for our break," Lacey remarked.

"Polite of it to wait."

Pete came out to meet us as we passed his barn. He took off his Kentucky Three-Day Event cap and ran a hand through his sweaty, reddish-brown mop, but there was no escaping the sort of hat hair one acquired after a long hot morning squashed into a riding helmet.

*All mine, ladies,* I thought, turning my cheek so he could give me a peck without his sweaty face accidentally touching my sweaty face, a fate we were both determined to avoid.

Pete grinned. "I'm disgusting."

"You and me both." I felt like I'd taken a dip in a hot tub and followed it up with a roll in the sand. "I'm showering; I don't even care if I have to take another one later."

"You're the soul of conservation."

"Drought's over, smartass."

Pete laughed ruefully. "Thank God. If we'd run out of water, I have no idea what would've happened."

I shrugged. There were enough real catastrophes to keep me busy; I didn't need to rehash all the might-have-beens.

Pete held open the door for me, and I sighed with pleasure as the cold air came billowing onto the patio, raising goose bumps on my sweat damp skin. I loved air-conditioning. It was probably my favorite thing in the entire world. Especially this year, which seemed even hotter than usual.

Pete hadn't been joking about the water holding out. Plenty of farms *had* lost their water this past spring, especially out west in the drier counties. Spring had been almost as nerve-racking as a hurricane season this year. What would come first, a blazing wildfire or an empty well? That was the question on everyone's minds as we watched the leaden skies, coils of yellow smoke curving along the horizon, and prayed for rain.

The rains came in with a fury of their own at last. Now we couldn't get through a day without an inch or two dumping on the barn, fat tropical drops pelting our hard hats while we tried to keep working the horses. At least the plants were happy. Horse country reinvented itself in the course of a week: the pastures went from topaz to emerald, the training tracks went from dust storms to canals, the nights went from a tense, silent waiting to a cacophony of jubilant frogs. The smoke cleared from the sky and we all knew we'd survived another fit of Floridian nature.

Already, though, the terror was starting to fade from memory. That's how we all stayed in Florida year after year, while the rest of the country watched in horror and said things like, "Only in Florida," and "How do people live there?" Easy: we had selective memories. The only thing we knew we couldn't stand was snow.

"Remember three weeks ago when we weren't dying of heatstroke from the insane humidity?" I reminisced, leaning into the refrigerator for an extra dose of chilled air. A rumble of thunder shook the plates in the cabinets. "And it wasn't raining every day? Wasn't that fun?"

Pete shrugged, throwing himself down on a chair by the kitchen table so he could worry at his broken half-chap zipper more comfortably. "I'm almost out of Keratex from dealing with soft soles on half the horses in the barn, if that's what you mean by fun."

I eyed his fingers as they fumbled with the recalcitrant zipper. "You should get new half chaps. Those are toast."

"When I sell Mercury."

"*If* you sell Mercury. I'm not sure that buyer is serious."

"I need her to be serious. He's perfect for her, anyway. He'll kill in the green hunters this winter, and I don't want to do it. I can't *afford* to do it. I'll give Amanda a half share if I have to. We'd both make some money that way."

"What does she care if she makes money? I don't know how anyone affords the winter hunter/jumper circuit if they're not loaded like Amanda. She'd lose money showing him and she'd still be just as happy when he sells." I pulled a pair of Diet Cokes out of the fridge and set one in front of Pete. He was still trying to get out of his leggings. "You want a straw so you can drink it while you're playing with that half chap?"

"I think—I—got it!" He wrenched the zipper open at last and kicked the half chap across the kitchen. The wet leather folded against the wall beside the fridge, where it was closely followed by its mate, and then a pair of dirty jodhpur boots. "Never buying the cheap ones again, I swear. The zippers go within six months."

"You get what you pay for," I observed, high and mighty since my parents had bought me a very nice pair of Irish half chaps for my birthday back in the spring. "If Amanda's girl buys him, get some like mine. Worth every penny."

"I need every penny," Pete said morosely.

I settled down at the table and cracked open my Diet Coke. "When is this going to stop being a struggle?" I asked. It was a question for the universe, for the eventing gods, for no one at all, but Pete answered me anyway.

"When we marry rich," he said, and when I gave him a dirty look, he just grinned and shook his head.

There was a knock at the door and then Becky poked her head in, ghostlike in a silver rain poncho. She held out a large express mail envelope. "Mail for you, Pete."

I started over to the entryway to get it, but Pete beat me to the punch, practically running to snatch the envelope from Becky. She shrugged and went back out into the rain. I wondered for a moment what was so important that she went to get the mail during a thunderstorm, then dismissed the question in favor of the more immediate one: What was so secret that Pete was disappearing into his office?

I sat down on the couch with Marcus to wait, pulling at his silky ears, eyes trained on the office door.

The rain let up and the sun came out again, and still I waited.

Pete came out at last, looking just as tired and careworn as he had beforehand. Or was he? Were his shoulders a bit straighter, was his chin a bit higher? "What was in the envelope, Pete?" I asked.

Pete went into the kitchen without replying. When he came back he had two beers, and put one in my hand.

"There's going to be a sponsorship offer," he explained, rolling his bottle around in his hands. "So far, there's a contract for me."

"For you?" We were a package deal, he'd said.

"So far. Yours is coming."

A likely story. "Who is it with?"

Pete took a breath, tried to bite back his excitement. "Rockwell Brothers."

I felt my mouth drop open. "Holy *shit*, Pete. Holy *shit*."

"I know, I know, right? It's crazy!" For a moment he let all his joy show, and I knew how he was feeling. It was the same way I'd be feeling if I had just been taken on by the biggest equestrian company in the United States—complete and utter jubilation. Cloud nine. All that jazz.

I hadn't been taken on, though. Not yet. I took a long, bitter pull of my beer. "Congratulations," I offered, hoping I sounded happy for him—because I was, I really was happy.

I was just feeling a little left out.

"They're going to make you an offer, too. Mr. Rockwell assured me of that."

"Wait, there's an actual Mr. Rockwell?"

"Of course there is. Who do you think the company was named for?"

"I just figured it sounded fancy," I muttered. "Are you two, like, bros now?"

"I don't think Mr. Rockwell has bros. He's just your standard industrial millionaire."

I started to point out that we didn't know any industrial millionaires, but the phone rang, the actual house phone that we only used for rare business calls that couldn't be trusted to our spotty cell service, and Pete jumped up, leaving my hand cold where he'd been holding it.

"Hello, Mr. Rockwell!" he announced. "Yes, I just received the package—yes, of course—" Pete walked into the kitchen without turning back, closing the door behind him.

Marcus clambered up onto the couch beside me, taking Pete's place with a sigh of long-suffering canine relief. He loved Pete, because everyone loved Pete, but a beagle does not enjoy losing their position in the spotlight. He showed this by replacing Pete at every single opportunity, creeping onto his pillow in the night if Pete got up for a drink of water, slipping his nose under my elbow the moment Pete vacated the couch, stretching out his hot-doggy little beagle body from end to end to take up as much space as possible, hopeful he would deter Pete from wanting to sit down on the couch again. It often worked, too.

*You don't need him*, Marcus told me now with his melting brown eyes. *I am all you'll ever need. Let's run away together.*

I rubbed his warm ears. "You're terrible and I love you. Do you think the Rockwell brand needs a beagle mascot?"

It wasn't a bad idea. I ought to float it to them. The Rockwell Group had long ago moved beyond Rockwell Brothers Saddlery and Rockwell Equestrian Wear and Rockwell Country Lifestyle. Surely a beagle fit well into this lifestyle branding. It couldn't *all* be corgis, although they'd definitely cornered the market for the past few years. Everyone wanted a corgi.

"Corgis don't have your adorable tail," I told Marcus, pulling on his long, whippy tail. He snatched it away and gave me an aggrieved look. I leaned over and gave the white tip at the end a little tickle. "Come on, you could be a brand ambassador too, with this cute white patch!" Marcus huffed and wiggled to the other side of the couch, tucking his tail under him for good measure. He put his chin on the armrest and side-eyed me.

"You're making a big mistake, Marcus."

Marcus closed his eyes.

Dismissed by my dog, I looked back at the television with unseeing eyes, wondering what was happening in the kitchen right now. Maybe Mr. Rockwell was busy explaining that he didn't want us both. It wouldn't be the first time.

We'd spoken with a rep from another company a few months ago, one who hadn't gotten back to us. The rep had explained her bosses really liked the idea of a built-in team, a couple competing both together and against each other. It made for fantastic press, she said, human interest stories that could be marketed beyond the usual equestrian magazines. Karen and David O'Connor had gone to the Olympics together, for heaven's sake, and then they'd been all over the news, even on interview shows talking about being married and eventing, like that combination was some sort of Olympian accomplishment in and of itself. That was the type of thing these big fancy brands were interested in. The upscale-living extension of the equestrian world, the houses "where Hermès might not mean a saddle, but a scarf," the rep had explained earnestly.

I had nodded attentively and pretended I had always known Hermès made scarves.

So Pete and I had agreed: selling ourselves as a team was the thing to do. Was it kind of weird to present ourselves as a couple in order to get money? Lacey thought so. Becky thought so. I ignored them. I needed a fat check and a new cross-country saddle, not a lecture on the dangers of combining love and business.

The company eventually passed on us, but whatever. The married-couple eventing phenomenon existed—someone would want us.

Of course, Pete and I weren't actually married, but I couldn't see any reason why that should matter. We were a team.

Yet right at this moment, sitting alone in the living room looking at a closed kitchen door, our relationship didn't feel much like the model of teamwork. I glanced over at Marcus again. He'd been watching me through half-closed eyes. Now his mouth fell open in a toothy beagle grin, tongue lolling. *At last you realize, I'm the only one for you.*

"It's weird, right, Marcus?" I asked. "It's not just me?"

He yawned, his round jowls peeling back like a lazy old lion's.

"Thanks, Marcus, your support is appreciated."

I sighed and looked around the room. No allies to be found here. This house had belonged to Pete's grandfather, and the cross-country photos decorating the walls were all black-and-white images of the venerable horseman and his long-gone mounts, leaping over old-fashioned ditch-and-walls and massive logs. I wondered why I hadn't hung up any of my own eventing photos. I'd had a pretty good year so far, and Pete's year had been sensational.

We'd started out so close. Regina and Dynamo had been neck-and-neck in the standings, glaring at each other from across the middle aisle when we shipped them together in the head-to-head trailer. The tall mare and the stocky chestnut gelding had a rivalry that extended beyond anything I'd ever aspired to with Pete.

Then, in April, Regina stepped up to Advanced. I was saving Dynamo's step-up; Regina was younger than him, and had more years left in her joints. And while there wasn't always a huge difference between the two levels, I felt left behind as Pete began to embark on the career of his dreams.

I knew there were stunning shots of Regina's first run at Advanced on Pete's computer, but no prints went on the walls.

It felt strange that for all this year's success, the house we lived in remained solidly in the past. Neither of us had bothered putting down any roots here. Maybe it was just our insane work schedules. Or maybe there was a darker reason. What if we hadn't decorated the place because neither of us had ever really expected to stay?

I got up from the couch, trying to shake away this unwanted idea, and walked over to the tiled foyer. I peered out the narrow window at the jumping arena glittering in the watery sunlight, the tidy lines of the training barn behind it, the live oaks arching their protective branches over its eaves, even a nodding horse head as someone leaned over their stall grill to admire the view.

Briar Hill was perfect. We just hadn't had time to decorate, I assured myself.

The kitchen door opened, and Pete came back into the room, phone in one hand.

His face was ecstatic, and my heart leaped into my chest. "What did they say?"

Pete beamed at me. "I'm going to England," he said excitedly. "I'm going to *England*!" He threw up his arms and whooped.

Marcus clambered up from the floor, and the two of them began howling together like a pair of idiots while I stood on the cold tile of the entryway.

After a while, Pete noticed that I was not howling along. He came over and swept me into his arms. "Jules? I'm sorry. I didn't think. I'm sorry—" I leaned woodenly against him, feeling his heart thump with a happy anticipation he could not help. Nor should he have had to, but I couldn't share his joy.

I was too busy panicking.

"What am I going to do?" I asked, my voice muffled against his shoulder. "While you're in England?"

"Mr. Rockwell said they'll be calling you too," Pete said reassuringly. "I don't know what he has planned for you. But I know he has something. Don't worry. And I'm only going for the summer. It's not forever."

"When?"

"A few weeks."

Pete in England—I'd be up to my eyeballs handling both his horses and mine. That was fine, though. What was another dozen horses? The real problem was that Pete was going, and I was not. Up until about five minutes ago, we came as a package, or not at all. He'd said so over and over again.

"Let's have another beer," Pete suggested, and untangled himself, heading back into the kitchen.

I sank down into the sofa cushions, folding Marcus into my lap for comfort. The world was spinning too fast and it was taking Pete with it, someplace I couldn't follow, where I wasn't wanted, where I wasn't good enough.

*Yet.*

"You're mad at me?"

I blinked. Pete had a funny look on his face, half surprised, half resigned, as if he might have known he couldn't expect anything better from me.

I hated disappointing him. "I'm not mad," I said, and found it was the truth. "I'm just . . . well . . . I'm envious. And I'm scared," I added. It took effort for me to admit it. At least give me credit for that much.

"If you think this means anything is changing with the farm, or our plans, then Jules, you have to believe me—" Pete's expression got very intense and he put his hand on my arm. "I'm fully invested in us—in our partnership here, in making the *farm* the center of attention, not . . ." He paused.

"Not *you*," I supplied.

"Not me," he agreed, regretfully. "I've been very adamant that you're part of the deal."

A heaping order of Pete with a side of Jules. The broccoli to his filet. No one wanted the broccoli. It just came with the good stuff, whether you asked for it or not. I felt my throat tightening. I was choking, I couldn't breathe, I couldn't swallow, I couldn't ask Pete just how much he'd had to plead in order to get his girlfriend in on the deal. I picked up my glass and stood up, desperate to get away.

Pete's hand fell away from my arm. "Don't go stomping away mad," he warned, his voice tense. "This isn't worth fighting over. We both know it's only because I have an Advanced level horse, and you don't."

"I don't *yet*."

"You don't yet. You think I don't know that? Jules, honey, sit down and let's be rational."

The R-word. Didn't he know me by now? I needed some time alone so I could nurse my disappointment in peace. I needed some space where I could let the tears overflow and no one would try to comfort me. Dammit, I just needed to be allowed to wallow in my misery for a little bit.

"Jules," Pete said pleadingly. "You have to believe that they've got a plan for you. You're going to get your invitation. They're going to take us both on this fall. They told me there was going to be an offer. We just have to wait and see what it is."

"You think so?"

"I've been telling you so. Maybe they just had to work out the logistics. Maybe you're going to come along—"

"With you?" I turned and looked at him.

He bit his lip, uncertain.

I laughed. "I don't think so either."

"It could be—"

"There's no point in speculating," I snapped, losing control of my be-nice button at last. "Can we just not talk about it?"

"I'm sorry," Pete said, and his voice was genuine. "I just really, really want to know."

"You and me both," I said, but inside, something had begun to soften. Pete, I realized, was just as worried about my future as I was. Here he was at a moment of personal triumph, and he was waiting anxiously to find out what was happening to me. Outside of that one shining moment when he'd gotten the offer, he hadn't spent another second celebrating his good fortune. He'd sat on his happiness and waited to see if mine would match it.

"Thank you for worrying about me," I said, my voice a little bit ragged with emotion. "Don't think you can't be excited for yourself, though."

Pete gave me a half smile, a dimple appearing on one cheek. "You know I'm scared to death to do this without you, don't you?"

My jaw dropped. "You can't be scared to go to England and train . . . that's the dream, Pete!"

He cocked his head, quirked his eyebrow, and regarded me with that quizzical gaze of his. "It was the 'without you' part that I've been worrying about, Jules."

Evening chores went by at a snail's pace, the sun blazing down as if a storm had never come through. By the time we were finished cleaning up, Lacey was muttering something about throwing herself into the pool fully clothed. I stayed in the barn alone, putting away some laundry on the tack room shelves, trying to work up the courage to go back to the house and face Pete after the way I'd treated him earlier. I knew he'd be tired after showing horses to Amanda the Hunter Princess (my name for my least favorite contact of his, who was always showing up looking for hunter prospects from his revolving door of off-track Thoroughbreds). He didn't need any attitude from me.

Barn Kitty, my newest animal friend, sat on top of the washing machine and watched me fold saddle pads. She was a small, orange-striped cat who Pete had rescued from a feed store parking lot and brought home for me. I thought Barn Kitty was a cute name. My old trainer Laurie used to have Barn Kitty Tabby and Barn Kitty Gray Boy. Lacey thought we should have named her Garfield. Lacey wasn't allowed to name my animals for a reason.

"I was the worst, Kitty," I told her as I tucked the last saddle pad atop the pile. "He basically told me he couldn't imagine going away without me, and I asked him *why*. I didn't even recognize that he was saying he needed me. I was only thinking about training. Horses and training. That's all I ever think about. Why does he even want me around?"

Barn Kitty yawned.

"I deserved that."

With laundry duty finished, I flipped out the lights, made sure that the cat flap was unlocked for Kitty's nocturnal hunting, and stepped out of the tack room. I looked up and down the barn aisle, its uneven paving swept clean after evening turnout, expecting to see only an empty barn.

There was a man in a black suit standing in the aisle, a silhouette with the setting sun behind him.

# 5

I TOOK AN involuntary step back and nearly toppled backward over the concrete sill of the tack room. Ah, my catlike grace.

"Can I help you?" I asked, hoping my voice didn't sound as much like a twelve-year-old's to him as it did to me. I got squeaky when I was nervous, and being startled by a stranger did nothing for my composure.

The man ignored any squeaking. "Jules Thornton?" he asked. "I'm Carl Rockwell."

The breath went out of me. I clung to the doorframe like a deflating balloon stuck in a tree branch, only a few pieces of wood between me and the ground.

Carl Rockwell cocked his head. He was waiting for me to reply.

I managed to draw a shaky breath. Good start, Jules. Now to find my tongue. "Mr. Rockwell," I managed. "What a surprise."

An unwelcome surprise. He had just called Pete a few hours ago. Why was he showing up in person? Rockwell must be here to let me down politely.

Or maybe my news was so good, so much better than expected, that they had to tell me in person. Maybe they were buying me an Advanced horse? I dragged my attention back to Carl.

"Sorry," I said. "Long, hot day. Let me get you a water. Or a Diet Coke? Do you want to sit down? The tack room is hot but—" I inclined my head toward the dark room, thanking the eventing gods that Lacey had cleaned it out a few days ago. I couldn't have borne showing a Rockwell a cobwebby tack room. These were the people who produced magazine spreads on Country Lifestyle, after all, and believe me, that did not extend to spiders and mud. I wasn't sure what sort of country they lived in, but it sure wasn't mine.

Carl Rockwell didn't seem interested in real country, though. "I only need a few moments." He looked around at the empty stalls. "I was hoping to see your upper-level horses?"

"Everyone's outside."

"That's fine. Lead the way."

We marched out of the barn, across the barn lane, and up to the black-board fence on the other side. I gazed down the slope of the big pasture, hoping the herd hadn't chosen this evening to roam down to the clump of oak trees at the bottom of the hill. There was no way the man in shiny black loafers next to me was going to pick his way down this mini mountain to get a look at my horses.

Luck was with me—the geldings were grazing just a few hundred feet away, clumped closely together so that they could join forces in the ongoing fight against biting flies. I found Dynamo's shining red rump among the herd and pointed him out. "The red chestnut is my upper-level horse. He's been at Intermediate all this past season. We've had two wins, a third, and a couple of fifths and sixths."

"When will he go Advanced?" Carl asked.

I hesitated. I couldn't tell this guy I was babying Dynamo, that I was afraid to make the move and launch what would I feared could be a brief Advanced career. But how much of that was just being overprotective of my favorite child? Why was I *really* waiting? I could be jinxing my horse by not believing in him. "In October," I decided. "He deserves an easy summer, then we're aiming for October at Sunshine State."

He nodded and pursed his lips, eyes roving over Dynamo's muscled form.

He wasn't a big horse, but he was built strong and tough. Anyone could see he'd hold up to the rigors of several more seasons with a little luck and a lot of good care. I was silly to hold him back.

"My real up-and-comer, now," I said hastily, pointing at Mickey, "is that tall gray horse. He can jump the moon. I see big things for him. So do his owners. They're very supportive. I'm sure you've heard of Carrie Donnelly? She's a part owner."

Rockwell shifted on his feet and gazed impassively at Mickey. "Ah yes," he said after a moment. "Danger Mouse, isn't it? Only at Training, though."

"Training's in the bag," I said quickly. "He's ready for Prelim. Advanced in three years, barring injury."

Carl Rockwell grinned, the first sign of human feeling to cross his face since he'd arrived. "I know this song."

"You know it's a solid plan, then."

"With the right training and the right person on his back."

I tilted my head and bit back about twelve inadvisable retorts. *Deep breath, Jules.* "He's getting excellent training. I think you'll find that as a trainer I'm—"

"A solid jumper," Carl interrupted. "With a rough-and-ready style that would have gotten you to the Olympics in the eighties. But this is the twenty-first century. 'The Military' event is history. Endurance day is gone. The long format is never coming back. You need precision. You need obedience. You need hair-trigger responses— and that's just on the cross-country." Carl turned to me, his dark eyes calculating. "It's all about the dressage, Ms. Thornton." He pronounced it DRESS-age, like the British. Like Pete. Like I was starting to do when I wasn't paying attention. "Of course, you need to go clean on the cross-country and show jumping, and your courage and sense of pace are outstanding."

He looked back out at the grazing horses, leaving me to stare at the white skin along the edges of his precisely manicured sideburns. The lines of his haircut, along with the lines of his suit, the lines of his carefully motionless face, were as regimented as the movements of a dressage test. It left me wondering what on earth the Rockwell requirements for my dressage might actually be.

Something horrible, I thought. Something outrageous. I couldn't do it. If he wanted some kind of dressage commitment, I would send him on his way. That wasn't why I was in this game.

But then Dynamo picked up his head and looked back at me for a moment, his jaw still, grass poking out from either side of his mouth. All of the hopes and dreams that had been tied up for years in that horse came flooding into my mind. This was our chance. I nodded at Carl, and he cleared his throat before he went on.

"Additionally, there are a few members of the board who have concerns about your business acumen. You need clients with big horses if you're going to show off our products. Or you need to be able to attract fans to buy into a syndicate. That takes people skills."

I bit my tongue.

"I would like to see a few more horses with upper-level potential in your barn," Carl said. "Still, the general opinion is you're a rider with promise." His tone made it clear he regretted the general opinion. "And so we are prepared to consider you as a Rockwell rider in the upcoming season—with a few improvements."

For a moment, the world was spinning and there were spots in front of my eyes.

"What do you want me to do?" I asked, wetting my dry lips with my tongue. "To improve, I mean."

"A summer training program."

*In England,* I thought. *In England. He would've said, though. If you're offering England, you* lead *with England.* "Where?"

"Seabreeze Equestrian Center, near Orlando," Carl Rockwell announced, still watching the horses instead of me. "For three months."

The spinning sensation came back, but this time it wasn't out of excitement.

"You will take two horses. I expect one to be Dynamo, the other can be one of your young prospects. The gray is fine, since he's a Donnelly horse. We've worked with her before. We've made arrangements with Grace Carter, the trainer there. She'll take you on as an apprentice. You'll do dressage and learn to apply it to your jumping, get more effective in both. She'll also give you a course in client relationships. You'll perform an exemplary Second Level dressage test on the older horse. The kind of test you can win an Intermediate event on—*without* help from your jumping scores. Do that, and we'll evaluate . . . and we'll see."

I stared at his profile. He didn't turn, didn't bother to meet my gaze. He was the money; he didn't have to.

Still, he was asking too much. "Apprentice" was just a fancy word for "working student." He wanted me to be a working student again? No. Absolutely not. I had my own working students, not the other way around. Angry words rose to my tongue, and I took a breath to even things out before I said something regrettable and Jules-like. There was no point in getting mad, but surely he could be made to understand: what he was asking was impossible.

"I'm not an apprentice," I said evenly, using his fancy word. "I'm a trainer. I have clients, I have my own—*apprentice*. What you're asking me to do is a little inappropriate considering my current standing and what I've already accomplished."

Carl shook his head gently, a ghost of a smile crossing his face. "What you've already accomplished? Are you saying you've learned everything you need to know? If you're planning on staying what you are—a passably acceptable local trainer—then you're probably right. You've had a good run with the horse you've had since you were a teenager, and he's a good horse who's probably capable of greatness. You've sold some nice amateur packers. And you can continue to do that, but you're not going international if you don't take any steps to improve your dressage. You'll be successful enough, but you'll never be the professional that you want to be, or that you seem to think you already are."

He looked at his watch, sighing. "I have to be on the road to Tampa. Have you decided against the offer?"

I bit my lip and looked down at the horses. Mickey got a little too close to Jim Dear and received a small nip on his rump in response; he shook his head and trotted away a few steps to safety. Even in those few steps his beauty and grace were apparent, while his foolish youth was all too obvious in the way he looked back at Jim in mournful astonishment. He was a talented horse with unlimited potential, and his owners had entrusted him to *me*—for as long as I could prove myself worth that trust.

Meanwhile, everything that Carl had said to me rang true.

I was nobody. A few good finishes at Intermediate, but I hadn't even been able to make the regional championships on a horse as good as Mickey. That was saying something, wasn't it?

Still, to give up my independence and go work for another trainer, someone I'd never even heard of . . .

Carl was done waiting. He turned to me with undisguised impatience. "This is the offer, Ms. Thornton, and then I'll leave you to think about it. You study and ride under Grace this summer, prove that you've improved your dressage, prove you have the skills to run a successful business, and you'll be one of our ambassadors. You'll have bespoke tack and clothing, plus financial assistance . . . I'll have the offer emailed to you." He paused, considered his next words, as if he wasn't sure he ought to share them. "We thought about sending you with Peter, but it wasn't the right program for you. His is for seasoning on cross-country, to prep him for a four-star. But you don't lack for daring. We have no doubt you can get a horse over any fence. We *do* doubt you can always do it safely or effectively on these technical courses you'll be facing at the four-star level. We need to be assured you're in perfect control of your horses before we make you an offer. So . . . you have our number. Let us know."

I bit my lip as Carl got into his car, slammed the door, and drove away.

I stood there in the gloaming for a long, long time, watching the horses fade into shadows.

# 6

"SO YOU'LL GO," Pete said, slathering pancakes with butter. "You'll go, and I'll go, and we'll come back this fall and have an actual shot at life without bankruptcy."

"So go? Just go to wherever this barn is and muck this woman's stalls?"

"And get a nice refresher in dressage, and get saved from financial devastation."

I rolled my eyes.

"Jules, I know we don't talk about finances much, but can I be really honest with you?"

I wished he wouldn't. "Sure."

Pete set a plate of pancakes in front of me. "I'm broke."

"Join the club." I drowned the pancakes in syrup. Pools of sugar, just what I needed for supper.

"No, I mean seriously." Pete settled into the chair across from me and made healthier choices with his syrup-to-pancake ratio. "I was kind of waiting to see what Rockwell offered. It's not a lot, but if both of us get a similar package, it will cover event fees for a couple of our horses and save us on equipment costs. You'll be able to bring in some clients based on the good PR, and I'll be able to cover costs on my sales horses. Plus the name recognition will help with sales. And thank God, because otherwise . . ." He trailed off. "I'm this close to having to give up the farm and find a job riding for someone else."

I stared at him, pancakes forgotten. He'd never told me things were this bad. "Pete—"

He looked away, as if he couldn't bear to meet my gaze.

The kitchen door slammed back on its hinges and Amanda the Hunter Princess came bounding into the room, all gleaming boots and Tailored Sportsman breeches and blond ponytail.

Pete told me to look the other way when Amanda came over. She was a good contact, he said. She could sell his horses to a whole new market.

She was incredibly skinny and still managed to have a nice ass in a pair of riding breeches, which was quite an accomplishment, I said.

Pete shook his head at me and the conversation was over.

"Good news!" Amanda trilled now. "I was in the barn chatting with Becky."

I frowned at her. A likely story. No one chatted with Becky. Becky was not a chatter. She thought small talk was for weaklings and fools.

"Becky says hello," Amanda added.

*Liar,* I thought.

"Anyway, I was in the barn and a client called me and good news! Had to come tell you!"

"Tell me?" I raised my eyebrows. Amanda was still looking at me for some reason. She was Pete's business partner, not mine. "You mean tell Pete?"

"Tell you, silly! I have a client for you! She's so great and she has a horse who is just dying to be an eventer!"

I glanced back at Pete. His face reddened, giving him away at once.

I sighed. "Well, that's very . . . unexpected," I said carefully, turning up the corners of my mouth as far as they would go. "I guess I thought you would partner up with Pete on client leads."

Amanda went on beaming, evidently still amazed at the wonderful news she'd brought me. "Well, you know, she doesn't really like male trainers. She's kind of particular."

"Particular . . . how?" "Particular" was not a word you wanted to hear when describing a potential client. Particular was the opposite of hands-off, laid-back, understanding—*those* were the words you wanted. "Would you call her difficult?"

"Oh, I don't know." Amanda plopped down at the kitchen table and slid the dressage manual Pete had been reading around to face her. She flipped through a few pages, wrinkled her nose, and laughed up at Pete. "I don't know how you spend all day doing this."

"I don't spend all day on dressage," Pete protested. He smiled at her benevolently. "But dressage is exactly why Mercury is such a nice horse, and why you like him so much and why you're going to tell your student to buy him."

"And then you're going to take me out to dinner in thanks," she said, practically sparkling with delight.

I narrowed my eyes. "So, about this client?"

Amanda looked blankly at me. Then her eyes went round with surprise, as if she'd just remembered what we'd been talking about. "Oh! I'm sorry, Jules! About Tony. Tony Pinto, isn't that the funniest name for a horsewoman? She's from Naples. She breeds Gypsy Vanner horses, I am *not* even kidding you, she actually *breeds* these spotty draft horses! I can't even! Anyway, she has a crossbred who is just not what she expected. He's five years old and moves like a Hackney. I am not kidding. His knees go up to *here*. Terrible. She really only drives now and wanted to sell this guy as a hunter, but of course with that kind of trot he's going nowhere in the hunter ring, I don't even *care* how flashy he is. But he's big-boned and he's really beautiful if you like that sort of thing."

We all shook our heads simultaneously; none of us liked that sort of thing. Amanda laughed with delight. "I know, right? But a lot of people *do* like paint horses. Or pinto. Is it pinto or paint? One's a color and one's a breed but I always forget which." She shrugged. "Anyway. She's going to come see you tomorrow. She's only in town for a couple of days. If you can make him an eventer and get him sold, she'll make it worth your time, I promise. She has friends and they all have cash."

Amanda left on that tantalizing note, turning down Pete's over-friendly (in my opinion) offer to make her a plate of pancakes. The kitchen faded a little when her larger-than-life presence went bouncing out the door; the lights grew dimmer, the yellow wallpaper was less sunny. I liked it better that way. I started on my pancakes.

"Maybe you could suggest to Amanda that she come during business hours," I said after a few minutes of silence.

"Do we really have business hours around here?"

I glowered at him, but he kept his eyes on his plate. After a while I tried again. "Did you ask her to find me a client?"

Pete pushed his empty plate away and fixed me with a steady look. "I'm just trying to keep this place afloat. I thought if you were making more money, I could ask you to contribute a little more to expenses."

That stung. "You didn't tell me things were that bad. I would have tried harder."

Pete rubbed at his forehead. "Would you have, though?"

"What's that supposed to mean?"

"You don't do things you don't like to do."

I took the plates to the sink. For a while I splashed around, washing dishes and making a mess. I cracked a juice glass and threw it in the garbage, enjoying the shatter. Pete sat at the table, staring at the wood grain. I finished mopping up the water I'd gotten all over the kitchen, at a loss for what to say.

Pete spoke up first.

"So you aren't going to consider the offer at all?"

"I never said I wouldn't talk to her. She's got a horse, I've got open stalls."

"The *Rockwell* offer," Pete said, voice strained.

He was gazing at me steadily, without a hint of his usual humor. "You mean, to go and be a working student all summer."

"Yes." He leaned back in his chair and folded his arms across his chest. "And gain a sponsor for fall."

I shook my head. "It's not even that great a sponsorship. A saddle and some money, it's not like they're buying me a horse. I'd be better off gaining some paying clients."

"It's a start. And a new saddle, and maybe appearing in some magazine ads . . . for God's sake, Jules." His voice was rising, his face flushing, and I realized with shock that Pete was really, truly angry with me this time.

He pushed up from his chair and slid it back so hard it hit the wall with a bang. "Jules, you can be as jealous of me as you want and it will never, ever affect me, I promise you. But for you to throw away an offer like this is absolutely batshit crazy, and not only that, it's insulting. It's insulting to Rockwell and it's insulting to *me*. We both have to succeed if we want to keep this place, don't you know that? What happens if my grandmother turns it over to us, like we want? What then? Taxes and insurance and repairs . . . do you realize we're actually going to start *losing* money when this place is ours? We're going to have to work a hundred times harder just to make ends meet."

He sat back down and put his face in his hands. I sat very still, riveted, staring at him. I'd never seen Pete so angry. I'd never seen Pete so passionate.

I'd never heard him call the farm *ours* before.

He sighed into his hands. "Things are only going to get tougher."

I looked down at the floor and saw his half chaps lying there, the broken zipper still stuck halfway. Those stupid cheap half chaps. This stupid, stupid life.

I hadn't known he was tapped out. We didn't talk about finances. He ran his barn; I ran mine. Pete's grandmother owned the farm, and she had an ultimatum on his head: make the United States Equestrian Team in the next year, or find a new place to train so she could auction the farm off and move on with her life. She was bitter after a lifetime as an eventing widow, but she'd held off on selling the place, hoping Pete would fail and go do something more sane and safe, like show hunters, or attend law school. It wasn't fair of her to make Pete's life a nightmare just because her marriage had been difficult, but I was starting to figure out that life wasn't fair.

I wanted to do my part. Especially if Pete saw Briar Hill Farm as *ours*. But . . . a working student gig? I leaned back in the hard kitchen chair and closed my eyes. I couldn't go back to that life. I'd come too far, and I just couldn't go back.

Pete didn't know what he was asking me to do. He came from a riding family, he came from a childhood where horses and showing were normal parts of life, not dearly cherished privileges earned through a combination of sweat, tears, and social exclusion. He'd never been left behind to muck and water while the other kids rode. He'd never been laughed at for riding in Walmart hiking boots because actual riding boots were too expensive. He'd been on those rides I'd watched leave the barn without me. He'd been well-dressed and turned-out and looked the part I had longed for. He might have broken half chaps now, but his childhood had been far more forgiving than mine.

Mine had hurt, and I couldn't forgive any of it.

"I'll get this client," I heard myself say, as if from a long way away. "Things will be fine."

Pete lowered his hands and looked at me, and his face was so pale and drawn, my heart crept up into my throat and stayed there, choking me. "If you don't get this client," he said softly, sadly, "then you have to go this summer."


We faced opposite sides of the bedroom that night, and in the moonlit glow, I stared at the blank walls where we had never hung any pictures, in the bedroom we had never had the courage to decorate, for fear, I was realizing, we might have to leave it behind. For a long time I didn't sleep at all, I just looked

at the pattern the moonlight picked out through the half-closed
blinds, the spectral leaves dancing across the drywall, and thought
about the things Pete had said.

About our farm, about our money, about my leaving.

Ever since I'd lost my farm, I'd tried not to think of anything
as permanent. Barns could blow away, houses could tear apart.
Horses were loaded onto trailers and never seen again. Books were
scattered to the four winds, their shredded pages festooning the
hedges and drowning in puddles. Everything could collapse at any
minute; that was the lesson I'd learned last year.

I loved living at Briar Hill, and Pete was happy to have me here,
so I'd left it at that. There were no guarantees, though, that this
would last through tomorrow, let alone for years to come. Even if
the house and barn and fences stood for another fifty years, someone else might be sleeping in this bedroom, other horses might
be standing in the stables and grazing in the fields. This might be
Pete's farm someday. It might not. Either way, I'd never thought of
it as my farm. Maybe Pete saw things differently. Maybe Pete saw
our lives as more intertwined than I had ever imagined.

I rolled over and studied the back of his head, long hair in need
of a trim, curling darkly against the white pillowcase. *My partner,*
I thought. Was he my partner outside of the house? We shared
things inside these walls. We used the same tube of toothpaste;
no one said anything about who'd bought the last loaf of bread or
who'd picked up the milk or whose turn it was to buy peanut butter, although occasionally we did bicker over extra-crunchy versus
creamy. (Pete was learning to live with crunchy, and I knew he
would be a better man for it.)

Out in the barns, though, we did our own thing. My barn was
my barn; Pete's barn was Pete's barn. I didn't go borrowing hay
when I was running low, or rummage around in his tack room,

as tempting as that was, because we were running our own operations out there. We had two different businesses, with our own bank accounts and our own plans.

Then again, I thought, what about when we went to horse shows and events? We went together whenever we could. We presented ourselves to the world, to the media (such as it was), to potential clients, as a team. Look at Rockwell: that nonsense never would have come up if Pete hadn't told them we were a package deal. I would have just kissed Pete goodbye and held down the fort until he came home.

Pete took a deep breath and shifted, and I slid a little closer to him, pushing the sheet away; the air-conditioning was doing its best, but it was too warm for two people under the covers. He was comforting to be near, even in his sleep; I could lie awake and imagine catastrophe after catastrophe, and Pete would dream on, reassuring in his enviable ability to just relax, just be quiet, just be.

I had no such ability. There were questions about life to be analyzed, while the clock silently flicked through its numbers. Like: What did "our farm" mean, exactly? Were we a settled couple, then? Were we going to . . . I didn't know, get married or something?

I thought about being married to Pete. More questions arose to keep me awake. Did he consider such a thing possible, or even inevitable? Would he be crazy enough to link himself to me permanently, or at least legally? Pete, who thought my moods were funny. Pete, who let trouble roll off his shoulders like a duck surfacing from a pond, while I flapped and floundered in the shallows, always fighting unseen enemies. Pete, of whom one internet commenter had once remarked, regarding his improbable affection for me, "Well, he doesn't *seem* like a masochist . . ."

We shared bread and peanut butter and toothpaste and a bed. We bickered and made up. That sounded like marriage, when one came right down to it. I wasn't sure what else there was to being married.

Just legal things. Like property.

Would my name go onto the property, with all the rights and responsibilities that entailed, once his grandmother was happy and the inheritance was approved?

I thought of being part owner of all this land, and my heart beat a little faster. My poor lost farm had been nothing special, in the grand scheme of things. A clutch of acreage that was close to Ocala, but not part of the rich, rolling horse country the world celebrated. There was no equestrian street cred, no country life social cachet, in my rural route address, tacked onto my rusty mailbox with reflective numbers from the hardware store. It had been a tiny slice carved from a once-mighty ranch, its pastures cut into little farms and dotted with mobile homes because that was what the market out there could bear, and my neighbors had been hobby farmers and hermits, some trying to scrape out a living on the outskirts of the equestrian epicenter, some trying to hide from society behind high fences and security cameras. It was typically weird, nowhere special, forgotten countryside.

Briar Hill, in contrast, was smack in the heart of horse country. I could easily have gone my whole life coming to these green hills for riding lessons, and then trailering home again after my hour was up, the meter run out on my time in the sun. Imagine staying here permanently—something I'd never allowed myself to consider. Imagine my name on the farm—a wish only a genie could grant.

I'd never be able to repay Pete if he put my name on the farm. Not if we were married for a hundred years and I was the nicest wife in the world. (Which everyone, I think, would know was a little out of my range.)

Pete sighed and rolled over in bed, his arms reaching out to catch at me. I wiggled backward and stretched against his solid warmth. What a feeling, to be loved! What a feeling, to be safe!

All he wanted of me was to give up my freedom for three months, to go work for someone else, to put up with her demands, to train and train and train and put a professional sheen on my dressage. All he wanted of me was to help carry the burden of the farm, the home—yes, it felt like home now—he was trying so hard to keep. All he wanted of me was to make this sacrifice for the both of us, now, so we could stay here, safe, forever, in a home we would never have to give up so long as we were willing to work for it.

I closed my eyes and put my hands over his. Maybe it wouldn't have been so much to ask if I'd been anyone else. But what he was asking me to give up was nothing less than my identity. I'd shed the skin of the poor girl who begged for rides, but the replacement was still flimsy and new. I'd be lying to us both if I'd said I wasn't scared I would lose it.

I'd give it one last try. I'd prove to him I could turn business around. If I could get more horses in my barn, I'd look more attractive to other owners. The more owners I had, the more attractive I'd look to sponsors. There would be money. It would work. It could work. It had to work.

# 7

IN THE MORNING I pretended to feel a burning urge to be at the barn. I managed to race out of the house and to the annex barn before Pete had properly rubbed the sleep out of his eyes.

It was five thirty in the morning, and Ocala was dark as night.

I rarely got up this early, and I never went to the barn this early, barring a horse show that required extensive early-morning prep, but there were some things more important than sleep, and one of those things was *not* discussing what had happened, or what hadn't happened, last night. Or, for that matter, what was *going* to happen.

The horses, who had spent the night thinking up new, devious ways to make my life impossible, were overjoyed to see that I'd gotten out of bed early. There was a chorus of whinnies from the pasture gates as my boots crunched on the gravel. I stood under the orange glow of the streetlight outside the barn door and listened to them sing their good mornings into the predawn silence. Down the hillside at the next farm, a few broodmares returned the favor, and then a ghostly choir of ever-more-distant neighs rippled through the damp morning air. We were waking up the neighborhood.

I fumbled in the darkness for the light switch and flung the shadowy barn into fluorescent daylight. The barn cat flicked her tail and rushed into the hay stall, surprised by my early-morning interruption of her important mousing duties. "Sorry," I called to Barn Kitty. "I should have told you I was coming to work early today."

Since I was alone, I made the executive decision to behave badly, and brought in all the horses in two big groups, lead ropes and horses trailing behind me like a Central Park dog-walker out with her charges. The horses nibbled at each other, squealing when they liked it and squealing more when they didn't, spooking at the shadows cast by the orange streetlight, and generally acting as if they had never been handled in the dark before.

It was nice to have something to concentrate on. The only thing that mattered was bringing in the horses. I wasn't going to think about anything more than five minutes in the future. Not even that. I wasn't interested in the future at all, I told myself, hanging up the last lead rope. Until I decided how I'd respond to Rockwell's offer, there *was* no future. I was standing on the edge of the precipice. I was gazing out into the darkness, squinting as I searched for a glimmer of light. I was . . .

. . . being licked by a barn cat.

I shook Kitty off. "You're insane," I told her. "What cat does that? That's not a cat thing." Barn Kitty, ignoring my silly human talk, ran ahead of me and stood outside the tack room door, orange-striped tail twitching with Meow Mix anticipation. "You're right," I conceded. "Breakfast time."

It was nice of Barn Kitty to bring me back to reality. I had horses to feed. That in itself was a reassuring thought. I loitered along the way to the feed room, dishing out smooches and ear rubs to the horses, their affection made loud by their greedy hunger.

"Good morning, my love," I told Mickey, pausing by his stall. The big gray gelding shoved his muzzle against my chest, happiness trumping good manners, and rumbled a low nicker that all the other horses picked up in unison. *Food, please!*

With the feed dumped and the horses tearing through the hay I'd thrown in the night before, there wasn't much to do for the next hour. So I settled down on the stoop of the feed room and listened to the sounds of horses chewing, snorting, and stamping their hooves. Maybe I fell back asleep for a little while, I couldn't say. It might be the closest to meditation I'd ever get, dozing off while horses lived their quiet lives around me.

When Lacey appeared with the rising sun, she didn't ask why I'd started chores so early. She just said good morning, grabbed a brush box, and got on with the day. I didn't know how much she knew, and I didn't ask. I wasn't ready to talk about it.

Training went on as regularly scheduled. The "big horses"— the horses with the most potential—first, then the client horses, then, in the heat of midday, I would take out the greenies who were just taking their first steps on their sport-horse journey. I saved babies for later because high temperatures tended to take the spring out of their step when they felt rambunctious. You have to work with the weather, or it will always work against you.

I took Mickey out early because I thought he'd cheer me up, but the idea backfired. His lead changes were sloppy, and I was having a hard time holding him together through his transitions. He felt completely strung out around turns, collapsing out of the corners instead of rounding his body through them.

"He keeps wanting to drag his hindquarters behind him," I complained to Lacey, who was trotting around the dressage ring on Maybelline, warming up the mare for me to school next. "You think he's off?"

Lacey had been my working student long enough to know what was expected of her at such crisis points. She obligingly pulled up Maybelline and held the fussy mare in check while I trotted, then cantered, Mickey away from her. He wallowed through the arena on his forehand as if he was hauling a plow.

Lacey shrugged when I pulled the horse up and looked for her opinion. "He looks even in both directions, but he sure is strung out behind. Just like you said. He could barely drag himself onto the left lead just now."

I nodded grimly. "Well, it could be . . ." I trailed off, mind wandering through all the potential issues that might be troubling Mickey until I found one that I could live with, at least as a temporary, not-the-end-of-the-world diagnosis. "Maybe he's just tired. He's been showing most of the year. You can handle Maybelline. I'll take this guy back to the barn myself and give him a nice bath."

Lacey nodded eagerly, happy to take on the mare and probably even happier that I concluded Mickey was worn out, not broken. She knew all about the best-case-scenario approach. As she started her horse's trot work, I turned Mickey for home. He didn't *feel* particularly tired, despite my expert diagnosis. I pushed away the nagging notion that I was completely wrong.

As we rounded a bend in the drive, he picked up his head suddenly, ears pricked, and neighed a greeting. I followed his gaze, and saw Pete riding up the road on Regina.

I didn't want to talk to him. I turned Mickey off on the side path that ran up to one of the cross-country gates, as if we'd meant to go hacking in the fields all along.

None of our current situation was Pete's fault, but right now I didn't care. He was a better rider than me, he was a better gamble than me, he had better horses than me, and he was going to get farther than me this year. That should have been all right—after all, there was that awful bargain his grandmother had forced on him. It was more urgent, for both of us, that Pete succeed as soon as possible. If he lost the farm, I'd be right back at square one. Pete's success was integral to my own.

But that didn't make it any easier for me to watch him soar ahead without me. I didn't want to follow him. I wanted to ride alongside him.

There were trotting hoofbeats behind me, and then Pete was bringing Regina back to a walk next to Mickey, who slowed his pace and turned to admire the regal liver chestnut mare.

I looked at Pete and he smiled tentatively. I felt a wave of disappointment in myself. He was a thousand times nicer than I was, and we both knew it.

I moved Mickey closer to Regina, ignoring the mare as she pinned her ears, and put my hand on Pete's thigh. His muscles were hard beneath the stretchy material of his riding breeches, and I wanted to sigh aloud. When was the last time I'd really let myself focus on Pete, and the way he made me feel, rather than Pete, the business partner I rode horses with? When would I stop making everything a competition?

Maybe never. Could a person change their nature? "I'm really trying," I told him. "I really am."

"I know," he said gently.

# 8

I SPENT THE whole morning alternating between excitement and dread. Amanda emailed over the info on her the client she was recommending to me, and the woman, one Tony Pinto, was coming up this afternoon. If anything, after this, maybe it would be easier to tell the difference between "Paint" and "pinto." Otherwise, though, my feelings were very mixed. On one hand: Hooray, a new client! I'd have a new summer project to get ready for some starter events in the fall, get him going Novice level over the winter, sell him as a nice Christmas present for someone, and start the new year with some cash in pocket. I'd also have a few extra dollars each month from board and training fees. What wasn't to love?

On the other hand, I couldn't imagine that any client coming from Amanda would be easy to handle. Amanda's clients tended to be in another stratosphere, financially speaking. I worked with professionals who had a little extra money to play with horses. Amanda worked with daughters of Hollywood and high finance. Even if Tony Pinto was just another horsewoman, if she was used to playing with Amanda, she was used to playing with big bucks.

The Gypsy Vanner part made me nervous too—the overgrown draft ponies with their black-and-white coats and feathered legs seemed like large living toys, the kind of thing a wealthy woman with My Little Pony dreams tended to go for in a big way.

Tony was supposed to arrive around one o'clock, when I was usually sneaking back to the house for a break from the sun and sweat, so I settled into the tack room rather reluctantly while Lacey headed home, Marcus trailing behind her. Left alone to wait with only a rumbling box fan for company, I cracked open a Diet Coke and flipped through my training book, reading old entries and mentally working out a training schedule for Tony's horse. If he was already jumping courses, we'd be ahead of the game, I thought. Maybe in July we could find a dressage show to get him used to showing, and then in September, the events would begin.

I tipped my head against the wall and gazed at the calendar until the numbers blurred and finally faded into darkness.

*"Hello? Hello!"*

I snapped awake and spun around in my chair, frantically pushing my loose hair from my face. I glanced at my phone on the desk. It was 2:05. She was over an hour late. I guess taking a nap hadn't been the worst idea.

I saw her in the doorway and immediately changed my mind. The nap had been a very, very bad idea. This was not the sort of person you wanted to catch you sleeping.

The woman glaring at me from the barn aisle was tall, thin, and completely terrifying. Long red nails tapped impatiently on the doorframe. Long black hair framed an equally long, narrow face, with a sharp nose, dark eyes, and a peevish expression on her downturned mouth. I took in her irritated stance, her impractical black blouse and loose trousers, and the clanking array of silver bangles on her wrists, and one thought rang in my brain: *Oh shit.*

"Well? Are you Jules's groom? She is supposed to be here to meet me. I told Amanda I would be here at one o'clock on the dot. I go to the barn, there is no Jules. I talk to a groom, she says go here, go there, she is in another barn. Now I am walking through this empty barn in the dirt, wasting my time, when I should be getting this meeting done so I can get back home. Can you go and get Jules, please? Tell her I am in a very big rush."

Her voice was big, imperious, demanding. Her Spanish accent made her vowels sharper and her words faster, and so her rapid demands made my heart rate skip up to high gear, flushing my cheeks and sending a tremble to the tips of my fingers. If she'd been a horse, she would have been nervousness personified, a spooky, impatient, opinionated, impossible mare I'd do anything to get out of my barn. I was supposed to do business with her?

"*Well?*"

I stood up and licked my dry lips. "I'm Jules. You must be Tony."

She regarded me for a moment. Should I have said Ms. Pinto? Well, that wasn't how the horse business worked. She wasn't my superior. She was my client, not the other way around.

She snapped her fingers. "Well! You are not what I expected. Neither is this barn. I hope Amanda is not wasting my time. I have to get back to Naples. I have a closing to get to. I have big clients waiting for me. Show me what you can do for me and let's make it fast."

I took a few deep breaths. I would be nice. I would be polite.

I would be good. "Let me show you around," I suggested. "Of course, this isn't a large barn, but we do have all the great training facilities around the property . . . the cross-country course, the jumping arena, the dressage ring . . ."

"Where are these things?" Tony whipped her head back and forth, as if the riding rings would magically appear in the center of the barn aisle. "I do not see anything like that here. Only this dark barn. You should light it up," she instructed. "It's no good for horses, this darkness."

Strange words from the queen of darkness in her black robes, I thought. "Oh, we have lights." I flipped the switch for demonstration, as if electricity was a new and impressive concept, and the fluorescent lights flickered to life. "I leave them off when we're not working, to conserve power."

"You should leave them on. Horses like lots of light. At my barn, we have the big windows." She peered into Mickey's stall, and the gray horse glanced at her incuriously before he went back to his hay. She frowned at the window at the back of the stall. "Bigger windows than that little one. To let in the light. And we have skylights also." She looked up at the roof's cobwebby rafters and sniffed. "This is not good. I expected more, from Amanda's recommendation. I am used to good barns."

"I can leave on his stall lights," I said hastily, and flipped up the switch next to Mickey's stall door. A wan lightbulb lit up the stall, turning Mickey's luminous gray coat a dirty yellow. "I can get him a nice daylight-type bulb, so he feels at home." I felt like an idiot just saying the words, but Tony nodded in appreciation.

"It's good. You'll get the light. And what about this cross-country course? I see arenas on the way in, all the way back there?" She pointed into the glaring sunlight beyond the barn door. "That's where you ride? It's too far. Why do you go so far? You need something closer. You waste too much time with all this back-and-forth."

Well, this was fun. I really enjoyed being told all the ways I was a total screwup as a horse trainer. Especially the parts I couldn't control. "I think the extra hacking time between the arena and the barn is good for the horse," I improvised. "It gives him a built-in warm-up and cool-down time, without having to keep looking at the walls of the arena. He understands that ring time is work time."

*Not half bad, Jules. It might even be true!*

Tony looked at me like I was insane. "I do not think this is necessary. But if you like it, okay. And the cross-country? I need to see it. Quickly, I am running very late."

I glanced over at her Lexus SUV and put the kibosh on asking her to drive out to see the course. It was a showpiece, not an actual off-road vehicle. If she got manure or mud on that baby, it would be my fault, and she'd probably make me clean and detail it myself, telling me all the while she was late and I needed to hurry it up. Still, there were only two easy ways to survey the cross-country course without a leisurely thirty-minute walk: on horseback, or by vehicle. I certainly wasn't going to put her on a horse, and my truck was back at the house. Tony looked at her watch and back up at me, her eyebrows coming together in an elegant frown.

I held up a finger and pulled out my phone, calling Lacey.

She answered after a few rings, sounding utterly panicked. I guess I did usually text her instead of actually calling. "Jules? What's wrong? Did you get hurt? Why are you calling me? Shouldn't you call nine-one-one? Can you speak? Jules! Speak to me!"

I rolled my eyes. "I called you because I'm in a hurry. No one's dying. Can you please borrow the golf cart from Pete's barn and hustle down here?"

"Is it that lady?"

"Yes."

"Is she awful?"

I couldn't help but grin. "Of course."

Tony bristled. "Can we hurry up, please? I have been telling you I only have a few minutes. If you want my business you are going to have to give me better service than this. Amanda would never—" I tuned her out.

"Is she a total psycho?" Lacey breathed, obviously having heard the complaints for herself. "I'm going to get the golf cart. It's right out front. Are you sure you don't want to just kick her off the property and be done with it?"

"Mm-hmm, thanks, please hurry," I replied, and Tony narrowed her eyes at me.

"You were not listening to me," she scolded.

"I can only listen to one person at a time," I explained, slipping the phone into my pocket. "Sorry about that, my groom was talking in my ear."

"You tell her to wait until I am done and then she can talk to you!"

What was happening? Did Tony Pinto think I was a servant or something? Was she possibly from the past? That had to be it. She was a time traveler who thought grooms and horse trainers were beneath her aristocratic notice. That didn't explain how she knew how to drive a car, or her modern clothes, but it was still the only plausible explanation for the way she was speaking to me.

I had to be *nice* and I had to be *professional* and I had to *kiss her stupid ass* if I was going to survive this summer. *Don't—go— all—Jules!*

"Oh look, here comes my groom with our ride!"

"It's about time!" Tony checked her watch theatrically, as if she would die if she had to stand in my horrible little barn another second.

"I am supposed to be in Naples right now closing on this house! I am making an exception for you, but only because Amanda assured me you were just the right person for Baby!"

"Baby?" I asked. *Oh, don't be that horse's name. Please don't let that be the horse's name.*

"Baby, he is my horse, you know this!"

I slid into the seat Lacey vacated and waited for Tony to settle in, tucking all her extra swaths of fabric beneath her. A horse named Baby . . . Horses named Baby tend to be spoiled beyond belief. They usually nip, they always kick, and when they don't get their own way under saddle—well, let's just say they choose a variety of ways to show their displeasure, including balking, bucking, rearing, crow-hopping, bolting, and, of course, throwing themselves flat onto the ground in a massive tantrum. It's just the sort of thing that happens with horses named Baby. I can't explain it. I don't make the rules.

"Have you done any eventing yourself?" I asked casually, hoping to take her mind off the time.

"Oh no, never." Tony shook her head vehemently. "I only do hunters. For years. And now I drive. I don't know why I did anything else! Driving is an *art form*. You must be extremely sensitive to drive. Only great equestrians can drive well. It is nothing like riding. Anyone can ride a horse."

I bit my lip and said nothing. *Very good, Jules.*

Good girls get paid, bad girls go broke.

We bounced over a narrow track in the grass and came to the top of the hill above the broodmare barn. I brought the golf cart to a stop and pointed out the fences. "You can see most of the course from here. The full course has Novice to Prelim options, and there are a few Intermediate-sized spreads out there too. It goes into those woods over there, and the beginning and ending jumps are near the jumping arena and the other barn." A smile came to my lips as I looked over the green hills, dotted with wooden fences.

"This is no good," Tony said. "We need to go look at the jumps. Why did you bring me all the way up here? You are wasting my time! Take me down to look at the fences."

Deep breaths. "It will take at least forty-five minutes to look at all the fences. I know you're short on time, so I thought this was the best way."

"Take me to see that one, right there." She pointed with one red talon at the nearest fence, a maxed-out Prelim picnic table I privately called The Nightmare. It was situated on top of a slight rise, so it was painfully difficult to give a horse the long stride he needed in order to stretch over the wide jump. With a bad distance, a horse was liable to panic and lurch hard on takeoff, meaning the landing was tough and just might fling a rider right over his head. I didn't take young horses over The Nightmare. I didn't take anyone over it, in fact, but Dynamo . . . and we'd only done it two or three times.

"That's not a jump your horse would go over," I said. "Now that fence over there, that's one of our Novice—"

"Are you refusing to show me that fence?" Tony turned her dark eyes on me for the first time since we'd driven away from the barn. "I don't think you want my horse. A trainer who wanted my horse would be taking me more seriously."

"Of course I want your horse," I said stiffly. "Because you're in a hurry, I'd like to show you the fences your horse would be training over."

"Why can't he train over that fence? He already knows how to jump! You think he's not good enough for your big ugly fences? He's a good hunter, you know. I bred him myself. You think I can't breed a horse?"

*Fine!* I slammed my foot down on the accelerator and we went jouncing down the hill. Tony shrieked, grabbing for one of the struts, her silver bangles catching the sunlight.

"Let's go see the fence," I growled.

"Be careful, I almost fall out of the cart!"

"So sorry!" I sang out. "Hang on, here's another bump!" I floored the pedal and the golf cart actually achieved a glorious half second of airtime. We came to the earth again with a crunch and kept sailing down the hill. Tony, holding on with two hands, finally shut up.

We made it to the picnic table and I hopped out, clenching my fists so she couldn't see how my hands were shaking. My face was red, my heart was pounding, and my blood was up—I wanted to tell her off in the worst way, inform her that her stupid clumsy horse could *never* make it over this fence, not unless he sprouted wings from his shoulders, and then I wanted to leave her here to trudge back to the barn in the hot sun. Maybe it would *rain*, too, maybe a nice obliging thunderstorm would blow up out of that rare cloudless sky and drench her to the bone, just for good measure.

Then what? I'd feel better.

I wouldn't have a client, though. I'd be right where I started. Pete would be so disappointed in me. And I'd have to go to Seabreeze.

I stood very still and let Tony walk in a circle around the jump.

She shook her head and clucked at me. "This is so stupid," Tony finally announced. "My horse should not be jumping things like this. Too big, too hard. It's dangerous. Why would you do this to a horse? I think you're a bad trainer. I think Amanda was wrong about you. Maybe it's all eventers, I don't know. Maybe it's not just you." She held up her hands helplessly. "I don't want you to think it's just you, okay? Maybe you're good. But this . . ." She looked back at the picnic table. "This is wasting my time."

The blood was pumping in my forehead and my vision was swimming and I actually had to hold the golf cart to steady myself. "Are . . . you . . . fucking . . . *kidding me?*" It burst out of me before I could stop it. "What did I say to you? I said this wasn't a good jump for your horse! I said he'd never go near it! You haven't listened to a word I've said to you! All you've done is bitch at me and complain at me and make shit up—all this 'Oh I have to be in Naples' and 'Oh rich people are counting on me' and 'Oh I wandered around your farm for an hour looking for you.' What, are you, an idiot? You couldn't find me on a farm with two barns? This is not my fault. You being stupid is not my fault. You being a terrible human being is *not my fault.* So just . . . just stop," I finished, having run out of steam, having run out of anger, having run out of the passion that had clouded my vision momentarily, left only with sick, painful, nauseating regret.

*Oh, what have I done. Oh my Godly God, what have I done.*

# 9

I CALLED CARL Rockwell as soon as my hands had stopped shaking. No time to reconsider, no time to try to butter up Pete, no time to get out of this. I'd tried to fix things, and I'd failed—I'd failed *hard*. Even I was amazed at the degree to which I'd messed up with Tony, and I was well aware of my shortcomings in the charm department.

I leaned against the barn door and dialed with bloodless fingers.

"Ah, Jules." Carl's voice was plummy and rich on the other end of the phone. "You've had time to consider our offer. What do you think?"

What did I think? All I had ever wanted was my freedom. Now I had to choose—the financial backing to keep climbing, or the freedom I had been struggling to hang on to for so long.

I looked down the aisle at my content horses, pulling at hay, nosing at their box fans. Every one of them could have happily lived like this forever, dozing through their day and grazing through their night, their athletic prowess and their superb minds an eternal secret. But I couldn't live like that.

"I'll go," I said resolutely. "I accept." My voice was loud; Dynamo lifted his head and looked at me, dark eyes inquisitive. "I'll bring the gray and the chestnut."

"Excellent!" Carl's voice was neutral. I wondered again if they really wanted me. It didn't matter—they had me now. "I'll inform the office and get in touch with Grace. You'll receive an agreement in a few days—make sure you sign it and get it back to us." He paused, then continued in a warmer tone: "Ms. Thornton, it's a pleasure to welcome you aboard Team Rockwell. I hope it's a long partnership."

I thanked him, hoping he couldn't hear the tremble in my voice, as I slid down the doorframe and settled into the hot dust.

"Oh, I'll also send along the fitting sheet for your new dressage saddle," he added. "Get those measurements back ASAP. These things take time, and we want you fitted for winter."

A custom dressage saddle! It wasn't the cross-country saddle I'd wanted, but hey . . .

Once we'd said our goodbyes, I allowed myself a grin. Sure, the news wasn't great. I'd just tied myself into a season of drudgery, and I had no idea how it would work with the farm and my other horses. But either way, I was getting a custom Rockwell Brothers dressage saddle. And maybe next year I could talk them into that cross-country saddle.

P ete was making a mess in the kitchen when I came inside, closing the front door on an electric-blue dusk.

"You stayed out late tonight," he observed. "I made pork chops. I tried to bread them, but . . ."

We peered into the frying pan. I shrugged off the mess. "We can scoop the breading up and pile it on the pork. Same difference."

Pete brightened. "That's my girl!" He turned from the chops to me. "What happened with Amanda's client?"

"What did Amanda tell you?"

Pete got very busy with things on the stove again. I'd figured.

"I called Rockwell," I said. "It's done. We have an arrangement."

Pete put the spatula down again, turned, and put his arms around me. He was hot from the stove; I was hot from the summer night; together we were two sweaty people, but I rested my chin against his shoulder, soaking in the safe feeling he gave me. He would be leaving, and I would be leaving, and I would lose this . . . at least for a little while.

After a little while of just standing close together, listening to the fat pop in the pan, Pete spoke in my ear. "Jules, this is the right thing to do."

"I know. But it feels wrong."

He stepped back and looked at me carefully. "I know this is scary, but it's just the summer. It's not forever. You're not going backward . . . you're just sticking a bookmark in here and picking up another book for a few minutes."

"For a few *months*." I sat down at the kitchen table, feeling limp. Something about walking in on Pete while he was cooking me supper had struck a chord of new anxiety, something even worse than giving up my freedom to be a working student. This had become home, and Pete was a part of home. Did I have to lose another home so soon? "I won't see you all summer, and I won't even be here to keep the barns running."

"We have people to keep the barn running." I noticed the lack of a plural. "Our careers need this step."

"What about us?"

"Us? We're fine. We'll be so busy, it'll all fly by before we know it. And we'll be stronger at the end of it, because we'll be more secure. We'll be farther along. This fall, everything is going to be better."

He kept saying "we" until I was practically choking on the lump in my throat. Who knew I'd become so invested in that word?

Pete studied my pale face for a moment, then he turned for the fridge. "You need a beer."

Beer! That was exactly what I needed. Several of those, please. I accepted the cold bottle and waited until several sips made their way into my empty stomach and were busy working their magic before I spoke again. Pete spooned the fried-pork-chop slop onto plates and added some mashed potatoes from a pot on the back of the stove. Comfort food, I thought. Just what the doctor ordered.

"You're smiling. Things can't be that bad."

I stuck out my tongue at him. "I'm drunk already. Is this better?"

He shook his head. "Silly. Relax already, will you? We can do this."

We carried our plates out to the living room and settled down on the couch. I piled butter onto my mashed potatoes and watched it melt into a golden pool of greasy goodness. Everything was better with butter. My entire mood was better just looking at it.

Then Pete messed it up again, being supportive when all I wanted to think about was mashed potatoes. "You made the right choice, you know."

"I never *had* a choice." I put my plate back on the coffee table and snatched up my beer. I didn't want butter, I wanted bubbles. "It's this or they won't take me. And I have no other offers—

nothing that will pay the bills. Shiny Pony wants to give me free shampoo—great. That will save me a total of ten dollars a year. Some Etsy company wants to give me free stock pins and earrings. I mean, are they for real? My brand ambassador offers would be exciting if I were a Pony Clubber. But for trying to run a business? Rockwell is the game changer, and thank God for you, or they never would have looked at me." I paused long enough to take a pull of beer. "They're my only option," I realized slowly, "but they're also my best option. They're a dream come true. I'm out of my league, and I'll never admit that again, so just shut up. If they think they can mold me into the rider they want . . . how can I say no to that?"

Pete raised *both* eyebrows. "You think you're out of your league?"

I shrugged. "Maybe. Everyone wants to ride for somebody like Rockwell. I always thought I had the talent, but now, if you're asking me if I have the right horses and the right record for this kind of company . . . I don't know."

"Do you still think you have the talent?"

I bristled. "Of *course* I do, Peter Morrison! I have enough talent to ride the pants off anyone else on their roster, including you!"

He laughed and planted a daring kiss on my forehead. "Thank God. For a minute there you sounded so resigned, I thought the real Jules had been kidnapped. Eat up. We can figure out the horse stuff later."

# 10

I TOLD THE girls the next morning.

Their reactions were typical of their very different personalities. Lacey nearly burst into tears, then wrapped me up in a sweaty hug and wished me good luck. Becky barely smothered a smirk and said she thought it was an excellent plan and she was glad I had swallowed my pride enough to accept a working student position.

I let the deeper insult go with only a handshake and a half smile, because Becky and I had been getting along surprisingly well this past year. Having settled on being a barn manager rather than a trainer, and devoting her life to making horses happy, if not making them superstars, Becky actually seemed thankful for her time as my working student. I was aware her resentment hadn't been entirely unfair. I hadn't been the celebrity-on-the-make I'd thought I was two years ago. I'd oversold myself to her, and when she had grown understandably resentful, I'd gotten nasty with her.

Those scars were slowly healing.

Maybe we'd both been naïve then. Maybe we were growing up. Whatever the change had been, we were now able to hold actual conversations without wanting to rip each other's throats out, and that was real progress.

Still, Becky was capable of some serious barbs in her speech, and they usually hit their mark.

"You think I need the dressage, do you?" I joked now, keeping my voice light.

Becky looked up from her coffee, eyes dancing with delight at provoking me. Old habits died hard. "You never win the dressage and you need the extra control on cross-country, so that's the piece you need to fix. Makes sense to me." She went back to her coffee, the matter closed. Cool, logical Becky. My opposite in every way imaginable.

Meanwhile, my possibly emotionally disturbed best friend was having a sob-fest in the bedroom. All I had to do was follow the wailing. Under a Kentucky Three-Day Event poster, Lacey was curled up in a ball of pillows and plush ponies.

I sat down on the bed, displacing a bay plush pony to the floor, where it lay headfirst next to my boot. I immediately felt remorseful and picked it up again, setting it gently in a fold of Lacey's white comforter and smoothing its mane and tail. I couldn't help it. The damn thing was a pony. You don't just let ponies fall on the floor.

I wasn't so soft with humans, however. It was part of my charm, or lack thereof. "What are you bawling about?" I asked, not unkindly, if not with the greatest sympathy. "You're not the one who has to spend the summer in a sandbox and mucking out someone else's stalls." Well. I considered. "Okay, not the sandbox part, anyway."

"That's the *problem*!" Her voice was muffled by feathers and linen. "What will *I* do? Sit and wait for you?"

I laughed and patted her on the back. "If you told me you were crying because you're going to be so busy this year that you're going to die of exhaustion, I would totally buy it. But sitting around and waiting? Absolutely not on your schedule."

Lacey's heaving sobs paused, and she drew a ragged breath. "What?" she asked, turning her head sideways to regard me with suspicion.

"Lacey! Please! It's not like I'm closing shop just because I got a new job, or whatever this is. I'll be gone three months. You'll have to hold down the fort. That means taking care of the horses. That means riding. That means everything."

She rolled over and blinked at me. "Everything?"

"Who else is going to do it? You're promoted, Lacey. You're officially my barn manager. And you don't get to say no. I need you."

Lacey gasped and launched herself at me. I endured her bear hug, thinking how very different we were. If my old trainer had announced that she was leaving town for three months, I would have assumed I was the only logical choice for barn manager and moved heaven and earth to make sure *she* was aware of it, too.

Lacey, on the other hand, just went to pieces the moment the status quo was interrupted. She was sweet, and that was nice, but I thought this level of emotion would be an exhausting way to live. I'd keep my cold, calculating ways, thanks very much.

"So where is this place?" Lacey inquired, having calmed down considerably upon the news of her promotion. She had to be old and wise now. She was a manager.

"Somewhere near Orlando," I said with a grimace. "Not even in Ocala or West Palm—how legit can this chick be?"

"Maybe it's for the better," Lacey suggested, picking up her phone. "That way no one knows you. You can stay under the radar all summer. What's the name of the place?"

"It's Seabreeze Equestrian Center."

Lacey's thumbs flashed over her phone screen. "Here's their website. Did you even look?"

I shook my head. I had been pretty much staying offline since the whole *Eventing Chicks* nonsense escalated. There wasn't anything online I wanted to see right now.

"Looks nice," she said, holding up the phone so I could see the photo of a large stable. "Too nice for you."

"I can still fire you."

"You need me now. You're stuck."

Boy, I was. I flipped through the barn's website, full of pictures of serious-looking hunter riders and show jumpers, white ponies and . . . trail horses. Trail horses? That was strange. I saw only a few dressage pictures, but what was posted was pretty impressive. I squinted at the captions. The only dressage pictures were of the trainer, Grace Carter. She looked fiercely intense, from what I could see of her face. Super.

I showed Pete the website as we sat in the kitchen after the afternoon break. "Pity me," I told him. "She looks scary."

"She's a hell of a jumper, too," he observed, flicking through photos. I could tell he was impressed. "Maybe you're not going to just spend the summer in the sandbox, like you were afraid of."

"Hah, yeah right. I'm probably just going to muck stalls all summer until I forget all my bad habits in the saddle." Still, I felt a tiny flicker of hope at his words. Most of the pictures were of show jumping. From the look of things, Grace Carter didn't spend too much time on dressage. A funny sort of place to go and spend a summer on remedial dressage, I thought. Maybe Rockwell had messed up; maybe they were sending me to the wrong summer school.

I clicked idly around to show Pete the amenities. Nice barn, nice covered arena—"Hey, riding in the shade ain't bad," I admitted. "But no cross-country course, and no place to gallop," I concluded morosely, looking at all that very final perimeter fencing, surrounded by forest, with no fields to speak of. "Why am I being sent here, again?"

Pete gave me a kiss on the forehead. "You're going to be a great dressage rider, babe," he said. "Think of it as a complement to your amazing jumping. Apparently, I'm the one who has to practice my cross-country. Imagine if they'd told *you* that."

I shrugged, but he was right—I'd probably be twenty times as pissed off if they'd told me I needed a cross-country boot camp. Although I still wouldn't complain about a trip to England.

Pete got up and slipped into his jodhpur boots by the door. "I'm going to start evening chores. See you at dinner."

I waited until he was gone before I started clicking around the blogs. Pete thought spending any sort of time online was a massive waste of time, and of course he was right, but I was weak-willed, and also I didn't feel like going outside to face the dirty stalls waiting for me.

The Eventing Chicks had left me alone since the last event. They'd left Pete's ass alone, too, which was nice. Today the front-and-center post was a top ten list about Area 2 trainers ("Top 10 Reasons Area 2 Trainers Are Dressed for Success"). Total clickbait, of course, but I clicked anyway.

The first two trainers were given props for their traditional Australian oilskin-and-Wellington boots looks. They'd had a wet season up north and the Virginia/Maryland circuit of old money and glamorous eventing venues had been up to their knees and hocks in mud. I couldn't afford an oilskin, but I could certainly appreciate the look. I clicked ahead to the third slide.

A smiling blonde turned the full force of her pearly whites toward the photographer, one hand holding the reins of a priceless mahogany bay warmblood, braided and polished to a fare-thee-well. The horse wasn't the subject, though. Her gleaming Rockwell Brothers field boots, deerskin-seated Rockwell Brothers breeches, and glorious blue tweed Rockwell Brothers riding jacket were.

My mouth went dry, both at the thought of wearing such amazing riding gear, and of being on par with her as a Rockwell-sponsored rider. If this cover girl walked into my shadowy tack room and saw my consignment shop bridles and rain-stained saddles, she would probably think she had stumbled into an equestrian haunted house.

Who was she, and was I going to have to meet her? Work with her? Be nice to her? I crossed my fingers for an answer in the negative and read the caption.

*Rockwell Brothers from head to toe? If this is your dream, meet your soulmate: Amy Rodan has been ambassador for the prestigious outfitters for the past two years, and we're in love with her new tweed look. Watch out for her this fall—she's headed to Olde England this summer and we hear she'll come home more suave in the saddle than ever.*

I shoved the laptop away and shut the lid with a click, but I knew she was still in there, gleaming and glamorous and *going to England with Pete.*

Wait until the Eventing Chicks found out. They'd have a field day matching them up, planning their wedding, and naming their three children (and more importantly, their three children's ponies).

All while I was barn-slaving down in Orlando, riding dressage for some trainer I'd never heard of.

Suddenly, mucking out my own stalls seemed like the most relaxing, calming exercise in the world. I needed back into the real world, and as far away from the one in my computer as possible.

# 11

GETTING READY FOR a summer away from the farm meant there were a million projects in the works, give or take—some horses were being sent to colleagues while we were gone (always a dicey maneuver, since the colleague might do a better a job with the horse and lose you the ride), mounds of tack to be sorted, cleaned, repaired, and packed; and, of course, plenty of time spent making sure our newly promoted working students were prepared for every eventuality.

Becky would at least have a groom to assist her, which was necessary since Pete had more horses. Down at our barn, Lacey was going to be on her own with five horses. Not an insurmountable task, but since she would be riding as well as doing the barn chores, she was going to add an extra level of busy to her life. I arranged for Mikey, Pete's groom, to do the chores on Tuesday to give her a day off. That meant she had to pitch in with Pete's stalls twice a week to make sure that Becky and Mikey got a day off, too. Not ideal for a work schedule, but not unusual. Horses don't take time off from their business of eating, pooping, tearing down fences, and forgetting everything we've ever taught them, and so neither can we.

"You've got the feed store number," I said, flipping through a checklist I'd made during an insomnia-fueled bout of organization.

"Yes."

"And the hay man."

"Yes."

"And Lester, the other hay man, in case Tony's hay looks bad."

"For God's sake, Jules, I already order the hay. Of course I have everyone's numbers!"

I fell silent.

What could I say? Of course Lacey knew how to run the barn. She'd been doing just that for nearly a year, and I hadn't even realized it. I was just feeling a mild panic, and why not? Leaving home, even to go just a few hours away, was scary. I couldn't imagine how Pete must be feeling.

I found *that* out a little bit before lunchtime, T-minus four days before our departure. I was riding Jim Dear up to the jumping arena, intent on having as much fun as possible before commencing my summer of dressage hell. We were walking up the barn lane on a loose rein, two relaxed souls on a humid midday in June, the taste of rain on our tongues, utterly at peace with the world.

So naturally when Jim noticed the horse half-hidden by a thicket of turkey oaks along the lane, he jumped out of his skin and nearly deposited me on the gravel. As it was, I had to snatch at the neck strap of his martingale and caught myself just in time.

Jim, realizing that the phantom tree-monster was only Rorschach, a strapping spotted horse he had schooled next to plenty of times, immediately reverted back to relaxation, casually snatching a bite of grass to prove how chill he was. It took me a little bit longer to regain my composure.

While I was busy taking deep breaths and working the adrenaline out of my fingertips, Pete had turned Rorschach's white face toward us and was smiling sheepishly at me.

"Having a little thoughtful alone time?" I asked, pulling up Jim's head with some effort. "Thinking about how much you'll miss me?"

"You, home, ice in my water, things like that," Pete replied.

I grinned, but privately I would have preferred it if I was not grouped with ice cubes. "I can pack you an ice-cube tray," I offered. "You'll have all the comforts of home."

"Not quite all of them." His gaze intensified for a moment, taking me in, and I had the half-embarrassing, half-flattering notion that he was memorizing me. It was a shame he hadn't picked a cooler time of day to do it. I tucked some wisps of loose hair back under my hard hat and wondered if he would also strive to remember me as I looked showered and fresh.

Okay, that was hardly ever. I'd give him that. Just like I would always have this image of Pete first and foremost in my mind, Pete as he was this moment: a little red-faced himself, coppery hair peeking from beneath his riding helmet, sitting relaxed and comfortable on horseback, clad in breeches and boots and polo shirt.

And quirking his damn eyebrow at me . . . "What?" I snapped.

"Memorizing me?" he asked teasingly. "Afraid you'll forget me while I'm gone?"

"Hah, as if I should be so lucky," I drawled. "Too bad I see your twin in every sweaty horseman in town."

"There won't be many sweaty horsemen where you're going, will there? I'll have to be the only one on your mind after all."

He was right. Seabreeze Equestrian Center was so far out of horse country, it wasn't even in your typical suburban boarding stable territory. The equestrian center was plumb in the middle of Orlando vacationland. I'd looked it up and Google Maps wouldn't lie—at least, I hoped it wouldn't, since I would be hauling two horses there shortly.

"Maybe my taste will start running more toward sunburned English tourists in Speedos," I teased. "Hey, maybe you can turn into one of those over there."

"Might be hard to get a sunburn." Pete sighed. "They say it's going to be one of the wettest summers ever. I don't expect to see much more sunlight before fall." He squinted up at our blazing yellow sky. "The opposite of here, that's for sure."

He sidled Rorschach up alongside Jim Dear and we looked through a break in the oaks, out over the valley. The sharp lines of pastures, the ovals of training tracks, the rectangles of arenas, were laid out before us in a quilt of horse country life.

"I'm not sure I'd go," Pete said softly, "if it wasn't to save all of this. It feels like too long, too far. Anything could happen."

"Hey." I reached out for his hand. "It's going to be fine. Nothing will happen. And even if it did, Becky and Lacey and Mikey have things under control. Plus I'm only two hours away. Not even that."

Pete nodded and gripped my hand, pressing hard. I could feel all of his nervousness, all of the fear he didn't want to show me. Flying overseas with horses was no laughing matter. He'd never done it before, and the stipend he'd had to accept didn't extend to taking along a groom who was experienced in that sort of thing. A friend of a friend who was heading over to train for Burghley had booked the same flight, and offered the services of her groom if Pete had any trouble, but he was essentially sailing off into the unknown without a helper, and abandoning the farm he loved in a time of crisis.

I understood. I'd lost my farm. "This is the right thing to do," I told him, speaking with far more confidence than I truly felt. Someone had to be the tough one, and as usual, it was me. "This is how you'll make the team. And keep the farm for good."

He turned back to me, eyes suddenly twinkling with amusement. I blinked, startled at the rapid change in his demeanor. "Did I tell you, my grandmother sounded almost proud of me when she found out I was going to England? I told her last week. I actually thought she was going to congratulate me, but she stopped herself and just told me I'd find England cold and dreary after living for so long in Florida." He chuckled. "I told her I remembered from last time I trained there and she just snorted, but I think she'd forgotten I went. I almost think she'd just let me keep the farm now, whether I made the team by the deadline or not, but she's so damn stubborn that she won't break her own promise, even if it would make everyone involved happy—even her."

I let myself daydream for a minute that Pete's grandmother would give up her ridiculous ultimatum. Without that worry, he could have slowed down, worked less, pushed himself less . . . maybe not have had to go to England after all?

But that was crazy thinking. Even if the farm was secure and truly his, there would still be bills to pay, clients to win over, horses to acquire, events to win. The overhead was too high for us to ever sit still. The training he'd get in England, free of charge, would be priceless in the long run. The name he'd build for himself as a Rockwell rider would gain him business, horses in the barn, money in the bank. The same went for me. We both had to go.

For now, though, we were able to sit together, boot to boot, hand in hand, and look out over the valley while our horses pulled lazily at the grass. I didn't complain when Pete clenched my hand so tightly I thought my bones might break. We were together for just a few more days. I'd take the bruises over the loneliness.

# 12

THE BARN'S DRIVEWAY was marked by a demure green sign, a white-painted dressage horse prancing into an extended trot, with hand-painted serif letters declaring "SEABREEZE EQUESTRIAN CENTER—BOARDING—LESSONS—SALES" beneath its dainty hooves. The concrete drive and black iron gate, left open to admit students and boarders, would not have looked out of place in Ocala. What a shame that wasn't where the farm was actually located, I thought morosely. This place was no Ocala.

The traditionally equestrian barn entrance most definitely looked out of place on this four-lane highway, surrounded by golf courses and vacation villas, their low-slung tiled roofs huddled behind stucco walls that ran along the roadside for miles. Just opposite the driveway, a guard shack nearly hidden by lush stands of palm trees stood sentinel for the residents of a luxury subdivision. Off to the west, behind a distant line of longleaf pines, a tall resort tower loomed against the cloudless blue sky.

"What on earth is that place?" I asked, but no one answered. I was alone in the truck. My request to bring along Marcus had been brusquely declined, which did not endear my new boss to me. I hadn't met her yet, but from the emails we had exchanged, I already assumed she was a total bitch. Dogs and horses went together like peas and carrots, or bran mash and carrots if you wanted to keep things horsey. Marcus gazed at me reproachfully when I drove away with two horses and not him, but I knew from Lacey's texts that he was already blissfully asleep in her bed. I was going to miss him way more than he missed me.

No matter what my boss turned out like, though, it was going to be hard to complain about the facility—I could see that immediately. I pulled the truck through the gateway and into a shady forest of live oaks. Off to the right I could see a little bungalow crouching behind a century-old tree, its antique walls shining with white paint, green trim, and topped with a gleaming new metal roof. Surely someone who took such care with a historic bungalow couldn't be all bad.

I slowed down on the advice of the green-and-white "5 MPH PLEASE" sign. Behind me, the horses were quiet, not doing their usual are-we-there-yet dance, as if they were taking in their new surroundings with the same irresistible feeling of pleasure. This was posh, they were thinking. Much fancier than the cramped old barn they slummed in back home.

Now the trees ended and the barn appeared. My eyes widened in appreciation. I'd seen the photos, but seeing it in person was ten times better. Before me was a massive double-aisle barn with high ceilings and tidy rows of barred windows running down the outside walls; a second-story porch with three doors and three windows opening onto it, which suggested I'd be living right upstairs; and an adjacent covered arena, plus an outdoor dressage arena and jumping arena side by side just outside the barn doors. Directly ahead there was a parking lot, and at the far end, a machine shed and hay barn. On the right-hand side of the parking lot, narrow paddocks ran beneath more oak trees. A sensibly designed show barn, set up with everything at hand.

A few horses looked up from their paddock hay and whinnied hello to the horse trailer, and Mickey and Dynamo promptly whinnied their replies. Soon the air was reverberating with the neighs of several dozen horses, most of which came echoing from within the barn.

I pulled the trailer up alongside the barn, longways across a half dozen parking spots, and turned down the radio. I waited for a minute or two to see if someone would come out to greet us. I'd need to know where to park, where to bring the horses, where to put my things. The whinnies died down, and we were left in the afternoon quiet, just waiting.

I'm not good at waiting.

There wasn't a soul in sight—not a groom, not a handyman, not a boarder, and definitely not a trainer. My heart rate was going slightly bonkers. I was supposed to live here for the next three months, and I couldn't even get up the courage to climb out of the truck and find whoever was in charge.

The truck wobbled a little as someone, probably Mickey, shuffled impatiently, and I knew I had to get on with things. I was a horsewoman. I had responsibilities. I didn't have time to be afraid of the future.

I hopped out of the truck, turned my ankle on the concrete, and bounced around on one leg, swearing, for at least a full minute.

When I pulled myself together, my new boss was watching me from a few feet away, looking mildly disappointed.

"Oh," I gasped. "I landed wrong. I'm Jules?"

"Are you sure?"

I wilted under her mocking tone—for just a moment. Then I bristled. I bit back the sharp reply on the tip of my tongue. "I'm sure," I said. "Are you Grace?"

"I certainly am," the woman replied crisply, folding her arms across her chest. I felt flustered all over again. Did she want me to leave? Was this all a mistake? Or a test of how our relationship was going to play out over the next three months?

I was the student, I was the student, *I was the student* . . .

I swallowed hard and stepped forward, hopping a little as my ankle protested. I held out my hand. "It's nice to meet you," I said earnestly.

Grace smiled thinly and took my hand, her dark eyes narrowing to take me in. Her lashes were long and elegant—in fact, everything about her was rather long and shabbily elegant, even the loose strands of brown-blond hair that had overgrown their short crop and curled alongside her ears. Her legs, clad in worn dress boots and plum-colored full-seat breeches, were coltishly long, but she moved gracefully—as a woman who has spent her life riding probably should move.

Yet somehow, she wasn't what I had pictured, drawing from the handful of dressage competition photos posted on the farm's website. In those, a dressage rider of old-school elegance was executing perfect half passes and tempi changes with a set jaw and no-nonsense eyes, and gracing the presenter with a tight smile when she was accepting a bouquet of roses and a silver cup. Her top hat was always perched perfectly atop a tidy dark bun, her lipstick was always applied perfectly, her spotless stock tie was always pinned with one shining pearl. Grace Carter was the Original Dressage Queen in those pictures.

In real life, I suspected, there was a little more humor, a little more strain, a little more sadness.

She looked more human than I had expected. That was probably a good thing.

Settling in horses is a chore any groom learns to do in their sleep: at every showground and at every clinic there's the same ritual of spreading shavings in the stall, hanging the water buckets, putting away the horse, throwing in hay, asking the horse to please eat the hay instead of running in circles like a ninny, wincing as the horse runs in circles like a ninny and grinds manure and spreads wet shavings all around the fresh clean stall, then giving up on the horse and going to fetch the tack trunks.

Dynamo was putting on his usual giraffe routine. Although he'd gotten better at going to shows over the years, he was still a little bit of a problem and right now he was trying to peer over the top of the twelve-foot stall walls by craning his neck as high as it would go. Every now and then he squealed, lashed his tail, and trotted in a tiny circle around his stall. It was annoying, and at the same time I couldn't help but admire the way his muscles stretched under his gleaming coat. Everyone here would have to admit I could certainly condition a horse.

Mickey was just eating hay, walking around from time to time chewing a mouthful, looking through the stall bars at me, then going back to the pile for another bite. He'd been taken from his barn and deposited into a new home, and he didn't care one little bit. He was also filthy, because the first thing he'd done in his stall was poop, and the second thing he'd done was roll in the new bedding *and* the new poop, but I contented myself with the knowledge that, even dirty, Mickey was in good shape, too.

Dynamo whinnied anxiously, his high-pitched voice setting off a flurry of replies from around the barn. A towheaded man, obviously a groom or a stable hand, turned to scowl at my horse, then noticed my eyes on him and went back to toweling the dust off the bars of a stall across the aisle. I remembered dusting stall bars while other girls went riding and my toes curled inside my scarred paddock boots. I shook my head hard, to send the memory away. I wasn't sixteen anymore, and I wasn't fighting for my place in this barn. I just had to get through the summer and I could get back to my real life.

"Hi," I said cautiously.

The groom looked around, then at me. "Hi," he said.

"I'm, um, Jules," I said.

"Okay." He paused. "I'm Tom."

We looked at each other for a moment. He was very tan, with sun-bleached hair that was almost white. His eyes were bright, pale blue. They studied me like I was a new kind of animal. Finally, he asked, "Are you . . . do you need me for something?"

I eyed the two tack trunks I'd deposited in front of my horses' stalls, which Grace had informed me I could wedge into the riding school tack room. Wherever that was. "I think I need a home for my things?" I suggested, wondering if anyone had actually been told I was coming.

"Oh. Maybe you should ask Margaret. Or Kennedy. I need to get through these stalls before we feed dinner and it takes forever." He gestured with the towel, to show me how hopeless the job was.

I was about to ask where to find Margaret or Kennedy when a bright voice broke in behind us.

"Hi! I brought you a wheelbarrow."

I spun around, startled. There was a slim, brown-haired girl, clad in the usual Floridian groom uniform of ragged jean shorts and cotton tank top, waiting for me in the aisle. She put down the wheelbarrow and held out a hand. "I'm Anna, Grace's assistant manager." She smiled. "You're the new working student, I guess."

I forced a smile, even though being reminded I was a working student for even one second was excruciating. Couldn't they have said it was an internship? Or I was on a retreat? A dressage retreat, now that sounded pretty good. That sounded a lot less like I was mucking stalls in exchange for riding lessons. "I'm Jules," I said, taking her hand—small, but hard, like a horsewoman's hand should feel. "Nice to meet you."

If Anna knew I wasn't sincere, she didn't let on. Maybe I was getting better at this. "I can show you where the school tack room is," she offered. "It'll be tight but we can wedge these guys in there. We have some spare saddle racks, too. You don't have to keep your saddles locked up . . . no one goes in there but us. Tom?" she called. "Did you meet Jules?"

"Sure," Tom said. "We met."

"Tom's a hobby marine biologist," Anna confided. "He works with horses because they remind him of big dolphins." She grabbed one trunk handle and I hefted the other. "Also, he doesn't talk to humans often. So whatever he said to you, I promise that counts as meeting him."

I grinned. "I guess we had the perfect meeting. He told me to go talk to someone else."

"Kennedy or Margaret?"

"Anyone but you or Grace, I'm guessing."

"Kennedy's an instructor, among other things. Margaret's our other groom. She won't have much to say to you, either. It's not personal, just Margaret." We heaved the trunk into the wheelbarrow, where it teetered, not quite a fit. "The school tack room is down at the end," Anna said, and she picked up the wheelbarrow handles again.

"Do the lesson kids go into the school tack room?" I was imagining sticky fingers on my tack.

But Anna shook her head. "Oh, no. We do all of that—we tack up, we clean the tack. It's a show-up-and-ride kind of program."

My saddles were more worn than the school tack, but they looked right at home tucked into the wall of jumping saddles. When my Rockwell saddle arrived, it would live in my house with me, I promised myself. Wherever that might be. The note in the measuring guide said it would be ten to twelve weeks before the saddle shipped out—putting me back home by the time it arrived. Something else to look forward to.

The apartment turned out to be one of those second-floor doors I'd seen while driving in. Anna popped open the screen door, which creaked with the enthusiasm of a burglar alarm, and attempted to show me its finer points. "There's a couch, there's a bed, there's a microwave," she recited brightly. "You have a window looking over the barn."

"I can do night-check from up here," I joked, crossing the little box in six steps and looking out the big window. There was Dynamo, eating his hay now but still pacing and trying to look over his walls. There was Mickey, taking a nap. How did I get so lucky with that horse? He'd gone from psycho to reliable in just under a year. "Just glance out and take inventory to make sure they're all still here."

"I do that every night before bed," Anna said seriously. "But I still go downstairs and do night-check. We can switch off. Grace does it on Fridays, because she has late lessons."

"Does she teach a lot?"

"It's getting busier. For a while we were really slow, then she got the ponies and started recruiting from the prep school up the road. Kennedy runs the pony school, though. Grace handles the adults." Anna backed out the door. "I'll help you bring up your boxes. Then we can start on the afternoon lesson horses."

Dreams, Wishes, Magic, Douglas, Splash, Martinique, Rainbow. These were the horses and ponies I tacked up, led to the covered arena, held at the mounting block, and handed off to riders young and old, one by one. Three white ponies, as perfect as any show pony could be but still seriously green, ridden by some tough-jawed twelve-year-olds who looked up for any rodeo challenge. An elderly warmblood who hadn't tucked up his lower lip in a decade, plodding under a content fifth grader who looked destined for a life of leisure riding. Two bay warmbloods with a little more pluck who carried out teenagers ready to jump the moon. A speckled Appaloosa who carried his broom-tail with pride and his tiny rider with care.

One by one I led them out and one by one they went off to the covered arena for their lessons. A woman with a bush of curly dark hair stood in the center and shouted good-natured commands and solid advice. The riders seemed to adore her. The horses flicked their ears in her direction and stood still when she gave one-on-one lectures.

I watched the lessons in a lull between tacking and untacking. The instructor looked completely at ease, totally in her element, casting a spell over her students. Kennedy, her name was. She smiled a big toothy smile and waved at me. I waved back and ducked inside the barn, embarrassed at being caught, embarrassed by showing interest. She might try to corral me into teaching with her, and that was lower on my priority list than cleaning sheaths. "More power to you, Kennedy," I muttered. "That's no job for me."

In the outdoor ring, Grace was standing in the center of a cluster of jumps, roaring at an adult rider on a powerful chestnut warmblood. I wasn't a warmblood person, not when Thoroughbreds still existed, but there was no denying this was a gorgeous horse, all muscle and power and four flashy white socks. At Grace's command, the rider pulled the horse into a tight ball of energy and flung it at the jumps, leaping around the course with impossible elegance. I lifted my eyebrows, impressed. That was more like it. Kennedy could keep her kiddies and her ponies. If I had to teach, let me teach grown-ups how to get it done.

Anna handled the adult riders' horses, tacking them up and carefully cooling them out after each lesson. Occasionally I spotted Tom moseying along with a wagon full of hay or a pitchfork in one hand, and a gray-haired woman with a firm jaw and a quick step hustling between tasks, who I guessed must be Margaret.

After each lesson, I hosed down the ponies in a bank of wash racks clustered in the center of the barn, near the tack rooms. Everything was easy to find—sponges, buckets, bottles of liniment, rubbing alcohol, sweat scrapers—so there was no need to stop anyone to ask for direction. A barn like this, where everything was kept in its place, made a groom's life easy.

Without meaning to, I was already slipping into a quiet rhythm, as if I was supposed to be here.

I wasn't, though, I reminded myself. I slicked the water from shaggy Douglas's back and pictured my own barn, my own horses. What was happening right now? It was four o'clock in the afternoon and we'd had storms earlier.

Lacey would be making her way to the barn to start evening chores. She'd feed early and turn everyone out, then do the stalls so the barn would be clean and ready in the morning. She'd pet Kitty and look up at the clear Ocala evening, and then she'd walk back to the house and make dinner with Becky. She'd give bits to Marcus and let him lick the plates, even though she wasn't supposed to because Marcus was much fatter than any farm dog should be.

As for Pete? Pete was still at home. He'd be at his barn, helping Becky pack up his trunks, getting ready to leave in a few more days. He'd be five hours ahead of me soon; sitting at his lonely table in his lonely barn apartment while I was still out here in the hot Florida afternoon. Would he feel as lonely and lost as I did right now?

I hadn't been alone at night in more than a year. Before Pete, there'd been Lacey. Before Lacey, there'd at least been Marcus. Now I didn't even have my dog. I just had the window overlooking the barn, where Dynamo and Mickey would be blanketed in darkness, hardly a comfort. My eyes prickled and burned and I turned away just as Grace walked into the wash rack, her dusty dress boots spattered with orange clay from the arena.

"You managing okay?" she asked, placing a hand on Douglas's wet neck, fingering the way his woolly senior citizen's coat coiled into pin curls. "Sorry there wasn't an orientation or anything. The afternoons are busier these days. Truth is, we're glad you're here, because we really needed an extra hand."

I brushed my hand across my eyes and blinked away my misery. She'd never see me cry, that much was for certain. "No problem. Everything is right where it should be, so that makes it simple to jump in and get to work."

Grace smiled, fine lines crinkling around her sharp brown eyes. I'd started out with flattery, and she recognized the move of a young woman ready to fight for her survival. Horsewomen didn't miss much, did they? "Thank you very much. We work hard to keep the place in order. I'm sure you'll fit right in."

A voice called out from around the corner, some adult student, imperious and used to being answered immediately, and Grace rolled her eyes at me and strode away, brushing horsehair from her palms as she went. I watched her from under Douglas's neck, seeing her stop short as a woman in Tailored Sportsman breeches and field boots came rushing around the corner from the tack room and began relaying how upset she was to find her favorite saddle pad had been used and put back on her saddle unwashed. Grace nodded seriously, as if this was the biggest problem she'd faced all day, and by the end of the interview I was starting to think it really was, either because she was such a skillful barn manager or because so little went wrong in this suburban horse utopia that a borrowed saddle pad really was a nightmarish transgression. I thought about the girls at my childhood barn, all of whom seemed to steal from one another and sabotage each other's show prospects with as much dedication as they practiced their equitation rounds, and wondered if that was just my barn.

I'd assumed it was all of them.

Anna stopped to listen in and I asked her if the case of the borrowed saddle pad was, indeed, an unusual occurrence.

She looked at me as if I had sprouted three heads and started speaking in German. "Have you been at a boarding stable before? A borrowed saddle pad is the very least of how badly these people behave." She nodded at the woman who was now listening to Grace with her arms crossed, eyes narrowed. "That's Stacy Hummel. She owns Fallon. Really talented jumper."

"Stacy is?"

"*Fallon*," Anna corrected me, and giggled.

Stacy's pale blue eyes found us. "Yes, girls?" she asked, interrupting Grace. "You need something?"

I turned red. Luckily, Anna was more graceful. "I wanted to tell you I found the shoe Fallon lost last week," she said easily. "I'll leave it on his stall door for you."

"Thanks!" Stacy smiled, showing glimmering white teeth, and turned back to Grace.

"Did you really find his shoe?" I asked as Anna and I slipped around the corner. "Was that just dumb luck?"

"Oh, no," Anna said. "I'll just put any old shoe on his stall door. We have a bucket of them in the tack room. She won't know the difference. But it's always a good excuse. These ladies love horseshoes."

I s it awful? Are you dying?"

I rolled my eyes at Pete, but the apartment was dark and I wasn't sure he got the full effect. I was too tired to get up and flip a light on, though. He'd FaceTimed while I was stretched out on the battered apartment couch, watching old episodes of *Friends,* so now he was seeing me by the blue glow of the television. Exactly how you wanted your boyfriend to see you on the first night of your summer apart, I know, but I was seriously wiped out.

"I am dying, yes, thank you," I told him. "Send help. Send chocolates. Send alcohol."

"I could come and pick you up," he joked.

"Please don't even joke about that. Either do it right now or don't mention it again."

His smile faded; even through the darkness I could see I'd made him feel bad. "I'm sorry, baby."

I told him I was fine, things were fine, the barn was lovely and the people were nice and the horses were super. The chores were hard because there were just so many horses here, but there was plenty of help and I would get used to it soon. My riding lessons were going to start tomorrow and I was sure I'd get the dressage up to the level Rockwell wanted it and be home at the end of the summer ready to tear up the winter eventing season.

"I'm really proud of you," Pete said, and he sounded like he meant it. How like Pete to put aside my initial refusal, and give me all the credit instead.

"How is Lacey?"

"She's large and in charge. She rode every single horse this morning and they all looked great. I think she's really going to get somewhere with that chestnut mare she likes so much. Maybe the other one as well."

"She's a mare whisperer," I said, stifling a yawn. "I'm keeping her forever to ride all my mares."

"Mares aren't so bad," said Pete, the rider of perfect princess mares. "You just have to give them a reason to listen to you."

"My commanding presence isn't reason enough?"

"No, a real reason. Not like a gelding reason. A gelding is like, 'Oh, you have carrots, let's go do all the work!' A mare wants to know that if the two of you got into a death match, you'd win."

That sounded about right. I just wasn't altogether confident that I would win a death match against most of the mares I knew. "Well, I'll tell you in a few days. I have to ride a mare here, apparently. I'm getting some novices to school on the flat every day."

"Speaking of novices, let me tell you what Amanda did with Mercury this afternoon . . ."

I tuned him out and turned my attention back to *Friends*. Monica and Chandler were in love in London and no one knew. London was in England, and Pete was going to England in a few days . . . without me. It would be nice if Amanda wasn't keeping him company. "Really good job, Amanda, three cheers," I said absently when Pete stopped talking.

"Did you forget I can see you?" Pete asked. "I can see you're watching TV."

Oops. I grinned. "Um . . . I miss you?"

He laughed. "Sure you do, Jules. Sure you do."

# 13

I WENT DOWNSTAIRS later in a good humor, but it only lasted about halfway through night-check.

Night-check meant plodding up and down the aisles with a wheelbarrow, throwing hay and making sure everyone had water, was alive, that kind of thing. It was part of barn life and I usually didn't dislike it, but tonight I felt more drained after a day of working for Grace than I had ever felt at home, even on the hottest, most miserable day of summer. Yes, I'd done more today than usual—there were more stalls to muck, more buckets to scrub, more horses to groom and tack and wash down—but the tiredness I was feeling went deeper than physical labor. Now I could tell I was lonely, and I was homesick, and, I thought, those two things were the reason why I felt so scared—a fear that was sucking away at my long-nurtured ability to work, and work, and work.

My phone was buzzing in my pocket, and I realized it must be Pete, calling me back. It was the most reassuring thought I'd had all day, making my heart lift even as my throat tightened. Yes, it had to be Pete: Pete missing me, Pete wishing he hadn't made me go, Pete saying let's go home, let's not do this, let's tell them we're good enough as we are, we can find our own way forward.

My arms were full of hay and there was nothing I could do but speculate as I made my way down the barn aisle, stall by stall, sliding open the doors with effort and flinging a flake of hay in. All I could do was build up what he might say, and what I might say in return, with all the fevered imagination of a romance novelist crafting her happy ending.

I finished with the hay, put the wheelbarrow away, and sighed. I was done at last.

I dug my phone out of my pocket.

I read the message and then I read it again. I didn't understand. I put the phone back in my pocket and went upstairs, flicking off the lights, leaving the horses draped in shadow, crunching at their hay, utterly content. Must be nice.

Did you know he was going out with her?" I demanded. "Did he say why? Did he say not to tell me?"

"I didn't know," Lacey said. She sounded apologetic, probably because she never should have sent me that post from *Eventing Chicks.* "I kind of thought *you* knew, and maybe you'd send it to him since he doesn't use social media much. I was hoping I could get you to blow up at me, not him."

I felt like the tired old couch was going to swallow me up, and that would be fine. I pictured the photo Lacey had texted me again. Pete and Amanda, sitting across from each other at the Horse and Hound in Ocala, smiling chummily over their drinks. I'd been gone *one day.*

"They're probably talking sales horses," Lacey said. "You know he wants to move Mercury before he leaves. I'll bet he tried to finish the sale and Amanda wanted to do it over dinner. She's always trying to do things over dinner."

That was true. Amanda did say "Let's talk it out over dinner" a lot. But Pete always said no.

"Maybe you're right," I said, exhaling. "I just don't trust Amanda. In general. You know?"

"It's not a jealousy thing," Lacey agreed. "I get it. She's just . . . a lot."

"All the pearls and makeup," I said, warming to the subject.

"The BMW."

"Seriously, what twenty-something girl is driving around Ocala in a BMW?" We laughed, but ran out of steam quickly. There was a long pause.

I imagined Lacey on the other end of the call, draped across the sofa, Marcus lounging against her chest. Suddenly, I missed my dog with a sharp pain in my stomach. "Is Marcus with you?" I asked.

"Of course he is. He never leaves my side. I tripped over him earlier and spilled a Coke all over the tack room. Took me half an hour to get it all cleaned up."

There would be ants, I thought immediately. And then: I was a terrible dog mother, leaving my sweet beagle like that. "Does he miss me?"

"I'm keeping him too busy to miss you. I just gave him a new pig's ear and he's at the end of the couch getting the dye all over the cushions. Becky's going to freak when she sees it."

"Where's Becky?" I leaned my cheek against the refrigerator door, letting its coolness soak into my hot cheeks. "She out in the barn?"

"Doing night-check. She's been gone forever. Probably Barsuk pulled off his wraps again. He's got to go on stall rest, did I tell you?"

"No! What happened?" Pete's young horse, Barsuk, was a gorgeous iron-gray gelding who seemed to get himself into trouble constantly.

"He was out galloping around like a fool in his pasture and . . ."

I stood in the kitchen until my feet ached, leaning against the fridge and listening to Lacey. By the time I hung up, Becky had come back inside, shrieked at the mess Marcus had made of the pillows, and Lacey and I had shared a laugh. Same old Becky, same old everything. The only thing different was my absence.

*Pete's home,* Lacey texted a few minutes later. *No Amanda in sight.* I typed back *thanks* and let it go.

Still, if only that message I'd dreamed up during night-check had come true. If only he'd missed me enough to tell me to come home. I leaned against the arm of the sofa and closed my eyes, imagining the homecoming we would've had. The reunion we were missing out on right now.

*B*oom! *Boom! Boom!*

"Holy shit, stop kicking!" I was halfway across the room before I realized I had been asleep on the sofa, and there was no way all that banging was a horse. These were deeper, louder sounds, and they were coming from the opposite direction. I rubbed my eyes, noticed the news was coming on, which meant it was ten o'clock and I'd been asleep for approximately five minutes, and staggered over to the front door.

The western sky was aglow with fireworks.

"Oh my God," I breathed. I hadn't seen fireworks like this in years. This was no Williston Fire Department Independence Day at the athletic field fireworks display; this was more like New York City on Independence Day. A huge white explosion filled the sky, and a few seconds later the resultant *boom* shook the doorframe under my fingertips. It was beautiful, and for a moment I let myself just take it all in. I'd loved fireworks when I was little. Why had I stopped loving fireworks? Oh, right, animals hated them. Speaking of which . . . the horses downstairs would be absolutely freaking out. I wasn't sure how I was going to soothe two aisles full of horses, but I guessed I better get my ass downstairs. I slipped my bare feet into my paddock boots and went clumping down the steps yet again without bothering to zip them up.

The barn was nearly dark now; only the two night-lights high in the barn's rafters cast their dim glow down on the stalls. It would be light enough, though, to tell me which horses were running around their stalls, panicking as fireworks shook the barn's walls every few seconds. The Fourth of July was a horseman's nightmare. Today was only a Tuesday in June, but apparently *some* kind of event was being commemorated. A little warning would have been nice. We could have given everyone probiotics to keep their stomachs happy even if they were stressed, and kept the spookier horses inside, maybe even give out a few judicious doses of tranquilizer, depending on how loony they had been during past holidays.

I peered into Dynamo's stall, right at the foot of the stairs, first.

As I expected, his head was up and his eyes were wide, looking into the gloom with surprise and jumping a little when I popped up out of nowhere. "You heard me coming down the stairs," I chided.

"You knew it was me." He whuffled his nostrils at me, his usual way of saying hello, and then reached down for another mouthful of hay. There was a *boom* outside, not quite so loud as the others, and he picked his head up again, gazing through the bars and down the barn aisle, but he didn't stop chewing.

Maybe the fireworks weren't close enough to be that much of a problem. It was possible I had overreacted. I watched him a moment more, then, satisfied he wasn't going to freak out, I moved down to Mickey.

Same thing. Eating, watching the light show as best he could from inside the barn, paying attention, but not overly concerned. He gave me a friendly nod of the head. "Good boy," I told him. "You sure had me fooled."

I went down the line and saw that my two horses were the only ones who had even noticed the fireworks. A few horses were actually lying flat-out and snoring.

By the time I was done checking the stalls and paddocks, finding only snoozing or munching horses where I had expected widespread panic, the fireworks show had ended. As I climbed the stairs, I caught a whiff of sulfur in the air. I looked west and saw a bright orange glow, like a city I hadn't known about had erupted just a few miles away. Above it the pyrotechnics smoke was hanging in a ragged cloud.

"Is this going to be a regular thing?" I asked the night. "Because those horses were just not concerned at all." It was very strange.

There was a rattle behind me, and I turned to see Anna stepping out of her apartment, feet shod in fluffy slippers and hands tucked into a hoodie pocket. She was dressed as if the night was about twenty degrees cooler. "Watching the fireworks?" she asked.

"I wasn't really," I said. "I was checking the horses, but none of them seemed to care."

"Why would they?" Anna cocked her head. "They happen every night."

My jaw dropped. "Every night?"

"Of course. That's Disney World over there. They always have fireworks. Different times, but still, every night. I still come out and watch them sometimes. I like to think about the people on vacation. They don't even know we're right over here, with our horses, watching the same show they are."

Well, that was the most bizarre thing I'd ever heard of. Standing on the rickety deck outside a barn apartment, thirty-odd competition horses below me, two professional arenas before me, and somehow I was close enough to see, and hear, and *smell* the fireworks at Disney World.

"Florida," I said, because sometimes that's all you could say.

Anna laughed. "Florida," she agreed. Then: "You want a glass of wine?"

This surprised me a little, because I hadn't figured Anna was quite at drinking age. But that was her business. I almost said yes, but it was late, and I was already feeling the depression creeping back into my thoughts. There was no telling what I might do next with a little wine in me. Get on Dynamo bareback and try to gallop back to Ocala, maybe. "Not tonight," I said. "I should head to bed."

Anna's face fell a little. She said goodnight and shuffled back inside. I felt guilty, but Anna might as well figure it out now rather than later: I wasn't the sort of person people relied on. I was just Jules, who couldn't quite get over herself, no matter how much she tried.

At least I was aware of it now. A year or two ago, I couldn't even have told you that.

# 14

MY FIRST RIDING lesson was the next morning, after stalls were done.

I wasn't in a dressage kind of mood (although who ever is, I would argue). The morning had started at six thirty with feeding, turnout, haying the paddocks, and stalls. The horses went out to individual paddocks for a few hours at a time, where they mainly stood around looking pathetic and longing to come back indoors. Anna said they were just spoiled babies. She stated this with affection, as if a horse who refused to stand outside and be a horse was somehow adorable.

"Go be a horse!" I told a big bay warmblood mare as she moped at the gate, gazing toward the barn. The mare whinnied at me and pawed at the gate, rattling the metal.

Margaret tramped by, leading another horse. She side-eyed me. "You okay?"

I tried to think if Margaret had said anything else to me up to this point. "Fine," I said.

She shook her head and kept on walking, the horse at her side jogging sideways with anticipation.

The bay mare I'd just turned out kicked the gate again.

"Knock it off!" I snapped, annoyed that she was refusing to just enjoy her few hours of freedom.

My coworkers were just as disappointing as the horses. Tom, the pale-haired, ultra-tan groom I'd met yesterday, didn't say much, just padded about on surprisingly light feet and whispered to the horses. The spare, gray-haired woman, Margaret, had plenty to say to Tom, Grace, and Anna, but didn't give me the time of day— other than giving me those skeptical looks. She took off as soon as turnout was over and was huddled over some Western saddles in the machine shed at the far end of the parking lot. Over paper cups of coffee in the school tack room, Anna explained Margaret was repairing some used saddles she'd picked up for the trail-riding business.

At least Anna spoke to me, even after I'd turned down her offer of wine and gossip last night.

"Margaret's kind of a trail expert, so she and Kennedy trade off on leading the trail rides."

I'd been meaning to ask about that. "How does a big show barn like this have trail rides?"

"It's mainly for corporate retreats and company parties," Anna said. "Not exactly open to the public."

"Still, it's kind of weird . . ."

"Gotta diversify to keep up in this world," Grace said crisply, coming up behind me. "Not all of us can live in Ocala and make a living selling horses to each other. Someone's got to keep horses in the real world." She tucked a silver-shot strand of hair behind one ear and gave me a once-over. "Thanks for dressing tidy. I've had students think it was okay to wear pajamas to do morning chores."

I stiffened under her assessing gaze. "I run a tidy barn at home," I informed her. "Pajamas don't fall under professional attire."

"But tank tops and cut-offs do," Anna said slyly, tugging at a loose thread on her shredding khaki shorts. Grace cast her an affectionate smile before turning her attention back to me.

"After the stalls are done, be tacked up on your young horse by ten. Breeches and boots, please. I'll meet you in the outdoor dressage ring."

Anna and I watched Grace march out of the tack room, graying blond hair swinging above the collar of her polo shirt. I glanced over at Anna and saw the admiration on her face. "She good to work for?" I asked. "Seriously, you can tell me."

"She's the best," Anna said. "But we better hustle or she's going to be down here asking questions."

More, more, more! You must lift with your seat as well as your legs! You must get him in front of you and keep him there—if not, you'll never get the transition. Leg! Leg!"

I was lifting with my seat, I was lifting with my legs, I was lifting with my goddamn subconscious mind, but Mickey was not lifting back. Or allowing himself to be lifted. Or whatever the hell that meant. And what was really maddening was that he felt great. He felt fantastic. He felt as good as he'd ever felt in the dressage arena . . . but since Grace was completely unimpressed and shrieking at me like a banshee, this apparently meant I had no idea how to ride. At least, not in Grace's estimation.

She had been standing in the center of my twenty-meter circle of hell for the past twenty minutes, repeating her instructions over and over while I tried and failed to lift Mickey into a graceful walk-canter transition. Mickey was tired, I was tired, we were both sweaty and cranky and ready to throw in the towel, and it wasn't even eleven o'clock on our first morning.

I nudged Mickey deeper into the arena's corner, asking him to wrap around my leg and bend his spine. What Mickey *did* was jerk his head against the bit and slide out of his smooth trot into a rocky, uncoordinated gait. What Mickey *did* was fall apart completely and stick his nose in the air. What *I* did was give him a solid kick in the ribs. What *Grace* did was shout, perhaps inevitably.

"Stretch your leg down! Down! This is kindergarten stuff!"

I stretched down, down, down. Something in my hip lengthened as far it could go, snagged, pulled, and then stretched a little more. Something painful. I went on stretching down, down, down. My hip was on fire.

"Inside leg *now*! And *now*! Good! And *now*! Yes! Good!"

I squeezed with my inside calf as she shouted and sure enough, I started to feel something new: movement from Mickey that was bigger and grander than anything I had ever felt before. "Hey—" I started to say. Mickey overarched his neck and stuck out his left shoulder.

"Left *rein*!" Grace cried, nearly distraught. "Hold him together! Inside *leg*!" I held, I lifted, I squeezed, I felt for that feeling again, and suddenly Mickey was at least two hands taller and his crest rose before me in a glossy arch, white and curved as swan's neck, while his back raised and shortened until I was floating on a cushion of air. I hardly dared to breathe.

"*Yes!*" Grace roared. "*Again!*"

I pushed, I lifted, I held my outside rein firm. Another stride, then another, on this new massive warhorse that was carrying me to battle.

"Leg back, ask to canter!" Grace was nearly leaping up and down with excitement. "Draw his energy up and channel it forward into your hands! Let your hands be the bit! Hold his mouth so that his energy rises! Send him forward, then close the door! Now! *Leg!*"

Did I do all of that? I certainly tried. Mickey rocked back, then up and forward, and then we were cantering, a collected, rocking-horse canter that made him feel like his legs were constructed of springs.

It was the greatest feeling I'd ever had. I closed my eyes. My fingers held the reins like two pieces of live wire. His mouth tingled at the other end, the corners of his mouth, the softness of his jaw, the curve of his tongue all vibrating beneath my hands.

"Leg! Rein! Leg!"

I legged, I reined, but I could feel the perfection falling apart and the canter unraveling. His shoulder pointed out. His nose came up. His back flattened. He was breathing like a bellows.

"Trot, then walk." Grace sounded unsurprised.

We jounced down to a walk and I let Mickey have his head. He stretched his nose to the ground, leaving me with the buckle in my hands. "That felt different," I said, in the understatement of a lifetime.

"Yes, but your goal is for that to feel normal," Grace said. "That was your horse truly engaged and on the bit, not faking it with pretty head carriage. He's a racehorse, so he knows how to arch his neck and look pretty, and you've done a good job of lifting him off his forehand—for the most part. But you're only getting him halfway there. What you just had—that's what you want to strive for in all your dressage work."

I nodded, feeling energized again despite the sweat pouring down my back and neck. I wanted to feel that again. I wanted to feel it all the time. "How long will it take?"

"For this horse? He's still a greenie. Novice level. You have years ahead of you."

"And my chestnut? He's much more advanced."

"Then he should be there already."

*Well,* I thought, *obviously he isn't. Or we wouldn't be here.*

Maybe he was at least close? God, I hoped so.

Grace was studying my legs with a contemplative look I found troubling. She stepped forward and patted my thigh. "Drop your stirrups," she commanded. I thought she was changing the length of my stirrups, so I complied. Then she deftly popped the stirrup leather right off its bar.

"Hey!" I protested.

Grace yanked the other stirrup leather free. "Your legs are tucking up when they should be stretching long. I'll give you your stirrups back when you don't need them anymore."

I blinked, uncomprehending.

"Oh, and one more thing." Slinging the stirrup leathers over one arm, she unbuckled Mickey's flash noseband and pulled the little strip of leather free of its keeper. Mickey opened his mouth and yawned, his tongue curving beneath the bit. "That's right, baby," she chuckled. "Stretch that jaw."

"No flash?" I asked. All my horses went in flash nosebands. Everyone's horses went in flash nosebands. I could not think of a single person who didn't ride all three phases of eventing with that little extra piece of control, unless maybe they were riding the show-jumping phase in an English hackamore, a piece of equipment I hadn't yet used and found distinctly unnerving.

"He doesn't need a flash." Grace smiled beatifically at me,

pocketing my precious noseband. She could at least hand it to me. Those things were hard to keep track of once separated from their bridle. "A flash keeps him from opening his mouth. He needs your hands to be so sensitive he doesn't *want* to open his mouth to escape them."

I digested this. "You're saying I have rough hands."

"I'm saying you've gotten sloppy." Grace went back to her mounting block with my leathers slung over her shoulders, my stirrups chiming cheerfully at her side. She settled down and smiled at me from her seat. "I know what you can do. What I don't know is why you're not doing it properly. I think you're just missing a whole lot of basics. That and you never take lessons, so no one has been yelling at you to keep you in shape. You're sloppy, end of story. So let's go back to the beginning. Don't look so surprised. That's exactly what Carl said to you, and I know it. We talk. Fix the basics and we'll have a top rider, he said, and he was right."

"How basic are we talking here?" I asked, gathering up my reins. Mickey tossed his head and I resisted the urge to bonk him in the side with my heels, which were now hanging in the air about six inches from his rib cage.

"Let's talk about transitions first," Grace said. "Walk-halt-walk transitions. He's done enough trotting and cantering today."

I resisted the urge to scream. It was going to be a long lesson. Without the flash noseband, without my stirrups, the ride simply fell apart. Gone was the great elevation and connection of a few minutes ago. Now, every transition was an opportunity for disobedience—at least, in Mickey's eyes. He ran through my quiet requests for halts, and when I got tired of requesting and started demanding, his mouth gaped open like the fierce-eyed charger of a Roman statue, he threw his nose in the air and pinned his ears. I found myself on the losing end of tug-of-war.

Grace shook her head as if it was just as she'd suspected.

"That's enough. We can do the chestnut this afternoon, after lunch," she finally announced. "Let's say two o'clock?"

Hottest part of the day? Why not. "Sounds good," I agreed, as if I had a choice.

"Excellent," Grace said briskly. "Loosen your girth and give that poor tired horse a walk to cool out."

I did just as she said, like a novice rider who didn't know the basics of cooling out my own horse, leaning over to unbuckle the girth and drop it a few holes, then nudging Mickey into a plodding walk. We went inside and he kept close to the covered arena's white PVC railing. It looked like a racetrack, I thought, its top rail curving in gracefully to keep the horse away from the footing's edge. If Mickey saw the resemblance, he didn't react; he just flicked his ears at a few mockingbirds in the tall pines just behind the arena. Mainly, though, he kept his head low, worn out with the effort of soaring like an eagle and arguing like a toddler.

I patted his hot neck where his white coat had gone gray with sweat. I was suddenly very afraid of my lesson this afternoon. If I'd done so poorly prepping Mickey at Training level dressage, who knew how badly I'd done with Dynamo at Second Level?

"He can't be that bad," I whispered to myself. "We've won at Intermediate, after all."

*You never won the dressage, though,* a voice whispered back.

A little before two, Grace called me to let me know I wasn't to tack up Dynamo with my own dressage saddle, but with a certain old brown one I'd find in the school tack room. I dug around under the jumping saddles with misgivings, sure I wouldn't like what I found, and was proven correct when I unearthed an ancient saddle of German lineage. I lifted the jockey looking for a saddler's stamp and found no name, only that the saddle had been made in West Germany. *West* Germany, if you please! This was an antique piece of tack from the old country, which could mean only one thing—it was built like a tank and hard as a rock.

Margaret was standing at the whiteboard by the tack room, writing a note about a pony with a lost shoe. She paused when she saw the German saddle in my arms. "Riding in The Colonel?" she asked, and I could hear the capital letters.

"Don't tell me it has a name," I said.

"Oh, yeah. One of Grace's old students named it that years ago. Better than some of the other nicknames it's gotten." She tapped the rock-hard pommel with the dry erase marker in her hand. "Let's just say this old fellow can bruise your baby-maker if you hit it wrong."

I made a face. "No," I said. "Let's never say that."

Margaret laughed and went back to her note.

In the crossties, I piled Dynamo with protection from The Colonel's flattened panels—since the saddle's wool padding had long ago compressed into rock-hard felt. He rejoiced in a gel pad nestled atop a thick pillow pad, but there was nothing to protect my backside from this saddle. To say nothing of my front side, if something should go very wrong out there. I began to see Grace's evil genius.

She smiled when I led Dynamo into the ring, and the smile did not fade when I gingerly lowered myself into the ancient saddle. I was already feeling a little banged around after riding without stirrups earlier. Even in my own saddle with its knee rolls and thigh blocks to help keep me in line, I'd been bouncing like a beginner at times. Dynamo mouthed the bit, exploring his newfound freedom from the flash noseband that usually kept his jaw closed, and flexed his neck, arching his elegant muscles in pleasure.

I narrowed my eyes. *Et tu*, Dynamo?

"This horse is looking for room to grow," Grace declared, watching him from the mounting block. "He's immensely talented, but he's been constrained. You've taught him to move in a beautiful frame, but you haven't let him stretch into himself. He's holding himself rigid. You need to let go and trust. Jules, have you ever trusted a horse, completely and fully?"

"Of course I have," I retorted. "*This* horse." I thought of all the cross-country courses we'd galloped together, feeling like one being joined together. We couldn't have gotten where we were today without trust. "If I've ever trusted anyone, it's been Dynamo."

"Have you ever ridden him without a bridle?" She sounded genuinely interested, as if riding without a bridle was something a normal human might voluntarily do.

"What? No. That's crazy."

Grace shrugged. "Everything we do with horses is kind of crazy. It's not my thing, but you should talk to Kennedy sometime. Okay, let's pick up a working walk and see how sensitive you can keep those hands. I don't want to see his nose flip up one time."

We got down to business and I jounced painfully through the next forty minutes, learning very quickly my suspicions regarding The Colonel were correct—I felt even the slightest lapse in perfect position. There was a sweet spot right in the center of that saddle. Once I found it, I never wanted to let it go, but the elusive feeling of perfection kept sliding away from me.

"Not bad," Grace finally pronounced as I circled her for the six hundredth time, making a huge effort not to gasp like a winded marathon runner. "This horse doesn't have a lot of natural talent, so you've been holding him together. Now we're going to teach him to do it himself. He needs to do a little more of the heavy lifting."

"Well, that doesn't sound so bad," I joked, feeling a rising sense of relief.

"Oh, you'll work for it," Grace promised me. "But it will be worth it. A little rebalancing and suppling and you'll think you have a whole new horse beneath you. You'll be wondering why you waited so long to get a little help. His jumping is going to improve, too. I'm looking forward to seeing this. Carl told me he was a special horse, and he was right."

This was a little confusing. I'd spent the past year thinking that Mickey was the special horse in the barn, the youngblood who would change everything. Now both Carl and Grace were saving their praise for Dynamo, the horse I had thought was at the end of his career. "This horse?" I asked. "I mean, he is, but . . . he's an Intermediate horse. He cuts things close at the Advanced level heights and spreads. He won't keep it up at Advanced for too long. Now, Mickey, in a few years—"

"Sure, in a few years," Grace said. "But you have a horse here, right now, who isn't using himself to his full potential because he doesn't know how, and you don't know how to get it out of him. And that's why you're here. We're going to unlock Dynamo's real talent, and set you two loose on the world."

Inspiring words, and game-changing ones, too, if they were true. I couldn't help but hope so. I loved Mickey, but wasn't it nice to dream my first child might still be the first one to take me to the top? I gave Dynamo a hug as Grace went out of the arena, wrapping my arms around his wet neck and pressing my hot cheek to his mane. "Maybe she's right," I whispered to him, and he cast one ear back to listen to my soft words. "Maybe you've got the big jumps in you, after all."

I cooled out Dynamo slowly, as the hot breeze blew across the road and the arenas, no clouds in sight, no rain to speak of, and found a free paddock so I could turn him out for the couple hours before supper. He walked around the little sandy enclosure for a moment, cast me a doleful look that clearly asked what I'd done with his massive green pasture, and then went down, knees first, for a roll in the sand.

When Dynamo was working at a flake of hay, tail swinging lazily at the flies, I went inside and begged for an hour off so I could get some food for my sad empty cupboards. I would never be able to make myself do it after work tonight. Luckily, Grace took pity on me and gave me directions to town.

"Come see me when you get back," she added as I headed out of the barn. "We need to talk about your riding lessons."

I threw her a friendly wave. I was happy with the riding lessons. I was sure it would be a good chat. Heedless of my grimy, sweaty-soaked breeches and half chaps, I hopped into the truck to drive the five miles to the nearest grocery stores.

By the time I reached the end of the highway and turned onto the main drag, I was deep in vacationland. All-you-can-eat Chinese buffets, discount ticket booths, a shoe store with a fifteen-foot-high sneaker kicking a twenty-foot-tall soccer ball mounted on its roof . . . a mess of commerce surrounded by sunburned tourists walking everywhere, in the crosswalks, on the sidewalks, in the sunburned grass. There was even one family, bafflingly, strolling down the concrete island in the middle of the road.

"I am not in Kansas anymore," I muttered.

I turned up the tourist road and passed a succession of hotels advertising free theme park shuttles and continental breakfasts before the familiar sign for a Publix appeared. Finally, something I knew. I pulled into the lot and parked the truck amid a collection of plain white sedans—rental cars—and out-of-state tags from all over the United States plus Canada and Mexico, walked past yet another discount ticket booth, and found myself in a gift shop. Mickey Mouse beach towels and Donald Duck T-shirts seemed to have edged out the groceries. I paused, bewildered and wondering where the food had gone, and a fast-talking New Jersey family promptly rammed a shopping cart into my heels.

"Hey!" I jumped and rubbed at my assaulted heels, examining the leather of my field boots to be certain the cart hadn't damaged them. Satisfied they were unscathed, but still pretty pissed off, I fixed the father with a glare. "Watch it, huh?"

The entire family looked back at me with unmistakable disgust. Even the toddler looked shocked that I would speak to them. Then they kept walking into the store.

"She stinks," the toddler said to his mother in a clear, ringing toddler voice.

"Yes," his mother said. "She sure does."

I looked down at myself, then back at them. Dressed as I was in my tank top, breeches, and orange-dusted riding boots, with drops of dirty water dried into dark circles on my arms, I would still have looked perfectly normal in Ocala. But here, two hours south and a world away, that sunburned group in Crocs were the norm and I was the strange one.

I didn't love this turn of events. I was not the tourist here. I was a Floridian—from the real Florida, not tourist-trap Florida. It all just made me feel more homesick. The last bubbles of euphoria over Dynamo's supposed potential popped. A serious urge for comfort food took over.

I followed my nose to the fried chicken.

# 15

FORTIFIED WITH GREASE, fat, and a generous hit of caffeine, I presented myself in Grace's office a little before evening feeding. The office was upstairs, next to Anna's apartment, and much the same as our studios, minus only the galley kitchen. The window looked over the stalls and Grace had stationed her desk at the back of the room, so she could swivel her chair and look down at the barn. I hadn't realized she was able to see us while we were working. It was a disquieting thought.

Where an old brown couch sagged in my studio, Grace had stationed bookcases that strained beneath the weight of her equestrian library. My eyes roved hungrily over the titles and then blurred, remembering my own shelves of books, tossed into the night by the hurricane, the pages scattered across my lost farm like drowned confetti the morning after a party.

I shivered.

"Cold?" Grace came in behind me, shutting the door. "I keep it chilly in here, I know. I've always loved the contrast between air-conditioning and the summer heat."

"I do too," I admitted. "I'm not cold."

Grace slid into her chair and gestured for me to take the other one. "So. First day. Interesting lessons. You had a few ugly moments out there today."

I remembered the big moments: the perfect canter on Mickey; the moments of pure collection from Dynamo. What had been ugly?

Grace saw my face change. "The shift from coercion to partnership is not going to be easy. Think about the moments when you tried to make Mickey do something and he said no."

Well, that had been most of the ride. I was trying to think of the good things—wasn't that what we were supposed to do as trainers? Praise the good, ignore the bad, keep working for the "yes" moments?

"They weren't great," I admitted. "But it wasn't all bad."

"It wasn't," Grace agreed.

I waited, but she didn't say another word. *What do you want?* I wanted to snap. *Just give me the magic words and make this whole summer disappear. Tell me what to do and I'll do it. Tell me what to change and I'll change it.*

"What?" I finally burst out. "What did you see that you'd change?"

"I saw a lack of trust. A reliance on artificial aids. Maybe a lack of horsemanship."

I looked at my dirty fingernails. I looked at the floor. I looked anywhere but at Grace. It was her job to tear me apart and it was my job to sit and listen. Just one more reason I hadn't wanted to come here, for those counting.

"Your chestnut horse doesn't dislike you," Grace went on, "and that's a good thing. The gray horse, the young one, he watches you when you're around him, in the barn, grooming, working on other horses. He's okay with you on the ground. But under saddle? It's not the same. You don't have what you think you have. He's listening to you because he isn't sure what you might do if he doesn't. He's worried about you." Grace took a sip from a mug that had been sitting on the desk; old, cold coffee, another little thing we had in common. "Take away some of your weapons, and he decides you're not as scary. Then we get the resistance, the disobedience."

"My *weapons*?" I leaned forward despite myself. "Excuse me?"

"The flash noseband, in this case. Nothing too sinister but still . . . you used it against him. It's not exactly a tool of cooperation, is it? Strapping a horse's mouth shut?"

"Every horse in this barn goes in a flash noseband! I've been in the tack room!"

Grace smiled. "And does anyone else in this barn plan on riding one of these horses at the highest levels of eventing?"

I bit my tongue, willing myself to calm down. "I assume no?"

Grace shrugged. "You want to be the best, you have to work harder than the rest."

"And will I be the only one at an event without a flash? You don't think they're used for a reason?"

"Strive for perfection at home, prepare for reality at the horse show."

Fair point. I nodded reluctantly. "I see."

"Do you? Just like that?"

I was a good working student, willing and compliant and eager to learn. What would that sound like, if it were true? "I'd like to fix . . . whatever needs fixing. If it's my hands, or . . ." I trailed off, hoping she'd finish the sentence.

"You know what needs to be fixed?" Grace searched my face, and I flushed in response, feeling as if she could look right through my skin and see how I wanted to mock her, see that I thought she was full of it, see that I wanted to run from this room and never come back.

"What?" I asked, when she said nothing more. My seat bones, I thought. My stirrups, my shoulders. Not enough core strength. Too much reliance on my hands. Slouching forward. Slipping to one side, bringing back my lower legs. The usual complaints.

"Your attitude."

This again! I hadn't even done a thing to deserve it, not here. I'd minded my own business, I'd done what I was told, I hadn't raised my voice at a person or a horse or a dog or so much as a mosquito. How could the problem still be my attitude? Was my face permanently painted in a sneer I couldn't see?

"You thought it was just something technical with your riding."

"Yes," I choked.

Grace shook her head. "Your riding is scrappy but accomplished, like Carl said. You lack polish, but your seat is strong. Your instincts are correct. It's just you and your horse—you have the wrong attitude about horses, and with Mickey, it shows. With Dynamo, we can do some exercises and I can show you how to get him out of his frame and into a more natural movement. He's bound up in himself right now because you put him there, which is natural when you've done all your own work and didn't have a professional coaching you. It's fine.

"I'll get you started and you can take some regular lessons with a dressage coach back in Ocala—I will insist and make it part of your final agreement with Carl," she added, seeing the immediate protest on my face. "You know you have to, so don't be a baby about it."

"What about Mickey?" I asked, pushing my protests about riding lessons away.

"What happened with you two?"

I looked down at my lap, unwilling to share. I knew what it had to be, though.

"Go on, spill it."

I dug my fingernails into my palms, forcing myself to remember that autumn day at the horse park, our first event of the season. We'd already been struggling together since I started him the summer before, and things didn't go well.

Mickey hadn't wanted to move, hadn't wanted to do anything but throw himself around like a bronco, his mind stuck in a loop of pain, and we couldn't find a way to move him past his memories so that we could show him his hooves were fine, and competition didn't have to hurt anymore. I remembered the shock widening Mickey's eyes as Pete brought the crop across his chest. A few minutes later, fatigued from being backed up for so long, he stepped forward . . . and realized there wasn't any pain at all. Backing up Mickey broke his feedback loop. It let him move forward.

Grace's eyebrows went up as I explained that awful day.

Had it been the wrong way to fix things?

Pete had said Mickey and I had a connection. He said we'd come so far. What if he was wrong, and Grace was right? We'd thought we were fixing things, but what if what Pete had done— what *we'd* done—had put everything back together wrong?

"It seemed brilliant," I said wonderingly after the confession.

"Like we'd found this way to break through to a horse who was basically having a manic episode. But . . . you don't think it was."

"It's a cowboy trick." Grace shrugged. "At least, I've seen a cowboy use it. And you're right, it works . . . if all you need is for your horse to listen to you when you shout. But Jules, if you want to be a truly advanced rider, if you want to be an international event rider, I think you need more. You need an ironclad partnership. You need a horse who will walk through fire for you because he *wants* to, not because he finds you scarier than the fire."

We were quiet for a few minutes after that. Grace sipped at her cold coffee. I looked at the ribbons on the wall, the horses jumping through the decades in dime-store frames, the dust-covered books, and considered the possibility I'd been doing everything wrong.

I didn't like the idea. I wasn't going to discount it entirely, but I wasn't going to give it too much credit, either. I *was* a good rider. Grace wasn't right about everything. It was still that simple.

I wiggled a little in my chair and tried to look dejected. "What do I do next?"

Grace smiled. "Back to basics! We're going to perfect your seat and work on your relationships at the same time. Your horses will thank you. Their backs will thank you. You can sit a little heavy on them when you're posting, did you know . . ."

Grace went on about everything I was doing wrong. I looked out the window over her shoulder, at the rows of stalls and the backs of dozing horses, and pretended I was home at Briar Hill.

# 16

A WEEK WENT by, and things became routine. Pete flew east and settled at his training farm in England, and I got used to thinking of him that way: a person far away, across an ocean, a person who saw the sun and the moon at different times than I did. I talked to Lacey less and less; she was in perfect control up at the farm, and she didn't need or appreciate my rapid-fire questioning about training, feeding, the consistency of manure in the stalls.

Seabreeze Equestrian Center was a surprisingly drama-free barn for most of the day. This might have been because the boarders had very little to do with their horses until the late evening. There were about twenty boarders, much fewer than there used to be, according to Anna, and they showed up mainly for riding lessons and careful, brief rides in the covered arena after work.

Their horses were a largely placid lot of well-trained warmbloods who knew where to put their hooves in every corner of the arena. They went around their twenty-meter circles and their circuits of the arena rail with their necks arched and their ears out to one side, their eyes glazed over in the manner of work horses who have walked this route too many times to count. They jumped their fences with a kind of resignation, placing their hooves in exactly the same spots over and over while their riders gripped enthusiastically with their knees and buried their hands high up in their manes, eyes shining with the fever of childhood dreams come true.

There was plenty of bickering in the evening, which I overheard while I was grooming and cooling out the lesson horses, but none of it was about me; no one really noticed the new working student. I guessed as long as I wasn't riding their horses, I didn't really matter.

I figured it was better to *not* be noticed by a bunch of wealthy boarders. Boarding stables could be cutthroat places, full of infighting and cliques and politics and ever-changing rivalries. There was a reason I'd escaped for my own piece of countryside isolation as quickly as possible. After growing up among cats with their claws out, all I wanted was peace, quiet, and no one else anywhere near my horses.

That wasn't really an option for the women who rode at Seabreeze and lived in the imposing subdivisions nearby. Their houses were candy-shell pink and beach-sand beige, decorated with columns and arches and Mediterranean flourishes; their dogs were designer, their breeches were designer, their saddle pads were designer. Their lives looked incredibly boring to me, almost as boring as their horses' lives. Luckily, Kennedy took most of them on trail rides at least once a week, and everyone came back from the woods with pricked ears and lifted tails, happy for the change.

The other half of the barn's stalls were taken up by Grace's lesson and trail horses, working for an ever-growing contingent of afternoon and weekend riders. Kennedy's group lessons went until seven o'clock on some weeknights, the arena full of trotting horses and bouncing children. On a few mornings, she took out a group trail ride, adults shuttling in from convention hotels and clambering into the battered Western saddles Margaret toiled over so lovingly, laughing at the "team-building" exercise they had to get through before the afternoon work session and the evening cocktail hour back at their hotels.

"I love trail rides," Kennedy told me on a sultry afternoon as I helped her tack up the trail horses. I wasn't sure about the Western saddles, but she showed me how to make sure they were positioned correctly and the girths were secure. Kennedy was different from everyone else at Seabreeze—she had a big personality, a head of big curls to match, and an appreciation for horses that went far beyond their capabilities in the show ring. "When I came here, a few years ago, no one even knew we *had* trails at this farm. But it's all open land for a good ways back there." She pointed across the parking lot, to the forest rising behind the machine shed.

"Are there any jumps out there?" I asked.

She grinned. "Logs, sure. If you ever get the free time, I'll take you out there."

Tempting. But in the first week, at least, I wasn't granted any free time. I scuttled from one task to the next, always on call whether I was needed by Grace, Anna, Margaret, or Kennedy (Tom never seemed to need me). The boarders called out commands no matter what else I was doing; students' parents asked me questions about horse care or riding clothes; the trail riders asked me if it was okay to ride horses while drinking or if that counted as a DUI type situation.

This barn had a strange, impermanent atmosphere. Things at home felt very predictable (at least, as predictable as farm life could ever be), but here, new faces were always coming around corners, new voices were always asking questions. I felt disoriented by the constant need to speak to people, to be polite, to come up with solutions to the problems of missing stirrup leathers and poorly fitting hard hats and how to get a big enough Uber XL to cart an entire group of software engineers back to the Brazilian steakhouse on International Drive for their farewell luncheon.

Still, I was settling in at Seabreeze, which had felt like an impossible feat a week ago, to say nothing of a betrayal of sorts, but it was a reassuring feeling to let go of some of the tumult and unhappiness, to know the routine by heart.

On a sunny Tuesday, after morning chores and before afternoon lessons, Anna and I tacked up a few boarded horses for Grace and she woke them up from their stupor for half an hour or so. Under the blazing sun of the outdoor arena, which had more forgiving footing than the covered arena, Grace put them through upper-level paces—warming up with shoulder-in and haunches-out, bringing their bodies together with walk-canter-walk transitions, then finally moving on to fifteen-meter circles, counter-canters, half passes, even pirouettes if the horse was far enough along. I watched from the barred windows of stalls when I should have been mucking out. Grace made dressage look exciting; she could make a trotting horse look like a warhorse plunging into battle, and a walking horse look like a king's mount carrying the monarch through the city while his people cheered and threw roses at his hooves. She made a cantering horse look like Pegasus come to earth.

I wasn't sure what I had been doing all these years, but it sure as hell wasn't that.

When I wasn't puzzling over Grace's ability to make dressage look like something I'd actually want to do, I was wondering why on earth she was training these horses in such upper-level movements. Some of these horses were capable of a Prix St. Georges test, but they were almost all show jumpers and their riders would have been completely over-faced by a Second Level test. Only one or two of her students could go out in the arena and impress me with their ability or understanding of their horse. Most of them just seemed to be out there for the fresh air.

I brought it up to Anna while we were taking a break between stalls. It was ten o'clock in the morning, and Grace was riding Vizcaya, a massive gray gelding, in the dressage ring. The horse was pounding his way through an extended trot, flinging his toes toward his eyeballs, while Grace sat serenely in the center of the saddle, looking for all the world as if she'd been Photoshopped into the scene. "I saw Vizcaya being ridden by his owner yesterday," I said cautiously. "She seemed a little more . . . timid than Grace." She had only walked and trotted the big horse, in fact, and taken him back into the barn after about twenty minutes, looking winded and slightly terrified.

"Oh yeah." Anna shrugged. "Lena's not really a show rider. She just likes to get on and hack around."

In the arena, Vizcaya was brought down to a prancing collected trot at C. Grace coupled him up until he looked wound so tight he might burst, then let him explode into a canter in the corner. He plunged down the long side of the arena like a thundering god.

"He looks like a lot of horse for a pleasure rider."

This was an understatement. He looked like a lot of horse for *me*.

Anna cracked open a Diet Coke and took a long drink, then

settled for another shrug, consigning Vizcaya's unlikely owner to the whims of the universe. "She loves him. Grace rides him three days a week and keeps his brain active. It works out for everyone."

"Does she do that with a lot of the horses? The boarders, I mean."

"Almost all of them. Some of them she shows, too, if they want her to. But she doesn't show much anymore. She's thinking—" Anna lowered her voice and looked around, as if any boarders were ever in the barn at this time of day. "—she's thinking of letting me show a couple of horses at the end of the summer. She might let you, too, if you talk to her about it. It would be great practice for you. You're only riding two horses a day!"

That was because I was spending the rest of the day mucking, cleaning, feeding, tacking, hosing, and sweeping. Always sweeping. I managed a smile. "Maybe. If she thinks it's a good idea," I said noncommittally.

"Oh, I'm sure she would. And she has plenty of horses to ride. The owners are always asking for more time on her schedule. Toby only gets two rides a week and his owner wants another day. I bet she'd give that day to one of us if we asked."

"You can have him." Anna loved Toby, and I had no interest in riding him, so I could easily pretend to be generous. "I'll wait for the next one."

Anna smiled. "Thanks, Jules. I owe you one."

She went back to the stall she'd been working on and slipped inside, setting the Diet Coke can on the gap between the stall bars so she could get back to mucking. I figured I ought to do the same thing—we were only halfway through stalls and someone was going to have to drop everything to hose and dry Vizcaya in a few minutes. But Anna's words made me curious about something, and with Grace out in the arena, I had the perfect opportunity to snoop.

The lesson office was unlocked, a tidy little closet next to the boarders' tack room with a desk, a fridge, and a few filing cabinets. Kennedy used the office to keep track of the constantly swelling ranks of students and trail riders; Anna said Grace had let her share the upstairs office for a while, but Kennedy's constant energy proved to be more than Grace could handle in one small space. I thought I could sympathize with Grace on this one. Kennedy was a bundle of excited nerves on the slowest days, always up for a new project when the rest of us were daydreaming about naps. The little broom closet where Grace kept the files that didn't fit into her cluttered office upstairs was a perfect place to let Kennedy spark and fizz without disturbing anyone else.

Grace's lesson calendar lay open on top of Kennedy's, but that wasn't what I was looking for. I already knew the day's training schedule—it was written on the whiteboard by the crossties each morning, so that Anna and I knew who to get ready.

I went for the filing cabinet.

The top drawer said *Bills,* which could have been mildly interesting, but the middle drawer was what I was looking for. *Contracts.* I already knew there were legal documents in here; Grace had said she was trying to convince Tom to drag the heavy filing cabinets upstairs because she didn't like having these files so accessible. Tom was holding out, and I didn't blame him—and right now I wanted to thank him for it. I slid the drawer open slowly, counting on (rightly) the squeal of rusty metal.

Vizcaya's file was the third one in. I pulled it out, marveling at the thick wedge of paper inside. None of my contracts were half so thick. Stealing a glance behind me to make sure Anna hadn't come around the corner, I started flicking through the typewritten pages.

There were numbers there, and they were big enough to make my eyes pop. Vizcaya had been imported from Germany, at Grace's cost, but every single one of those costs had been paid back and then some. The horse was sold to Lena, according to the documents, with the understanding that he would be boarded with Grace, trained by Grace, and shown at the owner's discretion and the owner's cost by Grace or a rider of Grace's choosing. It seemed fairly obvious that a rider of Grace's choosing would not include Lena herself.

"This is genius," I admitted, slipping the document back inside the folder. "Goddamn genius." Grace had figured out how to get wealthy women to buy horses they couldn't ride, and then pay her to ride them. Wasn't that essentially my business model, just on a much larger scale? (And a little bit more manipulative?)

Maybe there was more for me to learn here than just dressage.

I was just sliding the file back into its place when my phone rang, and for once the damn thing wasn't on silent. The electronic tango sounded like it was being broadcast around the quiet barn on the PA system. "Shit!" I stuffed the file into the drawer and slammed it shut. "Hello?" I hissed into my phone. "*What?*"

"That's my loving girlfriend!"

"Pete!" My tone turned contrite. "I'm sorry, I was just—" I saw motion in the corner of my eye and spun around. Anna was peering in, looking interested. I dove for the lesson book. "I was just in the office checking to see what horses to groom for this afternoon," I explained, raising my eyebrows at Anna so that she knew I was talking to her as well as Pete. "It's so quiet in here, the phone scared me to death."

Anna gave me a thumbs-up and went back to work. From down the aisle, I heard hooves clopping on pavement. "Oh shitty shit. The boss is back. Pete—"

"You have to go, I know." His voice was resigned. Far away and resigned. He was on the other side of the ocean. Couldn't I let Anna catch Grace's horse this time?

"I can grab a minute." Just not in the office. I scurried next door, to the boarders' tack room, and sat down on a tack trunk. The humming air conditioner would drown out my voice in case anyone was looking for me. "I miss you. What's your day like?"

"Cold and wet." He sighed. The slight trace of British accent his voice always carried had grown more noticeable. "Like every day. I'm spattered all over in mud."

"Because you fell off?" I teased.

"Yeah."

"Oh."

"Regina came to a screeching halt at a big square table and I went right over her shoulder. It was . . . embarrassing."

"I guess so. But Pete, everyone falls off." I tried to remember the last time I'd fallen off. "I'm probably due myself."

"This was my second fall this week."

That was sobering. "Both cross-country?"

"Yeah." Pete was quiet for a moment. There were clicks on the line. I imagined seagulls and dolphins and ships between us, traversing the Atlantic, listening in on our conversation while we admitted how disappointed we were in ourselves.

"Everyone apparently thinks that Dynamo is a better horse than I'm letting him be," I confided. "That I've been failing him and keeping him from his full potential."

"Who said that?"

"No one's said anything just like that." I was cheered by his surprise; that meant he wasn't secretly harboring the same thoughts. "But close enough. They think he's the horse worth investing in, not Mickey."

"I guess that's good, since he's already upper-level. It saves you time."

"It keeps me on your level. You and Regina. Sorry, we're going to be chasing you all winter at Advanced, if things go down the way Carl and Grace seem to think it will." I laughed. "This is going to be a better season than I thought!"

Pete chuckled, but it sounded forced. I shifted the subject back to him. "So does Regina have a problem with the tables over there? Are they really maxed out, or is the approach tricky, or . . . ?"

"Deb seems to think it's me."

Deb was the hotshot British rider he was training with. I did not know much about Deb besides the fact that she was the most attractive forty-five-year-old woman I had ever seen, and she could apparently stay on any horse over any obstacle ever presented. Between her and Amy Rodan, I felt like Pete had been sent to some sort of Ken and Barbie Equestrian Center. My jealousy was allayed only by the simple fact that Pete seemed pretty much terrified of Deb and her barbed tongue.

"If Regina doesn't think the fence is safe, she's going to stop to protect *you*," I said heatedly. "That's what a boss mare does."

"And I agree, but Deb has pointed out, several times, that if Regina is the boss then I am not. It's hard to argue with that, Jules. I just have to get in charge. I'm . . . just not sure how to change the relationship Regina and I already have."

"You should talk to Lacey," I said seriously. "She knows mares. She's up there having the time of her life with Maybelline and Margot, and both of them just had me completely stumped before she took over."

"Maybe I will." Pete sighed again. "Listen, Jules—"

"Wait a sec—"

"Jules? Jules?" Grace's voice was right outside.

"Oh shit, I have to go."

"Okay." Pete sounded miserable. I felt horrible for leaving him like this. "I miss you, Jules."

"I miss you, baby," I said, and I meant it. "I miss our life. Let's get through this and get home, okay?"

The door swung open and I smiled angelically at Grace. "My boyfriend," I mouthed, pointing at the phone. She nodded but didn't remove herself from the tack room door.

"Okay," Pete was saying. "We can get through this."

He didn't sound as sure as I had, though. I hung up the phone and began apologizing effusively to Grace, citing time zones and teatimes and demanding British trainers, but in the back of my mind, I was wondering just how bad things were for him in England, and how much longer he'd turn to my fumbling, inadequate words of comfort, when he had the beautiful and in all probability much more human Amy Rodan sitting across from him at supper.

The summer grew more complicated, just like that.

# 17

THE *EVENTING CHICKS* blog was getting too personal for me to ignore. After Lacey sent me their post about Pete having dinner with
Amanda—which did turn out to be about selling Mercury to her client, meaning I'd gotten all worked up over nothing as usual—I found
myself opening their site more often. Most days, there was nothing
about me or Pete. But at least once a week, Pete's new life in the UK
seemed to get an update. Today I'd managed to avoid checking for
anything new, but after I'd gone upstairs for the night, exhausted by
a long day's work, I couldn't stop myself from visiting the blog.

Tonight, the headline was tailor-made to piss me off.

Keeping up with #SweetPete and #FlawlessAmy?
Amy Rodan's groom dishes on their excellent

adventures in her new blog post from the other side of the pond!

I wished it was an actual, paper magazine so I could crumple it up and throw it across the room. Flawless Amy? *That* was the hashtag? If she was so flawless, what did she need with remedial cross-country camp alongside Pete?

The post was innocent enough. Amy's groom wrote about driving into the local village to try out a pub quiz and bemoaned the amount of mud they were dealing with. She described a kind of horse everyone in England seemed to have called a "hairy cob," which sounded just like a Gypsy Vanner. It made me wonder what Tony Pinto and her Baby were up to. There was a picture of Amy smiling from the saddle, the wet, green fields rolling away behind her. Pete and Regina were in the background, talking to Deb. He looked very serious.

I zoomed in on him for a minute or two, just taking in his familiar lines.

Then I scrolled down and read the comments.

KRAZEE_EVENTER: OMG this post is literally life!!!! Loving this for Amy and Pete!

TazzyMyHorse: #FlawlessAmy is my hero and love seeing her riding with a good guy like Pete, thanks for the update!

LiveToRyde: Wanna see Amy and Pete together back in the USA, hurry home we luv u!!!

For a moment, I was tempted to make my own comment. I'd make my username JulesTheBitter and let them know what I thought of all their Amy/Pete shipping. Didn't anyone remember me, or had the bit of success and notoriety I'd achieved with Dynamo simply vanished with the end of the Florida winter season?

I tried to tell myself it was a bunch of teenagers who didn't even know me, didn't know that I was back here waiting for Pete, riding dressage dutifully every day, grooming horses and practicing what Grace called my "soft skills" with the boarders and students, which was really just perfecting my ass-kissing game, as far as I could tell.

But the bitterness kept creeping in as I scrolled. It wasn't as if my relationship with Pete was a secret. *Eventing Chicks* had cheerfully reported on our unlikely matchup plenty of times over the past year. There was even a mention, if you combed back through the archives, which of course I would never do in the middle of the night when I couldn't sleep and all I could think about was Pete on the other side of the ocean and my throat ached with the effort of choking back a sob of loneliness, of Pete's strange and dogged pursuit of me last summer, before the hurricane, before my old life was blown away.

I was tired of the perception that I wasn't good enough, and with Pete, it had only grown worse. Two years ago I was fighting the critics who said I didn't have the background or the training to be an upper-level event rider. Two months ago I was reading the criticism that I wasn't good enough for my boyfriend. Now I had simply been dismissed as yesterday's news.

I closed up my laptop and the comments went dark, but I knew the people were still out there, chattering about the characters in my life as if I didn't exist, as if I'd been written out of the story many chapters ago. I thought about calling Lacey but it was past ten o'clock, and if she wasn't in bed by now, she ought to be. She had horses to feed in the morning, same as I did. Pete was certainly in bed; it was the wee hours in England. No one was awake but me and the fireworks. I went onto the porch, stepping carefully on the splintering boards, to watch them pop and fizzle in the distance.

I closed the door behind me and jumped; there was Anna, leaning against the wobbly railing, gazing at the starbursts in the distance. She turned and smiled.

"I didn't know you were out here," I said apologetically.

"It's a big porch, there's room for both of us." She waved me over with an openness I envied. "Come and watch this beautiful show we get for free every night. And if you look north at just the right time, you'll see lightning, too."

"Sounds exciting." I picked my way gingerly across the decking, wishing I'd slipped on some sandals, and settled next to Anna. Almost immediately, two massive explosions of pink light were upstaged by a flash of lightning that seemed to light up the entire sky. "Oh shit!" I exclaimed. "That was gorgeous!"

Anna was laughing. "God, I love living here."

I laughed too. "You can't be serious."

"What?" Anna looked at me curiously. "We have everything here. We have an amazing barn right in the middle of town. We're right next to one of the most popular vacation spots in the whole world. Look at these fireworks we get to watch! Sure, it's made our business different from most barns, but that's okay. We're living a totally unique life here. We're doing things no other show barn has ever done. Aren't you having fun with it?"

A rainbow of sparkles floated across the western sky. "Not really," I admitted. "I like Ocala. I like being in the middle of horse country, nothing but horses in every direction. Have you ever been there?"

"Sure, it's nice. But it's hard to stand out when you're doing the same thing as everybody else."

We were quiet for a minute, while the fireworks wore themselves out in a cannonade of a grand finale. The smoke curled through the orange glow of the distant parking lots, and the last of the thundering explosions rolled past into the quiet woods behind us.

"I'm not trying to do anything different," I said after a little while. "I just want to be an event rider. That's all I am."

Anna went on gazing out at the horizon, at those flame-colored lights glowing up from behind the pines, a different world within our reach. Too close for comfort, if you asked me. "I want to be different," she said finally. "Doing things the same way as everyone else isn't good enough anymore. The world's changing."

"I don't want the world to change," I said stubbornly. "That's why I want to stay in Ocala, maybe go to upstate New York in the summer . . . it would be easier to compete year-round that way."

"Don't you think that world's too little?" Anna lifted an eyebrow. "You really only want to show horses?"

"Yeah . . . so?"

"So, I just think maybe you could do more with your life than chase ribbons."

"And what makes you any different?" I snapped. "Girl who works in a show barn? You're one step above me, so I muck more stalls than you. That's about it. Oh, and I have an actual career as a trainer back home, so . . ." I let the "so" trail off, partially to be mean and partially because I didn't have anything else to say. *Eventing Chicks* still had me feeling like my entire career was something I'd made up.

Anna drew back and I saw her hands fist at her sides. I almost felt bad for being rude. But those damned commenters were in my head. I scoffed when she said, "I think you're being really nasty for no reason, and I'm going to bed."

"You're the one who said my world was too small," I reminded her as she walked away.

"If you can't see beyond winning some ribbons, then it is," Anna said. "Why'd you let them send you here, if you have such a great life in Ocala?" She opened her door, paused, and glanced back at me. "Honestly, when I see you riding with Grace, I think you're a little delusional about how great you think you are."

*Wow.* "Goodnight to you, too," I said, as Anna slammed her door shut.

Anna was cool to me the next morning, but I didn't let it bother me. I was tired from lying awake half the night anyway. She could've been hurling insults at me in between dumping feed into buckets and I wouldn't have been concerned. All I wanted to do was go back to bed, fall asleep, and get away from the fears that had plagued me all night long. After we'd finished feeding, she went off to talk to Kennedy, and left me to turn out the horses with morning paddock time. I decided to grab Douglas first, who just happened to be stabled next to the lesson office where Kennedy was sitting, going over the day's schedule and listening to Anna whisper in her ear.

"Hey, Dougie," I said softly, as the curly-headed old horse shoved impatiently at my chest. The only time he had any get up and go was when it was time for turnout, which was kind of ironic since the only thing he did in the pasture was stand at the gate with his head pointed toward the barn, gazing longingly at his empty stall. "Let's take it easy for a sec, okay?"

Kennedy's reliably loud voice floated out of the office. "I wouldn't worry about it, once summer is over—"

A horse whinnied from across the aisle. I threw the noisy beast a scornful look over my shoulder. He snorted at me. I turned back to Doug, fumbling with the halter in my hands.

"None of you have the sense to keep quiet. No chill at all . . ." I hushed up quickly as I heard Anna's voice.

"Grace told me she was going to ask her."

"Well, if Grace told you, that means you're still part of her plans, doesn't it?"

I buckled the halter behind Doug's ears and pulled at the long mane hairs bristling from underneath it, straightening them out with unusual care.

"I just don't want to get replaced."

"I don't see how you could be replaced. She lives in Ocala."

They were talking about me! I bit my lip and went on stroking down Doug's mane as if he had to be turned out for the show ring.

"If Grace gives up this farm and moves to Ocala, then what? What if Grace is just hedging her bets?"

There was silence. Kennedy sighed and said something I couldn't hear, but that was fine. I'd heard enough.

I led Doug out to his paddock, letting him prance beside me like a pony twenty years younger, pondering what on earth Grace might be trying to use me for.

G race made her move a few hours later.

"You should come to supper," she said casually, walking over to where I was working. She leaned against the open stall door. "Come over tonight."

She'd been quiet all day, glancing over at Anna and me as we worked, eyeing us with an appraising gaze. It was unnerving. Anna wasn't fond of it either; I could tell. As the day had worn on, her shoulders had begun to hunch and she'd pulled in her chin, as if she was trying to get smaller and smaller. It was odd; most of the time, Grace and Anna were as close as a mother and daughter. Closer, if you considered how rarely I even talked to my mom.

Maybe Grace was going to use me against Anna to get her own way. I wouldn't put it past a clever trainer. Setting two horse girls at each other's throats was relatively simple. And Grace hadn't built up a barn and business like this one by being kind and thoughtful. Judging by that boarding contract I'd seen, she was capable of just about anything. It made me like her more.

But . . . dinner at her house? Did we really want to do this?

"I mean it," Grace insisted, when I didn't reply right away. She came over and took the pitchfork out of my hand, leaning it against the wall with finality, as if supper was happening right this instant. "You've been working nonstop since you got here. Don't think I haven't noticed. We've barely had a conversation that wasn't about work. I don't know a thing about you! Come over tonight after you've finished up and we'll have a nice meal and a chat."

When she had finally wrangled a nod out of me and went off to ride, I looked over at Anna, who was scrubbing water buckets in the nearby wash rack. Anna met my eye for a moment, then dropped her gaze back to the buckets. Her mouth was set in a thin, sullen line.

"Everything okay today, Anna?" I asked, walking over with the buckets from the stall I was cleaning. I threw the water down the neighboring wash rack so that she didn't think I was adding to her workload.

"I'm fine," she said shortly. "Just hot, I guess."

"Summer." I leaned back on my heels, trying to think of something to say that might take the heat off me. "I heard Tom's going to the Keys tomorrow. Did he tell you?"

That worked. Anna was outraged. "In the middle of the summer? Who said that was okay? Grace never lets anyone leave during summer vacation, especially now that we have so many more kids around here."

"Grace asked Margaret and me if we thought we could cover for him. I wasn't going to say no. That's no way to treat a work relationship, even if it means a little extra work on my end. He said he'd owe me one."

Anna laughed, a short, bitter laugh. "You'd like everyone to owe you something, wouldn't you?"

I furrowed my brow at her. "What's that supposed to mean?"

She shrugged, maybe regretting her words already. "Oh, I don't know, I just get the idea you're always a businesswoman first. Like you're looking for the deals, and the partnerships, instead of friendships. There's nothing wrong with that, I'm just saying . . ." She trailed off, looking flustered.

I picked up my water buckets. "I know it looks like that," I told her, shrugging. "I'm sorry about last night, by the way."

I could have elaborated. I could have said I was short-tempered and bad at normal conversation because I wasn't used to having friends. I could have explained that at the barn I grew up at, I was the help and no one saw me as their equal, and being here didn't feel much different. I could have explained that if I was prickly and didn't want to hang out with her at night or philosophize about working with horses, none of that had anything to do with her personally. And if Grace was planning on buttering me up for some kind of off-the-books deal unrelated to the Rockwell sponsorship, Anna shouldn't for a moment think I was going to steal her relationship with Grace. I didn't want it. I didn't *need* it.

"Right," Anna said. "Thanks." She went back to scrubbing buckets, and I felt dismissed. It was like a pattern repeating itself, straight back to childhood, and I didn't want to live through it all again.

I teetered on the edge of the wash rack, on the edge of saying something more, on the edge of being honest about my feelings with someone besides Lacey and Pete.

"Oh, Jules?"

I spun around. Grace was leaning around the barn door, eyebrows raised. "Yes!" Saved by the boss, before I did something silly and emotional.

"Can you ride Ivor for me?"

"Ivor?" I couldn't have heard that right. Ivor was Grace's horse.

Anna slammed two buckets together with way more force than was necessary.

"Yes, can you just give him a nice thirty minutes on the flat? Nothing too strenuous. I won't have time for him today."

I couldn't believe this was happening. At the same time, I was slightly embarrassed at my own reaction. This must have been what Lacey felt like when I first started putting her on my good horses for hacks. Wasn't I past all this?

"No problem," I called, straining to keep my voice calm. Just another horse to ride. "I'll take care of it as soon as we're done with stalls."

"Thanks, hon." Grace disappeared back outside.

I walked down the aisle with my water buckets, carefully avoiding eye contact with Anna. But I could feel her gaze on my back, boring holes through me, daring me to turn around. I had a strong suspicion Anna hadn't ridden Ivor much.

Maybe not at all.

Of course, riding Ivor meant that I didn't have time to ride Mickey before the day really heated up, something I'd been promising him I would do on the days we didn't have lessons. He hated working in the afternoons, when the sun was blazing and it was impossible to work outside. The covered arena seemed to be where everyone preferred to ride, but the footing was a little hard. I sweated in the sunlight most days, preferring to baby their hooves and legs. We were used to heat, I reminded myself. We were Floridians.

Still, this was serious weather, enough to make the most summer-loving of horses and humans reconsider their home state. Every summer was a little different, and as the year went freewheeling into July, this summer's weather pattern was favoring heavy storms after sunset, rather than the typical midafternoon storms.

Without the midday clouds boiling into a three o'clock thunderstorm to break the misery, the heat built up with the speed of a spring wildfire. It didn't take a heat wave to crank the mercury up into the nineties—that was just normal weather. At one o'clock, when I'd have time to ride Mickey, the temperature in the outdoor arena would feel like one hundred degrees. We would be stuck—skip work or deal with the white-hot heat.

The answer to that one was obvious. Faint heart never won Fair Hill.

I guessed Grace wouldn't insist on the stirrup-less German antique saddle when I rode her favorite child, so I pulled my saddle, which had been reunited with its leathers and irons, out of my locker and settled it in front of a grooming stall. I found Ivor's bridle, girth, and back pad from Grace's stash in the school tack room, and added those to the pile. All the while, Anna stalked past on various chores, not meeting my eye. It was a shame riding Ivor would be the final wedge that drove us apart—I wasn't particularly looking forward to spending the rest of the summer working with someone who resented me—but I was still thrilled at the thought of riding him.

Ivor was not an easy horse, and it was just one of those peculiarities of horse people that made riding him such an honor. His brain was not always on his work, or even where he was putting his feet—keeping him focused was his rider's number-one challenge. Keeping him in check was the second. He was a horse of boundless energy and almost frightening strength, and, of course, he was a stallion.

For all that strength and ebullience, though, and even with the strike of stallion status against him, he was an awfully nice horse. He was friendly, interested in people (mainly in eating their ponytails, I remembered, tucking mine up into a bun and shoving it under my hard hat). He stood politely in the crossties while being groomed and tacked up, although he did like to crane his neck around and watch the groom at work, especially if he thought that he could get a ponytail or a sleeve into his mouth. If he did catch a shirt, he didn't really bite down like a lot of mouthy stallions. He just held the fabric in his lips and gazed at you with beguiling brown eyes, his white forelock falling over his lashes, expression as innocent as a foal.

Well. Anyone who has ever handled a foal knows they aren't even the least bit innocent. They are imps out for trouble. Ivor, for all his height (seventeen-two hands high, thank you very much) and all of his bulk (body like a bull's), wasn't really out for trouble. He just wanted someone to be his pal and play with him.

"I'm not that person," I warned him, slipping into his paddock. Ivor, who was occasionally a brilliant white but was today wearing his more usual color of gray-brown, looked up at me from his napping place in the mud next to the water trough. "I'm not your buddy and if you rub all that mud on me, so help me . . ."

He trotted over, neck arched, and squealed when I slipped the halter behind his ears. "Studdish today? I must have mare on me."

Ivor gave me an encouraging rumble from deep within his chest. I gave him a friendly smack on the neck that was also a reminder to behave himself. "Get a grip, you dumb jock. I have two legs, not four." I gave the nose chain a little jiggle to make sure he knew it was there, and we set off for the barn.

In the dressage arena, walking a boarder's horse on a loose rein, Grace waved from horseback. "Good girl!" she shouted.

One hose-down later, which left us both dripping wet and the drain clogging from all the mud, I managed to hoist my saddle up onto Ivor's back and got him ready to ride. The saddle pad soaked through with water immediately, even though I'd tried to towel him dry. No choice, though—the beast had been too filthy with wet mud to even consider grooming, and I knew Grace wouldn't appreciate her good horse going out to the arena dirty. I managed to get his bridle on with only a minimum of noseband-eating, pulled gloves over my wet hands with some difficulty, and we headed for the dressage ring.

Anna poked her head out of the feed room as we went by. "Good luck," she called. "Don't let him do anything stupid."

I held Ivor up for a moment, eager for a chance to normalize relations. "Got any advice for me? I'm not sure how this happened, but I'd rather not get dumped."

She shrugged and went back to dipping lunchtime grain. "I've never ridden him," she reminded me. "Guess you better ask Grace."

Guess so. "Thanks anyway," I told her, or told the back of her head, and moved on.

Ivor had the biggest movement of any horse I'd ever been on. Even his walk felt more like a springing trot than Mickey or Dynamo's. He moved away from the mounting block like a huge, glorious panther, and I felt my body swaying all over the place. I quickly dropped the stirrups I'd picked up when I'd mounted, and tried to loosen up my hips and lower back. If Ivor was built with springs instead of joints, I was going to have to develop matching ones in order to sit his gaits.

It only took a couple of rounds of the dressage arena to start feeling comfortable on him; by now, Ivor had lost interest in walking and was starting to gaze around him, looking for diversions: butterflies, mockingbirds, pine needles, dry rattling leaves falling from the magnolia tree near the top of the arena. Grace was now out in the covered arena, still riding one of the boarders' horses; I could see her watching me whenever she came down the long side in my direction, not bothering to hide her curiosity. It didn't make things any easier. Learning to ride a new horse is one thing. Learning to ride a new horse who is also your boss's favorite horse in the world while your boss is watching and thinking critical thoughts, is entirely another.

"Well, let's trot," I told Ivor, gathering up my reins. Ivor collected into my hands and pressed off into a working trot that felt a little bit like when Mickey left the starting box for a cross-country round. It was big, it was bold, it was so full of impulsion that for a second I thought I was going to be left hanging in the air while the horse whizzed away into the future without me, a cartoon cutout hovering above the arena for one perplexed half second before I hit the ground, Wile E. Coyote style.

But once I got used to the scope and size of his stride, it wasn't that bad. And once I got over thinking that it was too much trot, and started to think of it as just the right trot, I suddenly realized that it was the greatest trot in the world and should last forever.

Which was when the wandering brain of Ivor got bored again.

I wasn't paying enough attention, too busy enjoying the trot of the gods, or I would have noticed Ivor's ears waggling, Ivor's shoulder popping toward the rail, Ivor's spine shifting ever so slightly, as if he was preparing to turn into the arena or do a shoulder-in. In fact, he was prepping himself for a pretty epic spook at a pile of magnolia leaves.

I caught onto him right before he pulled the cord. "What are you doing?" I snapped, and gave him a boot in the ribs to straighten him out, lifting my hands as I felt him lifting his front end, and that was all simultaneous, somehow, with his snort and his spin, made a thousand times more difficult to ride due to his sheer grace and poise as he easily performed a 180-degree turn. A clumsy horse might have stumbled his way through it and given up halfway, but not Ivor. Ivor was both committed and capable.

Thank God I was too.

As I straightened him out, cursing him to the heavens, I heard a ripping peal of laughter coming from the covered arena. Grace, amused at my expense. That was fine. I rode past the barn entrance and glanced inside; there was Anna, glowering at me like a ghost in a horror film. That was not fine. But I shook her out of my mind and went back to enjoying the horse that was underneath me, this time with a little more respect and attention for the sheer nonsense he was capable of.

The rest of the ride was much simpler. I stayed with Ivor, and I made sure Ivor stayed with me. As I cooled him out, it occurred to me that *that* was probably the most basic definition of the most difficult levels of dressage.

# 18

THE STEPS TO Grace's house were sagging and creaky, spotted with a furry coat of green moss in places, but the broad porch was clean-swept and shining with a fresh coat of paint, and the front door sported a wooden welcome sign with a carved dressage horse trotting over the letters. I admired the wicker rocking chair and love seat that sat on a worn oriental rug next to the door, and the old bookshelf that housed an impressive collection of mud boots and clogs on the door's other side. There was a boot jack and a boot scraper. There were a few bits sitting in a small round bucket, waiting to be remembered and grabbed on the way back to the barn. There was a knotted coil of orange hay twine lying on top of a pair of scissors. The little things that identify a horsewoman even before she opens the door.

I tapped at the ancient screen door, but Grace was already there, opening it up and letting out a blizzard's gust of ice-cold air. So she spent plenty of money on her air-conditioning, even though her house was a little shabby. I identified strongly with Grace's priorities.

Inside, there were horse show ribbons everywhere—on the lamps, on the walls, on the edges of picture frames. I settled down onto a sagging couch festooned with a racehorse tapestry throw, and leaned over to examine a small trophy gathering dust on the end table: Virginia Hunter-Jumper Association 1982 Championships.

"You're from Virginia?" I asked, while Grace stepped into the little kitchen, glassware clattering.

"I was just there showing," she said, bringing me a glass of iced tea. "I was born in Florida. This was my grandfather's farm." She glanced around the bungalow. "This was his house."

"You come from a horsey family?" That shouldn't be any surprise. Most successful trainers did. It was much easier to become an accomplished equestrian when all the basics—ponies, saddles, trailers, show fees—were provided for you.

"Only my grandfather. My parents couldn't understand it. But he'd always had horses. There was an orange grove, too—that's houses now. And a hundred acres of cattle pasture—that's a golf course." She looked sad at the thought.

Another horsey grandfather, I thought. My grandfather lived for golf and deep-sea fishing. Life was so unfair. I adjusted myself on the broken springs of the couch. "The house is really nice. I like the . . . I like that picture there, by the TV." I pointed at the large framed photo: a black-and-white scene of horse and foal, girl and grandfather.

"My grandpa and his favorite mare." Grace smiled at the

memory. "Sassy Susan. He let me ride her when we went to check the cattle."

"That sounds nice," I said awkwardly, and turned my attention to my iced tea. Grace excused herself to check on dinner.

A few minutes later we were seated around an old dinette set. Grace started dishing out macaroni and cheese from a Corningware dish. Real macaroni and cheese, with brown spots on top, and flecks of bread crumbs here and there. I had eaten a lot of mac and cheese in the past few days, but clearly we were in different territory from the store-brand boxed stuff. "I hope you don't have a problem with carbs." Grace chuckled. "Every now and then I get a girl who won't touch pasta. And I wonder what she thinks she's going to live on when business gets tough. Hell, I still live on it."

I had to laugh at that. "A horsewoman who won't eat ramen or mac and cheese had better figure out a way to eat oats and hay. At least she can get the owners to pay for the horse feed."

"And how are you doing with owners?" Grace asked pointedly, placing a breast of fried chicken on my plate. "How's your business doing up there in horse country?"

I was a little taken aback by the question. "I'm doing . . . okay," I replied slowly, not sure how to answer. The truth wasn't that simple. "The hurricane hit me hard," I admitted. "I lost clients, didn't gain many back. I have six horses in the barn and half of them are mine."

Grace shook her head. "That's a bad ratio."

"I know." I dug into my food so that I wouldn't have to talk. There was silence for a few moments, punctuated by clinks of cutlery.

"I can help you," Grace said after a few minutes, as if she couldn't be bothered with any more preamble.

I looked up, but her attention was still focused on her plate. "What?"

"I can help you. If you're interested. I run into buyers from time to time . . . they're looking for investment horses, but they're looking for something beautiful, something they can admire and point out to coworkers and say 'That's mine.' Sometimes, the horses they want would be better suited for eventing. Or their paycheck would be better suited for eventing. No offense. You know what I mean."

"None taken." Eventing wasn't cheap, but it wasn't show jumping either, not the way Grace's clients were used to it, with thousand-dollar show days spent in Wellington or down the road from Briar Hill, at the big showgrounds around Ocala. I was tempted by the idea of a pipeline of clients, since I was so incredibly bad at picking them up on my own. "So how would that work? You'd just refer the owner to me, and then we could work out a training agreement on our own?"

Grace smiled indulgently. "I'd want to be a little more hands-on than that. These are my students, you see. I take care of them, find them the horse they want, make arrangements so they can ride the horse when it isn't in training. We would have to make sure they feel included. And I would need to be named in the contract for the purpose of commissions and withdrawal fees if they chose to leave the program without proper notification. Legal things. We don't have to talk about that right now. I was just wondering if you were receptive. Of course, if you don't have the room or if you think you're going to be filling up your barn on your own, that's completely understandable."

Of course there were Legal Things. Of course there were commissions and fees. Of course it would all be tangled up in Grace's strange business plan. Whatever she was doing, it was clearly working for her; I just wasn't sure I wanted to be caught in someone else's web.

Even so, it would be silly to cross out an opportunity now. I'd only been here a few weeks, what did I really know about the way she did business? There was plenty of time left in this apprenticeship. "I'd be interested in talking more," I offered. "Maybe after we've spent a little more time working together. It might be I'm not the rider you're looking for."

"Oh, I think you're plenty good enough to ride the horses I have in mind," Grace said cheerfully. She paused for a bite of mac and cheese. "And you're going to get better. Otherwise I wouldn't have let you ride Ivor. You can learn a lot from Ivor."

"Yeah, about that—he's a damn nice horse, Grace. You're very lucky."

Grace smiled again, but this time it was less welcome-to-my-spiderweb and more oh-I-love-my-pony. This was that universal smile all horsey girls get when someone tells us our pony has a pretty forelock or a nice trot. "Thank you. I know I am. I've had Ivor for a very long time, and it's rare I don't manage to make the time to ride him. But I have to admit, I was curious. I wanted to see what he thought of you."

"Thought of me? Is he like, a litmus test kind of horse?"

She nodded. "That's exactly it. And he liked you."

"Oh. Well, I'm glad." What else could I say? I filled my mouth with a huge heaping forkful so she would go on talking.

"We all like you," Grace went on, obviously unaware that Margaret thought I was an idiot and Anna thought I was stealing her best friend and Kennedy thought I should go on trail rides instead of eventing and Tom didn't think about me at all. "I know this wasn't your choice. But I think you'll be glad you came. On many levels. Both when you've improved your dressage and your horses, and when you're reaping the rewards of networking outside of your usual circle." She got up and went to the kitchen, then reappeared with a bottle of sparkling wine and two glasses. "It's not champagne, but it's close. Let's drink to new connections, and stepping outside of your comfort zone. I think you'll find there are very useful people out in the *real* world. The next time you're wondering where to find clients, look outside of Ocala. There's much less competition here. And plenty of money."

There was a long pause while we considered the uneasy relationship we both had with money.

"This place won't last forever, either," Grace said eventually. I looked at her questioningly.

"It's expensive, staying here," she explained. "This used to be farm country and now it's a resort community. I'm fighting to keep the farm going, but if I can expand to Ocala now, I'll be ready if developers and taxes force me out in the end."

The silence that settled over the room was heavy. We drained our glasses without the celebratory air they'd been intended for.

After dinner, Grace walked me to the door and we stood on the porch for a few minutes, admiring the dusk creeping through the live oaks. "This is a lovely setting," I admitted. "I wasn't thrilled to leave Ocala, but standing here, I can almost pretend I'm there."

A high-pitched train whistle pierced the evening from far away, and Grace laughed. "Steam train and everything?"

"Is that what that is?" I'd heard it early that morning, as well, along with a few other mystery whistles and what sounded like a race car or two.

"The Magic Kingdom steam train. The sound carries when it's damp. On some nights, when the wind is out of the west, you can hear the music from the parades." Grace shook her head. "I know it's crazy for you. It was crazy for me, too, when I first came back. When I was a little girl here, the only sounds you heard this time of the night were the cattle up the road. And the whip-poor-wills."

I cocked my head, listening, but the night was uncommonly still. "Are there still whip-poor-wills here?"

"Not anymore." Grace put her hand on the porch door, ready to head in for the night. "They're too shy for all the commotion around here. But when I was a kid . . . this was a real wild kingdom. Bobcats, bears, eagles. Now even if you go deep into the woods back there, you won't see any of them. We're civilized now, I guess."

"Civilization is overrated," I said.

"Are you going to think about my offer?"

"Of course," I said. "I'll be thinking about it."

"What if I asked you to answer me right now?"

I glanced at her curiously. "I guess I'd say no," I admitted. "I've never really thought of myself as a partnership type person."

Grace sniffed. "Watch and learn, child. Insisting you can do everything on your own isn't just arrogant, it's immature. Maybe you'll learn that this summer."

"Whoa," I said, holding up a hand. "I didn't mean to offend you—"

"Goodnight," Grace interrupted. "You have the summer to think about it." Her voice was cool.

Dismissed, and annoyed by it, I walked back to the barn with the sound of the steam train whistle still piercing the quiet night. I tried to imagine the noise and clutter of Orlando intruding on Briar Hill. Poor Grace, returning to her childhood farm to find it surrounded by houses and lit up at night by fireworks. That would probably make anyone kind of crazy. Hopefully this wasn't going to be a rift in our relationship. I felt like I had enough trouble.

# 19

ANNA WAS STILL short with me the next morning, which meant I wasn't forgiven for having dinner with Grace while she was relegated to lowly night-check duties. If only she knew the way that dinner ended!

Then again, Grace had looked me over and deemed me worthy of partnership, and whether I took her up on it or not, even with her irritation that I wouldn't agree right away, I was definitely feeling more like myself again. Even the prospect of today's dressage lessons couldn't bring me down; on the contrary, I felt energized and ready to give the sandbox another shot. I raced through my side of the barn aisle, turning over my stalls in record time, and I was already hanging up my pitchfork while Anna was still working her way through her row of stalls, all ready to get Dynamo tacked.

I hooked the crossties to Dynamo's halter and got busy with the curry comb. Horse grooming is ideal thinking time. Wars could be averted if presidents were handed a grooming box and a very dirty horse and told to spend an hour getting things straightened out. Grooming Dynamo this morning gave me plenty of time to consider how disappointed Pete would be in me if I rubbed last night in Anna's face.

"But really, Dynamo," I said, whisking away dirt with a dandy brush while he leaned into the action, loving the rough fibers on his muscles, "this is about respect. Anna has no respect for me. She's younger than me, and she's not as experienced as me, and she should be respectful if Grace gives me work she can't handle. It's not my fault she can't ride Ivor and she doesn't have a farm of her own that might make Grace some money someday. Why is her snotty attitude my problem? Why do I have to be the nice one?"

That was the problem with being a better person—sometimes the rules just didn't make any sense.

Dynamo ignored my complaints, shifting his shoulder so that I'd give the muscles there a little more attention. I knocked the brush against him harder and he wriggled his upper lip in appreciation. Dynamo didn't care who respected me. He didn't care if my pride was wounded by some eighteen-year-old. He just wanted his rubdown. I liked that about my horses.

My gung-ho, let's-do-this attitude disappeared the moment we got into the arena.

The only way to describe the morning was "airless," unless you wanted to throw in "stagnant" or "hellish" for good measure. I hadn't really noticed it in the barn, where the profusion of stall fans and the overhead ventilation kept the air at least moving.

Outside, wood smoke from the construction site next door was hanging low in still, humid air. In the covered arena, there wasn't a breath of moving air.

Even Dynamo, the reliable Floridian, felt the weight of the atmosphere and decided working was out of the question. Every other stride, he dug his head down hard against the bit, demanding I carry him. He shoved his nose toward the ground, nearly tripping himself at the trot, paying more attention to pulling on my shoulders than actually keeping his own feet on the ground. I grunted at his weight and stuck my heels into his ribs. Every thump of my boots got his head up again, but it never lasted more than a stride or two. Every time his head dropped, a certain part of my anatomy slammed against the rock-hard pommel of the old dressage saddle with what I was certain would be lasting effects. I pulled up out of desperation and loosened the reins, letting Dynamo drop his head as he'd been demanding, and wiped the sweat from my eyes.

Grace was dismayed. "Oh, Jules, he's going like an old school horse today! What's wrong with you two? You have to pull it together."

"Honestly, Grace, I think he's asking for a day off. This weather sucks." I fought to keep a pant out of my voice.

"Well, it's too late for that now. You can give him tomorrow off. But today he's going to have to give us at least five minutes of a nice collected trot, and you're going to have to prove that you can get it from him." Grace's voice had an edge to it.

I stretched my legs as long as I could get them, reaching back with my heels so I could touch Dynamo's long muscles that stretched under his abdomen. Grace had placed my leg there on our first lesson, showing me where to apply pressure and how the muscle lifted, raising his entire back and, by extension, his body. The motion forced my legs so far back that I felt an electric jolt of pain in my hip joints, but I figured I'd stretch out eventually and get used to it. Once upon a time, I'd been a little girl on a pony who couldn't get her heels down, and now look at them . . . my heels dropped toward the ground like an obedient sheepdog every time I touched the balls of my feet to anything hard—the rung of a chair, the lower bar of a fence, the curb of a sidewalk. They were probably permanently disfigured if you asked a doctor, but they were perfect for a horsewoman. So my hips could join the party—if I could get through the first painful stages of settling them there.

I winced now as I brought my legs back, glancing down past my hands to see the angle it set me at. My upper thigh was perpendicular with the ground, my toe invisible behind my knee. I lifted my heels against Dynamo's sides, squeezed my fingers closed on the reins for a scant second, and sat deep on my seat bones, feeling his rolling spine right through the wool and leather of the dressage saddle.

Dynamo's body came together, lightning dangling between my fingers and my heels, pressed into equine form by all the effort I could muster, and I carried him that way for two strides, six strides, eight strides, ten, turning him into a circle to help him hold the balance as the straightaway started to trouble him. My chin was down and my eyes were concentrated on the ground just a stride or two in front of his sweat-darkened poll and wobbling ears, which wasn't right, I knew—I should have been gazing confidently into the future, seeing five and ten strides ahead so that my body could signal to him where to put his hooves next—but I'd fix *that* later. I'd worry about me some other time. Right now, this was all Dynamo's show.

"Beautifully done," Grace said, finally sounding impressed, and I lifted Dynamo's frame once more in a half halt before bringing him down to a measured, flat-footed walk. I let the reins slip through my fingers as he stuck his nose out, begging for room to stretch. "I told you he would come around fairly quickly once we fixed a few of your flaws. Once we get your eyes off the ground, you'll be unstoppable. Then it's just a matter of building up his strength, and adding in lots of transitions and lateral work." She smiled gleefully at the thought of all that dressage. "He could be doing a Prix St. Georges test in August, not just Second Level. Do you have a shadbelly coat?"

I bit back a groan. All that dressage might be Grace's idea of heaven, but at that moment all I could think about was Pete, leaping over the fieldstone walls and the muddy ditches of England's countryside, and I was so jealous I could hardly stand it. So what if he was worn out and always on call and his nerves were shot trying to please his trainer? At least he was getting to have some fun.

"I do have a shadbelly," I said, "but I left it back in Ocala, since I only need it for three-day events."

"You can send for it. This horse would look so elegant with a rider in a nice tail coat."

I couldn't really imagine getting through the complexity of a Prix St. Georges dressage test, and I hated wearing that shadbelly, with those silly long tails falling on either side of the saddle. But I'd cross that bridge when I came to it. For the meantime, I leaned over and loosened the girth on my saddle. Dynamo heaved a sigh of relief as I gave his rib cage a little more space to expand, and shook hot sweat from his head. "Any other rides today?"

"Yes," Grace said crisply. "I want you to ride Splash and Mirage, in that order. I want you to do everything you just did on Dynamo, but with those two, you'll have to work that much harder. You can use stirrups again, but keep the old saddle. It will be good for you

to keep practicing until you get your lower leg where it's supposed
to be. Just thirty minutes each will do fine. Ride them out here, and
then do their legs up in alcohol wraps. This ground is hard."

Didn't I know it. "Um, but I won't have time to ride my other
horse?" I asked this in case there was some sort of oversight. Maybe
she had forgotten she hadn't given me a lesson on Mickey today.

"That's fine." Grace shrugged. "He's young yet, he can have
an extra day off."

I dismounted and pulled the tail of my shirt loose from my
breeches, rubbing it along his eyes as he brought his head down to
rub it against my thigh. "Don't want sweat in your eyes, baby," I
murmured. "That'd sting."

Grace sat down on the mounting block and sighed. "It's too
damn hot for this. Be sure to put some alcohol in his rinse water."

I wanted to put some alcohol in *my* water. "Okay."

"And tell Tom to stop what he's doing and harrow the arena. I
want to ride Ivor and the footing is all choppy."

If I had hoped I was going to get another spin on the stallion
(had I? My disappointment told me I had), that was apparently
off the table. Maybe if I figured out what the hell I'd been doing
wrong today, I'd win back the chance. "Okay," I said again, and led
Dynamo into the barn.

Tom and Anna were in the last stall, fixing a broken waterer.
"Tom," I called, ignoring Anna's smirk—she must have heard the
line about my lower leg through the stall windows—"Grace wants
you to harrow the dressage arena."

"Right now?"

"Right now." I led Dynamo past without stopping. Even the
barn seemed like a sauna now. I could feel how red my cheeks were.
I must have looked like a Pony Clubber on the verge of sunstroke,

instead of a native Floridian who'd been working in the heat for years.

Margaret went stalking past, buckets over one wiry arm, face morose.

"Why is it so smoky?" I asked her.

"Construction site getting busy next door," she said. "They're burning off the pine and the cypress. It'll be this way the rest of the summer."

"What about the rain at night?"

"Just makes it smoke more." She marched off.

Dynamo slammed his head against my side, trying to rub the sticky, sweaty, itchy bridle off. I fumbled at the straps with wet fingers and managed to slip it over his ears. "It's July, so maybe we'll get lucky and it will rain all afternoon. A good monsoon to clear it out, and we'll be able to breathe again."

"Smells like it did back in spring."

I jumped. Tom was standing at the end of the row of crossties, on his way to get the Gator, I guessed. "Looks like you had a fire really close to here," I said, skipping over the fact that he'd caught me having a one-sided conversation with my horse. It was just Tom. It didn't matter if he thought I was crazy.

"Yup. Almost lost the place. Burned right up to the arena. Still dry out there. Rainy season isn't doing its job. No good this year."

"This place they're building next door—is it going to take up the woods out back, too?" If so, I could see why Grace was starting to put out feelers for North Florida stables. The equestrian center would be surrounded on two sides by houses, and she'd lose the trail-riding business.

"Not yet," Tom said.

"Yet? Is it for sale?"

He shrugged. "It's Grace's," he said, his meaning clear as mud, and sloped off down the aisle.

I got back to hosing down Dynamo. The horse leaned into the cool water, sticking his nose into the spray to grab a drink and blowing the water out of his nostrils with a shake of his head and a powerful snort. I stuck my own head into the spray for a moment, letting the lukewarm water dribble down my neck and soak my shirt. If Lacey had been there, she would have laughed at me and asked if we were having a wet T-shirt contest. If Pete had been there, he would have wolf-whistled and I would have had to give him a punch on the arm, followed by a kiss.

But there was nobody around except Dynamo. I felt like I was seventeen years old again, my life all work, and no friends but my horse. It was a feeling that rose up so quickly from time to time, from the pit of my stomach straight to my brain, it could make me feel a little dizzy. What happened to my farm, my little family, my real life? Where had the last five years gone?

Dynamo lunged for the hose, his tongue sliding out of his mouth. I stuck the hose in his mouth and he grabbed it with his front teeth, holding it steady while he slurped at the spray. "This is weird behavior. You know that, right?" I asked him, but he was too busy drinking to so much as flick his ears at my words.

"I wish I were as simple as you," I told the horse ruefully, and lucky me, Anna walked by and commented cheerfully that I seemed simple enough.

# 20

ALL DRESSAGE AND no galloping made Jules a grouchy girl, and the horses were feeling the boredom too.

After another seemingly endless week of nothing but dressage, both my boys were feeling pretty sour. I was surprised one morning when normally affectionate Mickey didn't even turn to face me when I went into his stall to fetch him out for a lesson, and when I turned out Dynamo, he went straight to the back corner of the paddock and stayed there all morning, nose in the corner, hoping he was invisible and I wouldn't see him. I wondered if they were in cahoots, whispering through the stall bars after hours, *It's time to teach Mom a lesson.*

Between their lessons and Grace's lessons, my dressage improvement seemed to have plateaued. The horses weren't interested,

I was frustrated, and the glory days when I'd been allowed to use stirrups and ride Ivor seemed like pages from a history book, instead of two weeks ago.

Grace dutifully hollered at me for a couple hours a day, mounting me on a few school horses as well to put some mileage on them, but she said nothing more about a future partnership, and I wondered if I was failing at the apprenticeship before it was even half over.

"The horses are just miserable," I told Pete. I'd stolen a few minutes for FaceTime between throwing lunch hay and riding Splash and Mirage; it was late evening in England and Pete was done for the day. "I mean, I'm miserable too, obviously, but it really sucks to have to do this to my horses. They worked so hard all winter, and now they're paying for it by having to work even harder on the flat."

"Well, if it means you'll win the dressage, isn't it worth it? Think how much fun they'll have this fall." Pete was trying to be the upbeat one, but I could see the fatigue in the new lines around his eyes and mouth. He looked like he hadn't slept in a month, which, coincidentally, was just about as long as he'd been overseas. "Try being me," he went on. "Almost all I'm doing is jumping. On Regina's flat days, I'm getting on the boss's horses and schooling them over hunt fences. Sometimes I even make it over all of them."

"Do you get a day off?" I admit I was shocked by his exhausted appearance. We had worked our asses off at Briar Hill on a daily basis, so how much harder was he working now, for it to show on his face so clearly?

"I'm sure I'm meant to, but somehow things never work out that way." He looked over his shoulder, eyebrows shooting up into his reddish hair, then he turned back, muscles sagging. "I thought it was Deb looking for me."

"It's eight o'clock at night! Surely you're done. All I have to do after eight is night-check and turn out the lights. And throw extra hay. And top off waters. I guess that is a lot," I reflected. "But seriously, you should be done for the night."

"Last night Deb pulled me out of bed at nine thirty to clear up a mess her dogs had made with the trash. Said I should've brought the bins inside, so it was my fault."

Anger rose up in my throat, hot and bitter. I nearly threw my phone across my little room, but luckily I realized that would be counterproductive and steadied myself before any electronics met an untimely death. "That's not okay, Pete," I managed to say. "You need some boundaries."

He just shrugged again. "Less than two months and it's over, right, babe? How are you being treated?"

Pretty well, I thought. Grace's riding lessons were killing me, my horses were bored and angry, Anna was nice enough in person but watched me with narrowed eyes when she thought I wasn't looking, Margaret didn't know I was alive, and Tom didn't really seem to have an opinion about anything but manatee counts in the local springs. The boarders were their own private circus, constantly bickering with each other. The kids just arrived, rode their ponies, and left. The vibe here was kind of insane, but at least the work itself wasn't that bad. "It's weird," I said slowly. "I feel like Grace is trying to groom me for something. Invited me over and cooked me dinner, let me ride her big horse, offered me a business partnership after this summer is over . . . then she drops the nice routine and barely speaks to me outside of riding lessons. I don't know. It's just really strange."

Pete smiled, genuinely this time. "Maybe she just recognizes that you're a top-notch rider, and with a little fine-tuning from her, she's sitting on a gold mine, but she hasn't figured out how to monetize you yet."

I laughed and shook my head. "That's definitely not it."

But of course, once he said it, I didn't mind if it was true. I was all of those things, after all.

"Amy thinks you're probably getting more out of this summer than anybody."

My lip curled at the mention of his glamorous lab partner. Pete saw it and laughed. "Did you forget I can see you? Don't be jealous of Amy, babe, she's way too hot for me."

"That's really not helpful."

"Let me put it to you like this . . ." Pete looked around, as if to make sure there was no one to overhear him. From the looks of things, his dark little cupboard of an apartment was even smaller than mine, so I wasn't sure who else he might have thought was crammed in there without his knowledge. "Amy is not interested in a poor horse trainer. She's much more discriminating than you. And she didn't just come over here to work on her jumping."

"Oh no?" I was interested despite myself.

"She's looking for a title."

I burst into laughter. "Stop it! She's hunting for a lord like a heroine in a romance novel?"

"Wouldn't you?"

"Of course not! Think of all the parties they have to go to. I'd be a mess."

"You're definitely not royalty," Pete agreed. "But I love you anyway. You're very nice for a commoner."

"That's very kind."

"Feel better now? I have nothing to offer her."

"I feel much better, you idiot," I told him affectionately, and I did.

"Obviously, if you're calling me names."

"Oh, shut it."

I could've gone on like this with him for hours, feeling like we were back home on the couch on a rainy afternoon, waiting for the weather to pass so we could get back to work, secretly hoping it would storm all day and we could just lean into each other for a few more hours, letting the world turn without us. But Pete was knackered, that much was obvious from his drawn expression and red-rimmed eyes, and through my window I could see one of the boarders marching down the barn aisle, looking like she was in her usual mood (pouty, easily angered) and in need of a groom to fix everything for her, so I told Pete I loved him and to get some rest, and hung up.

There was the usual feeling of letdown and lonesomeness after—I'd gotten entirely too used to having that man around. Still, I smiled a little as I snagged my water bottle and slipped on my paddock boots. It was nice to have someone tell you they loved you, and that you were a tremendous rider and a potential gold mine. It could put a spring in your step as you ran downstairs to deal with a bunch of people who seemed to actively dislike you, before riding a herd of horses who were no more interested in the lessons you were teaching them than you were.

# 21

THAT FRIDAY NIGHT was stifling. We were prepping for a weekend of riding lessons and trail rides, but the truth was, everyone should have just stayed home and lolled around in their air-conditioning. A storm was dangling tantalizing fingers of cloud through the eastern sky, and rumbles of thunder went rolling through the barn, so low and deep the stall bars rattled in their frames, but in the west the sun was bright and cheerful as it scorched the earth at our feet, and the barn thermometer's arrow pointed to ninety-two degrees.

Nothing could be canceled in weather like this; summer was hot, everyone knew this, and ninety-two was perfectly normal. The thunderstorm to the east wasn't close enough to keep anyone out of the covered arena, and when I checked the radar on my phone, it showed the storm bubbling and popping in one place, unmoving, without the slightest inclination to drift a few miles west and cool us down.

So we were brushing horses and tacking up for the afternoon lessons, wiping sweat on our shirts and slipping ice cubes into our sports bras. It was the kind of day to make you rethink your life choices.

Instead, we just got a little more crazy.

As students started to arrive, a buzz went around the school tack room. Grace had posted the prize list for a little Seabreeze-only schooling show, the kind of show in which kids could get their first taste of equitation and hunter classes. They would learn fun horse show secrets in the comfort of their own covered arena, like the announcer's command, "Riders, please walk your horses," is always followed by "Riders, please canter your horses," and a lot of panicked looks from the kids who haven't nailed walk-canter transitions yet.

I didn't miss the hunter shows of my childhood, but it was July and I was feeling horse show withdrawal. I bellied up to the bulletin board while half the kids in the barn were out practicing their posting trot under Kennedy's watchful eye, and checked out the class listings in hopes there might be something fun for me to do. I found the options less than thrilling: there was short stirrup, long stirrup, rusty stirrup—every kind of stirrup for beginning riders. There were a few intermediate classes as well, but nothing for an advanced rider. I confided to Anna, who had moseyed over for a look herself, that I didn't find it a very inspiring show bill.

"It's not for us," Anna said patiently, as if I was some sort of idiot who needed to be humored, which was pretty much the way Anna said everything to me these days. "It's for the students."

"Aren't we students?" If there was going to be a show, I wanted a part of it. Grooming during a show, on the outside looking in, was a throwback to my old life, one I wasn't interested in reliving. Being left out in my twenties wasn't any more fun than being left out when I was a teenager.

Anna snickered. "Not in this case. We're the staff. You have to be okay with it, Jules."

I wanted to tell her that in that case, she needed to be okay with Grace inviting me over for dinner and letting me ride Ivor one freaking time. But I didn't say anything, and Anna headed off down the aisle with a saddle on her hip, ready to ride one of the boarders' horses. And by doing that, I guess, Anna made a good point. All week, she had been getting on client horses, while I was stuck with school horses who needed tune-ups. Ivor still remained Grace's private domain.

The entire situation smacked of manipulation to me; Grace had allowed me to ride Ivor that one time to give me a taste of just how good things could be between us. In the meantime, until I signed on to become her partner in crime—I mean partner in sales horses—I was relegated to the schoolies who had been going around the arena like battleships, with their necks stretched out in front of them and their hindquarters somewhere in the next county.

I let Anna have the extra rides without any dissent. I wasn't about to ask Grace if I could ride more and groom less—the few horses she was assigning me were punishment enough, especially since I was still riding in The Colonel, and a softer, modern dressage saddle was beginning to seem like an impossible dream.

At least with the school horses I was allowed stirrups. I was flying stirrup-free on Dynamo and Mickey, and Grace was still shaking her head over my legs. "Grow them longer," she would say, as if this anatomical feat was something I could simply will into existence. "Let your toes drag in the sand."

Since my toes were dangling a good four feet above the ground, this was apparently some sort of existential zen riding crap meant to enlighten me—exactly what I hated about dressage. Why couldn't we just get on and ride? Why did everything need to be some sort of metaphor? Why did I feel like the Seabreeze team and I were speaking different languages?

Horses were bullshit-free. That was one of the reasons I preferred horses to humans. Adding a lot of metaphorical nonsense took away from the simple pleasure of riding your horse and made it just as annoying as everything else in life.

Well, school horses needed saddles. I pulled out Douglas to get him ready for the four-thirty lesson. He dragged after me, sliding his shoes on the concrete aisle. "I couldn't agree more," I told him, and clipped him into the crossties. "You understand me, don't you, Douglas? You don't have time for that hippie-dippie stuff."

The ancient warmblood just closed his eyes while I dug the curry comb into his woolly coat.

"I bet your life got a lot more boring when you got too old to jump. That's how I'm feeling right now."

Douglas leaned into the hard rubber curry comb. He was due for another body clip; his senior citizen coat never stopped growing, and his sweaty fur made him itchy.

"All you want is to grow old in peace, getting regular massages, instead of poking around an arena doing flatwork."

He stuck out his upper lip and waggled it—*That's the spot,* he was saying. *Oh yeah, right there.*

"All this flatwork is killing me, too," I went on. "I've never been so bored. Dressage, Douglas, is the absolute worst. I hate it. *Hate* it, buddy. Grace and her long-leg obsession—I'm losing my mind."

"I thought you'd be more mature than this, honestly."

I jumped about six feet into the air and whirled around. Grace was watching me, arms folded across her chest. I felt my cheeks grow hot.

"Oh . . ." I said, and then: "Oh," again. This was bad. "I'm sorry if you think I was bitching about my job—"

Grace rolled her eyes. "I figured a rider who had gotten *almost* to Advanced would take things a little more seriously. Somehow, be a little more advanced than what you actually are. Now I'm interested in how someone with such a basic education made it so far, and got such a big-name client, too! You'll have to tell me about how you scored that gray horse of yours sometime. I already know how you got Rockwell's attention, but who helped you get a Donnelly horse?"

Was she joking? She had to be joking. I smiled tentatively, in case the whole thing was a haha-remember-that-time moment we would look back on with nostalgia. "Well, I don't have time right now, since I'm grooming your horses for you, but pencil in a few minutes on the whiteboard and I can catch you up on my bio," I said lightly. I broadened the smile to a full-blown grin.

Grace didn't grin back. "Get him tacked up and finish the rest of the four-thirty horses." She turned and walked away.

She wasn't joking, then.

I gritted my teeth and went back to rubbing Douglas. I was tired of this hot-and-cold game with Grace. I was great, I was partner-worthy, and then I was a worm, an immature brat, because I complained a little to a horse. To a horse! If a person couldn't complain to a horse, then we were running out of ways to let off steam dangerously fast.

I was riding Mirage, a downhill little Hanoverian cross (no one would say what the cross was, but I suspected Quarter Horse) around lunchtime the next day, when Grace came out and settled herself on the mounting block to watch. I tensed immediately, and the mare underneath me responded in kind, flattening out her spine and sticking her nose out. I heard a conspicuous sigh from Grace's direction and resolved to pull myself together. *Long legs, long legs, long legs,* I thought, trying to stretch my hips and knees downward as Grace kept telling me. Suddenly, I seemed to find the magic spot on the mare's side where I could press and ask her to lift her abdomen, and then her spine, up toward my seat.

She rose and flowed beneath me.

I smiled.

"Not bad," Grace called. "Give us a serpentine down the center. Three loops, nothing fancy."

Evidently we were having a riding lesson.

I dropped my leg again and asked the mare to bend around me, turning toward the center of the arena. In the center I rose two beats instead of sitting to change my diagonal, and despite a slight flick of her tail as I imperfectly returned to the saddle, the mare kept her composure and stayed in a round frame as we changed directions and bent to the right.

"Nothing fancy, I said, Jules," Grace said, but she sounded amused. She'd caught me trying to show off, and it hadn't worked— classic Jules.

We completed the third loop and, as Grace remained silent, I cued the mare up for a springy collected canter in the corner between A and K. She might be built downhill, but collected properly she was able to round into a pleasant rocking-chair gait that covered more vertical space than forward. I thought she'd be a natural for pirouettes when the time came. She enjoyed prancing like a carousel pony.

Then, suddenly, everything fell apart. She swiveled her right ear toward the bright sunshiny world outside the covered arena and just like that she was flattened out and skittering sideways into the center of the arena, her neck straight up and her mouth wide open. I could feel her heart pounding right through the flaps of the saddle. I hazarded a glance back—there was nothing there. The woods were silent and still, blackened pine stumps rising above new green palmetto growth. She'd spooked at nothing.

Annoyed, I thumped the mare in the ribs, to shove her back toward the abandoned railing, and opened my hand to draw her nose-first in that direction. "Shame on you!" I growled. "Get back over there!"

The mare complied, but without elegance or pleasure. *Whatever*, I thought, *I'll put her back into a canter and get her around the arena nicely a few times to make up for it.* I dropped my legs again, thinking *Long*, and managed to collect her up into a frame again. By C we were cantering along the short side of the arena, but I could still feel tension in her muscles; she was looking back toward whatever had spooked her on the long side. "Looking for trouble," I muttered. "Typical mare."

The spooking just kept coming, as if there was a monster on the far long side of the arena, somewhere right around E. Try as I might, I couldn't get her head back on her work, or me. She was too worried about whatever she imagined might be lurking in the woods.

I pulled up and let her walk on a relatively loose rein, not willing to give up much length lest she take off again.

"Something over there?" Grace asked.

Why hadn't she gone back to the barn? Didn't she have work to do? "I didn't see anything."

"She did."

"There's nothing over there."

"Maybe not, but she saw something that *could* have been something. And since she's in charge of your safety as well as her own, she tried to stay clear of it."

*My* safety? I turned and circled the mare near Grace. "How do you figure?"

"Mirage isn't looking to you for safety. She thinks you have no idea what you're talking about. You said there was nothing to fear, she said she knew better, and she'd handle things from here on out, thanks very much." Grace grinned, fine lines crinkling around her sparkling eyes. "Mares are in charge until convinced otherwise. You haven't convinced her yet. You haven't even begun to convince her."

I started to argue. Then I remembered the mares at home who seemed to ignore every word I said, to say nothing of every riding cue. So I couldn't ride mares. Big deal. I had geldings. There was no shortage of male horses who could jump big jumps in this world. I shrugged instead. "I guess we'll get there someday."

"Probably not," Grace said matter-of-factly. "You don't have the time. Just do me a favor and go easy on her mouth when she spooks. She's not going to stop spooking just because you yank on her face. That doesn't make anything less scary."

I chewed on my tongue and kept quiet.

"About the schooling show next weekend," Grace went on, as if I'd brought it up. "You can show Mirage and Emblem if you want. We're having dressage suitability and hunter under saddle. I think Emblem for the hunter under saddle; he's not up to working on the bit yet."

The show! Oh, I really wanted to show, even though it was just a ridiculous schooling show for beginners. I couldn't help myself. I was addicted to horse shows. "Can I take my horses in the low jumpers? Just to school?" The low jumpers class was something crazy like two foot nine—Dynamo would probably fall asleep over fences that size, but it would be so good to jump again. This summer was a hundred years long.

"No, you may not," Grace said. "You're not here to jump. And I don't think it would be fair to take your horses against some of the students. Olivia Johnson is riding in the low jumpers and she's only been schooling over fences for three months. What would you gain out of getting a blue ribbon over someone like that?"

I just really liked blue ribbons, I didn't have a reason. I was just made that way. I had a problem. I needed therapy. "Fine," I agreed sulkily. "Dressage suitability and hunter under saddle."

"After you get the short-stirrup kids mounted and in the arena," Grace promised. "You'll have plenty of time."

A horse show!" Pete mustered up enough energy to sound excited. "That's fantastic."

"Just dressage suitability and hunter under saddle," I hazarded. I curled my neck around the phone and dropped the hose into the next water bucket in the row. The horse inside the stall nuzzled at the bubbling water and then flung his nose upward, splashing me. "Stop it, you jackass!"

"Sorry."

"Not you, this nutjob horse . . . I swear to God . . ." I brushed water off the phone's face, opening up three games and my cross-country course app in the process. "Shit. Anyway. It's something to look forward to. I needed something."

"You have a Second Level dressage test in another six weeks to look forward to!" Pete reminded me.

"I will break up with you."

He laughed.

"So what's new in England? I saw online that you and Amy went to some lord's garden party. You forget to tell me about that?"

He chuckled at the barb in my voice. "Well, it was yesterday, and I haven't talked to you for two days, so I'm not sure how I could have forgotten to mention it. But it was stupid. Some investor of Rockwell's. We all had to put on our show togs and parade around like show ponies."

"The Eventing Chicks say your new breeches show off your ass beautifully."

"What did you think?"

"I didn't see any pictures of your ass. Just Amy's. And they did look really great on her, too. Tell Carl to send me a pair."

"Jules . . ."

"Hmm?" I started hanging up the hose, no easy feat with one hand on my phone.

"Are we jealous of Amy?"

"Just her media coverage." It was only half a lie. "I'm not at her level of fame. I only make the blogs when I preside over a groom fight, and that hasn't happened in a year." I deliberately left out all the snarky coverage about my supposed cross-country failures.

"You'll have plenty of blogs covering you this fall, when you're stepping out in Rockwell breeches, too." Pete chuckled. "You're going to be a model, I bet you never saw that coming."

"Not exactly a life goal," I said drily. "But free clothes are free clothes."

"And free training. Speaking of which, Jules . . ."

"You're exhausted."

"I'm pretty sure I'm dead already."

"Goodnight, Pete. Good luck."

"Goodnight, Jules. Same to you."

# 22

COMPETE IN A horse show, they said. It will be fun, they said.

It would have been nice to blame this one on someone else, but like so many other things in my life, I had no one to blame but myself. I'd been a whiny brat about not getting to show all summer, and now I was running from the covered arena into the barn while well-groomed and nervous mothers and husbands gingerly held the reins of well-groomed horses, as their children and wives fixed their hair nets and settled their riding helmets gently over their ears. Everyone was moving in slow motion but me, which was a good thing, because I had fifteen minutes to get Mirage groomed, tacked, and warmed up for the dressage suitability class. To say nothing about grooming myself.

The under-twelves in short-stirrup equitation were already

trotting around the arena, their weaving progress watched carefully by a dangerous crowd of doting tiger moms, by the time I had struggled into my white breeches and dress boots. I was already wearing my white ratcatcher, hiding it under a T-shirt (something had told me Grace would settle for no less than full formal attire for her schooling show), and when I'd come downstairs that morning to find a horde of children already nervously crowding the barn, I'd seen I was right. Every single one of them, even the newest of riders, was dressed appropriately for Pony Finals. The handful of adult riders who were already here, hours early for their midday classes, looked just as spiffy. I'd looked down at my denim shorts and scuffed paddock boots nervously—how often did you feel completely underdressed for barn chores?

Well, I wouldn't be shown up; I'd gotten upstairs and into the top half of my show clothes as soon as the horses were fed, and laid out my white breeches and gleaming black field boots, along with my dress coat, on the old brown sofa, ready to be shimmied into the moment Mirage was prepared to enter the arena. If Grace thought she was going to catch me out by having me show up to a schooling show in half chaps and paddock boots, she was mistaken. I would be on top of my game today.

What I *hadn't* counted on was how incredibly needy a group of eight-to eleven-year-olds would be when going into a show ring. Had I ever been this bad? Begging for help with my braids, with my bootlaces, with my garters, with my stirrup length, with my helmet buckles, with my show number, with my literally *everything*?

There was no way I'd been this awful, I thought grimly, adjusting the safety pins on Maddy's number so it sat evenly on the back of her jacket. I couldn't have needed all this extra help, because there was no one (most of the time) to give it. My mom helped me at the shows within reach, but once I started traveling across the state and the southeast with my trainer, earning my keep by mucking and grooming and braiding, I was on my own. How old had I been on that first horse show trip without my mom? Twelve? "Come on, Maddy, you can manage your own stirrup leathers," I said, and Maddy's lip immediately started to quiver. "Shit," I muttered, and got busy adjusting the leathers, trying not to think of the minutes ticking by.

"Bad word," Maddy chided. "Grace says you're not supposed to say bad words in the barn."

"She meant kids," I snapped. "Stick your toe in the stirrup and see if that's right."

"They're uneven." Maddy sighed gustily. "The right one is too long."

Somehow I got them all into the arena and moving under their own power. As the announcer called, "Riders, you are being judged," I was racing back to the barn, ignoring the death-glares from mothers who had been force-fed the notion that one never, *ever* ran in a barn (what did they think a barn was, a pool deck?) and leaping up the creaking, groaning, utterly frightening stairs that led to the grooms' apartments. Two minutes later (I was counting), I was racing back down in my boots and breeches, black show gloves in hand. I was ready—or almost, once the shirt came off—and now all I needed was a clean horse.

Please let there be a clean horse.

Mirage, thank all the gods of all the horse shows in all the universe, was an understated liver chestnut, not too red and not too brown, just something kind of muddy in the middle. It was a color that was custom-made for quick and easy grooming. I wasn't sure why we didn't breed all horses to this ideal. She could have just rolled in manure or mud and it would have made little difference— her coat would never gleam like copper under a summer sun, but it would never look like she'd been abandoned for weeks when she'd just been turned out for an afternoon, either.

The one problem with Mirage was her stockings—two over-the-top flashy white hind leg markings that reached all the way to her hocks, and that loved to turn a nice greenish brown when life was just a little more exciting than she was prepared for. A horse show outside her window, complete with an announcer talking over a loudspeaker, was exactly the sort of excitement the mare needed to . . . well, let's say it loosened things up a little bit.

I slid open her door and the mare barely flicked an ear at me; she was too busy gazing out her window toward the festivities around the covered arena. The rearview angle gave me a perfect view of what I was up against.

"Oh my God, why?" I had eleven minutes.

Everything would have been perfect if she hadn't stepped on the hose. Still, when I swung into the saddle just outside of the barn (bowing to riding school rules), my horse looked fabulous. I was the one who looked a little worse for wear.

Anyway, I thought the black coat didn't show the patches soaked with water *too* much. That was one advantage of wearing black. The huge smear of dirt down one leg of my white breeches couldn't be helped, so I would pretend it wasn't there. What was important was that no one could see my white shirt was soaked through, and that was primarily important because my bra had a design of small pink flowers on it. I'd told Pete it was too girly for words, and that was why he'd bought it, smirking, during a late-night run to Walmart. No one will see it, he said. It will be our secret, he promised. Jules has a silly girly bra, ha-ha-ha!

It would stay our little secret if I kept on my show coat. I wouldn't take it off until the paramedics were treating me for heat-stroke, and even then they'd have to cut it away.

Grace was graciously helping Anna and Tom catch the short-stirrup riders as they came out of the arena, allowing me time to trot one quick circle around the outside jumping arena while the judge prepped for the dressage suitability class. The class was the break between the short stirrups and the long stirrups, apparently to give the adults something to do while they were waiting around for the jumping classes to start in the afternoon.

There were about a dozen riders using the outside arenas to warm up, mostly adult students of Grace's, cantering about on horses who were a thousand times too good for them. At least half of the owners were weekend riders, but I had to admit most of them seemed very capable. There were plenty of sloppy hands and broken wrists and pointed toes in the mix, but all the same they were riding their horses competently and confidently, and wasn't that exactly what I always argued ought to be good enough for any judge?

Living here was confusing, I thought. I really couldn't get home soon enough.

Mirage had still been giving me hell about the far side of the arena, and I hadn't expected today to be any different, but I wanted a ribbon, preferably a blue one, so I was doubly determined to get her around the arena without any shenanigans. Luckily, she seemed so keyed up by the presence of the extra spectators and the alien voice of the announcer, I was pretty sure she wouldn't have time to spook at her favorite scary pine tree.

I was wrong.

We were trotting around on the rail, looking the picture of dressage suitability. Oh, sure, her eyes were popping out of her head and her ears weren't focused back on me but pointed forward, pricked as high as they could go, so she could keep her eye on the rapidly changing world around her, but at least the added stress was putting a spring in her step and a bounce to her collection she didn't generally have at the trot. No downhill mare today.

I didn't even see her flick her gaze toward the woods near E, I just found myself on the ground, the wind knocked out of me, while the blood hummed in my ears, drowning out the world.

I gazed up at the rafters until a face appeared. Anna's big blue eyes blinked down at me. Her mouth opened and words came out. "Are you okay?" I assumed. I couldn't hear her yet, and then all of a sudden I could. She was panting; she'd run over to check on me. There was shouting behind her, *"Whoa whoa whoa!"* in a deep voice that should have been Tom's but was actually Margaret's, the true tough old groom of the barn, who would forever put me and my conceits to shame.

"I'm fine," I wheezed, and closed my eyes and wished I wasn't.

The second-place ribbon from Emblem in the hunter under saddle class did little to redeem the day. I slogged through it, because I was Jules and slogging through endless work was what I did, and because I was too proud to stuff it and stay off horses for the rest of the day, but in my head I was back home, in my bed, with my pillow over my head and Marcus curled up at my side.

Still, I acted as if I was proud of my little red ribbon, and hung it up carefully on the bars of Emblem's stall, where he immediately tried to devour it. Emblem was a mouthy bay Hanoverian with a pea for a brain. I liked him okay, as far as I could like any project horse I had to ride for zero personal payoff and someone else's gain. He hadn't dumped me, which was now more than I could say for Mirage.

The fall haunted me. Sure, I hit the dirt from time to time. Maybe not regularly, but often enough to remember what it felt like in between incidents. The little liver chestnut mare had gone from a pleasure to ride to a fearful spook machine in the past week, and I couldn't figure out why. Throughout the evening, sweeping up the barn once the students had gone home, ribbons in hand, I chewed on the problem. Maybe her back was sore. Maybe she had vision problems. Maybe she'd been attacked by a squirrel and now she was afraid of the little monsters. Could be anything, really.

Anna came over with a broom and started sweeping alongside me. Tom and Margaret were sweeping diligently at the other end of the aisle. A late-afternoon storm had turned the clay walking area outside the arenas into an orange swamp, and then every single hoof and boot had brought the mess right inside, where it had dried into a layer of sticky flakes on the concrete. This was not your average mess at the end of the day. This was war: clay against humanity.

"Sure was a nice show," Anna said after a while.

"Not bad," I agreed, for the sake of politeness. Small talk! Lacey would be so proud.

"Your hunter under saddle round was really pretty."

"Emblem's a nice horse."

"I think Mirage and you might be going through something, though."

"I think Mirage is a bitch who needs to get it together," I said casually. Anna stopped sweeping and stared at me.

I passed her and kept going down the aisle, concentrating on shoving as much of the clay in one colossal sweep as I possibly could. I fixated on it, in fact, because the stare I was getting on my back was starting to make me feel nervous. "She's a nice mare," I offered. "I just think she's decided to be difficult, for whatever reason."

"Horses don't decide to be difficult just like that. They are re-acting to problems. It's our job to figure out the problem."

"And I think the problem is she doesn't want to work, plain and simple." I turned back to Anna, who was looking at me as if I had two heads and both of them were evil. "Not all horses are sweethearts who just want to be protected. I think you and Grace both are giving Mirage way too much credit with this 'oh boo-hoo I don't trust my rider' song and dance. I think she's taking us all for a ride, if you'll pardon the pun."

"I'm really sorry you feel that way," Anna said, and her voice was so icy it took me by surprise. "Maybe Grace was right about you. She usually is," she added. "Right about people. And horses."

"Oh really? And what does Grace think is up with Mirage? And with me?" I kept my voice low with effort; in reality, I was ready to start shouting. That would be bad, I reminded myself. That was not the good image I had been trying to portray while I was here. Although, I supposed, I probably just shattered that image by telling Anna I thought a horse was less than perfect and pure of heart.

"I think you're both wrong," Grace said, coming around the corner with her typically perfect timing. "I think Mirage is wrong, because she believes she has to protect you from whatever she thinks is lurking in the forest—clearly, Jules, the only thing you need protection from is yourself. And I think Jules is wrong, be-cause she believes Mirage is the problem. And I'm sorry, Anna, but you're a little wrong, too—for thinking the horse is never the prob-lem. Trust me, sometimes horses decide to be the problem all by themselves." She looked at me pointedly. "This isn't one of those times."

"So what's the problem?" I snapped, my nice quiet tone all used up. "What's wrong with the way I ride Mirage?"

Grace shrugged. "The same thing that's wrong with you and all your horses, Jules. You don't give them a chance to trust you, and you're in such a big hurry that you either scare them—that's the geldings—or you worry them—that's the mares. Mirage thinks you're going to get yourself killed, and her in the bargain, so she's taking the best care of you she can. Sometimes"—Grace allowed herself a chuckle—"she fails . . . but in Mirage's defense, she definitely thought you could hang on while she got you out of harm's way. She had faith in you this time."

"So I'm just not smart enough to keep Mirage safe?"

"Not to her. Goodnight, girls."

With that, Grace headed home, her clogs slapping against her bare heels as she faded into the blue twilight. At the other end of the barn, Margaret and Tom finished their sweeping and headed out to their cars, done with another day. Anna quietly swept alongside me, her eyes determined and her chin set, as if she was proud she'd said her piece and wasn't going to say another unnecessary word about it. We reached the end of the aisle and shoved the piles of red clay into the grass alongside the driveway, and then walked silently back to the nook by the wash racks to put the brooms away.

I didn't want to walk upstairs with Anna—that was one of the awkward things about our living side by side—so I lingered in the barn, touching the noses of horses as they shoved them inquiringly through the bars, all of them wondering why I was still there. It was past nine o'clock and fully dark now, a few flashes of lightning from far away glittering down the barn aisle every so often. The tall pine trees behind the property made it hard to watch lightning. At home I was on top of the world, looking out from our hilltop to see the clouds for a hundred miles in every direction. Here I felt low, hemmed in by the half-burned forest. I hadn't known one could feel so closed in on a flat Florida farm. Tonight, in the still, humid air, I felt positively claustrophobic.

I pulled out my phone to text Pete, see if he was still awake, but it was dead. I was alone out here.

The stairs creaked under Anna's feet, her shoulders sagging with exhaustion. *I could go now,* I thought. *She'll be inside by the time I get up there.* My aching feet began to make their way toward the stairs, almost by their own volition. I was suddenly aware of bruises, a sore hip, an aching elbow, the points matching precisely where I'd hit the ground earlier.

Still, I paused by my horses.

Mickey, previously my personal cheerleading squad of one, was currently too engrossed in his hay to even whinny at me, but Dynamo stepped up to say hello, pressing his nostrils close to my fingers and breathing his hot breath on my face. The sensation sent a wave of nostalgia and homesickness through my belly, not for Briar Hill, but for years past, for boarding stables and for my own lost farm, where, in the beginning, Dynamo, Marcus, and I had lived in contented isolation.

"I miss you, friend."

He sighed.

We spent maybe half an hour a day on the ground together, maybe forty minutes more riding in our daily lessons, but that was about the same amount of time we spent together at home, too. There was always work, there were other horses to ride, there was the unending pile of bills and show forms and half-hearted marketing attempts to deal with in the tack room or back at the house.

"Remember when it was just you and me?" I whispered. "Remember when it was Dynamo and Jules against the world? They said you weren't worth the time, but we showed them." Dynamo whuffled his nostrils in response, a perfect imitation of my own melancholy. "I wish we could show them again. I know that's what all this was supposed to be about, getting a perfect dressage score, la-di-dah . . . but it's starting to feel like something else. That woman wants to change more about me than just my position. She's got a problem with the way I ride, period. She thought I was one thing when I got here, she got all excited . . . then she decided I wasn't good enough. You don't think so, though, do you, buddy? You think we can get through this summer and go back to the way things were?"

Dynamo stepped away from the stall bars and went back to his hay, wagging his ears at me as he went. *No offense, Mom, but there's hay here.*

*Understood, buddy.*

I trailed my fingers along the bars as I went toward the stairs, listening to the chewing horses in each stall, and snapped out the lights at the foot of the staircase. The night-lights stayed on; every third lamp overhead was half-lit to keep the barn from ever being truly dark. That way I could look out my window and see the horses below, all night long.

I could see them, but I couldn't get close to them. For that, I had to come back down, slide open a door, and sink into a corner of a stall.

Maybe that's what was missing, that closeness.

# 23

I HAD TWO missed calls and multiple texts from Lacey when my phone woke up from its dead-battery slumber. Naturally, I assumed either Pete had died or the barns had burned down or both, but when I scrolled through the texts, I saw nothing so dire. Just Lacey asking if I'd seen it yet. Then Lacey saying everything was fine. Then: *Just call me, okay?*

I'd never known Lacey to be particularly vague, but no one was dead, and I was starving after the extra-long day. I thumbed a quick *what the hell is up* message to Lacey before moving over to the kitchen counter to get supper started. It was a ramen noodle kind of night, for sure.

The phone buzzed while I was running water into the pot. I ignored it, my thoughts still on the horses downstairs. I wondered if I spent enough time with Dynamo and Mickey, if there was more to our relationships than just our training sessions. After all, to work together on cross-country courses, trusting one another, we had to have a pretty serious partnership in place. I'd had it with Dynamo, but maybe it was faltering after all the recent neglect. Mickey, too . . .

The phone buzzed again.

"For God's sake, Lacey." I leaned over and read the message before it disappeared from the home screen.

The phone went blank, but I could still see the letters.

*Eventing chicks kno u r there*

The water overflowed the pot and frothed around my fingers. "Crap, crap, crap . . ."

The phone buzzed again. *Someone at show today saw u sent pic they put online SORRY!!!*

A horse whinnied somewhere downstairs, and another replied. I took a deep breath, my fingers tingling as the feeling returned to them.

"First," I said to the quiet little room, "the water."

I would make dinner. I would be a sensible and clear-headed adult. I would eat some noodles out of a plastic package well-seasoned with MSG and fake shrimp flavoring. Then, I'd deal with . . . with whatever the hell this was.

It was bad.

I didn't actually make it through dinner before I looked at the website. I got the noodles in the water and that was about as long as I could stand it before I grabbed the phone and started flicking through the blog's headlines. I didn't have to scroll far. Only one other story had been deemed worthy of this evening's equestrian gossip—something about Georgina Bloomberg, which I didn't even read. I mean, she was a show jumper, not an eventer, so what was the website bothering with her for? They had a lot of nerve calling themselves the Eventing Chicks if they were going to cover just any old equestrian.

Then there was the photo of me—a big Instagram box of a photo, taken at an angle by someone who didn't want to be caught snapping photos of random riders, especially random riders who had managed to get soaked completely through right before their class. I was lying in the dirt, looking up with a sheepish expression, while my horse trotted away, reins dangling, in the background. The classic "where's my horse?" pose.

"Damn you, Mirage," I muttered, and flicked down, because there were more, of course there were more.

A few of them just showed me shepherding children into the arena earlier in the day, when I was still wearing dry clothes—the same clothes I was wearing now, I thought, looking down at the Seabreeze polo and the dusty jeans and feeling a curious sense of déjà vu—there I was on the internet, looking very much the way I looked this very moment. They weren't terrible photos, although the brief captions indicated that everyone at *Eventing Chicks* headquarters thought it was pretty goddamn funny I was helping guard kiddies at an in-gate instead of prepping for the fall eventing season.

The last photo was the one I hadn't been prepared for.

I was standing next to Mirage, preparing to mount for the first time. I looked like I'd been caught in a hurricane on the way to the horse show. My hair was falling out of its braid, with wet tendrils sticking to my neck and the collar of my shirt. There was a delicate fan of dirt brushed against my wet cheek, as if I'd applied mud-colored blush—for a special look on a special day. My white breeches were marred by a dark arrow of filth pointing at my knee (or pointing at my ass, depending on which direction you decided the arrow was traveling).

That wasn't the worst of it, though.

The underwear showing through my soaking-wet breeches . . . that was going to be hard to overcome.

I groaned. How had I missed such an important detail of getting wet in white? I'd *known* I was wearing a silly flower-sprigged bra and if I took off my hunt coat, it would show through my thin white shirt. I just forgot about my matching pair of flower-sprigged underwear.

I put down the phone. Then I stuck a pillow over top of it. Then I threw my blanket on top. I would bury my phone in home furnishings and none of this would ever matter again. I would retire from eventing and help Kennedy run Western trail rides for corporate executives out of an English show barn. I would hole up here in Orlando and never show my face in horse country again.

"Just you and me and the spoon makes three," I told my bowl of ramen, which, thankfully, did not reply.

Lacey called around ten o'clock. I felt the buzzing of the phone from across the couch like an angry animal. I pulled it out from under its pillowy grave and put her on speakerphone so I didn't have to exert myself by lifting the phone to my ear.

"I'm no longer speaking to other humans," I said to the dark room, and to Lacey by extension. "I am running away to live in the woods. I will be a hermit with the bears and the squirrels. And I'm taking Mickey and Dynamo. You'll have to explain the Mickey thing to his owners."

"While they're remarkably understanding ladies, I don't think they're going to accept that Mickey is going to join you on a journey to inner peace."

"This isn't inner peace," I said. "This is giving up. This is me, giving up. I can't go back out in public after this."

"Jules, everyone wears panties, and sometimes they have flowers on them, because that's literally what underwear manufacturers produce. We're just consumers here. We're all the victims, if you ask me."

"What? No. Not just the panties. Everything. This whole situation. How can I come back from this? Everyone knows Rockwell is only taking me because of Pete. Everyone knows that even with Pete as the target, I'm not good enough to carry their name. And now they know I rode like crap at a local schooling show at a random barn in Orlando."

"Did you ride like crap?"

"Well, I fell off."

Lacey sighed. "Anyone can fall off at any time. Did you really ride like crap? What happened?"

I thought about it for a few minutes, my eyes searching the shadows on the apartment walls. What did happen? I failed to make any sort of impression on Mirage, for starters, and she dumped me in the dirt in the same place she'd been trying to get away from me for the past two weeks. I put in a so-so showing on Emblem, who thought all up transitions were for the hand gallop and all down transitions were for the walk, and everything in between was a good excuse to jog sideways, snorting. "I've only been riding these horses for a couple of weeks," I said. "They're pretty green still. It was probably crazy to show them at all."

"Why did you, then? Shouldn't Grace have known better than to have you show green horses like that? And anyway," Lacey went on, getting huffy in my defense, "why are you riding green horses? I thought you were supposed to be riding upper-level dressage. I thought that was the whole deal, to get your dressage going so you're ready for the big time."

I'd thought so, too. What the hell was going on? I was getting revved up, my voice hardening, my temper rising. I was ready to march down to Grace's door and start hammering with my fist until she came out and explained herself. "You're right, Lacey. I mean, seriously! Riding green horses in this awful old flat saddle like I'm back in the olden days, before anybody even knew what dressage or eventing was . . ." I trailed off, comprehension suddenly flooding my brain. "Oh."

"What?"

"This isn't about not being able to ride upper level." I cast about for any other way to word my thoughts, but there was only one thing to say. "This is about not being able to *ride*."

Ride, full stop. The word hung in the air between us, floating somewhere in the empty hills between Orlando and Ocala, challenging us with its true definition. Because we both knew the truth: riding was not sitting on a horse, riding was not wrestling a horse into a frame, riding was not getting a horse to go over a series of fences because he would prefer not to know the consequences for a refusal.

There was silence for a moment. "That doesn't make any sense."

It didn't make sense, but it did. Losing the stirrups, giving up the flash noseband, riding in a saddle without any blocking, schooling young horses in the very basics of flatwork . . . Grace was trying to put a polished foundation on me in a very old-world way. What had someone said about me? I was a scrappy, rough-and-ready type rider? Something like that. I'd learned to ride in stolen lessons and eavesdropping on clinics, by begging for rides and volunteering for tough horses. I'd learned to stay on through thick and thin, but had I ever really learned to ride in a classical sense?

"Oh, shit, Lacey. Am I the biggest fake in the world?"

Lacey snorted indignantly. "Don't let them get to you. There's nothing wrong with you."

I wasn't sure, though. The seed of doubt had been planted. I went to sleep slowly that night, taking a long time to close my eyes, unable to tear my gaze away from the pattern of barn lights on the ceiling. The shadows rearranged themselves into horses, trotting and jumping through the lonesome studio, every one of them a study of the perfection I wasn't able to attain.

# 24

I SPOKE TO Pete early the next morning, after he'd seen the blog, and he told me how much he missed me, and that he thought flower-sprigged underwear were cute, and, when he heard the rebellious-ness in my tone as I told him *someone* should have told me my underwear was showing and that everyone here was insane and I wanted to go home, he reminded me how much my staying here meant to the business.

"What does it mean for the business when everyone thinks that one half of the Briar Hill Farm team goes out with her underwear showing?"

"I'm sure it has happened to everyone," Pete said.

"So you've shown off your Batman undies in the jumper ring?"

"I—" He hesitated.

"Mm-hmm."

"Look, no one has sent me any texts about this post," Pete said, with a little too much emphasis on the word "this." "I think it's a nonissue."

"Who has been texting you about other posts?" I demanded.

"Oh, you know how people like to chat," he said vaguely.

I shook my head. Of course. The thing was, *everyone* in the industry read these stupid blogs. They posted their articles all over social media and you couldn't miss the really juicy ones. The ones with hundreds of comments underneath. I didn't even want to know how many comments my flower underwear had gotten. But I *did* know it couldn't be helpful to Rockwell when he was deciding if I could be the face of his high-end country lifestyle brand.

"Pete," I sighed, "don't you ever think, just for a teeny-tiny second, that this entire attempt to get me a sponsor is, in fact, cursed?"

"We're going to make it," Pete told me, "and it's because you were willing to make this sacrifice and get on board with their crazy plans for you. This sponsorship is going to get us there, Jules. I just know it."

He went on, fervent and inspired, talking for nearly half an hour about plans for the farm, the season ahead, how many points he'd need to acquire for championships, schemes to catch the notice of the equestrian team's scouts and get invited to their training camps in the coming winter. I listened while I worked my way through two cups of coffee, thinking I'd never heard level-headed Pete sound so excited about anything.

What could I do now, but live up to all his hopes and dreams? What could I do now, but show everyone who talked shit about me that I could do this, and then some? Wasn't that the reason I did everything, to show everyone they'd been wrong about me?

Was it? I didn't even know anymore.

Down in the barn, there was a note on the board asking me to ride Splash first thing. Anna was tacking up Ivor for Grace.

"Did she say to do anything special with Splash?" I asked her.

"Canter transitions," Anna said. "He's been sticky in lessons."

Splash put his nose through his stall bars and nickered at me suggestively. "Dirty old man," I told him, and gave him a scratch on the nose. He wiggled his upper lip on my palm, rubbing it back and forth until I thought the tickling might give me an accident. "You're bad," I said, and he leered at me, lifting his spotted lip over his nostrils to show his yellow teeth, asking me to rub his gum. Splash was a weird one. I gave the hard pink gums a good massage with my thumb until he pulled away, done with me, and went back to playing with his water bucket.

"Full of hay, I see," I observed.

Splash dunked a mouthful of hay in his fetid bucket and waggled his ears at me.

"Can't wait to clean that out," I went on, taking down his halter. "I'm sure it'll be waiting for me after our ride. This is just a little treat, to keep me sweet. Working on Splash and his sticky transitions."

I led him out of the stall, noticing what a complete mess it was already. A big part of me wanted to put Splash in the crossties, leave him there for fifteen minutes to nap, and get back here with a wheelbarrow to clean this stall out. But Tom was making his way down the aisle, slowly, with his wheelbarrow. It was going to get done. I didn't have to be the only one responsible for making sure the barn was clean.

And then I laughed at myself. "Come on, Splashie-boy," I muttered, tugging on his lead rope as the horse hung back. "Here I am getting obsessed with cleaning up after you when I'm supposed to be riding." I clipped him into the crossties two spots down from Ivor, to give the stallion (and Anna) some breathing room. "I'm getting this horse trainer thing backward."

"Maybe you're getting it right," Anna said.

"Maybe," I agreed. "Would you rather be cleaning up or riding?"

She picked up Ivor's breastplate, expression thoughtful. "I guess it depends on the day, and my mood."

Anna had a lot of moods. I never really knew if she was going to be pleasant or short-tempered with me. Today she seemed somewhat pleasant. I was about to ask her if a good mood meant she wanted to ride or muck out when a teenage girl came around the corner. Black-haired and skinny as a twig, the girl saw me with Splash and her dark eyes narrowed.

"Hi, Liz," Anna said. "You have a private lesson this morning?"

"Yeah," Liz said. "I thought I was riding Splash."

"I'm working on his buttons today," I told her. "He'll be a nicer horse for you in next week's lesson."

Liz huffed. "So who am *I* riding?"

"Check the board," Anna said. "I'll start tacking your horse as soon as I'm done with Ivor." She patted the stallion's neck, then sidestepped a nip as the horse went in for a taste of her arm.

Liz stomped away. I picked up a body brush. "Jeez," I said, whisking Splash's back with the soft brush. "Why did I feel like she wanted to murder me?"

"She really likes Splash," Anna said. "You know how teenagers get about their favorite horses. Honestly, she's been pissed at you ever since you started riding him."

"That was the week I got here!"

"Yeah." Anna finished bridling Ivor and set the halter over top, clipping him back into the crossties to wait for Grace. "She's hated you this whole time."

I rode Splash in the outdoor arena; Grace joined me on Ivor and gave me some pointers as she worked her own horse. Kennedy had Liz riding in the covered ring. I thought I noticed Liz staring at me a few times, or maybe she was staring at Splash. I wondered if I'd ever been that crazy-eyed over a horse I couldn't have when I was back at Laurie's farm. The answer was probably . . . although once I had Dynamo, I didn't have to look at anyone else's horses with jealousy. Maybe Liz would have that someday, too.

The day swept by, a series of chores and horses. We took a lunch break and I sat alone in my apartment, moodily eating a sandwich and looking at blogs. My underwear faux pas was getting more attention than my excellent first season at Intermediate. Who had realized that a rising star eventer was standing by an arena at an Orlando barn with her panties showing, and taken that photo? Had it been malicious, or was it just a joke to them?

There was a stirring next door; Anna would be heading down shortly to get on her horses for the afternoon. I went to the porch door and looked out. A hot wind was blowing around the barn, stirring the pale leaves of the scrub oaks lining the outdoor arena, and I glanced up at the sky. The fluffy white cumulus clouds were starting to cluster and congeal into something bigger than themselves. They were ambitious clouds. They knew their purpose and they knew how to make it happen with maximum drama.

"I get you, clouds," I told them. "But now I'm thinking you might be overdoing it a bit."

At least I didn't have to ride now, when the atmosphere was really cooking. Downstairs, I went into the school tack room and

studied the whiteboard. Six horses to tack for the three-thirty lesson, that wasn't bad, and then just three for the four-thirty. I'd
already mucked fifteen stalls and ridden four horses today, so the
grooming and tacking portion of the day was like my break. Still,
it was almost three, so I had to hustle.

I sighed and started piling saddles onto my arm. I was just
turning for the door when Kennedy came bursting in, her dark red
curls spilling from their ponytail and cascading wildly across her
Western shirt, the red-and-white button-down she saved for trail
rides. I didn't talk with Kennedy much; she was always busy and
usually late. Like right now.

"Can you help me?" she burst out, gazing upon me as if I was
the answer to her prayers. "I'm super late and we have a trail ride
in fifteen minutes."

"It's going to storm," I pointed out. Thunder rumbled from
somewhere far away, just to neatly illustrate my meteorological
prowess. "You'd better just cancel it."

"Not for a while. And I have five bigwigs from some corporate
conference on their way over. I need help tacking up. Please."

I held out my armload of English saddles. "Help me out of this,
then."

Kennedy helped me get out from under the English tack and
then we hauled the heavy Western trail saddles out of the corner of
the tack room, where they were stacked rather like cordwood, their
bristling cotton cinches slapping our legs as we stumbled down the
aisle. I could never figure out why Western saddles were so heavy.
You'd think a saddle designed for riding all day long across the
countryside would be as light as possible.

The trail horses didn't get the thorough show-ring shine that
the school horses did; we slapped the dust off with a body brush
and picked out hooves in the stall before throwing on their tack.

Each one had their reins knotted up into their throatlatch and were left free to nose at their hay, chewing it around their light snaffle bits. We had all six horses done in fifteen minutes. The corporate bigwigs were nowhere to be seen.

"They're always late," Kennedy said. "But at least we're ready."

"The trail riding's fun?" I asked. "I haven't been on the trails in years, besides cross-country courses."

"It's the best." Kennedy cocked her head at me, smiling. "You wanna come out sometime?"

I was actually tempted, but I just didn't have time. "Not really what I'm here for." I needed to concentrate on my dressage, get Grace's blessing, and go home.

I started down the aisle to get back to the school horses. Kennedy followed. "Let me help, it's the least I can do. Who do you need out?"

I rattled off the names of the horses and she set off to pull them out and get them in the crossties for me. When I was finished hauling all the tack to the crossties, she was clipping the last horse into place.

"There." She beamed. "A little less work for you, anyway. I really appreciate your help."

"Thanks." I pulled out a grooming kit and got busy on Douglas, the first horse in the row. The trail riders still hadn't arrived. "Guess our big rush wasn't really necessary."

"Oh, it was," Kennedy assured me. "We're always ready on time. That's one of our most strict rules."

"Ours? Or Grace's?"

"Ours," Kennedy said firmly. "Grace and I agreed on this one from the start—if they're late, they get their ride cut short or they pay extra. It's never our fault if they lose time. It's always the client's."

"That's pretty smart." I was impressed. "Do they ever complain?"

"Of course they do. But they pay. They're clearly the ones who didn't make their appointment. These guys today paid for me from four o'clock to four forty-five, and if they get here at four twenty and want to ride until five, they'll pay for that extra fifteen minutes. If you set high standards," Kennedy said seriously, "people will think more of you, and they'll pay more for the privilege of meeting your standards." She cocked her head. "I think that's them now. Thanks again!"

She dashed off down the aisle, grabbing her cowboy hat from a bridle hook as she went.

"So if I set higher standards for everyone I do business with, they'll respect me more," I told Doug, combing out his tail. "I just have to get more demanding of my clients." I laughed at the idea. Me, desperate for clients, setting up impossible standards for them to meet? "That doesn't make any sense at all. But what the hell do I know? I'm standing in someone else's barn, talking to myself."

A few minutes later, Kennedy was boosting the bigwigs, who were really just middle-aged men and women wearing jeans and sneakers, making fun of each other for looking silly in their white schooling helmets, into their saddles. They rode off down the barn aisle while I was still knocking dirt off school horses, once again left behind while the rich kids went riding. I gazed at the pony I was grooming. He swiveled a lazy ear toward me, decided I was uninteresting, and closed his white lashes over his dark eyes.

"We're better off here," I told him.

The pony didn't open his eyes.

# 25

I WORKED HARDER at everything. I shoved away the resentment I felt every time I rode into the dressage arena. I never looked at any blogs. I wrote short, carefully worded emails to Pete in which I told him I was becoming a dressage queen and he would have to watch out for me when he came back, because I was going to beat him at every single event, in every single discipline, and there was nothing he could do about it. He loved the emails and sent me back flowing rebuttals, describing how he and Regina would flatten me at cross-country now, then writing in a postscript at the end, *Of course I don't believe a word I've just written.*

My new focus was reflected in my horses. Mickey's eyes brightened and his coat took on a new shine, as if I'd been rubbing him extra hard in our grooming sessions, and Dynamo attacked every

movement I asked for with a renewed vigor. On our sixth-day riding lesson, he rose to the occasion quite literally, lifting his back
and carrying himself like a proud charger storming the battlefield,
and Grace, for once, stood silently and let us trot around the arena.

Or, at least, I thought that she did. I was so busy being carried
into the heavens by my winged chestnut that I might not have
heard her. I pushed away the unhelpful thought I had allowed to
crowd into my brain every day of my summer, that this was not
the same as galloping and jumping. The truth was, this was wonderful too: something equally thrilling but different in every way.

When truly ridden, without resentment or longing for another
kind of ride, dressage felt like a harmony that came only with re-
ward and almost no risk, a smoothness of silken movement that
was the polar opposite of the rigid, harsh piston movements of a
flat-out gallop. In a perfect collected canter, you sat in the center
of the horse and let him fill up all the space around you, lifting you
like a cloud on his rounded spine. In a racing-pace gallop, you balanced above the horse, his churning body too busy and rough to sit
upon. There was nothing wrong with that, but it was . . . different.
I didn't want to stop and ponder which might be better.

The truth might be I was a galloper. I lived for the open fields,
not the sandbox. That was okay; that was the *point* of all this.

I was catching on, wising up, joining the grown-ups at the big
table.

The summer was slipping toward its long, hot finale, the endless
yellow afternoons giving way to thundering evenings, and everything
in the arena was changing for the better. I could feel the difference
in myself; I was riding like a dressage pro, instead of a rough-and-
tumble old-school event rider who also knew how to lengthen my
stirrups and sit the trot, albeit bouncily, for the sake of getting to ride
cross-country the next day. I could feel the difference, and I could see

it, too—the horses were taller, and so was I, with longer legs and more elastic joints.

Then, suddenly, I was tired.

With a month to go, I was running out of steam. I'd been pushing myself as far as I could, mentally and physically. I'd devoted myself to doing everything Grace wanted, perfectly every time. My emails to Pete started to diverge from the relentlessly cheerful tone I'd been cultivating.

Finally we had a rough lesson, Dynamo's gaping mouth and upside-down neck making an appearance for the first time in weeks. I untacked him with a sour taste in my mouth; this was never going to end. Grace seemed to notice. The next morning she told me to tack up Vizcaya for my first schooling ride, instead of Mirage. I realized with shock I was off the lesson horses, and on the advanced ones at last.

Vizcaya was a challenging ride for me, and I could instantly feel why Lena didn't do much more than sit on him and walk around the arena hoping he wouldn't accidentally stumble into a trot or anything. His stride was big, his mind was alert, his body was round and quivering, ready for the slightest instruction from his rider. In fact, I thought, he was like a mousetrap, primed and ready to snap at the slightest provocation. Vizcaya had been trained to a hair trigger's precision, and it made him feel slightly dangerous, instead of what I would have expected—solid, knowledgeable, happy to perform.

"You feel that?" Grace asked. "You feel how all it takes is a touch of your leg, and he'll give you whatever you're asking for? *That's* dressage. That's what we're looking for. Your horses will do that someday, if you stick with it, and keep learning."

I didn't say what I was thinking: that this was one form of dressage, and it wasn't the one for me. I couldn't imagine making

Dynamo feel like this, like a quivering ball of energy just waiting to be directed. I sat deep and relaxed all of my aids, and Vizcaya came to a perfectly balanced halt, a leg at each corner, neck arched and holding the bit, and yet still I felt no relaxation. He was ready, ready, *ready.*

Vizcaya was a soldier, I realized. A soldier trained to go forth to battle no matter what the personal cost, no matter what fears he might hold, to do whatever his commander instructed without question or hesitation.

I dropped my contact and gave him a nudge with my heels, and he stepped confidently forward into his long-striding walk, reaching out with his neck until he found my hands again. Now *that* was reaching for contact. He positively craved it. He couldn't live without it.

Curious, I let go of the reins altogether and rested my hands on my thighs.

Vizcaya came to a confused halt, his neck elongated, mouthing the bit. He turned his head slightly and looked back at me, eyes questioning.

Grace frowned. "What are you doing? Pick up the contact and put him in a medium walk. I want you to feel the gaits of an upper-level horse so you'll know what you're looking for with your horses."

I picked up the reins, biting my tongue. I could hear Pete as clearly as if he was leaning over my shoulder, whispering in my ear, pleading with me to do the right thing and just shut up for once in my life. *Don't be snotty, Jules.*

"I don't want this in my horses," I announced, perhaps inevitably, even as I was sending Vizcaya into the requested medium walk. The horse held the bit like a red-hot coal in his mouth, waiting for me to half halt and ask for a transition into another gait, into a lateral movement, into a circle, into a seemingly endless list of movements that he might be required to perform at the drop of a hat, at any moment. He was like an honors student who had been pushed beyond the limits of sanity in his attempt to get everything right. "He doesn't want to think for himself. When I'm galloping cross-country, I need to have a horse who can make his own decisions."

Pete had told me a story once, about riding his grandfather's horse down to a sticky jump. He'd gotten them both into trouble and didn't see a way out. Luckily, the horse did. If I did all the thinking for my horse, eventually, my horse wouldn't be able to save me when I was out of ideas.

Grace looked amused. "You're not the first person to mouth that line, you know. And I'm going to tell you the same thing I tell every other know-it-all event rider who comes to me begging for help: you can win the dressage, or not. That's up to you. You want to compete internationally? You want to beat the Euros, who start riding dressage when they're in diapers? You want to beat the warmbloods who were bred for these movements and this obedience? You want to win these events, or do you just want to be an also-finished? That's your choice. I'm offering you the knowledge to win."

"How can I win an event if my horse has to wait for my instructions at every single jump? We're moving too fast out there for all of that." I shook my head. "I'm not saying I want a horse I can point and shoot, but—"

"Listen to me." Grace's voice sharpened. I had a feeling she was ready to march out of the arena and leave me to my own smartass devices. "One more time, I'm going to try and get this through your skull. You win the dressage, you have the precision you need to make the cross-country clear and within the time, you have the obedience and straightness you need to get around the show-jumping course, even with a tired horse. You win it all. On your dressage score. That's what you want. Forget *you*—that's what the Rockwells want. That's what your owners want. That's what every sponsor and every client and every buyer from now until the end of your competition days is going to want. What's it going to be, Jules? Because there are other riders out there who would love to get my time for free."

I bit my lip and dropped my gaze, watching Vizcaya's dappled shoulders move with careful precision around the arena railing. He was everything I didn't want in a horse—but I was trapped. Between what I wanted and what I needed. Between what I believed and what I had to do.

"I want to win," I mumbled, ashamed of myself even as I said it. But of course that was the only answer. When had I ever wanted to do anything but win?

"What's that?"

"I want to *win*!" I shouted, and Vizcaya trembled beneath me, not certain if I was shouting at him, not certain if that was some new command he had failed to memorize. I stroked his neck to comfort him, but he didn't seem to feel it and really, it didn't calm me as I would have hoped, either.

If I wasn't happy with myself, Grace was certainly pleased. She hung around while I was hosing Vizcaya down, watching me handle the big horse. "You ready to ride another?"

"Sure," I said absently. Riding was better than barn chores.

"You do well on Ivor," she said alluringly.

"I enjoy riding him," I said, aware of the understatement.

Grace was, too. She smiled. "Put your jumping saddle on him," she said, walking down the aisle.

I gaped after her.

Then I hustled to get my poor, neglected jumping saddle out of the tack room before she changed her mind.

I vor," Grace announced as I walked the big gray in a circle around her, ready to get the lesson underway, "is the very horse to illustrate to you why a jumper must have the highest possible dressage schooling. He's a talented jumper, but that's not why crowds used to gather when I rode him. He had a buck like a rodeo champion, and he wasn't afraid to use it anytime he got mad at me for telling him what to do."

"Wow," I said, shaking my head. "Look at you now, Ivor." His ears flicked back to listen. He was bent perfectly around the circle, his spine part of the circle itself, an elegant curve from poll to tail. He was aggressively talented. "You're a pleasure."

"He's still difficult at times," Grace warned. "He knows how to throw a tantrum. Give him his own way too many times, and he'll start demanding it. Any horse can regress. It doesn't matter how well trained they are, they're always happier to go backward than forward."

*Not likely,* I thought smugly. *He probably just gets tired of being told what to do all the time, and sometimes he can't take it anymore. Any reasonable creature would feel that way.*

"So you have to be on top of him, and be in charge, at all times. Especially when you're jumping. If he decides he wants things his way, you're going to end up on the ground. Like I said, Ivor's going to show you that submission isn't such a bad thing, and for certain horses, it's the only way to fly. Or . . . ahem . . . to avoid flying, if you know what I mean." Grace chuckled at her own terrible joke. Well, *somebody* had to. I kept a straight face without any problems.

We warmed up and started over a few low gymnastics. Grace hadn't jumped him in a few days, and he was obviously excited to get back to his favorite job. His enormous stride grew even longer; his tremendous impulsion reached rocket-ship proportions. But I maintained contact and order, holding him firmly between leg and hand, as Grace instructed, and his neck remained arched, his mouth remained soft, his body remained collected and ready to respond to my slightest command. When I told him I wanted four strides between two small verticals, he gave me four strides precisely. When I told him to shorten it up and give me five, he collected himself even more tightly and bounced through in five quick strides that felt more like bunny hops than a seventeen-hand warmblood's canter.

I had to admit, it was all pretty impressive. He was a horse of limitless talent, and it was exciting to have that sort of control over him. Exciting, but not necessary, I reminded myself. I could successfully jump Dynamo around this little course with no problem at all, and he wasn't a push-button dressage horse who was waiting for permission to draw breath. Grace's level of submission just wasn't for us, but I'd play with it for as long as she made me.

"Very good," Grace said when we had run through the gymnastics a half dozen times. "I think you're ready for a little course. Walk him for a few moments."

I dropped the contact and let Ivor walk around the arena on a loose rein while Grace scurried around the arena, lifting the jump cups on the fences from their usual short-stirrup height to rather more impressive levels. When she was through, I lifted my eyebrows at her. "What are those, four feet?"

"Oh, just." Grace shrugged, as if she jumped four feet every day.

It wasn't that I was uncomfortable jumping that high. It was just a little unexpected. Riders didn't hit four feet in the show jumping until Advanced level. I'd schooled Dynamo over higher fences, and hadn't always been entirely successful . . . although, supposedly, all that should change now that he was carrying himself more efficiently. I supposed it wouldn't hurt to practice the high fences on Ivor. "Let's do it, then," I said brashly. "Point out a course."

Grace picked up a broken dressage whip and used it as a pointer. "Vertical going away from the in-gate, square oxer, around the bush to the rustic poles, then over the roll top, the three-stride to an oxer heading toward the gate, and then wrap it up with the triple bar by the top of the arena." She smiled that beatific smile of hers, the one I'd learned meant she was well aware that she was pushing my limits. "And stay in charge every single stride, Jules. I can't emphasize that enough. If you let him take control, you're not going to finish this course without some dirt between your teeth."

I shrugged off her warning. If she thought this was my first day running around a show-jumping course, she hadn't been reading her *Chronicle* closely enough. I had this.

We cantered a circle at the head of the arena, as formal as if it had been an actual show, and then I let Ivor thunder up to the first jump. To my surprise, riding him away from the in-gate actually had a school horse effect on him—his stride grew a little sluggish, and his head came up a bit, losing the elegant collection that marked him as a heavily schooled dressage horse. I put my leg on, hard, at the last minute and he popped the vertical from a tight spot, a deer jump, straight up in the air.

I was rattled, but there was no time to lose my cool; we were already rolling toward the square oxer. Ivor was disconnected and sprawled out, but I figured that a big square oxer wanted a nice long stride, so I let him stick his nose out and find his own spot—

exactly the opposite of what Grace wanted me to do. Let's see if her big horse could think for himself.

Left to his own devices, Ivor's hand gallop became a thundering charge. He leaped for the oxer a stride too soon and nearly left me back on the front side of the fence. Straining to make it over the back rail, he smacked the pole and stumbled over it as the rail hit the ground at the same time he did. I landed hard on his neck, completely discombobulated. *Oh shit,* I thought. *I'm making a total fool of myself.*

Luckily, there was plenty of time to pull things together. I could chalk this up to not having jumped any big fences in a while if I just proved I could make it around the rest of the course without looking like a beginner who'd stumbled into the wrong riding lesson. I sat down in the saddle and used the turn around the potted shrubbery to collect Ivor and bring him back together. He was strong, but he was listening; I held him under rigid control as we cantered up to the rustic poles, and he waited until I released my hold on his mouth and gave him leg before he jumped from the base of the fence, neck and back arched in a beautiful back-breaking bascule. I hung over his neck, suspended in space for a split second, savoring that rare (to me) perfection of flight when a horse took a fence just right.

He landed on the wrong lead and I asked for a springing lead change as we looped toward the big green roll top. These were fences that could ride either beautifully well or horrendously badly, and I concentrated again on forcing Ivor to wait until he got to the very base of the jump before he launched. Again, the bascule. Again, the feeling of floating at the height of his arch. *A girl could get used to this,* I thought.

I didn't get the chance to get too comfortable, though. As soon as we turned toward the in-gate, Ivor's strides increased as if he was trapped in a tractor beam's gravitational pull, sucking him toward the exit and the comfort of his stall, and at that point I quickly lost my influence over where he was putting his feet. The three-stride combination seemed to rush to meet us, and Ivor scrambled over the first vertical, put in two massive strides before the big oxer, and launched himself into the air as if he was jumping a pickup truck. I clung to his mane like a burr, aware of how very amateur I must look right now, and fell hard against his neck when he landed like a ton of bricks on the other side.

Ivor, unfazed and full of run, bounded joyfully toward the in-gate, but we still had one more fence to get over. I dragged him to the right and his strides shortened, disappointed we weren't going to gallop right out of the arena. He flattened out, lacking impulsion, and I sensed trouble ahead. The triple bar was maxed out far too big to show up on an eventing course, but child's play next to some of the mad things they jumped in the show-jumping arena. I lifted my hands, dug in my heels, and did everything I could to lift him up into a frame that could fly over that fence.

Almost everything. The one thing I *didn't* do was see my strides correctly. I rode Ivor hard at the triple bar, but I didn't tell him when to jump. I thought giving him the tools to make it over would be help enough.

It wasn't.

He waited too long, or I failed him by not giving him the instructions he wanted, and threw in a chip at the last minute. Now we were at the base of the triple bar, now we were too close, and now we were jumping. He picked up his knees to his chin, that gallant horse, but it was not enough; he took down the first rail with a sharp rap to each hoof as he jumped. We made it over the other two bars, and cantered away, but already I could feel that his gait had changed. I pulled him up and leaned over his shoulder, looking at his clay-caked hooves.

There it was. White paint on his right coronet. I kicked off my stirrups and jumped down to take a look.

Grace came running over. "Is he okay?" she barked. "What do you see?"

"He rapped his coronet on the jump," I said, kneeling down in the clay. I ran a finger along the soft coronet, where the gray hair lay softly over the gentle flesh above the hoof. When I pressed a little, just above the streak of white paint on his hoof left by the jump pole, Ivor flinched ever so slightly. "I think it's just going to be a bruise," I called. "It hurts him a little but nothing too serious."

"Get him cooled out and get that hoof into a bucket of warm water and Epsom salts," Grace snapped. She folded her arms across her chest and looked down at me, her gaze icy. "I *trusted* you."

"I'm sorry," I said, choking a little on the words. I was, though. I was sorry I'd messed up so badly. I could have done that better. With a little time to get to know him, I could have given Ivor his head and let him jump that course without getting in his way. Instead, I'd thrown him right into my way of riding, without giving him any time to prepare. What a stupid mistake, with Ivor bearing the brunt of it.

Grace chewed on her lip, watching me for a moment. Then she shrugged. "If he's fine, we're fine. If not . . ."

Neither of us could imagine what the consequences would be if he wasn't okay.

"I hope you learned something, anyway," she said, turning away. "If anybody got hurt today, I would have preferred it had been you."

That was ice-cold." Pete shook his head. "Man, that sounds even meaner than anything *you'd* say."

"Oh my God, shut up." I carried the phone down the barn aisle, working my way through night-check. It was eight o'clock here, so it was past midnight in England. I didn't want to ask why Pete had decided to call me so late. I was just happy to have someone to talk to. I'd called Lacey earlier, but she'd been so worn out, she'd fallen asleep while I was still explaining the situation with Ivor.

Or maybe it had just been a really boring story I was blowing out of proportion.

"I do think you're blowing this out of proportion," Pete said, reading my mind. "I mean, the horse isn't actually lame? And she said that she wants you on him again tomorrow?"

"Yeah." I turned on a water faucet and dragged the hose down the aisle to top off water buckets. Everyone was drinking so much in the heat, I was tempted to just add a third water bucket to all of the stalls. It would save all this watering well after I was supposed to be done for the night, anyway. "She relaxed after it turned out he was fine. She said now that I've learned my lesson about keeping the horse under control, it's time for me to prove that I can actually do it. So I have to keep riding Ivor in this rigid frame. Then she wants me to do it on Dynamo." I sighed.

"And you don't want to do it on Dynamo," Pete guessed.

"God, no. That's not how Dynamo and I do things! You know that. We're a team. I show him the fence, he shows me the spot, and we jump."

"It won't be like that with every horse," he pointed out.

"It should be, with the good ones," I said. "It's like that with Regina, isn't it?"

"Yes." Reluctantly.

"Well, those are the only horses that matter," I argued. "What do I care if some packer knows exactly what I'm thinking? I don't need help making amateur horses. I need help making an upper-level horse."

"Jules!" Pete sounded astonished.

"What? Oh my God, what?"

"You just admitted that you needed help!" Pete looked around very quickly, as if searching for hidden dangers somewhere off-camera. "Admittedly in a completely backhanded way, but still! Holy shit, I think it's the end of the world! Fire and brimstone is splitting the dressage arena in half! The moon is falling from the sky!"

"Shut up, Pete," I told his grinning face, thousands of miles away and still mocking me with ease. "You just shut up."

# 26

THE HORSE SHOW flyer was hanging from the tack room's whiteboard when I came down from lunch the next day. Anna was standing in front of it, her face full of longing. She ran a finger under a class listing as I came up behind her. "What's that?" I asked, peering over her shoulder.

Anna dropped her finger, but not before I saw she'd been wistfully stroking the words *High Jumpers*. "Just a horse show Kennedy and Grace are taking some students to."

"It's really soon."

"It's just a schooling show. There's no early entries or anything. I've been to these a few times—the farm's really nice. About an hour from here."

"Huh." I looked at the flyer for a few minutes. "I wonder if it would make a nice refresher for Dynamo. It's already August and he hasn't jumped much all summer. We could probably both use the change."

Anna looked uncertain. "I don't know if Grace will like that."

"Who cares what Grace likes?" I was saucier than I should have been; I knew it even as I said it, but Grace had been stiff with me since the jumping lesson on Ivor. There was not a thing wrong with him—he'd been a bit ouchy the rest of the afternoon and then he was fine—but Grace seemed to think he'd escaped my careless jumping skills through sheer luck. Hey, if she thought she could hold a grudge, she hadn't seen anything yet. I could match her dig for dig.

"You *both* should care," Grace said from behind us.

I spun around, feeling my face turning tomato red. Okay, I could match her dig for dig but maybe not in person, while I worked for her. It would be more of a behind-the-barn kind of grudge. I tried to think of an excuse for what I'd said, but there wasn't an obvious way out. So I just plowed right ahead. "Can I take Dynamo up to this show, Grace? I think it would be good for him. And," I added with a burst of inspiration, "it would be nice to see how much his jumping has improved with all the dressage we've been doing."

Grace smiled, but it was a thin, cold smile. "What a wonderful idea," she agreed primly. "We'll also work on your jumping a little more with Ivor. I'm sure he has plenty more to teach you after yesterday's . . . *ride*."

I kept my mouth from twisting with serious effort. So she was going to bring that up! I saw her insult and raised her a challenge.

"Maybe," I said tightly, "I should take Ivor and show him too."

Anna hid a dramatic little gasp with one hand, but Grace just cocked her head and regarded me for a moment, her sharp eyes inscrutable. Then, as I was wondering if I should just go ahead and have my tongue removed from my head altogether, and if my laughable government health insurance would cover that, Grace nodded decisively. "Good plan," she pronounced. "I think you need a deadline to keep you serious. So you'll work him all week and then take Ivor as well. Anna will help you groom. High jumpers, right? Excellent."

Grace went off down the aisle, waving to Kennedy, who was pulling saddles out for a trail ride. Anna and I stared at each other in silence for a few moments.

"Oh, Jules," Anna said at last, her voice full of dread. "You really bit off more than you can chew this time."

"Are you kidding me?" I folded my arms and glared down the aisle at Grace's back. "Ivor's a jumping machine, and I know exactly what I'm doing. You're always forgetting I'm a professional."

But Anna did not look reassured. "The high jumpers is one point forty meters. That's four foot five. Do you even jump that high?"

I bit back a squeak and paused for a moment to pull myself together. "I might not . . . but Ivor does."

Pete didn't pick up his phone when I called him, so I tried Lacey instead. I was bursting to tell someone how I'd conned my way into a jumpers show, and Anna's scared-puppy look wasn't doing anything for me.

Lacey, however, did not sound very excited either. "I'm confused. You're going to start jumping again, halfway through a dressage apprenticeship?"

"Yeah, because I can do *both,* Lacey. That's what we do, remember? Eventing? It's dressage and jumping?" I settled down onto a hay bale in the hay shed, a place where I knew I could a) pretend I was working if caught and b) not be heard by anyone in the barn. "This is amazing luck. And I'm going to ride Grace's big horse. Which means I can show her I'm totally capable of riding her big scary horse that she thinks needs to be a total robot all the time."

"Um . . . why do you need to do that?"

"Because she's *wrong*! God, no one gets this but me."

"I'm sorry. I'm trying to understand. I just thought . . . I just think it would be easier if you did what you had to do, aced the Second Level test, and came home."

For the first time, I realized how very tired Lacey sounded. And no wonder—she'd been running the farm alone for weeks, riding my horses, taking care of my problems . . . all by herself. We might have four times as many horses here at Seabreeze as I had back at home, but I was also sharing the work with three other people. It made a huge difference. "Lacey, how is everything going? Are you and Becky and Mikey doing okay?"

"We're doing fine." I heard birds chirping, and a door slam, as if Lacey had just gotten up and walked outside. I pictured the front yard, the little patch of grass that ran down to the barn lane, the black boards of the pasture fence beyond, the barn and arenas off to her left.

"Where are you?"

"Walking back to the barn."

"At this time of day? It's lunchtime."

"I've been at the house since noon. I fainted earlier. Becky told me to go take a cold shower and a nap, but I'm feeling better now. She's riding the mares for me later this evening." Lacey delivered this news in a matter-of-fact way that did not stop me from sitting bolt upright on the hay bale, gripping the phone with white knuckles.

"You *fainted*?"

"It was heat exhaustion. It's like ninety-six degrees here today. No breeze. Not a cloud in the sky. It's been raining really late every day. I'm just going down to make sure everyone's got hay and water, and then I'm staying inside for the rest of the afternoon. I'll feed when it cools off."

"Lacey—" I didn't know what to say. It was hot here, too, but nothing really matched the airlessness of our old barn. And she didn't have the luxury of a covered arena. When horses had to be ridden, she had to go out in the sun—there was no way around it. "Be careful," I said weakly. "I'm really sorry that happened to you."

"It's okay," Lacey said patiently. I could hear her boots crunching on the gravel of the barn lane. "We're all okay. Just get the dressage test and get home, okay? We're all ready for fall."

The strangest thing about the showgrounds was not knowing anyone, or at least not recognizing anyone. I was used to the relatively insular world of eventing—at the big events and even the winter schooling events, you saw mostly the same people. Not that many of them would be considered my friends, but it was still comforting to know your enemies. I mean, your competition. I mean, your colleagues in the equestrian business.

So pulling into the showgrounds in Ocala was usually an exercise in heraldry, recognizing horse trailers, stall webbings, and saddle pads of the major and minor houses of eventing. I always looked forward to it.

Driving into the unfamiliar grounds of West Orange Equestrian Center, I quickly found that I didn't know a single person there.

This was the show-jumping circuit, a place I rarely found myself. I occasionally took horses to a jumper show around Ocala or Gainesville for a little tune-up, but it had been well over a year since I'd had the time or the horses to do anything like that. Most of the trailers had addresses from central and south Florida. I spotted Tampa, St. Cloud, and Valkaria lettered on the sides of truck cabs as I found a parking space out in a soggy pasture doing double duty as a parking lot. The farms of trainers who probably spent most of their winter season in Wellington, not Ocala, I figured.

I parked the trailer next to Grace's rig and jumped out. I had Dynamo alone in my trailer; Grace and Anna had brought Ivor along separately. Did Grace not trust my driving? I didn't know, and I told myself that I didn't care.

"No stabling," I told Dynamo, tying him up to the side of the trailer. "Only here for a couple of hours. Try not to do anything stupid."

Dynamo, who had slowly been mellowing out over the past year, decided this was an excellent time to get back to his old routine of behaving like a total fool. He rolled his eyes at me and lifted his head as high as he could to look around at the unfamiliar trailers and horses. After considering the scene for a moment, he opened his mouth and roared a loud, inquiring neigh that rattled my eardrums.

"Good God," Grace said, walking around the side of her trailer, a prancing Ivor in tow. "That was enough to deafen me."

I ignored her, too distracted by the sight of my future ride dancing on the end of his lead shank. Ivor's quiet composure and confidence was apparently an at-home feature only. We'd had a pleasant week getting to know each other better, and I'd thought we were ready to debut our partnership on the show-jumping course. Now he looked every inch the idiotic stallion, with his blood up and his attention far from the person he was supposed to be listening to. Doubt crept into my mind. Maybe my plan wasn't so great after all.

Grace mainly ignored his antics, giving him an occasional jerk on the chain shank whenever he threatened to take his hooves off the ground all at once. "He's an idiot, but he'll stand tied," she announced. "I'll put him right here, so he can look at Dynamo. It'll give him something to think about. Anna's going to pick up your numbers, and then she'll help you tack up." Grace took the chain off Ivor's nose and deftly tied him to a ring on the side of her trailer. "I'll see you out there!"

"You're leaving?" I was getting left alone at the trailer with two horses, one of them a stallion? Surely she would wait until Anna came back, at least.

"I have some friends to see. And I'll want to get a good spot to watch you and Ivor." Grace winked and turned on her heel, leaving me with a hand on Dynamo's shank and a helpless eye on the prancing, piaffeing Ivor.

I'd been set up to fail.

No, she had to know Ivor was all talk. She would never leave her big horse with me if she thought he might get loose or get hurt. Grace wasn't my biggest fan, but she would never risk Ivor's safety just to prove her point. She wasn't crazy, she was just sick of me.

Maybe she was actually trying to kill me.

I considered this as Ivor reached out a foreleg and kicked my trailer, denting the wheel well. It seemed well within the realm of possibility.

Dynamo whinnied again, his body trembling with the force of the blast. Ivor jumped as if he hadn't realized the other horse was there, then gazed at him, riveted. The two horses stared at each other like long-lost lovers.

"Great," I said. "You two keep each other occupied. I'll get started." I only had a half hour to get them groomed and tacked, if I was going to fit in a course walk. And there was no way I wanted to face a four-foot show-jumping course without walking the damn thing first.

# 27

IT WOULD HAVE been a lot easier to walk the course, though, if Anna would just come back.

I managed to get Dynamo groomed and tacked, although it would certainly have gone more smoothly if he wasn't dancing around at the end of his tie, swinging his hindquarters to and fro as he tried to get a look at the action going on in either direction. Ivor, for his part, mostly just pranced in place, tearing up the sod beneath his hooves and creating a hazardous working area for my feet. I got him saddled up with difficulty, using a saddle borrowed from the school horse tack room since my saddle was on Dynamo. It was a handicap I was not excited about, but that had seemed like a minor trifle in my initial excitement to take Grace's horse and win a ribbon.

I examined the new two-inch scar across the top of my field boots that one of his shoes had left. Well, *that* wasn't going to buff out. I looked around for the missing Anna.

She was coming down the slope from the stables, where the arena and registration were, with two manila envelopes in her hands. I crossed my arms and waited.

"Here you go," she said, waving the envelopes. Ivor snorted at her terrifying arm-waving envelope-flapping of doom, reared back against his tie, hit the end of it, and then threw a buck instead, one hoof ringing against the side of the trailer. Anna looked horrified. "Oops," she whispered. "I'm so sorry."

"As long as he isn't lame and the shoe's still on, I don't care." I snatched the envelopes and shook out the bridle numbers. "Did you get receipts?"

"Was I supposed to?"

"Oh my God, Anna. When you pay someone money you always get a receipt. It's a business expense. It gets written off on my taxes." I had a special file just for horse show receipts. It was a staggering sum of money, especially when you considered that all I came home with was satin ribbons. But I tried not to consider that. "Okay. I'll get them when I go up to walk the course. Can you stay here and babysit these monsters?"

"Grace wanted me to come meet some people."

"You can meet them when I'm riding." Horse shows were all about networking, but Grace knew full well that Anna was supposed to be helping me. I hoped I didn't run into her up at the arena. I really didn't trust myself right now. I might tell her exactly what I thought of her little games. "I'll be back in a few minutes."

"Okay," Anna said uncertainly, looking at the two goofball horses I was abandoning her with. She was lucky I hadn't left her to saddle them, too. I went marching up the hill toward the arena, the wet ground squishing under my scarred boots, weaving through the maze of horse trailers, horses, riders, and dogs.

I passed the registration tent, where two sunburned volunteers sat at a folding table and took payment, cheerfully accepting the archaic currency of personal checks from riders wearing the universal schooling show uniform of sun shirt, breeches, and field boots. The volunteers handed out bridle numbers in return, slipping them into the envelopes along with maps of the courses for each of the classes entered.

There was a horse-and-rider team in the arena when I walked up, hopping their way through a low jumpers class. It looked more my speed than the four-foot fences I was going to jump later, especially after spending nearly two months on a dull diet of flatwork, but cantering around a three-foot course wasn't going to do much for any of us. It wouldn't show if Dynamo was really going to handle Advanced courses the way Grace had promised, and it wouldn't show I could handle Ivor my way, working in partnership instead of demanding utter obedience, the way I'd promised myself. I wasn't sure if the most important thing at this point was winning the class on Dynamo or on Ivor, but I figured either way I'd go home happy.

Once the rider had left the arena, others on foot started lining up near the in-gate. I figured she must have been the last rider in the class, so I wandered over and joined them, trying to look casual. Not recognizing any faces in the crowd made me feel out of place. I could imagine the seasoned jumper riders muttering to each other, "And who is *that* chick in the beat-up boots?"

Pete would have said I was being ridiculous, and that everyone there was only worried about themselves, not me. "You think everyone's staring at you and judging you," he told me once. "But that's *your* bad habit, not theirs."

The class ended and the riders on foot around me surged forward, eager to walk the course. The jump crew went into the arena along with us, popping up the heights of the jumps, pushing out the spreads. A steward walked through with a tape measure, making sure everything met United States Equestrian Federation standards. It wasn't a recognized horse show, and most jumps were lower than the typical high-jumper classes offered at the big shows this winter, but people still had certain expectations as they prepped their horses, and the steward was being careful to make sure those expectations were being met.

It was a nice course, I thought, resting my hand against the last rail of the triple combination to check the depth of the jump cups. It wobbled a little but seemed secure—maybe a hard rub wouldn't pull the rail if one of Dynamo's hooves touched it. The final obstacle in the combination was a wide oxer—it was going to be the ultimate test of Dynamo's development this summer.

"Pretty big combination," a young woman said, putting her own hand on the rail. She was pretty, and pale, and stick-thin, looking more like a fashion model than an equestrian. I was unpleasantly reminded of Amy Rodan. She smiled at me and I smiled back without thinking. "It's my first time at this height," she explained, emboldened by my apparent friendliness. "I'm a little nervous about it. Well, really, I'm sick with nerves about it."

"It's not too bad," I comforted. "The poles all fall down. It could be worse."

"How could it be worse?" She ducked under the pole and stood between the first and last standards of the spread jump. She spread out her arms and laughed.

"What's worse than this? Grand Prix? Don't even tell me—my trainer seems to think that's in my future."

I smiled knowingly. "It could be a cross-country jump. Logs don't fall down when you hit them. *You* do."

"I could never. That's insanity." She climbed out of the spread jump. "You don't do that, do you?"

"Professionally," I said proudly.

"You're insane," the fashion model said, wobbling the jump pole once more. Now she seemed to take comfort in its motion, instead of worrying about it. "Absolutely insane."

I probably was, I thought, as we set off to inspect the next fence. Just not for the reasons she thought.

The trouble started while we were still in the warm-up arena. Of course, warm-up arenas are notoriously terrible places anyway. Kids crashing around without shouting that they're going to jump a fence until about two strides out, young horses having mental breakdowns over all the fuss and strangeness, general drama when two horses who have never met but *know* they are mortal enemies start a kicking rage-fest when they get too close . . . Warm-up arenas are like equine demolition derbies no one entered on purpose, but that everyone has to survive at any cost if they want to get on with the proper show. Or, you know, survive another day.

Ivor took the opportunity to remember he was a stallion, something that didn't really come up at home. In fact, I could not recall a single moment during which Ivor had lifted his head and so much as sniffed at a mare back at the farm. Here, it was all he seemed to be doing. The gorgeous, collected, on-the-bit Ivor of old was replaced with giraffe-impersonator Ivor, and there was nothing nice to be said about that. His belly-shaking whinnies didn't make me any friends either.

Grace leaned on the rail and watched, arms folded and eyes hooded. When I looked her way, she beckoned me over with one hand. I rode over with my jaw tight.

"You need to get him under control," she said, squinting up at me. "Use all of your resources. Hand. Leg. Seat. Get him in a tight circle, do some transitions, do some half halts, and remind him that you are the master. And then never let him go for a minute."

I nodded and rode off to find a corner where I could turn some circles, unhappiness seething in my belly. Ivor was betraying me. I'd really, seriously, ridiculously thought that we were friends.

But I did as Grace said, because things were spiraling out of control too quickly for me to get rebellious and try to do things my own way. After a few minutes of fifteen-meter circles and constant transitions, I had Ivor firmly between hand and leg. Maybe he wasn't as tautly under control as I'd gotten him back at the farm, but it was pretty close—and it was night and day with the rowdy stud horse I'd been dealing with before. I let him loose from the circle and we cantered around the arena at a stately pace, drawing a few admiring looks from spectators and riders. That was nice.

I took him over the warm-up jumps a few times at the same even canter, not letting him out of the rigid collection until we were at the base of the jumps. He popped over the vertical and the oxer like a firework, launching himself off his hindquarters and soaring over the fences with extraordinary power.

I brought him down to a walk, not bothering to hide my grin, and rode over to Grace. "He's ready," I told her.

She nodded, unimpressed. "Do all of those things in the ring, and you'll be fine."

*Fine!* I wanted to snap. *We're going to* win *this thing.* But I kept my mouth shut and looked around for Anna. She was supposed to have brought me Dynamo by now. "Have you seen Anna? With my horse?"

Grace shrugged. "Whatever you two cooked up is your problem."

I swore and jogged Ivor away, heading for the gate. I didn't know what Grace was up to now, but if she'd found some task for Anna that involved wandering off with Dynamo right when I needed to warm up, I wasn't going to be surprised. She didn't want me to succeed today. I wasn't sure why . . . Okay, I knew exactly why. I'd been acting like a bored princess who didn't have to listen to her governess and all her old-fashioned lessons. Fine. But still, she didn't have to torpedo my chances at this show. It would look good on her if I did well, wouldn't it?

I pulled up Ivor at the gate and walked him out, my mind racing. What if Grace wanted me to fail at jumping to prove her own point? What if she was trying to make me throw this show so I'd understand that her way was the only right way?

*You're being paranoid*, Pete would have told me. *You always think everyone's out to get you, and they never are. It's all in your head.*

Ivor was practically leaping up and down, his mouth hard against the bit, and I realized suddenly I'd tensed so hard I'd nearly sent him into a frenzy. Rule number one of riding: never ride when you're mad. I was breaking that one right now.

I ran a hand down his wet neck, dark with sweat. "I'm sorry, buddy. Relax. Shhh . . . relax."

Ivor did not seem inclined to relax. I was so busy being angry about Grace's supposed sabotage, I'd sabotaged myself. And wasn't that just typical. I was my own worst enemy, as ever.

"Jules! Jules!" I turned in the saddle and saw Dynamo's white-striped face emerging from behind the stable. Anna was leading him, waving her hand in the air. "Over here!"

I turned Ivor and we strode over to meet them. "What were you doing in the barn area? We're not supposed to go in there."

"Dynamo's flash broke. I went in to see if I could borrow one from the riding school."

"And?"

"And?" Anna pointed at Dynamo's bridle. "He's wearing a flash, isn't he?"

"I'm sorry. I'm a mess right now. It's just show nerves."

"Show nerves? But you're a professional." There wasn't a trace of irony in Anna's voice. She was genuinely surprised.

"Show nerves never go away," I admitted. "At least, if they do, it takes a lot more years in the saddle than I've had so far." I slid down from Ivor's back and we exchanged reins. "Pay attention to him. He was being a total asshole for a while."

"I got him." Anna smiled. "Dynamo was being a little bit of a lookie-loo, but otherwise he's a really good boy. You're lucky to have such a nice horse."

I swung into the saddle and leaned down to give Dynamo a hug, ignoring his damp neck. "I am," I said into his mane. "I'm so lucky to have him."

I hung on to that one irrefutable fact.

I was lucky.

Remembering I was lucky didn't change the core goal of the day—to show Grace she was wrong, and I could get Ivor around that course my way. With Dynamo fresh and warm, I got back on Ivor and we thundered into the arena like avenging angels.

All I needed was a sword to wave in the air. All the gray stallion needed was a brain.

Because he had apparently lost his somewhere in the warm-up arena.

Rolling up to the very first fence, it was obvious to me that I was not fully in control. Where was sensible, thoughtful Ivor, who anticipated my thoughts and tingled with sensitivity as we cantered elegantly around the arena? He'd been replaced by a wild animal with the neck of a giraffe, the stride of a cheetah, and the strength of a bull. I found out very quickly, as he scrambled desperately over the first vertical, way too close and way too fast to make it anything like his usual graceful bascule, that I was about to get carted around this course.

*Okay then,* I thought grimly, and stuck my heels in front of me and raised my hands to my chest, ready to water-ski. *I've been carted around before. I can salvage this and at least balance him up before the fences. We've been working together. We know each other now. We can go clear. We can manage this.*

Except that we couldn't.

With much hauling on the reins and kicking, I got Ivor to turn back for the second and third fences, two fairly pleasant-riding oxers decorated with garlands of silk flowers to look like a set of old-fashioned flower stalls. I only know that's what they looked like from the course walk. The view while actually riding over them was more like a flashing blur of red and yellow while I prayed to the eventing gods to get me through this course in one piece.

Slaver was flying from Ivor's mouth as I turned him, with all the finesse and grace of a Panzer tank, back toward the triple combination down the long side of the arena. He snorted and dug down on the bit, in the biggest hurry to get to a jump I'd ever seen in a horse, and my senses tingled with impending doom as we went roaring up to the base of the first of the three fences as if it was a feed bin overflowing with sweet feed and carrots.

He jumped like Pegasus taking to the air for the very first time—overexuberant, and without any apparent thought for where his hooves would eventually come down.

I grabbed mane and hung on, hoping for the best.

He landed so far into the combination that he had to take the next fence from a half stride, his knees pulling down the front rail of the oxer as he took off again. The impact threw him off balance and he landed hard, stumbling, his nose tipping toward the ground and my nose tipping toward his mane, only my rock-hard cross-country leg saving me from rolling right over his shoulder and hitting the ground. But even with my leg sticking like glue to his girth, I knew that nothing was going to save me if the idiot tried to keep going. I closed my fists on the reins, hauled back, told him *whoa!*—but it was too late to take control now. I'd already told Ivor he could do things his way, and the horse was bound and determined to finish the way he'd come in, like an utter oaf to my mind, but like a fighter and champion to his mind. Probably.

Instead of putting on the brakes and stopping before the big final spread in the combination, Ivor flung himself forward, put in one stride instead of two, and launched comically early. Comically if you were in the stands and were rooting for an impressive crash or two, that is. For me, seeing that Ivor had just convinced himself he was fully capable of jumping a good twenty feet into the future, it was just those quiet milliseconds between realizing you're going to eat some dirt, and the actual moment of eating said dirt, feeling the grit between your molars, tasting the tang of blood on your bitten tongue.

In that millisecond, three words were ringing in my ears, imprinting themselves on my brain: *I was wrong.*

He landed somewhere in the middle of the jump, the poles rattling and flying in every direction, and in the midst of this hard landing I went toppling off his shoulder, strong leg notwithstanding, and landed a few times on top of various poles. At least, that's what they tell me, and the bruises hold up their story. I just remember the heat of Ivor's neck as my cheek slid down his hot flesh, and the wooden poles clattering as they fell from their cups. The rest, as they say, went black.

I sure knew where I was when I woke up, though, and I wished my blackout had been a little longer, perhaps necessitating an ambulance ride, so that I didn't have to open my eyes and know I was lying on my back (and on a few jump poles) in a show-jumping arena somewhere near Orlando, with a crowd full of trainers, riders, horse show moms, and assorted hangers-on watching me with wide eyes and plenty of hushed gossip, while someone else caught the horse I had just botched riding so completely, and somewhere a trainer who had known all along that I was going to fail stood with her arms crossed and her eyes knowing.

I closed my eyes against the golden sky and tried to concentrate on what could move and how much it would hurt to move it—my ankles, my wrists, my knees, my elbows, my hips, and last of all, my neck.

I sat up, biting back a groan, and brushed the dirt from my face. The yellow sand clung to everything from my eyelashes to my lips. I blew out a mouthful and ran my tongue around my loosened front teeth. Wouldn't that be a charming look for Pete, if he came home to Jules the Toothless Wonder?

Pete. Oh God, what was Pete going to say? He was going to be furious that I'd played around like this, trying to prove I was better than the trainer I'd been sent to, when I had sworn to him I'd put my head down and work, that I'd concentrate on my lessons, that I'd get through this with flying colors so that I could come home to our life. I had promised him. I had said I would be better.

I had been trying to be better, and somewhere along the line my pride and ambition had taken over again.

I shook my head at myself, and that was when I realized just how much my head ached. The motion set my entire skull to throbbing, and I put my hand up to my forehead to rub at the pain. I found a lump there, already coming to life from beneath the skin, and snatched my fingers away at the flash of pain. Jesus Christ, I'd hit my head *while* I was wearing a hard hat. Riding someone else's horse completely against their instructions. At a show I had no business riding in at all.

I deserved some sort of award for worst choices in a single summer.

Then there was an EMT looking very serious and holding up her fingers in front of my eyes and asking a lot of questions I couldn't answer, and wouldn't you know, I ended up getting that ambulance ride anyway.

# 28

I GOT BORED very quickly.

Moping around because my head ached wasn't exactly my style. I was under strict instructions not to go back to work in the barn for a full forty-eight hours (an arbitrary number if you asked me), but by the end of the first full day on stall rest, I was antsy. I needed to get out, but where was I supposed to go?

The usual evening events were underway downstairs: Kennedy was shouting general abuse at the tween girls in her Sunday-afternoon advanced lesson, who seemed to thrive on her drill sergeant routine; Anna was cooling out Grace's last ride; Grace was out in the arena riding a new horse; and Tom and Margaret were prepping supper feed and pulling down night hay. It was a busy little community, happy enough without me, and I didn't want to face any of its residents.

I knew Grace was sitting on a pretty hefty lecture, one that I deserved. I'd gone against her orders with her own horse and could have very well brought him home with a serious injury. (The fact that he'd only gotten a scrape on one fetlock and some paint on his hooves was not at all an excuse, and I'd never try to make the case for it.) I knew that she had every right to cancel the contract she had with Rockwell, tell them that I was a lost cause and to sponsor at their own risk, and send me back to Ocala with my tail between my legs. And while part of me actually *wanted* that, anything to get out of another four weeks of dressage and servitude, I knew for sure that if that happened, there would be no living it down with anyone at home. I would have shown them that, once again, I was incapable of putting anyone first but myself.

I pressed my face against the barn window. Mickey and Dynamo were down there, already digging into their night hay, tails swishing against the evening flies. They were probably bored, too. Mickey, in particular, hadn't done any real work in days. I'd been so wrapped up in my show-jumping adventure with Ivor and Dynamo, I hadn't been able to spend time on Mickey. Talk about a failure of priorities.

What I needed, more than anything, was to go riding. My senses were out of whack. A bad fall, and an ambulance ride, and a bottle of prescription painkillers—that was a bad combination for doing some serious thinking and clearing one's head. The only thing that could get my brain working on all cylinders again was a good ride.

I'd just wait until they were done downstairs, and then I'd

sneak out on those trails I'd heard so much about. There was a full moon tonight; it was the perfect opportunity.

I tried to FaceTime with Pete before I took out Dynamo, but his connection was bad and we ended up talking on the phone instead. I wasn't sure if it was the lack of eye contact that caused our conversation to drift into a furious argument, or if it was inevitable I would just push him too far. All I knew was things did not go as I had expected.

Pete sounded even more tired than usual, and when I finally finished telling him about the horse show, his voice was taut. "Are you always this insane?"

"What?" I pulled the phone away and blinked at the screen, but his face wasn't there and I didn't know if he was joking. His biting tone suggested he was not.

"*Seriously,* Jules, are you always this insane?" His voice rose. "Can you never give it a rest? I thought you were lightening up, I thought you were starting to mellow out, and I think the horses did too. Now I wonder if you're ever going to be normal."

"I don't know what you're talking about." I did. I knew exactly what he was talking about, but his tone was scathing and I wasn't ready to be lectured. Not when I was trying to shove away this god-awful headache. Not when I was trying to figure out how to get everything back on track with Grace. If he'd let me finish, I would have told him I was going to fix everything. "I'm not insane. That's just plain mean of you. I've had a crazy summer with these . . . with these crazy people, and things got out of hand, but—"

"Have you ever for a second considered that you're just as crazy as everyone else? Crazier, even? I'm surprised they deal with you. I'd have kicked your ass out weeks ago."

"What the hell, Pete? What the actual hell. Do you not want me to call you anymore or—"

"You're being ridiculous." Now he was furious, I could hear it in the tightness in his voice. He would do anything not to blow up; he was always working on repressing his negative reactions and displaying a passive face to the world. He said it was the professional thing to do, but I thought he could probably use a good explosion every once in a while. Now I thought he might be gearing up for one, directed solely at me. "Don't try to make this about me. You asked my advice and I'm going to give it to you. And if you don't want to hear it, you can just hang up. Got it?"

I was clenching the phone so hard I thought I might crack the screen. "Got it," I bit out. "Go on then, Mr. Advice." Although I couldn't actually remember if I'd asked for his advice or not. Maybe it was just one of those Relationship Things.

"Good. Listen. Accept that you are at least part of the problem. If everyone else is pissed about something, that something might include you. You're a bad-tempered person, Jules. This isn't news to you. We have talked about it. You're a wonderful, passionate human, and a dedicated horsewoman, and I love you for those things. But you're an angry person. You *are*," he insisted, raising his voice as I began to protest. "You think the world is crapping on you all the time. You saw this summer as a punishment instead of an opportunity. When obviously, to everyone else, it was a huge, amazing opportunity to fix the one hole in your training résumé without costing you a dime, and actually paying you in the end. But you refuse to see it. You refuse help. You fight everything and everyone, Jules. And I just can't . . . Jules, I can't anymore." His voice faltered.

There was silence for a moment. I imagined the seagulls between us, crying to one another as the Atlantic crashed beneath their wings. My mouth was dry; my fingers were numb. "Can't what?" I croaked, licking my bloodless lips.

His voice was a whisper. "Can't do *this* anymore. This . . . us."

I dropped the phone. It clattered on the linoleum floor and I could hear Grace outside in the barn shouting about untacked school horses and I could hear neighing and I could hear hoof-beats in the aisle, hooves sliding on concrete like a beautiful tune I'd heard a million times before and would never tire of, but I didn't really hear any of it because Pete was four thousand miles away, separated by an ocean and a change of heart that I couldn't possibly register, couldn't possibly accept, couldn't possibly live with.

How *dare* he say such a thing? My bad temper rose up and shoved away my despair. I bent down, picked up the phone, put it to my ear. "That's not advice," I accused, interrupting whatever he might have been saying, or thinking. I wasn't listening.

"What?"

"You said you were going to give me advice. You said you had wonderful advice I needed to listen to. So I'm listening, but all I've heard are complaints. What's the advice?"

And then Pete started shouting. "Are—you—bloody—*serious*?"

"*Yes I am!*" I roared back. "You superior smug bastard!"

"I'm telling you," he said thunderously, "that if you're going to continue to be a self-defeating whining witch who spits in the face of everyone who tries to help her, we're through. How's that for advice?"

"And I'm telling *you*," I snapped back, my heart thundering in my ears, "that isn't advice! That's an ultimatum! And a pretty shitty one, too! What, you're going to break up with me over the phone? I should just go back to the farm and pack up and leave?

Because it's not happening. You made me a promise. You said as long as you had a farm, I had a home. Well *guess what*."

"I'm not . . . Jules. For God's sake." Pete took a few long, heavy breaths that I guessed were to indicate that the blowup, short and sweet as it had been, was over. And also that he wasn't breaking up with me, which was good, because that shouting was the sound of me panicking worse than I'd ever panicked in my life, in case he hadn't noticed. Not entirely about the prospect of losing my home and farm, either, it must be admitted. "Jules, there's nothing I can tell you about your attitude that can change it, except . . . that you have to change it. Fast. Right now. For all of our sakes. For the farm. For the money. For the horses. For your future."

I sighed.

"For our future," Pete said. "Fix it. Or things have to change."

R unning away?"
    I stopped dead, one foot in the stirrup and the other on the pavement of the barn aisle. Dynamo stood still, but he turned his head around inquisitively, and nudged me in the ass with his nose when he saw that I was just hanging, mid-mount, from his side.

Grace crossed her arms over her chest and waited.

I let my foot slide down from the stirrup. "I needed to go for a hack," I said. My God, did I need to go for a hack. Nothing else could save me now. "My head is much better."

"It's nine o'clock at night."

"I wanted to wait for it to cool off."

"The barn lights go off, they stay off," Grace reminded me.

"You know the rules. Not to mention you weren't even headed for an arena, were you, Miss Head Injury?"

Dynamo's nose was pointed to the far end of the aisle. Only the woods lay beyond that door. It was obvious where we were headed. "I was just going to walk him down the barn lane and back again," I said lamely, but Grace wasn't anyone's fool. Least of all, mine. A frown creased her brow and she regarded me in an almost motherly fashion.

"You're addicted to trouble, Jules. Has anyone ever told you that? You absolutely crave danger and doing things you're not supposed to be doing."

"Why can't I ride in the woods?" I asked stoutly, picking up my chin. "There's a perfectly good trail. A commercial-grade trail, if your advertising is to be believed. Might as well use it now, since those backhoes next door are going to make it pretty unpleasant in a couple months."

"As if that was the point." She stared me down with that steely gaze of hers. "We haven't been having a very productive summer. You've fought me. You've tried at every turn to assert yourself as the expert. I'm not sure why you think that's necessary. I don't know why you think that you, a girl barely in her twenties, could be a more experienced horsewoman than myself. I've been nice to you, I've been cruel to you, and I've let you get yourself into incredible trouble, but not once have you let yourself just listen to your trainer, work with your horses as you are instructed, and grow as a rider and a horsewoman. To say nothing of growing as a person.

"So you have a choice. You can get on that horse and ride out into the woods, or the arena, or wherever you think you need to be tonight. And tomorrow you can pack up and go back to your farm and go on being the experienced professional that you think you are. Or you can put that horse away, respecting my rules that say the barn is closed for the night, and you can go up to your apartment and you can wait out the two days until the doctor allows you to work again. Then we can start over. We have nearly four weeks left in this little exercise. Your dressage entries have been sent. Your check has been cashed. Your ride times will be published online and we'll trailer over to the showgrounds and make damn well sure that you put in a good showing for me, for Seabreeze, for Rockwell, and for yourself.

"And then you can go back to your farm knowing that you're a better rider, and you'll have your sponsorship for your show season. And all you had to do was give up your ego for four more weeks. Four weeks! Can you do that, Jules? Tell me, right now."

I licked my lips, which had suddenly gone dry and were burning in the hot night air. She was right. Pete was right. Everyone was right but me.

Four weeks was nothing. This was the rest of my life—all of our lives. "I can do that," I said. "I can do that. I'll do it." And to prove it, I reached up and unbuckled Dynamo's noseband, then picked up his reins to turn him, take him back to his stall, and untack him completely. Dynamo fluttered his nostrils at me, as if to say he'd known we weren't actually going out there. Even Dynamo knew better than me.

Still, Grace stood in our way, surveying me with a look that said she wasn't quite ready to believe me. Finally she stepped to one side, giving me a curt nod. "Untack your horse and put him away, then," she said. "And don't forget one word that I said to you. Because I know you're going to have a hard time shedding your little tough trainer act. Remember that, when I'm telling you that it's your third strike and you're out, got it? Remember that before you do something you'll regret for the rest of your life."

# 29

I SPENT THE next day holed up in the apartment, watching the barn activity from my window and imagining all the things Grace and Anna were saying about me while they laughed their way through the horses I usually rode. My competitive side couldn't stand the way they smiled at each other as they passed in the aisle. I had the old working student's jealousy running through my veins.

To keep myself away from the window, I retreated into the books lining the walls of Grace's office. I crept into her office whenever I saw her riding, safely occupied on horseback, and, confident I wouldn't be discovered, took my pick from the dusty shelves, brushing away cobwebs and tiny spiders who wanted to hitch a ride into my apartment. Behind the trophies and cracked photo frames of gleaming hunter ponies and shining jumpers, I found a treasure trove of old riding manuals. I turned yellowed pages and found black-and-white plates, on thick glossy paper, of the elegant seats of yesteryear: riders (mostly men) in loose breeches and hunt-top boots, their hands floating along their horses' necks in perfect automatic releases; their horses big-boned Thoroughbreds with flaring nostrils and pricked ears straining over massive fences with their forehooves neatly crossed beneath their chests, no one worrying about how square and even their knees were as they jumped. They were efficient and elegant machines, rough-and-ready soldiers who cleaned up well, born for their jobs and happy to do them.

I was supposed to look like them, a cool and collected horse-woman who could not be concerned by a fence, who could not be put off by a dressage test, who simply went out there and did her job better than anyone else. No one had changed the rules on them, though. No one had told them they had to be a Grand Prix dressage rider, a Grand Prix show-jumping rider, and also, by the way, just in case, be able to gallop a cross-country course. Back then, cross-country came first. It was so like me to be born in the wrong century, wasn't it?

I put the book I'd been studying next to the newest saddlery catalog I'd tossed on the scarred coffee table. The anxious-looking rider on the cover looked like she was jumping an entirely different fence from her cool-eyed, bored-looking hunter. Her hands were near his ears, her wrists were twisted, and her elbows were down near his withers; she was pinching with her knee and her lower leg had slid back the horse's barrel toward his hindquarters. "Grace Carter would send you back to short-stirrup," I told the girl.

She didn't care what I thought. She made more money in endorsements and sponsorships while she was catch-riding baby green hunters than I would make with a barnful of upper-level event horses. That was just the business we were in . . . for now.

Since I had regressed to talking to magazines, I decided I'd better talk to a human. I texted Lacey—no answer. She was probably riding. I texted Pete—no answer. He was probably riding.

I didn't really know anyone else who would answer a text from me.

Well, the phone was already in my hand. No one was there to stop me from making a mistake.

For the first time in weeks, I checked the blogs.

Lacey texted me back about a half hour later, after I'd already read the worst of it and was on to the more minor comments section. Her text notification popped up above the comment from LittleEqChamp I'd been reading: "Maybe this will finally teach Jules Thornton that she doesn't belong in the big leagues and one nice horse who does anything she wants isn't enough to make her an upper-level rider." LittleEqChamp's avatar was a glittery pink unicorn.

*What's up? I was riding Maybelline. Going awesome.*

*That's good,* I thumbed back. *I was reading about my horse show disaster.*

*Stop. Put down the phone.*

*Too late.*

The phone started buzzing and Lacey's phone number popped up on the screen. I hit the green button and the speaker icon at once, too lazy to bring it to my ear. "What."

"Are you seriously reading blogs? Why are you doing this to yourself?"

"I need to know what my adoring public thinks of me. Spoiler alert: they don't adore me."

"You had a bad day."

I snorted. "I'm having a bad year."

"Well, so what? It happens. People have bad years. Some people have bad decades."

"Excellent point," I agreed. "Maybe I've been having a bad decade and I didn't even realize it. Maybe a good decade is coming up. I'm due."

"There you go. Now stop reading nonsense on the internet. I can't babysit you, I have to start evening chores."

"Can I just tell you something?"

"What?" Lacey sounded wary.

"This is an inside job."

"We're talking in bank robbery terms now. Do you think it's that serious?"

"I think it's that serious. When everyone in eventing—"

"Everyone chronically online in eventing, which probably isn't your peers," Lacey interrupted.

"I'm not worried about my *peers*," I snarked. "I'm worried about the women with money to burn who want to buy into an upper-level horse syndicate to feel alive and need to show off to their friends on Facebook when their horse wins an event! Talk about chronically online! I *need* the likes and hearts addicts to like and heart *me*!"

"Okay, okay." Lacey sighed. "When the potential horse moms of eventing go online, you want to look good."

"Exactly. And someone knows that and they're trying to ruin me."

"You're really using the word 'ruin' and you're being serious, right?"

"I am being serious. And it's coming from this farm. Look at this post from last month: 'Jules Goes to Pony Club.' All about my early enrollment in No-Stirrups November. Who would know I'd been riding without stirrups all that time?"

"Wouldn't there be photos?" Lacey avoided snickering at the blog post title, which was how I knew we were friends.

"Too many other people around? It would have to be from weekends or after school, because otherwise it's just the grooms and me."

"So, who?"

"I don't know. Anna?"

"No," Lacey said. "Anna is dying for you to leave. She would want you to look good so your business pops without Grace's help and she can have her boss to herself again."

"Good point. So, is it a student? The grooms would not care." Tom and Margaret seriously lived in a club of two, and ignored me so easily it didn't even feel like a slight.

"A student," Lacey repeated. "Now, that's interesting. You're surrounded by them. The adult riders, though, you barely interact with them."

"Right, they ride and they leave. Some of the kids hang around, though."

We were quiet together for a moment. I'd missed this, I thought. Lacey and me, against the world.

"I'm reading it again," she said eventually. "Hang on. It *does* sound like a kid, don't you think? Like a teenager. You got any of those watching you?"

I thought about it. We had a handful of teenagers, around fourteen, fifteen—too young to drive, too old to hang out with the other kids. They moved in a pack before and after their lessons, and were rarely in the barn during the school day, when I would be riding.

Except for that one black-haired girl who liked to ride Splash.

What was her name? "Liz," I muttered. I remembered the way she'd watched me the day I'd ridden him during her private lesson. Like I was stealing her best friend. "Oh, yeah."

"You figure it out?"

"I think. What's this blogger's name? Do they have more than one of the stories?"

"L. S. Franklin? Hang on—yeah, she wrote the other one about the last horse show, too."

Franklin, Franklin, Franklin . . . it had to be her, right?

"I'm looking in the lesson book," I decided, and took the phone off speaker. I glanced out the window; Anna and Grace were both in the barn aisle, untacking horses. Even if one of them came upstairs, I had a couple of minutes.

I slipped into the office and flipped through the book until I found Saturday, her usual lesson day. I ran my finger down the names—there it was, under one of Kennedy's intermediate lessons. *Liz Franklin.*

"That's her," I breathed. "Liz is sneaking pics of me and selling my worst moments to *Eventing Chicks*. This is about a school horse, mind you. A *school* horse."

"Well, I guess she loves him."

"Apparently. I think this goes a little far, trying to wreck my reputation, but what do I know?"

Lacey giggled nervously. "What are you going to do?"

"I don't know. Kill her? I should kill her, right?"

"I think that's a little much."

"Push her in a mud puddle? Would that work for you?"

"Maybe that one. If you can do it without getting caught."

Speaking of getting caught . . . I looked out the office window and saw neither Grace nor Anna in the aisle. Tom and Margaret had their horses in the wash rack. Time to go.

I bounced out of the office and shut the screen door just as Anna appeared on the porch. She raised her eyebrows at the sight of me. "Jules? Aren't you supposed to be resting?"

I had the phone to my ear; I pointed to it as if I was trying to get reception, and walked to the porch railing. "I'm not sure I can do anything," I muttered. "But I really want to let her know I'm onto her."

Lacey wasn't so sure. "I think you need to let this go."

A horse-and-rider team were walking into the outdoor jumping arena. I eyed them. Speak of the devil . . . "She's here right now. She's riding. I can't believe it."

"Jules—Jules, don't actually do anything—"

But my blood was up. She was making a name for herself by shaming me online. There were a lot of guilty parties here: the *Eventing Chicks* website editors, the people who commented, they were all part of this . . . but they weren't right in front of me, sashaying along on Splash, who was moving beautifully because I'd been schooling him half the summer. I saw her mother standing along the rail, looking uncomfortable in high heels and a silky work blouse. I turned around slowly, slipping the phone into my pocket, pressing the red button to silence Lacey's protests, walking past Anna, who was still watching me with that worried look on her face.

"Jules, take it easy . . . you don't have to help feed tonight if you're not ready."

As if taking care of horses was the problem. I ignored Anna and started down the stairs.

I waited for her, sitting on a folding chair near the wash racks. The afternoon lesson traffic was starting to file through the barn and Margaret and Tom, picking up my slack by tacking horses, eyed me curiously but didn't say anything.

She was only in the arena for about half an hour, and came back inside flushed and happy-looking, her black hair slipping from its ponytail and resting on her slim shoulders. She was tall for her age, and almost painfully thin, with dark makeup accenting her enormous eyes. In her designer breeches and tailored polo shirt, her Samshield helmet with a pink monogram scrolling across the front tipped back and unbuckled, she was everything an Instagram generation could want out of an equestrian. Splash dipped his head, pulling the reins through her hands as he reached for her pocket, thinking her phone was a treat, and she laughed at him, showing off perfect, expensive teeth.

I clenched my fists in my lap, and wished I'd thought to change my clothes. Worn khaki shorts, faded tank top, battered sneakers flaked with shavings from mucking stalls—I should have pulled on my best breeches, zipped on my good boots, and found one of my old Green Winter Farm polo shirts, so at least I looked like a professional trainer, instead of a groom on hard times. Oh well, too late now. Liz slid down from the horse, handing the reins to Tom, and I stood up, ready to face her.

Her eyes caught the movement, and she turned. As soon as she saw my expression, she knew. I could see it in the blush that spread across her pale cheeks, in the way her eyes widened and her mouth fell open. She wasn't old enough to hide her fear yet.

I decided to try and keep things between the two of us. As Tom led the horse into the wash rack, I moved toward her. "I was just wondering," I murmured, "if you could tell me what the *S* in your pen name stands for?"

Liz took a step back, but the wall was behind her and she was stuck. "I don't know what you mean."

"L. S. Franklin isn't you?" I pretended surprise. "The cele-brated blogger of *Eventing Chicks*, always dishing the dirt from the hot equestrian scene in O-town?"

Her cheeks were burning now, but she kept her gaze lowered, refusing to look at me. "I don't know what you're talking about," she insisted. "Leave me alone."

"No, *you* need to leave *me* alone!" I spat, frustration taking over. "Who the hell do you think you are, writing all that about me? Taking pictures of me? No—" I jumped in front of her as she tried to step around me. "No, you stay here and explain your-self—"

"What the hell is this?" Grace came around the corner with Liz's expensively dressed mother. "Jules, what are you doing?"

"How dare you shout at my daughter," Liz's mother hissed. "Get out of here, or I swear to God I will have you arrested."

I stepped back and Liz rightly took the move for surrender. She jumped over to her mother and glowered at me from beneath her expensive helmet. "I think your groom has an anger problem," she said. Her blush had faded; with her mother on the scene and Grace looking like a thunderstorm about to explode, Liz was fully in control of the situation.

Grace frowned at me. "Well? What's happening here?"

A few more students crowded around; my raised voice had at-tracted a sizable peanut gallery and everyone who had shown up for afternoon lessons needed to know what the excitement was all about. I looked at them, well-dressed teens and women, their boots more expensive than half the horses in my barn, and I knew I wasn't going to get a jury of my own peers. Still, I tried. "Liz has been writing for a blog about me. She's been slandering me online."

Liz's mother laughed, a big showy laugh to let everyone know how ridiculous I was. "Liz? Write a blog? When would she have the time for that? Between drama society and riding and tennis? What, does she fit you in when she's waiting for the bus in the morning? Accusing a fifteen-year-old . . . really, I don't know who you think you are, but . . ." She turned to Grace as if she couldn't see the point in talking to me any longer. "You're going to have to do something about this one. We spend a lot of money for Liz to ride here."

"It was a mistake, I'm sure," Grace said gruffly. "I'll talk to her in private."

Liz peered at me through her lashes. "I think you should fire her. She's crazy."

"That's a little dramatic," Grace said briskly. "She stepped in front of you, she didn't push you down and try to knife you."

Liz's smile faded, and so did her mother's. "Grace, I have to insist that you do something."

"And I will, in private. I think we're done here. Liz, help Tom untack that horse. You need to get your hands dirty once in a while. You won't always have a groom." Grace turned on her heel and marched down the aisle. She didn't like being told what to do by her clients, I realized. She didn't like it any better than I did; she was just better at hiding it. I felt a sudden surge of appreciation for Grace.

"You're going to get fired," Liz whispered to me. "And Pete's going to dump you for Amy Rodan. You're going to be living in your horse trailer in six months, wait and see."

I spun back around. Liz was laughing, her friends were laughing, even her awful mother was laughing.

"You knew," I told the woman. "You know what your daughter gets up to."

She shook her head at me, impossible, humidity-defying curls flopping around her cheeks. "I don't know and I don't care. You're here to muck stalls and groom horses, not accuse my daughter of writing *blogs*. Who cares what she writes? All any of you do is play around in the barn, smelling like shit, and you think someone's going to take you seriously? This isn't the real world, honey, and you shouldn't take it so seriously. Do your job, keep your mouth shut, and move along."

I bit my lip. I bit my tongue. I tried so hard to keep quiet.

"Go and untack that horse. I don't like that Tom, and Liz doesn't have time. She has a tennis lesson to get to. I tell you, Grace is crazy if she thinks we have time to stand around here doing the staff's work—"

Then I lost it.

# 30

"UNTACK YOUR OWN goddamn horse."

Liz's mother gasped. Liz gasped. Everyone else in the barn gasped. The horses probably gasped.

I didn't care. At that moment, nothing mattered but getting away from them. I threw up my arms and waved them in a circle, vaguely indicating everyone in the barn aisle, in the equestrian center, in the tri-county area. "I won't take your shit for one more second. I have had enough of all of you, and I am going *home*!"

The crowd parted and let me stalk down the aisle, my arms still spread out like I was having my big evangelist moment. My head was swimming and my heart was racing and I knew I was right. These petty rich people with their petty rich-people problems and their fancy horses they couldn't ride and *wouldn't* take care of . . . and

278 | Natalie Keller Reinert

Grace! Grace was the worst of all of them, cosseting and aiding and abetting, petting and soothing, giving them every little thing their spoiled hearts desired, walking away rather than defending me, and then standing in the center of the arena and telling me I didn't work hard enough, telling me I didn't give enough to my horses, telling me I was bound to fail so long as I stayed on my current track, which, the last time I checked, was exactly the same as her track—to ride the best horses I could, to the best of their ability, to win ribbons, to win clients, to win a steady paycheck and a stable life.

So I'd had a rough year. So I'd lost most of my business. So I was walking away from a sponsorship—those people didn't want me, those people didn't need me, those people weren't going to be good to me. They were going to go on treating me just the same way Grace had, the girl they had to take on because someone else wanted them to, in order to get the rider they really wanted. They wanted Pete? They could have Pete. I wasn't going to stand in his way. He clearly wanted them too, or he wouldn't have signed off on this plan, wouldn't have insisted I agree to their ridiculous demands. I'd make my own luck. I'd gotten this far on my own.

There was a buzz of conversation behind me as I neared the end of the aisle, blinking into the evening's golden sunlight. Let them gossip, I thought, waggling my fingers at Dynamo's pricked ears as I walked past his stall. Let them chatter—and I blew a kiss to Mickey, who paused mid-chew to watch me go. Tonight, when they were all gone, when I didn't have an audience, I'd clear out, pull my tack and my suitcase and my horses and we'd go home.

There was a creaking on the steps behind me, and I turned around on the landing. Anna was running up the steps, her face white, her big eyes round. *Oh, Anna,* I thought.

"What?" I snapped.

"Don't do this," she gasped, clinging to the swaying railing.

*These stairs are really going to go sooner rather than later,* I thought. *Even the nicest barn is really crumbling once you get out of the customer areas.* "I already did it. Having a meltdown in front of clients is considered self-termination. I think Grace could legally run me off the farm with a shotgun now."

"How can you laugh?" Anna asked.

I didn't really know. Everything just seemed really funny right now. "What else should I do? I'm throwing a massive sponsorship back in a company CEO's face. That's pretty hilarious."

"This was going to be huge for your business," Anna reminded me. "Look, I know Liz did it . . . I've seen what she wrote about you, and I know it must feel awful to get laughed at like that. But people will forget! If you finish this and get the sponsorship, you can ride all winter like the big shot you want to be, and this summer will just disappear. You already said this was the answer to all your problems. That's why you were here. How can you let some teenager chase you out now?"

*Some teenager.* It was always mean girls, wasn't it? As far as I thought I'd come from Laurie's, this entire summer had just put me right back in that place. The butt of the joke, the poor groom. I could outride everyone here and they'd always find a way to strike back.

It was exactly what I'd been afraid of since the beginning.

"I guess I was wrong," I said. The laugher had faded and I felt hollow now, like all my emotions had fled. "This wasn't what I needed. It was the opposite, actually."

"You need the money," Anna said.

"If I get the money, I go away, right?"

She didn't waver. "Yes."

"Why do you want to be Grace's right hand so bad?" I asked. "You want me gone so I can't take Grace from you, but I don't want Grace or her horrible clients. I don't get why you love it so much, taking their bullshit day after day. They're not worth your time."

"I feel bad for them."

"Anna, you feel bad for everyone." I turned my back on her and headed for my apartment door. "You need to start thinking about yourself for once."

"I have what I need," Anna said. "I live here. I have horses to ride. I love my life. They have to drive here, when they have time, after working all day in cubicles. Wouldn't you be miserable too? Wouldn't you just have to yell at someone, anyone, to make yourself feel the tiniest bit better about how they spend their days, typing on a computer and looking at the same four walls? Think about that. How awful."

I had my hand on the screen door handle, but Anna's words got to me. Imagine that, sitting at a desk chair all day and doing other people's work for them, making other people money, while waiting all day for the half an hour you'd have time to ride your horse on the way home from work. We always joked about having real jobs, jobs with desks and chairs and air-conditioning, jobs where you actually had to take a shower before you came in or people would notice you were covered in dirt and hay and horse slobber—what a riot that would be, right?

But those people downstairs really lived like that.

"You might be right," I said reluctantly.

"So you can't be mad at them all the time," Anna went on. "Liz, there's no excuse for her. But the rest of them, the older ones . . . you have to humor them a little bit. That's what I do. And once they've ridden, and spent some time with their horse, they're usually much nicer. Then you can talk to them about their ride, ask them what they're having trouble with, and remember that the next time you school their horse. It's a good system. The horse gets better, they have a good time, everyone wins. Most of the time. Look at this place. Grace built this place on that system."

"Well, I'm really happy it works for you guys," I conceded. "But I'm going home."

"You're really leaving?"

"I'm really leaving." I opened my screen door and stepped into the apartment. "See you someday."


Of course, the first order of business was to call Pete and let him know I'd be driving home late tonight. The great experiment was over, the wonderful business opportunity was abandoned, I had failed to meet the promise I'd made him, but in all fairness, the promise had been made under coercion, and I didn't exactly work well under other people's regimes. It was kind of my calling card, right?

Well, if it was all over, I could live in the guesthouse with Becky and Lacey.

I looked at my phone for a long while and then decided there was no point making any calls when it wasn't one hundred percent charged—supposing we had to have a long conversation about what a wonderful decision I was making and how this would open up great new opportunities and in fact it was probably best if I just got going right now, so why was I waiting until tonight?

I laughed at myself; even I wasn't foolish enough to believe any of that. Pete was going to be furious. There was no telling what he might say or do when I told him I'd given up. I'd promised him I would stay. I'd promised him I would make it work.

I'd promised him and I had failed him.

The four thousand miles between us wasn't enough anymore. I needed to be on another planet, in another galaxy, in a whole new dimension, anywhere to avoid telling Pete what I'd decided, and to hear his reply.

So I plugged the phone into the wall and sat on the sagging brown couch for a while, gazing across the room at the cabinets where my handful of dishes were housed and wondering if I should bother packing any of them, or just leave them for the next poor bastard.

The sky grew dark outside and the apartment dimmed. A rumble of thunder split the quiet, and a few horses whinnied and kicked downstairs. Then the rain started up, roaring on the metal roof just a few feet above my head. I leaned my head down on the arm of the couch and closed my eyes. I'd just wait out the rain, and then I'd call Pete. I would definitely call Pete. I wouldn't do anything without talking to Pete.

When I woke up the room was nearly dark, with only the light filtering in from the barn window to pick out the furniture, sending shadows across the walls. I hopped up and looked out the window. The horses were fed, the ones who went out for the night were gone, and the aisle was swept. Evening chores were done, evening lessons were finished. It must be past eight o'clock.

"This is what happens when you plan a major life decision right before evening feeding," I told myself. But it was good timing, I supposed. Rule number one of leaving a barn job: leave as close to the dead of night as possible. No one wants to have to talk to a former boarder or employer on the way out.

I picked up my phone on the way out the door—no new calls, 8:23 P.M. Far too late to call England. I'd call Pete tomorrow. Or better, I would never tell him, I would just pretend it all ended early, and I would just act very surprised when Rockwell didn't sign me. Even better, I wouldn't go back at all, would never face Pete, would leave the country. I would disappear into the jungles of South America, just me and my horses, and never be heard from again.

"What's done is done," I repeated to myself, a helpless little mantra. Why was I second-guessing myself now? I'd painted myself into a perfect corner—I *had* to go home.

Alert horses watched me walk by with pricked ears and trembling nostrils, poised to whinny if there should be any signs of treats or grain, wondering if I'd come down so soon before night-check for some sort of delightful horse party. Maybe there would be extra hay! A few murmured encouraging sounds to me, but I didn't turn and look at any of them.

Until I passed the corner stall by the center aisle, where Ivor lived. Then the silence made me turn and look. Ivor, being a chatty stallion, always had something to say.

The stall behind the bars appeared empty. No gray horse looking at me, dark eyes glittering behind a waterfall of white forelock. "Ivor?" I asked, walking over and peering down into the stall.

Ivor, stretched across his trampled shavings with his lip pulled up and his teeth clenched, made a low rumble in his chest that was almost a human groan.

I took in the scene in a heartbeat: no manure in the stall, untouched hay, brimful water bucket, shavings tossed against the wall from pacing. "Oh buddy boy, you poor thing, don't you dare colic and die—" I was grabbing his halter from the hook and slamming open the stall door as fast as the words could leave my mouth. Ivor lifted his head to look at me, then let it drop again, his upper lip wobbling against the bedding. His pale coat was studded with dark patches of sweat.

"Poor boy, poor boy, come on, lift your head, lift your stupid giant heavy fucking head—" I urged him, struggling to get the halter on him. "Now get up, get up, come on, you have to get up now . . ."

I chirruped and clucked encouragingly, and Ivor obligingly

sat upright, but decided that was quite enough effort and stopped short of actually rising. I swung the leather lead shank at his hindquarters and he eyeballed me as if to ask if I was really going to be that much of a bitch.

"I am if you don't get up," I told him firmly. "You know the answer to colic is walking. Don't try me. You're a smart horse. Now up . . . up . . . let's go!" I swung the shank again, tickling his flanks, and with a reluctant shake of his head, Ivor put out first his right foreleg, and then his left, and then finally pushed off from the ground. He stood, trembling with anxiety and unhappiness, in the center of his chaotic stall, shavings dangling from the sweaty patches on his coat.

"Good boy, good boy!" I patted him and gave him an encouraging rub on the forelock. "We've got this. Let's go take a walk and see how you do." In my head, I was going through the steps I was about to take: walk him for a few laps around the indoor, gauge his level of discomfort, bring him back in to call the vet if he didn't loosen up and drop a little manure in what . . . say . . . ten minutes? Ten minutes, I decided. "Let's go do some rounds of the ring and then we'll see," I told him.

Round and round and round we go, the dance of the colicking horse and the subtly-trying-not-to-freak-out groom. It wasn't a dance I needed any refreshers on, despite a long colic-free period back at the farm in Ocala. I fed a lot of hay and had a lot of turnout and maybe some good luck (you didn't hear that from me)—what could I say? I just hadn't had any colics. Every other problem under the sun, but no colics.

Nothing knocks out a horse like colic, though. They can't handle a bellyache, and really just about anything can cause one. What had Ivor's tummy in a tangle? Maybe someone looked at him wrong earlier. Maybe his hay had some mold in it and he plowed through it anyway, because there wasn't any grass in his paddock to distract him. (I really was lucky to have those green pastures back home, wasn't I? Down here in Orlando, the sand just didn't have the energy to yield up grass fast enough to please all these hungry mouths.) Maybe the barometric pressure dropped abnormally quickly during the storm earlier, which gave him a headache, and the pain in his skull caused his gut to slow down, and wham, impaction colic. Who knew? Ivor wasn't telling.

What I did know was to take him for a walk and see if I could get things moving. Ivor seemed to know the drill, too. We went out into the dark covered arena, dimly lit by the couple of barn lights left on as night-lights, and he paced agreeably enough by my side, occasionally swinging his head around to take bad-tempered nips at his flanks.

"You can't bite a colic," I told him, but stallions don't like to be told they can't bite anything. He shook his head, his snowy forelock catching the light and sparkling. Such a fancy unicorn of a horse. Grace was hoping to breed him to a few mares next spring; I'd heard her chatting with a few of the boarders, trying to catch them up in baby fever. She was trying to grow a whole new segment of her business. There was no doubt Grace was a canny businesswoman, I had to give her that much.

"Walk on, buddy, let's go," I said to Ivor as we passed the in-gate for the first time. He jigged toward the barn, ready to head back to his stall already. It was safe there, he was thinking, and whatever was biting him from the inside wouldn't be able to follow. He would have forgotten that he'd been lying in his shavings a few minutes ago, hurting there as well. "Come on, a few times around to see if we can get a poo out of you. Don't you want to take a nice dump? Wouldn't that feel lovely?"

Ivor walked on, although he did not look as enthused about pooping as I would have liked.

We were on our second circuit of the ring when my phone buzzed. I pulled it out, saw the caller was Pete, and answered breathlessly. I burst out with my news first, not waiting to wonder why he was calling in the middle of his night. "Pete, would you believe I'm out in the riding ring walking Grace's stupid stallion?"

"The big beautiful gray you've been riding? Is he sick?" Pete saw no problem with skipping hellos and going straight to horse talk. That was one of the best things about Pete. Remember when I said I was never going to date a horse trainer? I was so wrong.

"Yes, that one. Well, I come down into the barn about ten minutes ago and wouldn't you know, he's down and he's been rolling, and he didn't touch his dinner . . ."

"Shouldn't you have pulled him out when he didn't finish his dinner? It's hours past feeding time."

"Well, I didn't feed tonight, so I didn't check to see if he hadn't finished—"

"Why didn't you feed? Weren't you going back to work tonight? Is everything okay?"

Ivor spooked elaborately at the shadow of a fire extinguisher mounted on one of the arena's support pillars. "Stop that!" I snapped. "He must be feeling better," I told Pete, changing the subject hastily. "He's spooking at stupid crap he sees every day."

Pete sighed. "Jules? How'd you get out of work tonight? Or do I not want to know?"

I looked at Ivor, admiring the darkness of his eyes, the smoothness of his broad stallion's jowls. Horses made better boyfriends, they never asked inconvenient questions. "I may have quit," I admitted finally. "Things were said."

"Things like?"

"Things like that I was quitting."

"Well, you can't. So you need to go . . . apologize or something, make her take you back . . ." Pete sounded panicky.

Panic took me aback. I'd expected another raging explosion. I didn't quite know how to respond to the obvious note of fear in Pete's voice. "Listen, it's fine. I'm not going to stay. I'll do without the sponsorship. You take yours, it's fine. I'll make up the slack on my own. I can—"

"Jules. Jules. Jules." Pete's voice was flat, expressionless, and the emptiness of his tone made me shut up immediately. Next to me, Ivor sighed, an eloquent sound of relaxation that normally would have made me jump for joy; we were nearly there, a manure pile was imminent, and then I could put him back to bed with some hay and leave him alone for a little while, enough time to get my trailer hitched up and pulled around to the barn, anyway. Except for Pete—"You cannot quit this, Jules. You promised. You promised me you'd do this."

"I tried, Pete," I protested—didn't he know how hard I had tried? "You weren't here—one of her students is the one writing about me online, and they were treating me like their servant . . . look, maybe I learned some things here. But I won't be spoken to like that. I'll fix things at home—"

"You finish this, Jules," Pete said, his voice dull and defeated. "You made me a promise. Don't you understand that things weren't working? Things were about to fall apart? You couldn't hold a single client, you couldn't make enough money to keep afloat, and I was running out of ways to keep the place going. I still am. We need this money. And more than that, I need to know you're serious. I don't think you are anymore."

"Serious?"

"About us."

288 | Natalie Keller Reinert

I couldn't breathe. I couldn't speak. I just kept walking, putting my boots down into the hoof-marked clay, and beside me poor gallant Ivor did the same, my four-legged white shadow.

Pete let the air between us hang silently for a few minutes, and then, as if he could not bear it, he spoke again. "I love you, Jules," he said softly. "But if you're not willing to do whatever it takes to keep the farm going, I can't pick up the slack for you anymore. You made me a promise. Keep it. Finish this. Then you can come home . . . not before."

He hung up.

I grasped the phone between white fingers for a few minutes more, wondering when he'd call back, but of course he didn't. Pete was the adult in our relationship, always doing the hard things I wasn't willing to face.

I looked at Ivor, plodding beside me with a lowered head, looking tired and bored and miserable. "I only like horses, Ivor," I told him. "I only like horses and Pete. Do I really have to deal with other humans in order to keep them both in my life?"

Ivor fluttered his nostrils in response. His ears waggled at half-mast. "You certainly look more relaxed now," I observed. "But why won't you give me a nice poop?"

"I know a trick," a voice called across the arena. "Are you ready to learn something from me?"

Grace lowered the back door of the horse trailer, letting the ramp touch the asphalt of the parking lot with a gentle bang. There were a few nervous whinnies from the barn in the distance; it didn't take much to alert a horse with a little show experience that a trailer was being opened. Ivor walked around me in a fast, nervous circle, biting at the chain on his lead shank.

"So now what do I do?" I asked, letting the leather slide through my fingers until he came back to a quivering halt next to me.

"Just load him up," Grace said. "Trust me. On easy colics, this always works."

"Come on, Ivor," I told the stallion, and started walking with purpose toward the dark trailer. He started to hang back, and I had a feeling we were doing something wrong, skipping a step— Grace really should have hooked up the trailer and turned on the truck, so the interior lights would come on—but then she stepped behind him and gave a chirrup, clapping her hands, startling the big horse into a jog. We hit the ramp at a smart pace, too fast for him to balk and change his mind, and then we were in the shadowy trailer, his hooves banging against the rubber mats and sending echoes through the hollow air beneath.

"Okay," I said. "We're in." Ivor shoved against me and I stuck my thumb in his chest to get some personal space. "Now what?"

"Wait a sec," Grace said, positioning herself at the rear of the trailer. "If nothing happens, I'll push the divider closed, so just be ready—ah!"

"What?" I asked, but there was no need; my ears and nose told me what was going on. There was a wet sound, and a whiff of half-digested grass. "Holy shit."

"Exactly," Grace joked, sounding pretty pleased with herself.

We stood in the darkness and let Ivor nose at the hay net hanging in the trailer. He plucked a few strands and held them in his mouth, considering whether he felt well enough to eat. The silence between us was a dark, looming monster; I felt my hands shaking and clenched my fists. I had to fix things, or it was all over. I'd have lost Pete, and if I lost Pete—oh sweet Jesus if I lost Pete what was left for me? The enormity of it had hit me at last, and I was afraid.

"I'm sorry," I said after a while, because I didn't know what else to say. And then, deciding the truth was all I could give her: "I was wrong."

Grace shifted her weight; I heard the ramp creak gently beneath her light feet. "About what?" she prodded.

*Thanks for making this easy for me.* "Everything," I said. "God, everything. Riding. Attitude. Screaming at your boarder. I have problems, Grace, people keep telling me I have problems, I'm too proud, I'm too arrogant, I don't listen, I'm awful, and—"

"Stop," Grace said.

"No, it's true, I—"

"I know it's true, but just stop doing it. Just stop. Fix it."

"It's not that simple."

"If you want something badly enough, it's that simple. What do you want?"

I wanted horses. I wanted to ride. I wanted Pete.

I wanted Pete.

She waited a moment and then prodded at me. "Do you want fame, fortune, Olympic medals? That's what you wanted when you came here. Do you still?"

I opened my mouth to say *Yes, yes of course* that was what I wanted. That was all I had ever wanted.

The words wouldn't come.

"I want to go home," I whispered. "I want to go home and be with Pete. I want things to be like they were."

"Like they were?" Grace sounded surprised.

"Better," I amended. "I want it to be better. *I* want to be better."

"Well," Grace said lightly, "what are you going to do about it?"

"Stay here, and finish what I started, if you'll let me." I waited, and with every second of silence, my heart crept higher into my throat, choking me.

"Stay then," Grace agreed. "I think you mean it this time."

# 31

THIS WAS A stupid way to live if you wanted to show people up.

After the night with Grace and Ivor, waiting for a horse to poop so he wouldn't die, something seemed to click into place. Sandy-eyed and dragging around the barn, feeling the lack of sleep even harder as the morning humidity leached the energy from my muscles, I made the rounds of the stalls, checking water buckets. Freshening the horses' waters was one of those mindless tasks that gave a person a lot of room to think, and I had a lot of thoughts to work through.

Starting with this: I'd been pushing myself, and horses, for all the wrong reasons. And at some point, the act of caring for horses had become more satisfying than riding. Maybe it wouldn't always feel that way—I remembered talking with Anna in the wash rack, weeks ago, and the way she'd paused, unable to answer me when I asked her if she preferred riding or taking care of horses. Maybe when I was back home at Briar Hill, or even back on the cross-country course, I'd feel more fulfilled by riding again.

But for the moment, I was glad Ivor was alive, glad I had a part in keeping these horses well and happy, and completely annoyed at myself for thinking that I was somehow proving something to the girls of my childhood by being a professional horsewoman.

This wasn't what those girls had been angling for. They'd never wanted to spend their days dealing with manure and filthy water buckets and medicating thrushy hooves and cleaning geldings' sheaths. They wanted their horses brought to them clean and scrubbed, but as for me , , , now that I admitted it to myself, I could see it was true: I *wanted* to do the cleaning and the scrubbing. I couldn't live with a barn that had a dirty bucket in it. I had to clean that bucket, immediately.

And things weren't going to change, even after this summer, to the point where I was going to be some sort of barn goddess who had barn underlings to do all the hard work. Even with Lacey to help out, I wasn't exactly shielded from barn chores. There would always be chores and it was really unlikely I'd ever make enough money to command an army of grooms to do it all for me.

I didn't even want that. It was someone else's ideal. It was *their* ideal.

The girls from that barn were gone, driving cars their parents bought them, visiting their horses at boarding stables, living a life I would never have wanted.

None of it had really mattered, I realized, and it was as if the summer air lightened and the sunshine filtering through the roof panels grew brighter.

The way I lived my life had to change. The way I saw the world had to change. All those old memories, all the rivalries and jealousies and real and imagined insults? I had to shove them aside. I couldn't be in this game with some sort of living-well-is-the-best-revenge philosophy anymore. It just didn't fit.

"I need better reasons," I whispered, watching the water pool into the bucket. "For everything."

That's all it took? He just needed to go into a trailer and wham, he pooped and was fine?" Lacey sounded exhausted—she always seemed to be exhausted these days—but Grace's amazing colic fix put life back into her voice.

"Well, we gave him a bran mash and walked him a couple more times that night, but yeah, in the end, he was fine. He just needed that first push to get his system moving again. She's hacking him out right now." I peeked out the window of the stall I was cleaning, to see Grace walking Ivor on a long rein in the outdoor dressage ring. "She says by tonight he'll be good as new."

"It's actually genius," Lacey said, bemused. "What horse doesn't poop the minute he gets in a trailer?"

"Exactly. We're going to use this one in the future. Although hopefully we won't get any colicky horses this winter. We'll have enough to do without testing out colic cures, right? All the events coming up, and I'll probably have to do some extra appearances or photo shoots for Rockwell once the sponsorship comes through— it's going to be busy!" The idea of being run off my feet sounded positively delightful. Busy meant successful.

Lacey was quiet. Over the phone, though, I could hear her breathing. A suspicion hit me and my stomach turned over. "Lacey? What's up?"

"Jules, I feel terrible," she whispered. "Only . . . this winter . . ."

Just like that, I knew. I felt the breath rush out of my lungs, leaving me gasping for air.

*Don't say it, don't say it, don't say it . . .*

"I'm going back to Pennsylvania after you come home."

By now I'd stopped pretending I was mucking a stall. I leaned against the wall boards, the reek of old molasses and mildew in my nostrils, head spinning. Margaret passed by outside, saw me conspicuously not-working, and gave me a hard, schoolmarmish look. I ignored her. My entire world was falling apart; I did not have time for her bitter glares. "Going back?" I managed to gasp after a moment. "Why?"

"I'm going to finish school." I could hear the tears she was biting back. Tears for me, the one left behind. "For equestrian studies. I'm sorry—I know you were going to keep me as barn manager, but I still wouldn't be able to afford to get a degree unless I move back home, and the local college has a barn management program now—my parents can help—and I am so run-down from this summer, and—God, Jules, please don't cry—"

Too late, I was crying, big snotty awful gasping sobs taking over my entire body, and then Lacey was crying too, and then I guess she dropped the phone, or maybe I dropped mine, either way we weren't talking anymore, just grieving for the end of everything, after all we'd been through. All that pain hadn't been enough. This summer was taking everything I loved from me, I thought hopelessly. I thought it had been bad last summer when the hurricane took the farm. Last year I lost almost everything I owned, but I kept Lacey and gained Pete. This year, it felt like if I wasn't careful, I was going to lose them both.

Well, I was losing one of them for sure.

Anna came slipping into the stall, her big round eyes soft with sympathy, and wrapped her sweaty arms around me before I could bat her away. Then, to my surprise, I didn't want to push her off. I just wanted someone to lean on.

I came to a few minutes later. Anna stepped back and blinked at me. "Do you want to talk about it?" she asked, clearly thinking someone had died. She picked up the phone at my feet and brushed off the shavings clinging to it before handing it back to me.

"My barn manager is quitting," I said, letting the words sound impersonal and businesslike. Then I choked and hiccupped, another sob. "My best friend is leaving," I admitted, nearly breaking down into tears again. I sniffled like a lost child. "When I go home, nothing will be the same. It's all ruined."

It's all *ruined*—that toddler reaction, the favorite toy lost. Lacey gone and Pete saying angry, undeniable things and Grace telling me I would never amount to the rider I wanted to be unless I changed everything about the way I rode and trained . . . I'd come here for a couple months thinking only of going home, but while I was away, home as I knew it was busily changing forever.

"I'm so sorry," Anna was saying, putting her hand on my arm, but this time I felt the sweat and the dirt between her palm and my forearm, and it was too much. I took a step back and picked up the pitchfork where I had leaned it against the wall, a lifetime ago.

"Thank you," I said. "I mean it. I just . . . I better get back to work, if I ever want to get done." *If I ever want to be done here, if I ever want this summer to end, if I ever want to just get back to the farm before anything else can change, go wrong, be ruined forever.*

Grace took me back to her house for coffee after the morning rides were done. She poured inky coffee into mugs won as horse show prizes, jumping horses decorating their sides, and sliced up a grocery-store pound cake with some cold strawberries.

"We'll call it afternoon tea," she said, setting the plates down on the homely little dining table. "The best decisions are made over a hot drink and some cake."

My generation tended to make decisions over a few beers and a plate of nachos, but who was to say we were doing things right? I took a bite of pound cake and found it was exactly what my diet was missing: butter, sugar, and eggs. "I'm ready to make some seriously good decisions," I declared.

Grace chuckled. "Good. Because remember when I told you to watch out or you'd make that third strike?"

I choked on my bite of cake. "Mm-hmm," I managed.

"Well, you got lucky with Ivor," she went on. "I hate to say it, but if he hadn't colicked and you hadn't found him, you'd be driving home today. Which I think was your plan anyway?"

I blushed and put down my fork. "I overreacted . . ."

"You bet you did. You know, they wanted you to learn how to deal with people while you were here, too. And I thought you were doing a pretty good job. I didn't know what the big deal was. Until yesterday."

"It was the blog," I said helplessly. "The things they said about me—"

"Were awful and rude, I know. And I'm embarrassed I have people like that in my barn. I thought better of them. Not a lot better, I know Stacy is a piece of work and you wouldn't even have believed Colleen, Maddy's mom? She tried to run this place out of business to save her own ass. She tried to burn the place down."

"No way—" I perked up. Now, *this* was a story I wanted to hear.

"Oh yeah. Not getting into it today, some other time. But anyway, Maddy's still here, because I figure Colleen's claws have been pulled and her money's still green if her kid wants to ride. Liz, too. Bad kid, good money. I don't just give people the boot. I figure out how to work with what I've got. The same with you. You're blushing pretty red right now, so I know you won't be pulling some stunt like that again. What would have happened if I sent you home, or if you went running home in the middle of the night?"

I shook my head. "Nothing good." I didn't even want to think about it. I remembered what Pete had said to me last night. The very thought of his words, and the tone they'd been delivered in, gave me a sick feeling in my gut. *You finish this, Jules. You made me a promise.* The cake on the plate before me suddenly looked a lot less enticing. I pushed it away.

Grace raised her eyebrows. She took a bite of her own cake and drummed her fingernails on the scarred wood of the table, as if she was buying time. I wondered what she was afraid to say, and picked up my coffee mug, looking for comfort in the strong black roast.

But Grace said nothing.

"My working student is leaving," I admitted. "My barn manager. She's going back up north after I come home."

"That's sad," Grace said. "Will you get a new one?"

I shook my head no. "No need. Not enough horses to keep one busy."

"Yet."

"Yet," I echoed. "When I have a barn full of horses, that'll be a different story." I straightened up, casting about for the rags of my old pride. I'd deleted the *Eventing Chicks* website from my phone's search history, blocked their accounts from my social media. I knew Liz would have choice words to say about me after last night, although I figured she wouldn't want to admit she'd been unmasked in the barn. Either way, I was putting it behind me. I was a rider. That was all. From this point forward, people would see me riding, or they wouldn't see me at all. "I have to make a new start."

"Finish this," Grace suggested. "Finish this, see it through, get their money, and see what happens next. Maybe you don't want a barn full of horses. Maybe you'll decide you only want a couple, but they'll be the right ones."

"Don't I need a barnful if I'm going to make any money?"

"What have I been telling you all summer?" Grace looked annoyed. "Do something different, change it up, stop playing by the same rules as all the other barns in town. It's not enough to be a good rider and a good trainer. You have to do something no one else does."

"What could that be?" We were riding in a sport with thousand-year-old traditions and expectations. I wasn't sure thinking outside the box was really appropriate or cost effective.

"If you don't figure it out between now and the end of summer, I'll help you decide," Grace promised. "Until then, keep your mouth shut and think about nothing but dressage."

So this was going to be the end of the movie: for the next three weeks, I would ignore the internet, ignore the boarders, ignore everyone and everything in favor of getting this dressage test as perfect as possible, getting the sponsorship, and going home. Along the way, I hoped, the solution to Grace's challenge would come to me. I would figure out what made me unique. I would find a way to distinguish myself from a sea of riders who all wanted what I wanted.

I rode Mickey and Dynamo in late-morning lessons, and the school horses and novices right through the hot middle of the day, while the skies rumbled around me and the clouds pretended they were going to let loose at any minute. August had come in a swirl of humid sea breezes and sullen yellow-cast skies, the storms hovering off to the north and the south and the east and the west while

the farm sat and baked, desperate for the relief of rain. The rain-
drops kept waiting until after dark to fall, when it was too late to
give us any respite from the heat, and I often did night-check with
thunder roaring overhead.

A boarder's horse was sold to a farm in Virginia and a paddock
came available, so I'd started turning my horses out overnight.
They loved the extra turnout time, but standing in the tropical
deluge with water streaming down their necks and backs meant
rain rot across their hindquarters, awful scabs that I had to pick at
and rub with a variety of topicals, each more noxious than the last,
none of which did a single thing to check the fungus, or bacteria,
or whatever the hell it was, in its spread across their tender skin.

I didn't like leaving them out all night in such weather, but the
alternative was to continue turning them out for two hours each
morning, and I thought they were getting stiff and rebellious with
such rigorous arena work and so little turnout time. Mickey had
been particularly obnoxious all month, and when I went into his
paddock in the early mornings, hoping to connect with him on
some deep spiritual level, he mostly reacted by farting and kicking
and bucking, as if he thought I'd come down to play with him,
horse-style. After a few close calls ducking his flying hooves, I'd
end up throwing a clod of wet sand at him to remind him about
Mom's Personal Space, and then he'd go sulk in a corner until I left
to get chores started. Grace laughed and said the hard work was
giving him big muscles and a big head. "You two are more alike
than you think," she chortled.

Luckily, our time in the arena was more and more productive.
My dressage was getting better—at least, my basics. I was still
struggling to get Dynamo into a true collected trot, but his walk-
canter transitions were becoming things of beauty, as he sprang
into motion like a gazelle, and his topline seemed to have lifted a

full inch. His back had changed shape, and the old German-tank saddle no longer fit him. "At least I never actually wanted children," I joked to Anna, sliding the hated saddle back into a shadowy corner of the school tack room. "Because that thing probably did some permanent damage."

I was still hoping for my Rockwell dressage saddle to arrive, although I knew it could be months before a custom saddle was finished—especially a free custom saddle to be presented to a brand ambassador who hadn't yet fulfilled her obligations to the brand. In the meantime, though, returning to my regular saddle filled me with pleasure, if only because it had some actual padding left in the seat.

I lost myself in the rhythm of working trots and medium canters, in ten-meter circles and shoulders-in, because I didn't want to think about the fall. I had no idea what going home would feel like, but I was afraid it would be more painful than triumphant. In the meantime, all I could do was ride.

At least the novice horses I'd been assigned had benefited from our hours together. A subtle shift in position, a little leg and a slight half halt, and Mirage bounded into a canter, her nose coming slightly ahead of the vertical, but, all in all, an accomplished, admirably uphill transition. I flicked a drop of sweat from my eyebrow and rested a bare hand on her hot neck, a grateful caress, a good-girl pat. She snorted with every stride, shoving her breath through her wide nostrils as each forehoof hit the ground—the satisfying sound of a horse enjoying her job.

I looked between her ears and sank into her movement and wondered what would happen if I didn't meet Rockwell's standard in my dressage test. It would change things, I thought. Pete would look at the time I'd wasted fighting, when I could have been learning and growing, and he'd see it as a promise broken.

He wouldn't kick me off the property, but he could still shove me out of his life. Lacey's bedroom was coming open; I could live in the guesthouse, with Becky. Pete would run his barn, I would run mine. I would be a tenant. I would wake up alone, breakfast alone, walk down to the barn alone, do the chores alone. Things might not be so bad, I reflected. I would have the horses. As long as I had the horses, couldn't I face anything?

I saw my empty mornings and my silent days and my lonesome nights stretching ahead of me, looking out the guesthouse window at the light in the kitchen, Pete sitting with his head bowed over the table, flipping through a dressage book, shutting me out because I hadn't lived up to his vision of me, preferring to live without me at all, if this was all I was, a person of endless jealousies and misplaced pride.

I couldn't, I couldn't, I couldn't . . .

I sat deep in the saddle and huffed my breath out—*hah!*—and Mirage skidded to a halt, remembering at the last moment to draw her hindquarters beneath her and pick up her downhill little nose. "Good girl," I told her warmly, and gave her a loose rein, letting her stretch her weary neck out, slapping the white foam from the sweaty reins.

I could change.

There would be only a few horses left in the barn. I could concentrate on them, concentrate *hard,* maybe use all that empty time to get to know them better, the way Grace wanted me to. There was a round pen up by Pete's barn I could hack them over to, play around a little with free-lunging, see if I could get them to come and talk to me the way Dynamo liked to. We'd do more dressage, now that I was starting to come around to the zen of it all—the way I could disappear into my horse's motion, shutting out the distractions of reality. When I was jumping, the outside world was my primary concern, whether it was finding the line to the next jump, or matching my horse's stride to the shape of the fence we were galloping toward. In dressage, as long as I didn't actually ride my horse right through the arena fencing, I didn't have to worry much about any obstacles but the ones in my own mind.

I looked through Mirage's waggling ears and smiled. That was the first freeing thought I'd had in a very long time.

I could change. I had already changed, but there was more to it than recognizing my motivation had been in the wrong place. I had to—I hated this—learn to be a little humble. I didn't think I could be a lot humble, if that was a thing. But I could occasionally listen to someone else for a change. I had learned to listen to Grace. I could learn to listen to Pete. I could admit I was less than perfect. It would grate at first, but I'd get over it.

I had to, or I'd be sitting alone before very long, gazing out the window at the life I'd once had, wondering why I'd thrown it all away.

# 32

WEKIVA HORSEMEN'S PARK had red-clay arenas, like the ones at Seabreeze, and black-board fences, like the ones back home at Briar Hill. It was a pleasing blend of the two farms. An announcer's tower stood above the hunter ring, where brown and green fences rose up from the puddles. A white tent next to it housed a card table where a prune-faced woman in a Florida Dressage Society polo shirt sat shuffling through a pile of manila envelopes. A small pile of ribbons in six colors, blue and red and yellow and white and pink and green, rose up at her elbow. Nothing too big and showy, no trophies, no grand champion rosettes; this was only a local dressage show for the handful of trainers who had made their Florida outposts in this out-of-the-way spot, too far north of Wellington and too far south of Ocala.

I took in their fancy custom-painted rigs and trucks as Grace drove into the complex and thought maybe Grace was right—these were the clever ones, who got out of the huge lagoon where they'd been unassuming, average fish and promptly found themselves the biggest fish in their new, smaller, more comfortable pond. Instead of following the horse business to where all the other horse people were, they'd followed the money to where the clients were—the weekend riders, the women with money to burn and dreams to chase.

I didn't want to leave Ocala, but I could see what Grace and these other trainers were doing, and the idea of finding a new business model was beginning to make sense. I just didn't know what it would be.

It didn't matter yet, anyway. First I had to get through this dressage test. First I had to prove myself in front of this judge, who apparently came up from Wellington for these shows. First I had to show Carl Rockwell that I hadn't spent my summer in vain.

The morning was slipping past in a shimmer of half-remembered moments. I was running a soft towel over Dynamo's closed eyes, wiping away the sweat and tears and dust of travel. I was tightening the girth on my old dressage saddle, running my fingers over its cracking billets and wondering if it would soon be replaced with a gleaming new model. I was slipping on my battered helmet, settling it atop my lopsided bun and tucking loose strands of hair into my hair net with white-gloved fingers. I was pressing my sweaty face against a cool towel I'd dropped into the soda cooler earlier, and refusing Grace's offer of lipstick to brighten up my pale face.

"You look like a ghost," she fussed. "It's not going to help your score if you look terrified."

"I've never worn lipstick," I whispered. There was some coffee and a granola bar inside me that I was pretty sure would make their way out again if I spoke any louder. "I'll wipe my face on my gloves and smear it."

Grace shook her head. "You eventing girls. Get on your horse, then. Maybe you'll feel better when you're in the saddle."

I wouldn't, I knew. I was going to be sick; the minute I felt Dynamo swing into a walk and my body swayed from side to side with his movement, I would lose my breakfast right down his immaculately groomed shoulder. I wondered if I could lean far enough over to miss him, and miss my polished boots. I'd never been so nervous in my life. I'd never had so much riding on one horse show. I'd never bet everything, literally everything, on four minutes in an arena.

In the saddle, everything was different. Dynamo ambled into a walk, I found my stirrups, my stomach settled immediately, and I lifted my gaze to smile at the beautiful world around me. At any moment a stirring song would begin playing and my animal friends would arrive to help me defeat the wicked witch.

Grace raised her eyebrows. "What just happened?"

"I thought I'd be sick." I rode in a circle around her. "I'm okay now."

Grace snorted. "Anyone would think this was your first time at a horse show. Of course you feel fine once you're in the saddle. That's how being a horsewoman works. Now, let's warm you up and get this thing done."

"Let's," I said, and picked up the reins, feeling I could ride down the center line in Wellington today and nothing bad could happen. I had trained for this, I was ready for this, and I was partnered with my best friend. How could I not feel fantastic, with everything on my side?

Dynamo arched his gleaming chestnut neck, his white-wrapped braids glittering under the hot Florida sun, and together we stepped forward to do battle.

It was magic," I told Pete. "There were no other words for it. It was the best ride of my life."

He leaned back on my sagging old couch and gave me a smile. "It was gorgeous. And that's a pretty blue ribbon to hang up, too."

"My first dressage ribbon, pretty special," I agreed, admiring the little scrap of blue satin.

I slipped the ribbon's clip over the battered window blinds. Pete had arrived home a few days before, and had driven down to see my ride without my knowledge. As I'd ridden out of the arena, my face flushed with heat and joy, my white gloves patting Dynamo's glistening hot neck, he'd stepped out from the shadow of the little tent and I'd nearly toppled to the ground with happiness.

But when I leaned down to greet him, his kiss was cool, and his hands were in his pockets when before they might have been on my thigh. Now I felt a curdle of fear in my belly that I'd nearly thrown him away with my own foolishness. I just hoped it wasn't too late. I didn't know what I'd do if I'd ruined everything.

"I have to go home soon," Pete said, standing up and stretching. "Sunday nights on seventy-five have the worst traffic. If I don't get going, everyone from Ohio will be out there already and I won't get home before midnight."

"I know. It's okay—I'll be packing up tomorrow and home on Tuesday." The words were like sugar on my tongue.

"Ready to be home?"

"Are you kidding? It's all I can do not to leave tonight." The word "home" kept ringing in my ears. I wanted him to say it again and again. Our home, our farm that we loved. It wouldn't be long now before it was ours in truth. Pete would have a fantastic winter season, the U.S. Team committee would send him to the spring training camp, and his grandmother would relent and give him the farm. We'd have to work like the devil to pay for it, but it would be ours.

"You've already held yourself back this long, why not wait another day or two, prove you can do it?"

My stomach turned over, but I smiled at him as if the barb didn't hurt. "Maybe I'll just stay another week, give you some time on your own."

He raised an eyebrow. "You don't have to go that far."

I watched him start for the door and realized he wasn't going to kiss me goodbye, wasn't going to so much as pull me in for a hug like he might an old friend. For a moment pride rooted my boots to the ground, then I darted forward and grabbed his arm as he went out the screen door. "Wait," I told him, desperate to get some glimmer of emotion from his masked face. "Just wait . . . I have to tell you something."

He didn't brush me away. He didn't pull his arm free. He leaned back against the doorframe and waited, taking me at my word, forcing me to say something, anything.

I swallowed against the lump in my throat. "I'm sorry for the way I freaked out this summer. All the back-and-forths, and complaining, when I just had to stick it out for a couple little months. I'll make it up to you. I'm so, so sorry."

Pete put a hand on the back of my head, pulling a little at my ponytail, then tipped me forward and kissed my forehead. "You say that a lot, love," he murmured, voice husky. "Can we start skipping the part where you go crazy and make all these apologies necessary?"

I closed my eyes tight against the tears. "Yes," I whispered. "Yes."

He tilted up my chin and kissed me softly, a ghost of a kiss, a sober, removed, if-only kiss. "Then pack up and come home."

Pete went down the stairs, the boards creaking beneath his feet.

I took a deep breath, waited until my hands stopped shaking, and then went back inside to change out of my show clothes. It was almost time to feed dinner.

# 33

"SO THIS IS it," Grace said without preamble, coming into the tack room.

I looked up from the trunk I was packing, a small pile of polo wraps in my lap. Grace settled down on a folding chair near the door and held out an escaped wrap that had tumbled into the doorway. "I guess so," I replied, taking the polo with a nod of thanks. "It's been a hell of a summer."

"Boy, I'll say." There was a rumble of thunder and we both cocked our heads, a mirror image of each other, judging the direction and the distance the sound had come from.

"Of course, to be really literal about it, summer still has a few months to go."

Grace smiled wryly. "The joys of Florida."

"It's home." I settled the wraps into the bandage holder in the tack trunk's lid. "You know how it is. We're both natives."

"A rare breed," Grace agreed. "My offer about sending you clients still stands, by the way. You proved yourself this summer. You were a tougher nut than I expected, but you cracked in the end, and you did some damn good riding."

I busied myself pulling a pile of saddle pads from under my battered old saddle, giving myself a moment to think without Grace's eyes on my face. She read expressions with unfailing prowess; she'd know I was uncertain about going into business with her and she'd want to know why. I didn't know why; I was just nervous of everyone and everything right now. I was going home, but things weren't going to be the same. Lacey would be gone; Pete had been away for months; we had said things to each other that weren't easily forgotten. I could let it all fall away without a second thought, letting him win the arguments if that's what it took to keep him, but in the back of my mind I would always know he'd been prepared to let me go. I'd always have to watch myself, and him. I didn't know if things would ever be as easy between us again, if our fights would ever be as meaningless, if going to bed angry would take on some fearsome new threat to be analyzed in the middle of the night.

I was too frightened of the future to plan for it.

"Don't let your ambition fail me now, Jules." Grace chuckled.

"I'm not. I'm just not sure what business is going to look like. I won't have a barn manager, and with Rockwell behind me, I'm sure to get some new horses in the barn—"

"You've changed." Grace didn't make this sound like a bad thing. "I don't think of you as a cautious person."

"Everything around me has changed," I admitted. I closed the tack trunk on the saddle pads and sat down on the lid. I lifted my gaze and saw that Grace was grinning, pleased.

"Are we seeing the world a little differently now?"

*A lot differently,* I thought. *All of it.* I nodded.

"That's fine. You can take your time. But before you go back and fall into old habits, let me just ask you this. Do you see a difference between the way you communicate with Dynamo and the way you work with other horses? Mickey, yes, but all other horses?"

"Well, I've had Dynamo longer . . ."

"That matters, but it's not quite what I mean. Dig a little deeper."

I thought. Mickey and I were doing well together. We'd had our problems in the past, but now . . . we just did our thing. I wouldn't say we were the world's most understanding team, but we got through our rides with a minimum of arguments, and he definitely liked having me around the barn. His morning whinnies were evidence enough. Although, I had to admit, now that I was one of the work crew and grain might come from just about anyone, his daybreak greetings were becoming a little more democratic. Just the other morning I'd heard him neigh a big-hearted hello to Tom, a greeting I'd previously thought was reserved just for me.

I felt a frown crease my brow. Maybe what Mickey and I had was nothing more than what any bearer of food might have with a particularly friendly, people-oriented horse. Maybe the bond we'd been building was really forged with sweet feed, and not trust.

"Dynamo does whatever I ask of him because he wants to be my partner," I realized, the words coming slowly, reluctantly. "Is that what you mean? And Mickey does most of what I ask, because he doesn't want to get into trouble."

The thought, spoken aloud, was crushing. But that was the way of the business, wasn't it? Training horses meant they came and they went, a revolving door of different personalities. What sort of partnership could you build with a horse who would be with you for just six months, or even a year?

312 | Natalie Keller Reinert

Grace was nodding, pleased with my answer. "You have a bond with Dynamo, but where did you get that? Not with riding. It was those afternoons you spent in the field with him. You understand his movements, his ear twitches, the way he cocks his head. And he feels the same way about you. How is Mickey, or any other horse you ride, ever going to forge such a connection with you?"

"How can I run a business that way?" I countered. "I need a barn full of horses to pay the bills, and they all need to be ridden. I can't sit in a pasture watching them."

"If you could, though, would they go better for you? If every horse you rode trusted you as Dynamo does, would you be a success?"

"Of course I would!" I'd be unstoppable, a world beater, with a barn full of Dynamos, who believed in me, who wanted nothing more than to take on the world with me.

"Aim for that, then," Grace said, leaning back against the wall and studying my face. "And when you have that success rate, and you're riding horses with a feel no one else can match, charge for that. And that's how you'll make a living when everyone else is scraping and pinching. You can't just do the same thing everyone else is doing. If I hadn't remade this business last year, I'd have gone under just like everyone else. This place would be a road to another housing development. Believe it or not, Jules, this used to be horse country. Now . . ." She shrugged. "Now it's survival of the fittest. Ocala might not look like this neighborhood, but trust me, the same things are happening. Florida is a developer's paradise. It could all end tomorrow."

I didn't know what to say.

"So listen. Before you ride a horse, spend a little time with him. Take him out in a paddock and sit with him. I have a feeling about you. I think you're better than you're letting yourself be."

"When?" My voice sharpened. What good was this advice, coming from a show barn trainer who didn't tack up her own horses? "I have a barn to run. I have chores. How do I fit sitting in a paddock with all my horses into a schedule?"

Grace gave me an assessing glance, her eyes resting on mine for a long moment. "Find the time," she said finally. "If you want to make this work, you'll figure out what's important and how to make time for it."

"I don't see you doing all this."

"Maybe that's my mistake." Grace shrugged and got up, heading for the door. "It's too late to change it now."

Grace's words rang in my ears that evening, as I sat in the apartment among my boxes, alone for one more night, waiting for the sun to rise on my homecoming morning.

Her advice was consistently solid, as I'd learned the hard way this summer. I was not a person who took advice, not from anyone. I was aware of this character flaw; I was working on it. I'd tried to prove Grace wrong again and again, but she'd always been right.

Outside the frogs sang from the steaming puddles as the evening thunder trailed away into the distance. Late August in Florida, another month or two of summer and then the arenas and fields would dry out again, the air slowly cooling off, and the eventing season would begin anew. I would be starting fresh, too, just a girl and six horses, taking on the world. I would be crazy not to heed Grace's advice as I began this next chapter. Define insanity: to continue the same failing strategy, again and again . . .

How could I follow her advice on this one, though? It would mean rethinking everything.

I sat with a notepad and a pen, making calculations on my

phone, glancing out the barn window every so often. Down below, stabled horses nosed at their hay, walked around their stalls, laid down for snoozes. I considered them, contemplating the problems we faced. The horses I wanted to be my partners lived their lives apart from me, save for the hour or two of contact when I rode, fed, turned out. In truth we were little more than casual acquaintances—hardly the trusted friends I made them out to be.

We needed time together, hours spent doing nothing but soaking up one another's presence.

I watched the horses move through their inscrutable patterns, their night routines that no one knew but them, and I could see a crossroads opening before me. To the right stretched the path I'd been planning for myself all along, the glory and the ribbons and the medals, won through the usual manner: build up the training business, fill the barn with other people's horses, ride as many horses in a day as possible, turn over sales horses as quickly as I could. I knew that road; I'd grown up with my boots pointed down its hard-packed clay, following in the footsteps of a thousand riders before me.

The road on the left led to a different sort of life. There were ribbons there, too—who was Jules without the chase for colored snips of satin?—but my days would be spent developing my relationship with a chosen few horses. The day I'd brought home poor, frightened Dynamo from the auction, I'd been on this road, and I'd never even realized it. I remembered sitting in the paddock waiting for him, I remembered the shivers tingling up my spine as he'd chosen me, nudging my neck with his nose, asking me to be his friend when it would have been easier for him, safer for him, to remain apart.

I wanted that feeling again. Was it only down that rutted side road, and would there truly be ribbons and glory at the end of it? Or could I end up in a rotting single-wide on two acres of wasteland, a skinny horse out front, a dreamcatcher in the window, haunted by the memory of endless potential I'd squandered?

I supposed that could be my final chapter either way. I had no real control of my destination. All I could do was choose my traveling companions, and the way we would work together to find our happy ending.

I got up and walked onto the porch, waiting for the evening fireworks to light up the sky. I deserved a pyrotechnics show tonight, a celebration that I'd made it through the summer, a sending-off party for the next stage of my life. But the skies were quiet, and I imagined words like "technical difficulties" and "unforeseen circumstances" offered as apologies to a crowd of disappointed celebrants, who had paid small fortunes to see their dreams written in the sky. My gaze drifted from the distant heavens to the nearby paddocks, a gray ghost flickering through the live oak limbs that could only be Mickey in his paddock, lipping at leftover hay in the darkness.

I owed him more than cowboy tricks and fast fixes. I owed all of them more.

I crept back inside and looked at my notebook again. I drank a beer and ran my fingers under numerals and letters. The fireworks went off at last, but I didn't get up; the time for celebrating had ended. It was time to make a plan.

The clock ticked on toward eleven. The television next door went silent; Anna went to bed. Pete had texted goodnight hours ago. I was on my own here, and if I was going to succeed, I was going to have to reinvent everything. And I would have to talk to Pete. I couldn't do this alone.

# 34

GOD, IT WAS good to be home.

Leaving Seabreeze was uneventful. No one cried or said they'd miss me. Kennedy gave me a short, but tight, hug. Margaret wished me good luck in a tone that implied it seemed unlikely. Tom reminded me that there was really good kayaking in the Ocala area and I should check out the local springs. I pretended I would but I knew I wouldn't have the time. Anna, impossible to read, tried to shake my hand gravely and ended up giving me a hug, too—longer than Kennedy's, and just as tight.

Grace patted my back and said I'd done all right. It felt like high praise.

Back at Briar Hill Farm at last, there hadn't been time to pretend things were normal. Lacey—drawn and thin, worn out from a summer of managing my horses alone—was already a wreck about leaving. And two days after I got back, she really did it. She really left.

This evening, newly alone in the annex barn, I turned the horses out for the night one by one, not bothering to rush, not taking them out two and three at a time as I used to. There was much less reason to hustle, after all. There were only five horses now, barely half an hour's worth of work if I ambled and gazed at the stars between each trip from barn to pasture. Barn Kitty sat in the aisle and watched me, tail wrapped neatly around her front paws. She wasn't sure yet if I was the same person who had left three months ago. That seemed fair. I wasn't sure yet, either.

The horses rolled in sand and shook the dust from their coats. Five horses. Mickey and Dynamo, Jim Dear and Hart, and the lone mare, Maybelline. I'd decided that chestnut witch was my great challenge in life. She'd had a nice summer with Lacey, and for a moment I'd thought of asking Lacey to take her up north and sell her. But Lacey let slip that she would have a stall and turnout space for just one horse when she went home, and I knew who Lacey truly loved.

So I'd told Lacey she could have Margot. It was the least I could do. They'd been together for more than a year, and watching them together was a pleasure. Lacey would press her face against Margot's shining mahogany neck, and the mare would delicately touch her muzzle to Lacey's cupped hands, lipping at her fingers, looking for treats, looking for salt, maybe just looking for love. When I saw them together, I remembered the old days at Green Winter Farm, when Lacey would have to lunge Margot for half an hour to get the bucks out; when the mare would get so excited over a series of gymnastics fences that Lacey would squeeze her eyes tight shut and just hang on for dear life; when Lacey had huddled underneath the mare's monogrammed cooler in the eye of the hurricane, her frightened face peeking out from beneath the elegant script spelling out her fancy show name.

I made sure Lacey took the cooler, too.

Margot had left last night, the semitruck growling in the little turn-around out front, Margot whinnying from her box, the driver sliding the tack trunk into the storage compartment, and Lacey crying unabashedly, sobbing onto my shoulder while I tried as hard as I could to keep all my own emotions reined in, safe inside where they belonged. After a few minutes, I gave in. We stood together under the orange glow of the streetlight and wept like lost children, and eventually the truck driver gave up on us and just drove away, the night echoing with Margot's anxious neighs and the startled replies of the horses left behind.

Lacey left this morning, still sniffling, eyes haunted, face white, jaw set. At least she'd have Margot to comfort her. At least she wouldn't be alone, way up north with the cold winter ahead of her.

At least I wasn't truly alone, with the horses around me. I looked back at the spot where we'd said our goodbyes, the ruts left behind by the horse trailer filled with puddles from the afternoon rain, the water winking in the barn lights, and then I turned back to the horses, reminding myself of why we worked so hard and why we gave up so much.

Dynamo and Mickey grazed head-to-head; they'd grown close after the summer at Seabreeze. Hart rolled a few feet away, groaning with pleasure as he dug his withers into the damp patch of sand near the water trough. Along the fence line, Maybelline leaned her elegant neck over the top board and squealed with Jim Dear, stamping a foreleg to let him know how completely deplorable and how utterly desirable she found him. Jim Dear, hopelessly ensnared, rubbed his lips along her mane when she let him, and ducked backward in panic when she changed her mind and came at him with bared teeth and pinned ears.

I left them to their flirtations and walked back to the barn in the gathering dusk. I finished closing up shop, switching off the fans, closing the tack room door, making sure Barn Kitty had a full cup of water for the night. She meowed rustily and wound against my bare legs, her fur surprisingly soft for an animal who lived such a rough and wild life. When I started up the barn lane, she stayed behind, watching me with golden eyes. Dynamo looked up and rumbled a nicker as I passed the pasture gate, and then I was alone, ambling up the driveway beneath the oak trees, as the stars came out one by one in the big Ocala sky.

Not quite alone: Marcus came padding out from a cool spot near the wash rack and joined me, his long ears flopping and his tongue lolling as he gazed up at me companionably.

The house was dark. I walked through the foyer, the living room, and the kitchen, flipping on lights, and finally down the hall to the bedroom. I started to turn on the overhead light, then paused, considered, and stepped over to switch on the softer floor lamp instead. "Pete?" I asked softly. Maybe he'd fallen asleep. He was still exhausted from England. But his jumping form looked fantastic. I'd watched him ride earlier today.

He hadn't come to see me ride, although he'd asked after the horses, politely, as if he were an acquaintance I'd just run into at the feed store. After three nights at home we were still stepping out of each other's way as if we were new roommates, tentative with each other, not sure how the other person viewed us anymore.

I'd kept my promise, but just barely, and I knew he was thinking about that every time he looked at me. I'd come too close to letting him down this time.

I'd lost Pete's trust.

320 I Natalie Keller Reinert

Still, we were home together. I'd wanted everything to be the same—no, better—but I didn't know how to make that happen. So I was quiet and polite, waiting for the chance to prove myself.

Pete rolled over on the bed and blinked up at me with shell-shocked eyes. It was the most emotion he'd shown me since I came home, and for a horrible moment I thought something had happened to Regina—but of course I would have heard; there would have been phone calls, requests for second opinions, the vet's truck parked outside his barn.

"Baby! What happened?" I fell onto the comforter next to him, taking his cold hand in mine, his reluctance to touch me, and my reluctance to make the first move, forgotten at once. Pete was hurting. Pete was *scared*. The realization set my heart pounding. Pete wasn't scared of anything.

Pete pulled himself upright and then lunged forward, pressing his face against my neck with a long, shuddering breath. I sat very still, shocked; he'd never done anything like this before and I didn't quite know what to do.

*Stroke his hair,* I thought wildly, *stroke his hair and his back and say soothing things.* "It'll be all right," I said uncertainly. "It'll be fine." What could he be worried about? There was nothing to worry about besides money and horses. "We'll figure out a way to get by. We've always managed . . ."

"If only that were the problem, Jules." His voice was muffled against my shirt, which must really smell of horse, I thought. I pulled back a little.

"What's going on?"

His eyes darted around the room, as if he didn't want to make eye contact with me. *He's breaking up with me,* I thought suddenly, an icy knife of dread in my heart. *He's fallen in love with Amy. He's fallen in love with Amanda. That's why he hasn't been looking me in the eye.* Why did Pete know so many gorgeous women with names that started with *A*?

"My grandmother died," Pete said emptily.

*Oh.*

He put his head back down and began to sob brokenly, and I let him, pulling him close against me, tilting my nose down to touch his soft chestnut hair, suddenly feeling a motherly urge to comfort that I'd only ever heard about before. Poor Pete, losing his grandmother, the one person who had never believed in him, when she'd finally been coming around and starting to appreciate the riding he could do! Poor Pete, oh poor Pete, oh . . . I went rigid, my skin prickling ice cold all over.

The farm.

*Don't ask about the farm,* I told myself. *Don't ask don't ask don't ask don't ask—*

"Pete . . . the farm," I whispered, unable to help myself.

He hiccupped like a child and swallowed a sob. "I don't know," he whispered, getting control of his breathing again. He sat up slowly, brushing at the tears on his face. "Jesus Christ, Jules, I don't know. I just found out she died and . . . I just kind of lost it. She hated that I did this, and we didn't get along, but I basically grew up with her and my grandfather. She raised me."

"I'm sorry, I shouldn't have asked, I'm so sorry . . ." I started to back away again, in case he still didn't want to share with me, but he clung to my hands. I sank back onto the bed and waited.

"No, no . . . this affects both of us." He rubbed his eyes. "We have to find out. Unless she changed something . . ."

I stared at him, waiting.

His blue eyes met mine, and in them, I saw the same fear I was feeling. *No,* I thought fiercely. *No, I won't let this happen.*

"We won't lose the farm," I told him, voice firm. I dropped

my walking-on-eggshells attitude. He was going to have to trust me now. "We'll fight, we'll do whatever we have to do. This is our home. We're keeping it."

Pete nodded, clutching at me for a moment, then drawing back, as if he was afraid of what I'd think of him. As if his emotions could be any more frightening than mine! "Stay here," I told him, pushing away from the bed. "I'll get us a couple of beers."

I went down the hallway, past the pictures on the walls, the images of his grandfather jumping through the years on horses long gone, and I felt that old shiver of fear. If only we'd hung up our own pictures, I thought. We'd have made this place our home in truth. Instead, the eventing gods had been angered.

I paused in front of one particularly impressive picture of Pete's grandfather, his horse soaring over a massive ditch-and-wall, the kind of terrifying jump that hunter/jumper trainers use to scare their children into sticking with the show ring. Like the riders I'd admired in that old book of Grace's, he had the firm, commanding style of a different age, his hands floating alongside his horse's neck, his legs firmly beneath him, his jaw set and his eyes fixed determinedly straight ahead. He looked like a man who was accustomed to giving orders, not taking them. He looked like a man who would never have taken nonsense from a client, or a boarder, or a student, or a sponsor.

A hand touched my shoulder and I jumped, but of course it was only Pete. "He was a great rider," I whispered, putting my hand over his.

"One of the best," Pete agreed. His voice sounded a little more steady; he was recovering from the shock already. I felt a surge of love for such a resilient soul. Nothing would ever get Pete down, not for very long. I'd like to think that despite my tempestuous temper, my ups and downs of agony and ecstasy, I could be the same way someday.

"What would he have done?" I asked. "If he lost his farm, what would he do? Would he give up?"

"He'd find some other way," Pete said. "He always found a way."

"Well then," I decided, lifting my chin. I squeezed his hand tight, taking possession, taking control, claiming what was mine. "That's what we'll do. We'll find a way."

# ACKNOWLEDGMENTS

This one is for all the Jules fans.

I never intended to write a sequel, and definitely not a series, when I wrote *Ambition*. But as the years went by and *Ambition* found loyal fans, the messages and requests began to pile up. "When will there be more Jules? What happens next?"

I didn't know what happened next, so I kept on writing other books—also set in Florida, also about equestrians—and tried not to think too much about Jules. But of course, a character that strong-minded never really goes away.

When Grace Carter and Seabreeze Equestrian Center became a part of my fictional world, I had an idea of what might happen next. And that's how Jules went to meet Grace. I think they're a match made in heaven, so thanks to everyone who waited for this one! I needed time to bring a character to life who was tough enough to boss around Jules.

For the setting, I'm thankful for the time I spent as a manager at Grand Cypress Equestrian Center in Orlando, Florida—a beautiful stable that existed in the never-never land between theme parks and a tourist strip. At Grand Cypress, we educated so many riders, whether they were local kids, busy working parents with hardly any time for their horse, or out-of-towners with some spare time to ride. It's no longer part of the central Florida horse scene, but there was a brief period in history when you could sit on your horse in a beautiful dressage arena, and watch the Walt Disney World fireworks light up the sky just a few miles away. Our struggle to keep this stable relevant and operating in such a rapidly changing environment inspired Seabreeze Equestrian Center and my trainer Grace, who was determined to keep her farm running despite the pressure from developers and a changing client base.

The original edition of this work was polished and made better thanks to the thoughtful editing of Caroline Bleeke. Once again, this beautiful new edition has been a team effort by the Flatiron Books crew. Thank you to Megan Lynch and the rest of my stellar team: Jon Yaged, Mary Retta, Maris Tasaka, Nancy Trypuc, Marlena Bittner, Malati Chavali, Emily Walters, Ryan T. Jenkins, Eva Diaz, and Keith Hayes.

Thanks to my fabulous agent, Lacy Lynch, and her wonderful team of Dabney Rice and Ali Kominsky, for helping me take this journey.

# ABOUT THE AUTHOR

Natalie Keller Reinert is the award-winning author of more than twenty books, including the Eventing and Briar Hill Farm series. Drawing on her professional experience in three-day eventing, working with Thoroughbred racehorses, mounted patrol horses, therapeutic riding, and many other equine pursuits, Natalie brings her love of equestrian life into each of her titles. She also cohosts the award-winning equestrian humor podcast *Adulting with Horses*. Natalie lives in north Florida with her family, horses, and cat.

www.nataliekreinert.com